THE ALIENATED ASSASSIN

James Ward

Copyright © 2022 James Ward

All rights reserved

The characters and events portrayed in this book are fictitious. Any similarity to real persons, living or dead, is coincidental and not intended by the author.

No part of this book may be reproduced, or stored in a retrieval system, or transmitted in any form or by any means, electronic, mechanical, photocopying, recording, or otherwise, without express written permission of the publisher.

Cover designed by James Ward with artwork purchased under licence from www.123rf.com

ISBN: 9798831531770

OTHER BOOKS BY THE AUTHOR

Writing as James A Ward
Nothing Serious
It's a Funny Old World!

Writing as James Ward
The Happiness Agenda

Writing as Bernard Fling
X Marks the Spot
Bernard to the Rescue!

Writing as James Alexander
Wait to Deceive
When the Devil Calls

CONTENTS

Title Page
Copyright
Dedication
One   1
Two   4
Three   9
Four   15
Five   21
Six   30
Seven   34
Eight   36
Nine   43
Ten   46
Eleven   53
Twelve   57
Fourteen   71
Fifteen   79
Thirteen   83
Sixteen   88
Seventeen   92
Eighteen   98

Nineteen	104
Twenty	107
Twenty One	113
Twenty Two	116
Twenty Three	124
Twenty Four	129
Twenty Five	137
Twenty Six	144
Twenty Seven	151
Twenty Eight	161
Thirty	166
Twenty Nine	175
Thirty One	179
Thirty Two	183
Thirty Three	193
Thirty Four	200
Thirty Five	207
Thirty Six	213
Thirty Seven	217
Thirty Eight	222
Thirty Nine	226
Forty	232
Forty One	237
Forty Two	240
Forty Three	248
Forty Four	253
Forty Five	256
Forty Six	262

Forty Seven	264
Forty Eight	266
Forty Nine	270
Fifty	273
Fifty One	276
Fifty Two	281
Fifty Three	287
Fifty Four	295
Fifty Five	297
Fifty Six	301
Fifty Seven	306
Fifty Eight	313
A MESSAGE FROM THE AUTHOR	318

ONE

'Mrs Plank is not a passionate woman.'

Colin Crimp looked up from his keyboard, a finger poised in mid-air. 'I'm sorry?'

'I'm telling you this because we're both men of the world,' Henry Plank confided.

This last remark came as something of a surprise to Colin Crimp. He had never considered himself a man of the world; far from it in fact. He liked the idea, but he couldn't really *see* it.

He sniffed tentatively, aware of something foreign in the air. Whisky. Mr Plank had been drinking again. He often drank, occasionally after breakfast, always out at lunch, but never in the office. That was his rule, and he stuck to it firmly. But not today. It was 11.30 in the morning, and Henry Plank was drunk; well possibly not drunk, but the sun was in his eyes.

'We men have needs that can't be satisfied in the real world,' said Henry sadly, easing himself into a chair opposite. 'Fucked if we do, fucked if we don't,' he muttered, fingering the buttons on his waistcoat, before lapsing into a long, uncomfortable silence.

'Right,' said Colin at last, feeling the need to say something, anything.

'I've done things,' said Henry, reviving. 'Things I maybe shouldn't have. Been places, too. It's all gone pear-shaped. You know what I mean, Colin?'

The young man stiffened. 'Not really.'

Henry surrendered to a filthy belch, then leaned forward, spewing a scud of whisky-scented breath across the desk.

'How long have you known me?' he asked, his big milky eyes closing into slits.

Colin shrugged. 'About three months.'

'Exactly! And in all that time have I ever touched you inappropriately?'

'Good lord, no!' cried Colin. He wasn't sure where this was heading.

'Of course not!' said Henry loudly. 'I only touch women. Anything else is unnatural.' He cleared his throat again. 'You're not unnatural, are you, Colin? Of course, you're not! Stupid question. You like women. The more the merrier, am I right?'

'Well, I suppose, I mean, I like women, yes,' said Colin, struggling to marshal an adequate response.

Henry licked a corner of his mouth, then pushed his tongue against a fat, lower lip. He rose suddenly, like a spectre in the fog, crashed two big, broken-veined hands onto Colin's desk and bellowed, 'What do you think to Karen? I mean, would you give her one – if the opportunity arose?'

Colin retreated into his chair, nostrils laced with the smell of whisky. Nothing in his short career with Henry Plank (Publishers) Ltd had prepared him for this moment. True, Henry could be a cantankerous man and his language occasionally ripe, but, by and large, he kept his head down and left others to do the heavy lifting in the office. He was married with no children, lived in a large bungalow on the outskirts of Fetherton, and was on first name terms with the vicar. Colin wasn't sure why that mattered, but Henry had mentioned it more than once as if it bestowed an importance that needed to be shared.

He liked a drink, and he rarely combed his hair, but he was a publisher and those were the sort of things publishers did. Possibly in other companies they also inquired after their employees' sexual preferences and discussed the shaggability of the secretary, but not here. Here, they published books no one else would touch, and charged their authors a fortune for the privilege. They worked long hours for little pay – at least

Colin did – and dreamed of better times to come. Possibly, one of these days, Henry Plank would publish someone famous, or rather they would become famous, and then rich. And so would Henry. If he were in a good mood, he might spread his newly acquired fortune among his workforce, such as it was: at present Colin, Karen and a quiet lad named Bob who had learning difficulties and smelt of fish.

Then again, he might not, it was an uncertain future.

'I'd give her one,' said Henry, collapsing into his chair. 'In fact, I'd give her two!' He turned his attention towards the ceiling, as if expecting to find her up there. Then he closed his eyes and released a long, despondent sigh. 'I don't feel well. I don't feel well at all.'

'Would you like a cup of coffee?' asked Colin, keen to steer their conversation into safer waters.

'I've been drinking,' said Henry. 'I shouldn't have, not in the office, but I couldn't help myself. You see, it's all gone pear-shaped.'

'So you said, Mr Plank. Is there anything … I mean … would you like me to do anything?'

Henry opened a big, vacant eye and swivelled it in the other man's direction. He licked his lips a second time, and said quietly, 'I'd like you to come into my office, Colin.'

Colin felt his stomach tighten. 'You're not going to touch me inappropriately, are you, sir?' he inquired.

Henry passed a hand across his face and slumped. 'Good God,' he sighed wearily. 'I need another whisky…'

TWO

Lambert Ticke sat at his desk, scratched his chin and scowled. He held up a piece of paper to the light and examined it carefully from all sides. There was little point in testing it for fingerprints, all supposing he had the equipment, which he didn't; too many hands had touched it by now. Ignorant hands. Well, all right, he corrected himself, not exactly ignorant hands because hands weren't sentient, not in the accepted meaning of the word, but their owners were ignorant, every one of them. He should know: he had worked alongside them for the past six months.

He smoothed the paper flat and ran his eyes down the page. It was – in a manner of speaking – a letter to his employer, Sir Edward St John Stark, ostensibly expressing the writer's support for a recent TV appearance. 'You'll have put the wind up your opponents, and got yourself in line for a BAFTA,' wrote 'Mervyn Ratt (Mr)'. It concluded, 'PS Any chance of a signed photo?'

It was a stupid letter, an irreverent letter – in Lambert Ticke's view a thoroughly impertinent letter – for it was a letter to the Prime Minister of the United Kingdom of Great Britain, Northern Ireland and All Her Colonies Beyond the Sea. That this was the author's opinion of the nation's current political weight had been underscored by his use of these words in 18-point capitals at the top of the page, followed by a large exclamation mark. Why that had been added, Lambert Ticke had no idea. Possibly it was the writer's idea of a joke. If so, he reflected, it wasn't a particularly funny one.

But that didn't bother him. What bothered him were not the words, but the gaps; not what was said, but what was not said: the unspoken threat beneath the surface of the three, self-indulgent paragraphs.

In his own, carefully considered opinion, Lambert Ticke was dealing with a dangerous man – and he could scarcely have been more excited.

This was the very thing for which the Correspondence Clearance Unit had been set up: to keep tabs on men like Mervyn Ratt, to filter out the sane from the not-so-sane, and the not-so-sane from the downright barmy. Not that Mervyn Ratt was necessarily barmy – not yet at any rate – but he was on a road without exits, a road that led to the very heart of a civilised society.

The remit of the CCU was simple: to carry out a detailed, psychological analysis of the nation's underbelly. There were bad people out there, people who, in the twenty-first century, would stop at nothing to subvert the institutions of government. It was the CCU's job to find those people before they stepped out of line; before they wreaked havoc.

True, this wasn't exactly how Lambert Ticke's colleagues saw their task, and to be fair, in this, they had the support of their job description: 'Your function will be to scrutinise all incoming correspondence and confirm that the writer's purpose in contacting the PM's office has been dealt with. We don't want people getting upset with us.'

He had tried to convince his 'department controller', Walter Cuff, of the need to widen their terms of reference, but Walter had just laughed and told him to 'stop taking the piss'. So Lambert Ticke had soldiered on alone, confident in his own mind that, unlike his colleagues, he had correctly understood the purpose of their mission. Let them treat it as a joke if that was the limit of their combined imaginations, but he would remain alert to the dangers posed by enemies within. (After all, that, he told himself, was what he was paid for.)

He held the letter by its long, outer edges, twirling

it beneath the glow of an angle-poise lamp, recalling the event that had triggered the writer's excitement. Two weeks previously, Sir Edward St John Stark had entered a BBC studio, mounted a pulpit and addressed the nation for a full sixty minutes on live, prime-time TV. To a filmed backdrop of a bright summer's day and a brisk movement by Elgar, he had answered 'unrehearsed' questions from friends in the audience, lacing his replies with the occasional 'joke' to show he had a sense of humour. The jokes weren't that good, but the nation had been duly impressed, or at least that part of the nation that loved its game shows and believed everything the newspapers told them. Normal people had switched off, gone to the pub, or got stuck into a good book.

Ticke's colleagues had dismissed the letter as a joke and, it having gone round the office twice because it was short and easy to read, it had been thrown into the tray marked, 'No further action'. A signed photo had been sent as requested, and nothing more was to be done.

But Ticke knew better and had retrieved the page while no one was looking. This man – Mervyn Ratt – hadn't written one letter, he hadn't written two or three, he'd written hundreds: to ministers, backbenchers, government advisors, the lot. (Every department had its own CCU, and Ticke had made it his business – on a weekly basis – to trawl through their files after everyone else had gone home. It took several hours at a time, but was, he concluded, well worth the effort.)

Ratt's output was prodigious. He must live alone and have no friends: the classic profile of the anti-social psychopath. (That Ticke himself lived alone and had no friends was neither here nor there. He didn't need friends, he had a doctorate in political philosophy, and understood the human mind.) Here, in the PM's office, the sea of correspondence had become an ocean. Half the letters in the 'No further action' tray had been written by 'Mervyn Ratt (Mr)'.

To his colleagues, the letters were the work of 'a pillock' with too much time on his hands and a ready supply of stamps.

But to Lambert Ticke, they represented the outpourings of a dangerous mind. This had been the premise of his as-yet unpublished masterpiece, *The Alienated Assassin*, the thrust of which was simple: if governments continued to ignore their electorate's concerns, as most western states invariably did, then bad things would happen. Put plainly: people would become alienated, and turn against the system. Having turned, they would hit back by whatever means available, and always on an escalating scale. Verbal complaints at first, or possibly a call to one of the mindless radio 'phone-in' shows. From there, an opening letter would be penned – rather verbose and not well-thought-out – followed by more thinking, and more complaints; succeeded by rejection and a growing belief that the system didn't cater to the man in the street.

It was hardly surprising, thought Ticke: you could get stoned out of your mind, climb into your 4x4 and mow down a family of five out on their bikes. If the magistrate was in a foul mood, you'd have your licence docked three points and possibly pick up a fifty quid fine. Defend yourself against an armed intruder and you'd end up doing twenty years. No wonder people were hacked off.

When the worm finally turned, the judges and the politicians would get it in the neck first, which was only fair. But after that, it would quickly become open season on everyone. That was when society would break down, and everyone would suffer. And it was that which he couldn't allow, not now, not ever. The judges and the politicians must be protected. It was a high price to pay, but that was life, and life was rarely fair. If it was, then he, Lambert Ticke, would be running the PM's CCU, not Walter sodding Cuff.

Of course, nothing like this had happened yet, but it was only a matter of time. Lambert Ticke had studied the human mind, and he had studied history, and his conclusions were sound: no-one was to be trusted, least of all the so-called 'experts' who claimed the main threat to law and order in the twenty-first century would come from organised terrorism.

It would not: it would come from disgruntled 'lone gunmen'. And if 'Mervyn Ratt (Mr)' wasn't a lone gunman, then he, Lambert Ticke, was a bearded haddock.

Ratt had to be stopped, before it was too late, and only one man *could* stop him. Lambert Ticke took a deep breath. His time had come.

THREE

'Mrs Plank has thrown me out. Told me to sling my hook. What do you say to that?' asked Henry, extracting a bottle of whisky from beneath his desk and sloshing some into a mug.

'Shouldn't you … I mean, do you think …' began Colin. He knew what he wanted to say, he just couldn't think of a way to say it politely. 'Why has Mrs Plank thrown you out?' he asked, cutting to the quick.

'Says I play around with other women,' replied Henry loudly.

'Do you?' inquired Colin, not sure it was any of his business, and less certain that he wanted to know.

"Course not!' cried Henry, and took another swig of malt.

'Well, then, you must say so,' advised Colin. 'Tell her it's a mistake, that she's got the wrong end of the stick.'

'If only it were that easy,' sighed Henry.

'Couldn't you make it that easy?' asked Colin. 'I mean, it can't be difficult. I've no experience of this sort of thing, but if you haven't been playing around and tell her so, she'll realise her error, surely?'

'It's the whores she can't accept, that's the problem.'

'*Whores?*' repeated Colin, feeling the ground shift beneath his feet.

'Her word, not mine,' said Henry. 'Quite frankly, they're lovely girls, you couldn't meet nicer, salt of the earth.'

'You've been seeing women of the night?' asked Colin, appalled.

'More late afternoon,' said Henry. 'Sometimes mid-morning. Never night. They prefer to keep office hours. Night-time's no good. They like to put their feet up and watch the telly, like the rest of us.'

'Prostitutes...', muttered Colin, who could scarcely believe his ears. 'You've been sleeping with prostitutes?'

'Escorts, Colin, escorts. There's a difference. Prostitutes are cheap old hags who work out of back streets. Escorts, on the other hand, are expensive young fillies who advertise on the internet. They own their own flats, take plastic and are often booked up for weeks in advance. You need to make an appointment, like the doctor. Only the medicine's sweeter!'

'When ... I mean, how long have you been seeing these women?'

"Bout six years. On and off.' He roared with laughter, an inappropriate response in Colin's view. 'More ways than one!'

'But why? I don't understand, if you're married...'

Henry threw him a sorrowful glance, gulped back another mouthful of malt and sighed. He seemed to be doing a lot of sighing, thought Colin, and sighed himself.

'I've told you already. Mrs Plank is not a woman given to displays of physical passion. It's not that she can't, just that she'd rather not. Not her cup of tea, if you get my drift. A good book suits her better, always has.'

'Haven't you, well, talked about it?' asked Colin. 'Isn't there someone you can see? I thought there were organisations.'

'Good God! *Talk about it?* Mrs Plank would sooner eat her own liver. Out of the question. She can't talk about it to me, what chance does a stranger have? I have a big drive, always have. It's a medical condition.'

'Aren't there tablets you can take?' asked Colin, desperately.

'No,' replied Henry. 'I must have women. It's homeopathic. Natural remedies, you see. Like that book, *Nature Knows Best*, by the Higgins girl. She knew.'

A faraway look transformed Henry's face. Colin remembered the title only too well, though for different reasons. In his short time at the firm, it was, he felt, the worst-written book he had handled. But as they were a vanity publishing company and the author paid all the costs, it hadn't bothered Henry in the least. Colin had suggested they reject it, but Henry had waved away his protest; even more so after Alice Higgins had delivered her work in person. Colin had reckoned she was at least a hundred (though Henry assured him she was only 52), and that if homeopathy were responsible for her looks, there was much to be said for chemicals. She had swept through the office in a thin flowing skirt, orange bandana, and a bra-less blouse, beneath which surged a sea of large, Amazonian breasts. Henry had remarked on them more than once.

'You didn't, I mean, not…?' ventured Colin.

'How could I resist?' confessed Henry. 'She all but had me over this very desk. I remember how she sat in that chair, and … what are you doing?'

At the mention of the chair, Colin had sprung up.

'It's all right, we didn't do it there,' said Henry. 'I couldn't manage it, nor could she, come to that. When you get to our time of life a little comfort's required. All right for you young people. You and Karen, you could do it there. I wouldn't mind watching, either, if you felt able…'

'Watching?' cried Colin. 'What do you mean?'

'I'd pay. Sixty quid should cover it, what do you think? Make an old man happy?'

'You don't know what you're saying. You've been drinking, I'll make allowances.'

Henry shook his head. 'Life's short,' he muttered despondently. 'Just one invite to the party. Don't do it now, never will. Can't do it when you're dead. Can't even get a good kip, 'cos it's not sleep, you know, when you're dead, it's just dead. I mean, good kip, you wake up, feel better for it. Dead, well, you don't.' He snorted crudely. 'I expect you have standards. Looking for love, that sort of thing.'

'Not necessarily,' said Colin weakly.

Henry shook his head. 'You're too young. Forget love, you

should be looking for a good time. Take Karen, for example. Literally, if you get my drift–'

Colin bridled. 'You shouldn't talk about Karen like that.'

Henry's face lit up. 'Like her, do you?'

'I didn't say that. It's just not right, that's all.'

'Got the hots for her? Can't say I blame you. If I were a younger man, I'd be after her, too. Doubt she'd be interested now, not even if I offered her ready cash. Well, I have, nothing doing.'

'You offered her money? For sex?' Colin was mortified.

'Only in a manner of speaking. Nothing definite, just a suggestion. Anyhow, she didn't come across, so no harm done.'

'Wasn't she offended?'

Henry shrugged. 'Took it in her stride. Why not? Woman of the world.'

Colin sagged. He'd been wanting to ask Karen out for two months, but hadn't had the nerve, and here was Henry announcing he'd offered to pay her for sex. And then he tightened, because something else had just occurred to him: Henry's wife was a co-director.

'What will happen to the firm?'

Henry heaved his shoulders. 'Soldier on,' he said. 'What else? Mrs Plank'll want her pound of flesh. Need to keep working till she sees sense, takes me back, water under the bridge, that sort of thing.'

'Do you think she will?'

Henry puffed out his cheeks.

'Who can say? Women aren't logical, they don't think straight. Might not be able to do the maths. May have to send her a letter, you know – setting out the salient points.'

The younger man slumped. This was all too much on a Monday morning. Monday mornings were bad enough without having to cope with all this, too.

Henry reached for the pipe he kept in a saucer on his desk. Congealed ash and whatever muck was in the mixture had, over time, dribbled down onto the plate to form a cement-like seal that had welded the saucer to the desk. The pipe itself, chipped in several places and vigorously chewed at one end, always made Colin shudder. The stench was awful and clung to his clothes for days after they'd been washed. Henry himself had no sense of smell, which was fine for him, but hell on those he floated past when puffing the dreadful thing.

Having tapped it on the plate, he had second thoughts, and discarded it in favour of the whisky. Colin gave a sigh of relief he would not have previously imagined possible.

'Now about our digs,' said Henry airily, leaning back in the chair with the look of a man strangely comfortable with his lot.

Colin looked up. A creeping sensation gripped his shoulders, then worked its way down his back. 'Digs?' he repeated.

'Well, Mrs Plank has chucked me out, I'm on the street, you live alone, I thought…'

'It's out of the question!' said Colin. 'It wouldn't be right.'

'Two men living together, I see where you're at. Neighbours might talk, get the wrong idea.'

This hadn't been Colin's concern, though now that Henry mentioned it… No, that was silly. Or maybe it wasn't; he had some peculiar neighbours.

'I'd make it worth your while. For the digs, I mean. Just a bunk for a few nights, nothing more. Fifty quid? All in. What do you say?'

'All in?'

'I can't cook. You'd have to do meals.'

'Fifty pounds a night?'

'I was thinking a week. Or part thereof. Flatmates.'

'I don't live in a flat.'

'I was speaking figuratively.'

'I'm a private person.'

'What you get up to is your own concern. I'm broadminded. I've seen it all before. 'less it involves animals.'

'*Unless it involves animals?* What's that supposed to mean?'

Henry waved his glass in the air, spilling drops of malt across the desk.

'Nothing at all. Sorry. Don't feel well. Forgive an old man.'

He stood up and took a deep breath, as if he were about to deliver a speech. At least, thought Colin glumly, it put some distance between him and the pipe.

'Make it a hundred, and you do all the shopping. What do you say? It'll only be a few days. Mrs P will come to her senses in no time.'

Colin shrugged. 'I don't know.' But he did. He thought it was a terrible idea, but he knew what he would say. Henry was gazing at him with those big, watery, dog-like eyes of his. Colin was too soft for his own good; he always had been. Besides which, he liked his job, and he liked Karen even more. Maybe this could work to his advantage. He wasn't sure how, but if the boss owed you a favour… So, yes, he knew what his answer would be, and he gave it, though with the heaviest of hearts.

'If it's only for a week…'

'Probably not even that. Two at the most. Three tops. Within the month, you'll see…'

Colin felt a huge weight descend on his shoulders. He didn't like this at all. This would be troublesome. And that was without all the other troubles that were heading his way. Troubles about which, at present, he didn't have the slightest inkling.

But they were heading his way nonetheless…

FOUR

Norah Plank was an angry woman. She had given 25 years of her life to Henry, and this was how he had repaid her: running around with other women, being rude with them, doing things with them, *to them*, that he had never done with her. And certainly not *to* her. True, she had never actually wanted to do that sort of thing, but that wasn't the point. You married for better or for worse in her opinion, and if worse (from Henry's point of view) meant an absence of filthy behaviour involving oral-genital contact and/or thrashing your partner's bottom, that was fine by her.

Henry had crossed a line that was not meant to be crossed, and he had done things that were not meant to be done. He had betrayed her, and in the worst possible way.

She had discovered his stash of DVDs at the back of the wardrobe (why were these things always at the back of a wardrobe?), each one wrapped in a brown paper bag, and placed inside a suitcase in which Henry claimed to have stored a few 'odds and sods'. Well, from what she had seen, the contents were most definitely odd, and her husband a complete and utter sod.

The DVDs had appalled her, featuring, as they did, orgies of naked, well-endowed couples grappling furiously – and often unnaturally, too, she considered – in all manner of places, none of them appropriate. Surely no one had ever had sex at a funeral? And with a recently widowed dwarf, for God's sake! Or on top of a moving bus at rush hour? It was ridiculous – and revolting, too. She had no idea Henry was such a beast.

Norah had never approved of sex. Quite frankly, the further away she was from sex, the better. And the further away from Henry Plank, the better still.

She wasn't sure what had been worse: discovering his hidden store of filth and the mobile phone he used for contacting his tarts – the swine had kept that with the discs, along with all their numbers and text messages – or the fact that he had not denied it when confronted.

'A man has needs,' he had told her.

'This isn't a need,' she had replied bitterly, 'it's a medical condition. You need help, it isn't normal.'

'Sex is perfectly normal,' he had retorted. 'It's not having it that's unnatural. I'm an animal–'

'You're that, all right!' she had yelled.

'With an animal's needs,' he had continued, undeterred.

That had tipped her over the edge. 'And which animal asks another animal to thrash it senseless with a horse-whip?!' she had inquired indignantly.

'I don't know what you're talking about,' he had attempted, but without much conviction. There had, he recalled, been one or two DVDs he had viewed out of interest – involving dungeons, flagellation and hot candle wax – and which some of his ladies threw in as an optional extra. It was the sort of thing that might have interested a high court judge, but did nothing for him. It didn't seem fair for Norah to mention it.

'I phoned Miss Crush!' she revealed. 'And that other whore, Lady bloody Spank!'

'They're of foreign extraction,' he had told her feebly. 'Latvian ladies. Nothing wrong with that. They came over when we were in the EU.'

'Well we've left now so they can fuck off back home!' she had countered bitterly. Norah Plank never swore, which convinced him things were serious. He'd opened his mouth to reply, then closed it again. She had him on the run. Even more so with her next remark.

'You won't get away with this!' she had warned him. 'Wait

till the vicar hears, and all your friends in the Party.'

That *had* frightened him. Henry was a councillor with high hopes of one day being selected for a safe seat. It was never going to happen, of course, but the delusion had long given him a curious pleasure. He was a churchwarden, too – a pillar of the community. She couldn't wait to let them all know what a sanctimonious old hypocrite he was.

But he had got in first. She still recalled the saddened look the vicar had given her when she told him during tea and biscuits the following afternoon.

He had studied her over his tortoise-shell spectacles and mumbled something about women of a certain age, and that the menopause was nothing to be ashamed of.

'What the hell are you talking about?' she had asked, finally extracting an admission that Henry had told him all about her 'delusions' and asked him for advice.

That had done it. She had dragged the Reverend Boulder into the bedroom – much to the poor man's distress – and shown him the contents of their wardrobe. Except that apart from Henry's old suits (most of which she had since shredded with a pair of blunt scissors) – and her extensive collection of pastel-coloured skirts – the wardrobe was bare. She had been stupid, of course, assuming he would leave the evidence lying around, but it was the last mistake she had made.

It was when the phone calls began that she really flipped. Henry had been quick off the mark, and soon all his friends – and hers, too – were calling to offer tea and sympathy. Not one of them had taken her side. Henry was a brilliant actor, she had to give him that and, without the DVDs and mobile phone to back her up, she had no proof of his transgressions.

Norah had been beside herself for days. Her first thoughts, once she had overcome her initial fury, had turned to murder. But Henry was a mason and knew a few judges, so the chances of her getting off, whatever the provocation, were slim; and she wasn't prepared to give him the satisfaction of knowing she was doing 20 years on his behalf, all supposing there were some way of him finding out from the black hole of Hell, where – if there was any justice in the afterlife – he was slowly frying to a crisp.

Drink had proved an unexpected ally. Norah rarely touched alcohol, but now she embraced it as a new-found friend. And as she drank, desperate for oblivion, she decided that if she couldn't kill Henry, then she would kill herself. The gas fire in the sitting room had always been dodgy, and often failed to light first thing. Easy enough to switch it on, sit back in her favourite armchair and just fall asleep. Then again, gas was dangerous. All it needed was for Henry to come home, light that foul pipe of his and the entire house could explode. It wasn't that she was much bothered if she took Henry with her – indeed the thought rather appealed just then – but their next-door neighbour was a retired teacher, 83 years old and still mowed her lawn twice a week. She didn't want the old dear's death on her conscience even if she wouldn't be around to fret about it.

That narrowed her options somewhat. Thanks to the government's ridiculous laws on how many painkillers you could buy at any one time, she had been forced to make several visits to several different chemists on several different occasions. It was, she thought, unnecessarily cruel of the state to ensure that, when one of its citizens decided life no longer held meaning, they were forced to spend several more days prolonging the agony.

At last she had gathered together what she had assumed to be a lethal dose – 382 tablets in all. It would have been 384, but halfway through counting them she had developed a splitting headache and decided it was silly to spend her last few hours in pain when the remedy was close at hand. She wondered if she had enough tablets to kill both herself and Henry, but decided against it. What would be perfect, of course, would be if she could somehow lay the blame for her demise at Henry's door. How satisfying to go to her grave in the certain knowledge that Henry was doing time for her murder. But that would take some planning, and Norah wasn't sure she was up to it. No, best to keep things simple. With that in mind, she had typed a letter to the local press, setting out Henry's aberrations in a detail that surprised her, bearing in mind she had no real grasp of their precise nature.

The letter written, she had poured herself another g&t. One thing led to another and, by the time she had knocked back her fifth double g (and significantly less t), she no longer felt suicidal.

Eventually, she broke off, and would have gone for a brisk walk were it not for the fact that she had great difficulty in standing upright.

Later that evening, when Henry failed to return, and she assumed the swine was out with one of his women friends, a fresh maudlin mood overtook her. She emptied the contents of 12 packets of Paracetamol onto the kitchen table, opened a bottle of vodka (the gin was history by now) and poured herself a glass.

She drank heavily for the next hour, preparing for the moment when she would swallow a lethal dose. When the time came for her to stand up and be counted, she could do neither and keeled over into a dead faint. Waking up the following morning, with the worst headache of her life, she was grateful for the tablets on the table and swallowed four. Not a lethal dose, but sufficient to ease her pain. When, an hour later, she had walked into her bedroom to discover Henry fast asleep – and realised he must have returned during the night without concern for her absence – she made up her mind. God had not intended her to kill herself. He had intended for her to exact a different revenge altogether.

The nature of that revenge came to her in an instant. It was brilliant in its simplicity and would be shocking in its enactment.

She spent several hours on the internet, tracking down the necessary materials, which included, at rock bottom prices due to a 'closing down' sale on one site, 100 litres of black paint. She didn't know if she needed that much, but better to be safe than sorry. And at 50p a tin, the outlay was scarcely to be fretted over.

Three weeks later, she was ready. On D-day minus 48 hours, she had telephoned for a locksmith and, by the time Henry came home that evening, the house was well and truly secured. She placed a small suitcase on the doorstep, and told him through an upstairs window, in language he'd never heard before, that if he stepped back inside the house she would cut off his testicles – emphasising the point by flourishing a large pair of blunt kitchen scissors, the same scissors she had subsequently used to shred the rest of his clothes.

Henry had taken the hint, and beaten a hasty retreat. She had no idea where he had spent the night and cared even less. That it had been on the floor of his own office and that the following morning he had lied his way into Colin's house was again of no interest.

What mattered to her now was the future.

She poured herself a glass of whisky. (The vodka had, by this time, gone the way of the gin, forcing her to paddle further into uncharted waters.) A lifetime of restraint could not be thrown off that easily, but alcohol was a great help.

Taking a huge gulp of undiluted malt, Norah Plank went over her plans one last time. It would take courage, it would take strength, but she was not unduly concerned, for she knew she had both. She would have to speak with their solicitor, of course, just to tie up the legal ends. He wasn't a mason, so wouldn't be in Henry's pocket. Of course, he was of the old school, and wouldn't approve of what she had in mind. But sod him; indeed, sod everyone. She had seen what a duplicitous lot people could be. From now on she was doing things her way.

Norah poured herself another whisky. She could get used to this way of life, she decided. Indeed, she mused, if she were to carry out the plan she had in mind without faltering en route, she might very well have to.

FIVE

Roger Caspin couldn't believe his luck.

'Just run this past me one more time,' he said. It was best to proceed with caution. Possibly he'd misunderstood something. It would be a shame to get his hopes up, only to have them dashed.

Lambert Ticke had a gleam in his eye, and, when he spoke, was breathless with excitement. Caspin had long considered him to be bonkers. These academic types often were; not grounded in the real world. It had crossed his mind more than once to have Ticke 'relocated' to another department, or better still, sacked. Anything to get him off his hands, the sooner the better, and as permanently as possible. The man was trouble, and a pain in the proverbial arse.

'Ratt must be stopped. I believe he's a threat to the PM's life.'

This was why Caspin had not removed him. He had read about men like Ticke. If you sacked them, they sometimes returned the following day armed with a pump-action shotgun and blew you away in the office. Caspin didn't want to be blown away in the office. He didn't want to be blown away anywhere, come to that, so felt it best to humour Ticke and avoid him as much as possible. If the man thought harmless letter-writers were out to kill the PM, then he was right to be wary. He'd put up with Ticke for the past 18 months only because he had no choice. Seconding him to the CCU had eased the pain a little, though Ticke had simply used the posting to peddle his crazy theories with renewed fervour. Still, from what Ticke had just told him, he might not have to put up with the cretin for much longer.

'You seriously think this Mervyn Ratt is planning to assassinate Sir Edward St John Stark?'

'I do.'

'Based on a letter asking for a signed photo?'

'It's a trophy. If you'd read chapter 14 of my book...' began Ticke, but Caspin cut him short.

'Yes, but why? If I'm to authorise action, I need to be sure of my facts. I need you to be sure of *your* facts.'

In truth, Caspin didn't give a damn whether Ticke was sure of his facts. What he wanted was for Ticke to make a complete fool of himself so that others higher up the food chain would chuck him out on his ear. That would take the responsibility out of his, Caspin's, hands, and ensure that Ticke did not return with malevolent intent.

'It's difficult to explain,' said Ticke. 'But if you give me leave of absence, I can nail him, I assure you.'

'When you put it like that, it's hard to say no.'

Ticke looked surprised, as if a resounding 'No' was precisely what he had expected.

'You'll want back-up, of course,' Caspin continued.

'Of course,' said Ticke, with all the assurance of a man who had never previously considered the idea.

'Where exactly does this Ratt bloke live?'

'Fetherton. It's a market town near Harrogate.'

'I like the sound of it.'

Ticke frowned. 'You like the sound of what?' he inquired.

'Whatever it is you plan to do,' replied Caspin, struggling to contain his enthusiasm. 'What *is* your plan? You have one, I assume?

'I thought I'd infiltrate,' said Ticke. 'Get to know him, find out what he's up to.'

'Fetherton, you say,' mused Caspin. This was getting better all the time. He knew Fetherton; it was within the recently created North Yorkshire Borders region. The chief constable was Peter Barrow, one of those politically correct types you could lead by the nose, because as long as something was even remotely suggestive of authority, he disapproved of it. The fact that he himself was a symbol of authority didn't seem to bother him unduly.

'Fetherton, yes,' said Ticke. 'As I say, if I could have some time off–'

'No problem,' said Caspin. 'How much time do you need? A couple of years? To really get yourself bedded in?'

Ticke frowned. 'I was thinking more along the lines of a month. Two weeks might do. I doubt it'll be a long haul.'

Caspin visibly slumped. Two weeks? That wasn't what he wanted to hear. Still, a fortnight was better than nothing. 'You'll be going incognito, I expect.' This was it, the moment of truth.

'I hadn't really thought.'

Caspin leaned forward. 'What you're doing is absolutely mad.'

'You think so?' Ticke seemed taken aback.

'But you might just pull it off, I wouldn't put it past you. There's just one snag.'

'Is there? What?'

'If anything goes wrong, we'd have to deny all knowledge of your activities. You understand, Her Majesty's Government must not be compromised. Nor, more importantly–,' Caspin broke off, and swivelled round to admire a portrait of Queen Elizabeth (circa 1958) that filled one wall of his office, 'must our gracious sovereign.'

Ticke nodded, though he looked confused. 'Of course. On no account.'

Caspin swung back. 'If you're captured–' he continued.

'*Captured?*' repeated Ticke shrilly. 'I wasn't planning on being captured. Who the hell is going to capture me?'

'You may be dealing with deadly forces,' said Caspin, a suggestion he immediately regretted, as Ticke's face clouded over. That wouldn't do, he didn't want the pillock going off the idea. 'But I'm sure you can handle yourself. My God, I wish I had a hundred men like you, we'd soon have the country back on its feet.'

Ticke frowned. This conversation was straying into unexpected territory.

'You'll need help on the ground,' said Caspin, reaching for the phone, then suddenly withdrawing. He tapped the side of his nose. 'Best if I do that later. Make a call, get things in place.'

Ticke looked puzzled. Caspin glanced from side to side, then leaned forward and said, in a hushed whisper, 'I know a few people, they owe me favours. I'll have a word in the right ear.'

'That's very kind,' said Ticke. 'Might I ask whose ear?'

'The chief constable is a personal friend,' explained Caspin. In fact, the chief constable was nothing of the sort, but Roger Caspin had access to files, and in those files were certain titbits which could, on occasion, be used to oil the wheels of government. He knew a few things about Fetherton's chief constable. Besides which, the politically correct could always be relied upon to do as they were told – that was why they were politically correct.

'So when might I get started?' asked Ticke.

Roger Caspin leaned back in his chair and gestured expansively. 'Any time you like. Mustn't let the grass grow under your feet. But remember, if the balloon goes up you're on your own.'

'No help at all?' asked Ticke, a little downcast.

'None,' said Caspin. 'You'll be like a wartime agent, because, mark my words Ticke, this is war. The war for decency and you're in the front line.'

He was rather pleased with that one. He thought it was total crap, of course, but just the sort of thing a madman like Ticke would want to hear.

Caspin stood up and offered a formal handshake. 'I hope this isn't the last time I see you,' he lied.

'Last time you see me?' repeated Ticke, alarmed. 'Why the hell should it be?'

'I'm sure it won't come to that,' said Caspin hastily. 'Piece of cake for a man like you. God speed!' He raised his hand a fraction, aware, for one awful moment, that he had almost saluted this nutter. Mind you, if anyone had been eavesdropping on their conversation just then, they might have imagined him, not Ticke, to be the nutter...

*****

'What the hell are they up to?' asked Conrad Blag.

'Difficult to say,' replied Felix Hapgood, shaking his head. 'We missed a lot. Damned static.'

'Run it through the printer, get a transcript,' said the other man, scratching his chin thoughtfully.

Hapgood pressed a few buttons, then watched the grey, metallic box pump out a length of paper. Remarkable what computers could do these days. He hoped the print-out would be a lot clearer than the conversation to which they had just been listening. They were always getting interference. It didn't help that they were forced to work from a basement seven miles out of central London and with poor reception when the weather was wet, which seemed to be the case on most days in this Goddamn-forsaken country.

He tore off the roll, scanned it briefly, then passed it to his boss. Blag studied the page, reading aloud:

'Threat ... PM's life ... you ... Mervyn Ratt ... assassinate Sir Edward Stark ... back-up ... Fetherton ... infiltrate ... couple of weeks ... might just pull it off ... deny all knowledge ... captured ... hundred men like you ... country sorted ... help on the ground ... make ... phone call ... things in place ... chief constable ... personal friend ... balloon goes up ... on your own ... this is war ... last time I see you ... God speed!'

Blag puffed out his cheeks. 'This is it,' he muttered. 'It's the Big One.'

Hapgood seemed less than convinced. 'I don't know,' he

countered tentatively. 'It's not very clear.'

His boss rubbed two large, hairy hands together, partly from excitement at the prospect of the longed-for 'Big One', and partly because, not for the first time recently, the central heating in their basement HQ had broken down. 'They're going to kill their own PM!' he thundered. 'How much clearer can it be? It's war, Caspin says so himself. Might be the last time they see each other. Could be a bomb involved, who knows? A hundred other men, too – that's a fucking army – and the chief constable's in on it. Sweet Jesus, it's hard to believe.'

Hard indeed, thought Hapgood despondently, and shook his head. He'd been with Blag long enough to know his fellow-American's thoughts on the perfidious nature of the British intelligence service, but this latest conclusion, he decided, might be taking things too far.

'We can't be certain,' he said. 'I'm sure I heard them say something about someone else wanting to kill the PM. They're probably just sending an agent in to check.'

'Check my ass!' responded Blag loudly. 'Something's going on. Never trust a Brit with a plum in his mouth. They're all in bed with the Trots.' He sucked at his teeth and narrowed his eyes into slits. 'And this other bloke – Tit? What kinda name is that? High-pitched voice, too. Shriller than a monkey with his balls in the blender.'

He sucked at his teeth again. 'Never trust a man with a high-pitched voice,' he roared, voicing another of his prejudices. 'Probably transsexual. Nothing would surprise me.'

'According to our records,' said Hapgood, who had already called up a file marked "British Security Services: Confidential", 'his name is Lambert Ticke.'

'Top man, too,' declared Blag, 'if Caspin wants a hundred like him.'

'Bit of an academic high-flier. PhD,' continued Hapgood. 'Went to Cambridge,' he added, and immediately regretted it.

'Cambridge!' bellowed Blag triumphantly. 'That settles it!

They're either traitors or butt-bandits, that neck of the woods, usually both. Other colleges ask: how many A-levels? Cambridge just wants to know: do you take it up the ass and would you strangle the Queen?'

Hapgood took a deep breath. Blag was onto his favourite topic, he needed steering back into the main channel. 'His file says he's single. No "significant other".'

'Not since Stalin turned up his toes,' suggested Blag, refusing to be shifted off course.

Hapgood shrugged, and said nothing. It seemed the safest option.

'And he's off to Fetherton,' muttered Blag thoughtfully. 'Where the Goddamn hell's Fetherton?'

'Yorkshire,' said Hapgood, back on firmer ground. 'Leeds way. Closer to Harrogate, I think.'

Blag rubbed his chin and looked none the wiser. He decided to change the subject. 'What do we have on this Ratt fella? Name doesn't ring any bells.'

'I'll have him checked, see what I can find.'

Quite frankly, Hapgood doubted they had anything on a man called Ratt, but he decided he would cross that bridge when he came to it.

'This Tit must be a sleeper,' mused Blag. 'Nipped in right under our noses. Clever bit of work. Gotta hand it to the Russkies.'

'I don't think Ticke is a Russian,' said Hapgood. 'And Mervyn Ratt doesn't sound like a Russian name, either.'

'Of course it doesn't, the Kremlin's not stupid,' thundered the other man. 'Probably short for Rattsky. Anyhow, doesn't have to be Russian, just a red.'

'I don't see the Russian connection,' objected Hapgood. 'They've nothing to gain from killing the British PM.'

'Don't you believe it,' said Blag. 'Your Russkie's been frozen out of world affairs for years. He's keen to get his nose back in the trough. The bastards will stop at nothing.'

'Could be the Arabs, of course,' suggested Hapgood.

'*Ay-rabs?*' repeated Blag loudly. He stroked his chin, and a faraway look came into his eyes. 'It would make more sense,' he conceded. 'Good God, Caspin in bed with the camel-shaggers, I hadn't thought of that...'

Hapgood tried to counter his boss's latest train of thought. Though he'd raised the Middle East connection himself, it was only an idle remark. 'I don't see Caspin as a traitor,' he said. 'It doesn't feel right.'

'You can't trust anyone,' said Blag forcefully.

'I trust you,' said Hapgood.

'Of course you do,' said Blag. 'You have to trust me. Didn't trust me, we'd get nowhere fast.'

A heavy silence fell for several seconds, broken eventually by Hapgood. 'You haven't said you trust me.'

'Goes without saying,' replied Blag.

'I'd still like to hear you say it.'

'You're in a funny mood.'

'Say it.'

'I trust you. God, man, it's this Tit fella we need to watch out for, not each other.'

Hapgood looked glum. 'So what do you suggest?' he inquired sourly.

'We need to tail him,' said Blag, ignoring the other man's reaction. 'See where he goes, who he speaks to.'

'I'll get the ball rolling,' said Hapgood without enthusiasm. 'Anyone in particular you'd like assigned?'

'Who can we spare?'

'There's Grogan, he's just back from sick leave. Raring to go.'

'Didn't he go bonkers and shoot a couple of our Spanish agents?'

'Something like that, but they say he's fine now, back on the ball.'

'Bit of a loose cannon, though. Don't we have anyone else?'

'Not really. But if we're just seeing how the land lies, it shouldn't be a problem. And he can handle himself, if things turn nasty.'

Blag shook his broad shoulders. 'We'll go with Grogan, then, to keep an eye on things. For the off. Once we know more, we'll send in the big boys.'

'Grogan *is* a big boy,' Hapgood reminded him. 'According to his file he's put on a few pounds while he's been off, and he already weighed in at 16 stone.'

Blag frowned. 'You know what I mean.' He wasn't in the mood for jokes. The security of the western world, and American interests in particular, wasn't a laughing matter. Murdering the British Prime Minister was one thing, but you didn't mess with the good old US of A. Or make light of those who did her dirty work for her. No, sirree.

SIX

Mr Cupperby had never heard anything like it in his life. He would have asked Norah Plank to repeat herself, but feared he had heard her correctly the first time.

'So it's definitely not illegal,' she inquired, leaning forward in her chair, studying him keenly.

Mr Cupperby blanched. 'Well, not illegal as such,' he conceded.

'What do you mean – as such?' she asked. 'Either it is or it isn't. Which is it to be?'

'It's legal, in the sense that it's not illegal,' proclaimed the lawyer in him. 'But is it moral, Mrs Plank? Is it setting the world a good example?'

Mrs Plank shrugged. 'The world is not my concern,' she told him. 'Getting back at my swine of a husband, that's what matters.'

Mr Cupperby struggled with his tie, searching for an adequate response.

'Couldn't you just cut up his suits?' he suggested desperately. 'Might that not be the more sensible option?' In truth, he thought it was no such thing. Mr Cupperby was a deeply moral man, despite his legal training, and the idea appalled him. It said much for his troubled state of mind that he spoke as he did.

Mrs Plank frowned. She'd cut up Henry's clothes already, but had no intention of telling the old fool. 'That's criminal damage, surely?' she said. 'He might call in the police. You're not proposing I break the law?'

Mr Cupperby retreated into his chair. His argument was impossible to sustain. Yet surely anything was better than what this lunatic woman was suggesting.

'You're planning to open up as a lady who – does things to men,' he said, unable to bring himself to complete the sentence.

'Domination,' said Norah helpfully. 'That's all I'm offering. I'm paying men to clean up my house and receive a damn good thrashing into the bargain. How can I lose?'

'Ah!' cried Mr Cupperby, wondering if, perhaps, his legal mind had not missed a trick. 'The administering of physical punishment – that could be deemed violent conduct. Grievous bodily harm, even.'

'But only if the man objects, surely?' insisted Mrs Plank. 'If it's not against his will, where's the harm?'

'The man may not be *compos mentis*,' argued Mr Cupperby, warming to his theme. He became quite excited. He might be on to something here. The use of Latin was always a good starting point. Most clients were unfamiliar with the language, as indeed, if truth be told, was he. But that didn't matter. He was a lawyer. People assumed he did know, and assumption was nine points of the law as his father, the late Mr Cupperby Senior, had often reminded him.

'I wouldn't thrash a loonie,' said Norah, dashing his hopes that he might have turned the tide. 'Loonies have rights, too, I know that.'

'I don't think one should call them loonies,' said Mr Cupperby. 'I believe the correct term is the less mentally able.'

Norah Plank shrugged again. Mr Cupperby couldn't help but notice how violently her bosom shook. It occurred to him – very briefly – that she was not wearing a bra. The thought was most unsettling. Mr Cupperby was a single man of 65, his knowledge of women negligible to the point of non-existence. (He had once had afternoon tea with a lady in Dewsbury, but had taken it no further.) There was no danger, he consoled himself, that Mrs Plank – braless or otherwise – would lead him from the straight and narrow; quite the reverse in fact. But he wished she would contain herself and, deciding she might not, he averted his eyes and thought of his garden.

'If they're mad, what do they care?' she pointed out. 'You can call them anything you like, they won't get upset, that's why they're loonies.'

Mr Cupperby marshalled the last of his troops and flung all he had at her, in one final charge. 'The law might argue that a man who asks to be thrashed is not in his right mind and therefore, *ipso facto*, the balance of his mental state is palpably disturbed.'

Mrs Plank eyed him clinically. 'But if a man *is* in his right mind, then he can ask for what he likes?'

Mr Cupperby's legal juggernaut squealed to a halt. He cast around for another Latin expression.

'*Aquila non capit muscas!*' he cried desperately.

Mrs Plank squinted back at him. 'What does that mean?' she inquired.

Mr Cupperby's heart skipped a beat. He had launched his final weapon, and had not anticipated any response. Most clients, when presented with such a cry, retreated gracefully and paid their bill. He had used the expression several times over the years and it had always served him well. No one had ever asked him what it meant.

He waved airily. 'The point is of no significance,' he attempted. A big mistake. Norah leaned forward, the devil in her eyes.

'What does it mean?' she asked. 'If you don't tell me, I shall go on the internet and look it up. And if it's not there I'll call one of those phone-in programmes on the radio.'

Mr Cupperby felt sick to his stomach. His mind raced. He thought about telling her he had forgotten, but realised this would make him look even more stupid than he already did. He toyed with lying, but the wretched woman had the look of someone who wouldn't take no for an answer even if the answer *was* no.

'An eagle does not catch flies,' he mumbled weakly.

'What's that got to do with anything?' asked Mrs Plank.

Again, Mr Cupperby's mind raced though not, it had to be said, reaching escape velocity. 'I don't know,' he conceded wearily. 'I'm confused. It's been a long day.'

'But I'm legal?' inquired Norah yet again. 'It's not against the law to thrash a man if he deserves it?'

'*Deserves it?*' Mr Cupperby paled. What house of hell was this dreadful woman planning to run?

'Asks for it, then,' said Norah, in the spirit of compromise. 'If he says, "Auntie, beat me with a frying pan," I'm covered by the law?'

'Auntie?' repeated Mr Cupperby, stunned.

'It may not be Auntie,' conceded Mrs Plank. 'It depends on the role-play in question. But am I covered, that's all I want to know.'

'As long as no permanent damage is done, then, yes, I suppose you are,' he replied, finally defeated. This was all too much for him. Ernest Cupperby had not entered the law in order to advise menopausal harridans on the rights and wrongs of thrashing men with frying pans. He had entered the law to make money out of misery and selling homes to first-time buyers. This was completely beyond him. There were days when he wished he'd taken up estate agency instead.

SEVEN

Chief Inspector Bernard Lunt was not a happy man. His haemorrhoids were acting up and his wife had joined a yoga class.

Linda Lunt was a woman who, from time to time, embarked on voyages of self-discovery. She looked inside and generally found herself wanting. What was worse, however, was that on these occasions she invariably found her husband also failed to measure up to her new, exacting standards.

'Meat is poison,' she informed him, on her return from Mrs Palona's class on Yogic Life Enhancement (whatever the hell that was) at the local evening institute.

'I don't think it is,' he replied, not so much out of a conviction that it was true, but more because he liked his steak and kidney pudding, his chicken and chips and his occasional bacon fry up.

'Fish is even worse,' said Linda Lunt, scotching his hope that cod would remain on the menu. 'The Government is pumping contaminated sewage into the sea, along with radioactive waste and something to do with the Pill. I can't remember what, but it's more than likely you'll turn into a woman,' she had declaimed vehemently while clearing the fridge of all offending items.

He had mulled over the prospect and considered its merits. There were worse things that could happen to a man, he reflected, than turning into a woman. It would give him access to bits and pieces he had long been denied. Of course, the notion was ridiculous, but a man could dream. He slunk back to the present.

'I can't fight crime on an empty stomach,' he protested.

'You won't have to,' his wife replied. 'Mrs Palona has given me several recipes, many of them based on seaweed extract.'

'Isn't the seaweed contaminated?' he inquired. It seemed a reasonable question.

'Apparently not,' she told him. 'It absorbs the poisons and converts them into environmentally friendly minerals. Seaweed will save the world. We'd all be much healthier if we ate nothing but seaweed. It contains all the vital nutrients.'

'That doesn't sound very likely,' he remarked, but his wife would hear no criticism of Mrs Palona, who, she reminded him, had spent five years in a Tibetan monastery where she had become skilled both in healthy cooking and the martial arts.

'She could kill you with a flick of her thumb,' said Linda Lunt. 'Though of course she wouldn't as she's a pacifist.'

Her husband frowned. 'If she's a pacifist, why did she learn how to kill a man?'

'That's none of your business.'

Bernard bridled. 'It will be if she does for someone. I'm a policeman, I'd have to arrest her.'

'Yes, well I hardly think that's likely.'

'She might lose her temper. If she's trained to kill with her bare hands, she may have some poor sod's head off before he knows it.'

'I've told you,' said his wife firmly. 'That's not going to happen. Not unless she's provoked, then it would be self-defence.'

Bernard looked at her, aghast, and was on the point of saying something else when he changed his mind. His wife was in a funny mood this morning, and there was no point in pursuing the matter. But alarm bells were ringing in his head. He wasn't sure why, just a feeling. A feeling about the future. A feeling that he decided it was best not to put into words.

EIGHT

Colin Crimp was feeling the strain.

Henry's week-long stay had lengthened into almost three and taken its toll. Henry snored – very loudly and for hours at a time. His personal habits, also, left much to be desired, and, quite frankly, didn't match up to those Colin had hoped for in the ideal housemate. He left his clothes wherever he stepped out of them: his shoes on the settee, his underpants on the bedroom floor. As for his pipe which, however many times he had promised not to smoke it indoors, he invariably ignited after a couple of malts, its foul stench followed Colin like a lovelorn stalker.

Colin doubted whether Mrs Plank would be in a hurry to see her husband return. Indeed, as the days passed, his concern grew. He recalled, with a shudder, the moment one of Henry's socks had materialised inside the fridge (along with a box of Chilean Chardonnay, which hadn't been there the day before, and was already half-empty). As if that were not bad enough, Henry had brought with him a stash of pornographic magazines which he read in the toilet, a room in which he seemed to spend an unnatural amount of time. Colin no longer felt clean in his own house.

'You have a problem with intimacy,' said Hugo Lake.

'I have a problem with dirty old men,' replied Colin.

Hugo Lake was a therapist, whom Colin visited once a fortnight to discuss his mental health, such as it was. They had been seeing each other for the past six months, ever since Colin's breakdown. (Or, rather, what the doctors had officially proclaimed as his recovery from breakdown.) Colin was an

English teacher by training, not an editor in a small publishing company. The latter was his route back to sanity, or, as Hugo Lake preferred to describe it, his 're-engagement with life'. To be honest, so far as Colin was concerned, any route that did not involve his re-engagement with the world of education, and in particular those monsters in human form who had comprised class 4C, Morton High School, Leeds, was fine by him.

'Have you spoken to the girl, yet?' asked Hugo Lake.

'No.'

'Why not?'

'The opportunity hasn't arisen.'

'You work with her seven hours a day, five days a week – what opportunity are you waiting for?'

'The right one,' Colin muttered. 'These things can't be rushed.'

'She can only say no.'

'That's probably what she will say.'

'So you fear rejection?'

'Of course I fear rejection,' admitted Colin. 'Who doesn't fear rejection? Would I be normal if I longed for rejection? Doesn't that show I'm a well man?'

Hugo Lake made a note in his jotter. *Fears reality.* 'Are you still writing your letters?'

'Yes. Every day. I get a lot of anger out of my system. It's very helpful, thank you.'

'How many have you written so far?'

'Five hundred and eighty two.'

'That's quite a haul. It may be time to ease off.'

'I don't want to ease off. There's still a lot I'm angry about. In fact, I was thinking of increasing my output.'

'Why not learn to accept your anger? Channel it into other pursuits. Karen, perhaps.'

'I'm not angry with Karen.'

'I think you are. You want Karen and she's not forthcoming. She goes out with other men. Lots of other men. Almost every other man from what you tell me. Even Henry

Plank has–'

'Yes, thank you, I don't need reminding. I'm a failure when it comes to women.'

'Is that what you think?'

'Isn't that what you're saying?'

'This isn't about me, it's about you.'

Colin slumped. This was how their sessions always went. Several months on and, quite frankly, he wondered what was the point. Hugo Lake rarely offered advice, preferring to parry question with question, constantly throwing him on the defensive. He sometimes wondered why he bothered, and suspected the man was a fraud. There were dozens of certificates lining his walls, but these things could be run up on a computer and the frames looked cheap. Was there really an organisation called 'The Society of Mental Health'? Or 'The UK Counselling Collective'? That one sounded decidedly fishy. And all those letters after his name: MSCo, TBA, SCMH – did they mean anything, or were they just invented?

'I'd like to suggest something,' said Hugo Lake.

Colin stiffened. He didn't like the sound of this; there was something in the therapist's tone that augured ill.

'Open yourself up to Henry Plank. Get things off your chest. He's an older man and may surprise you with his wisdom.'

'You *are* joking?' said Colin. 'His wife's just thrown him out for seeing prostitutes. I hardly think there's much I can learn. He drinks, reads dirty magazines and spends a lot of time in the toilet.'

'I'm not suggesting you embrace his moral code,' countered Lake. 'But he's a free spirit. Perhaps he can release the inner you.'

'What if I *am* the inner me?' replied Colin sadly. 'I mean, what if there's nothing more to release? What if it's all been released and this is it?'

Hugo Lake placed his notepad on the table, steepled his fingers and said, 'Life is a voyage into the unknown, Colin.

Journey forth and discover.'

Colin said nothing for several seconds. He was too busy thinking. What he was thinking was that Hugo Lake was a complete and utter pillock. The man had no more insight into the human mind than he had into nuclear physics. This was money down the drain. Fortunately, it was not his money, it was the NHS's. But that was even worse. Someone, somewhere, was limping around with a dodgy hip because people like Hugo Lake were raking off crazy amounts of taxpayers' cash for peddling twaddle. He wanted to tell this man exactly what he thought of him, and his ideas, and how pointless was the system under which they all laboured. He didn't, of course, because that wasn't how Colin operated. Instead, he nodded weakly, said, 'Yes, I see what you mean,' and felt his lack of self-esteem more acutely than ever.

*****

As it turned out, Hugo Lake's advice proved academic. Having mulled over the possibility of allowing himself to be surprised by Henry Plank's wisdom, both Henry and his wisdom went absent without warning that evening.

When ten o'clock came and passed with his lodger – who had stayed behind after work – not putting in an appearance, Colin wondered whether he should phone the police or just change the locks. In the event, he did neither and went to bed in a troubled state of mind.

He slept, woke, slept and woke again, finally sitting upright at 2.30 am and wondering whether a slice of toast might settle him. He was still pondering the matter when he heard a noise at the front door, and the grate of a key in the lock. Henry was home, a fact confirmed, a moment later, by a loud, sing-song voice that echoed through the house. The man was clearly drunk and talking to himself as he climbed the stairs. It was only when Colin heard a second voice – more shrill and frightful – that the awful truth dawned. *Henry was not alone!*

Dreadful though this conclusion might be, worse was to follow. As he shivered beneath his blanket, cursing those gods who had dragged him to this fork in his life, Colin heard his bedroom door creak open, and a groan of timber as stumbling feet approached.

A loud belch sounded nearby, and then a second closer than the first. Henry – and whatever loathsome creature of the night he had met on his travels – was advancing on his bed! Colin froze. What he should have done, of course, was to move very obviously and very noisily. Yet for some reason, every muscle in his body had locked.

What followed next was the most terrifying moment of his life: Colin felt the blanket lift a fraction and his mattress sag. *Good God! Henry and the tart were climbing in to join him!*

Finally galvanised into action, Colin coughed – very loudly – and whirled his arms, rolling onto his back and moaning as if he had just met the Angel of Death. Which, in a way, he had.

'What the fuck's that?' shrieked a sharp, female voice.

'Bugger knows!' replied Henry drunkenly.

'You've got another bloke in here!' cried the woman. 'I ain't getting into bed with two of you. That's extra.'

Colin felt a hand shuffle across the mattress, and fondle his hip. He stifled a morbid whimper. It was Henry's hand: big, rough and hairy. It was hard to imagine things could get worse.

'My God, it *is* a man!' muttered Henry. 'It's my landlord!'

'I ain't paying your rent!' yelled the woman. 'You're kinky, you are.'

'It's all right,' said Henry. 'He's asleep. He doesn't know we're here.'

'I don't care,' said the woman. 'I'm leaving. This ain't normal.'

'It's OK,' said Henry, recovering. 'I made a mistake. This isn't my room. It's a bigger bed, though. We could all squeeze in at a pinch.'

'I ain't squeezin' in anywhere,' said the woman. 'We all have our limits and those are mine.'

'He's asleep,' mumbled Henry, alive to a hideous, new possibility. 'He won't notice. He takes tablets. They knock him right out.'

Beneath the blankets, Colin bridled. How the hell did Henry know he took tablets? He hadn't told him. He hadn't mentioned any of his health problems, they were his own concern, no one else's. With a jolt, he realised Henry must have gone through his drawers. The bastard! He had opened up his house to the man and this was how he repaid him: rifling through his things and bringing home whores. And, worse still, trying to have sex with them in Colin's own bed in the middle of the night. Were there no limits to the man's depravity?

Possibly not. However, there were, it seemed, limits to those of the woman Henry had chanced upon. She was having none of this, particularly when she caught sight of Colin in the half-light and pronounced him, 'Some sort of monkey man,' and beyond anything she had ever clapped eyes on before.

Though this did nothing for Colin's self-esteem, it was at least the final straw so far as the woman was concerned. It was with some relief, tinged with anger and not a little regret, that Colin heard his uninvited guests stagger clumsily back across the room and out through the door.

He lay perfectly still for several minutes, fearful they might return. When it became clear that he was safe – or as safe as he could ever feel now – he pushed back the sheets, climbed out of bed, crossed quickly to the door, placed his head against it and listened. From somewhere far off, he heard the sound of Henry's voice, oscillating crudely. The woman's, too, though it soon became difficult to tell them apart.

It was all too much. Retreating to his bed, Colin climbed back in, pulled the covers up and tried to shut out the dreadful images running through his mind. Then, as an afterthought, he got up again, crossed to his desk, dragged his chair over to the door and wedged it beneath the handle. It wasn't much, but it was better than nothing. It might allow him a good night's sleep. Then again, he somehow doubted it.

NINE

Colin pondered his future glumly. The appeal of Henry Plank (Publishers) Ltd was not what it had been. Henry had slept in late that morning which, in the circumstances, was perhaps not surprising. Colin had skipped breakfast – for fear of waking his lodger – and had caught the bus into work alone. It made a pleasant change from his usual commute. Colin didn't drive, and, though Henry owned a BMW, he had left it parked near the office for what he called 'insurance purposes', though Colin suspected an empty tank and limited funds were more likely reasons. Their journeys in together, invariably at Colin's expense, with the suggestion that he 'add it to the bill', were never the highlight of Colin's day, and it was a relief to be free of the other man for a change. By mid-day, Henry had not put in an appearance, a turn of events which left Colin both relieved and concerned in equal measure. Not for Henry Plank's personal well-being, but for what might be going on back at his house. He wouldn't put it past Henry to have arranged a rave in his absence, or, more likely in his case, an orgy that would have put a team of footballers to shame.

Karen, in the meantime, had confided to him over a mid-morning cup of tea that her new boyfriend – a Spanish waiter by the name of Ferdinand – was treating her badly.

'I think he's seeing another woman,' she told Colin. 'I found lipstick on his Y-fronts, and it wasn't mine, I know. I don't use that shade of pink.'

Colin felt his stomach tighten. He ached for Karen to become intimate with any part of him, he wasn't fussy. For one long, painful moment he wondered if now might be the time to tell her how he felt; to reveal that he would never let another woman soil his underwear with her lipstick. He wouldn't put it quite like that, of course, and it was while he was trying to fashion an adequate response that she ended his hopes forever.

'It's nice having a friend like you to talk to, Colin. You know, someone who doesn't think about sex when he looks at me.'

He wondered what sort of look he was giving her just then, because it felt like a tap had been turned on, and everything that made him who he was had begun to drain from his body at speed.

Karen shrugged her shoulders. 'Men, eh?' she sighed. 'What can you do? Can't live with them, can't live without them.'

He had no answer to that, but it didn't matter because just then Bob drifted into the room, looking rather vacant. This was not an unusual look, Bob was invariably vacant. Henry employed him because he had 'special needs', which, as far as Colin could judge, Henry had interpreted as the need to be paid as little as possible, while performing a range of menial tasks: fetching, carrying, making the tea and, on occasion, dusting Henry's office.

To be fair, Bob didn't seem to mind. His previous employers had paid more, but they had expected more, too. Bob sometimes failed to turn up for days on end, having – according to his mother – forgotten he worked at Henry Plank's. As his job was largely one that could go undone for much of the time, it didn't matter. And when he did eventually turn up, he was always keen to work twice as hard, for even less money than before, simply to make up for his absence.

Karen had a soft spot for Bob, which dismayed Colin further. She was always putting her arm around the young man's shoulder, giving him little hugs. She never gave Colin a hug, though she was pleased to tell him, on more occasions than he cared to recall, that he was 'a good friend'. Colin didn't want to be a good friend, he wanted to be her wild and impetuous lover. He wondered – from the way she cuddled Bob – if she would treat him any better if he told her about his breakdown, but decided against it. With his luck, she would probably stop talking to him altogether, or leave the country just to be on the safe side.

Bob dropped a pile of papers onto Colin's desk. 'It's Mr Tipson's novel,' he said, and Colin sagged. Frederick Tipson was one of their more prolific – and appalling – authors. He wrote what he liked to call *crimes noir* – but which were little more than pornographic trash, which no normal publisher would touch with the longest stick they could find. To his certain knowledge, sales figures were in single figures for each of Tipson's books and even those, he believed, were purchases Tipson had made himself. What made Tipson all the more objectionable was the fact that, convinced of his literary prowess, he insisted on typing out every novel on an ancient Olivetti Dora he'd been given for his fourteenth birthday and had used ever since. Colin was forced to make corrections by hand, after which the manuscript was converted into electronic format for final printing.

'All great authors use a typewriter,' Tipson had told him on several occasions – both in person and over the phone – as if that transformed him into a great author himself rather than the talentless hack that he was.

While Colin studied the manuscript with some dismay, he saw Karen, from the corner of his eye, give Bob another of her hugs. It made him feel more miserable than ever. When she leaned in close and pecked the young man's cheek, Colin felt life couldn't get any worse.

He was wrong.

TEN

Lambert Ticke's dreams of glory had been put on hold for ten days while Roger Caspin set about clearing the way. Unfortunately, that way involved first finding the chief constable of the North Yorkshire Borders region, before reminding him that he, Roger Caspin, knew where at least three bodies were buried, one of them non-metaphorical. The fact that Peter Barrow had only recently – and quietly – been discharged from an alcoholic rehabilitation centre at the other end of the country had thrown a spanner into the works that had taken some time to remove.

Now, at last, it had been removed and Ticke was driving north. He had been given indefinite leave of absence – told, in fact, to take as long as he liked. Quite frankly, he expected his mission to be a short one, but it was nice to know he had the confidence of those in authority. Though frustrated by the delay, he had put the extra time to good use, scouring the internet for as much information as he could find on the practical aspects of constructing a home-made bomb. It seemed to involve a large amount of chemical fertiliser – conveniently available from any agricultural store – and, less conveniently, a detonator, for which several hours of online research had thrown up no obvious source. Still, no matter. His plan wasn't to build a bomb, merely to create the illusion that such a thing was possible.

Less theoretically – though no less ridiculously – Ticke had visited a West End actor's store from where he had purchased a boot-black beard that in no way resembled his own russet hair colouring, together with a grey stick-on moustache that in no way complemented the beard. A disguise might be necessary, he had considered, and, being the only suitable items they had in stock, he had reluctantly taken both. Still, these were small matters in the greater scheme of things, that scheme being to expose both Mervyn Ratt and his plot to assassinate the Prime Minister of the United Kingdom of Great Britain, Northern Ireland and All Her Colonies Beyond the Sea.

Roger Caspin had informed him, two days previously, that he had 'put a word in the right ear' and that it was 'all systems go'. Caspin's curious choice of language continued to baffle Lambert Ticke, but he dismissed it as the prattle of an inferior mind.

What would have disturbed him, however, had he not been blissfully unaware of it, was that the full might of American intelligence (or at least that part currently accessible by Messrs Blag and Hapgood from their basement HQ in Leytonstone) had been brought to bear on his personal laptop. As a result, his extensive research into the practicalities of domestic bomb-making had been mapped, logged and fumed over for the past few days.

'The guy's a homicidal maniac!' yelled Blag, whose blood pressure had soared to medically dangerous levels. Ticke's investigations had involved several forays onto Isis and Al Qaeda websites, causing Blag to chew to oblivion what little remained of his hard-bitten fingernails.

Even Hapgood had to concede that his boss's original fears – however unlikely – had grown more credible with every succeeding search for 'Bombs and how to make them,' interspersed with the occasional 'Assassination attempt, best way to proceed' and 'Where to buy a nuclear weapon'. (Ticke was nothing if not thorough.)

'Grogan'll have his work cut out to stop this lunatic!' growled Blag as he studied their findings for the seventeenth time. 'Wouldn't surprise me if he's planning to take out the entire Cabinet.'

'We'll have to tread carefully,' cautioned Hapgood, aware

that any rash moves would reflect on the two of them, not just his boss. He rather liked his current posting. It allowed him to indulge his love of the British theatre, his fondness for not being shot on the way into work, and the weekly delights of a Soho-based Miss Lulu de Flame, who knew which of his buttons to press and in what order.

'Tread carefully, my ass!' spat Blag, flaring his nostrils and wishing it was he, not Grogan, who might get the chance to gun down a Commie traitor in cold blood.

'Shouldn't we put MI5 in the picture?' suggested Hapgood. 'I mean, it's their neck of the woods, they might want to get involved.'

Blag gave a dismissive snort. 'Might as well phone Putin direct and ask what he wants for his birthday.'

'Even so,' attempted Hapgood, aware that his cause was already lost. He wondered why he even bothered.

'Even so, my Goddamn ass!' responded Blag, idly scratching his rump as if to reinforce the point. 'The less the Brits know about this, the better.'

Hapgood sighed and abandoned what little fight he had left in him. He closed his eyes and briefly fantasised about the lovely Miss Lulu. Blag had mounted his favourite steed again and was galloping into the sunset. Hapgood might as well dwell safely in his own head and enjoy himself while he could. Things were going to become a helluva lot more complicated before long. He knew that as well as he knew every freckle on the lovely Miss Lulu de Flame's small, perfectly shaped nose.

*****

At precisely that moment, a hundred miles to the north, Lambert Ticke pulled off the motorway and into the 'Happy Bunny' service station. Not that he was feeling much like a happy bunny just then. He desperately needed to use the toilet, having downed seven glasses of water before setting out. He had long ago read that drinking large quantities of liquid ensured the healthy functioning of the human brain. As a man who prided himself on possessing a superior intellect, Ticke had taken the message to heart and drunk like a fish ever since. One happy outcome was a soft and healthy skin, the envy of women everywhere. One not so happy consequence was an all-too-frequent need to urinate that often manifested itself at awkward times. Having already missed two turn-offs, he regretted lacking the foresight to pack a container of some sort to tackle the problem en route. Lay-bys were non-existent on this stretch of road and all the hard shoulders had been converted into smart lanes which, to Ticke's mind, were anything but smart, given the shocking death statistics that accompanied them. His bladder was now fighting its own duel to the death with his stomach, and he wasn't sure which one of them was going to land the fatal blow.

Fifty yards down the road, a blue transit van executed a sharp left-turn, much to the terror of a Volvo driver who had been travelling alongside without a care in the world.

'Pillock!' screamed Volvo Man as he slammed on his brakes, much to the fury of a Nissan driver just behind him and whose language, in turn, was even more choice. As both cars' bumpers locked – like rutting stags – the Volvo span in one direction, and the Nissan in another, dragging both into the middle lane where they forced a slow-moving Skoda into the fast, much to the surprise of a BMW driver travelling at 110 miles per hour only because he'd taken his foot off the pedal.

As the BMW struck the central reservation, thudding back into the path of a Waitrose lorry previously minding its own business, the pair of them met the still-entwined Volvo and Nissan, and the quartet skewed to a gut-wrenching halt, blocking all three north-bound lanes for the next three hours. (Miraculously, no lives were lost, though an unfortunate bowel mishap ultimately rendered the BMW a complete write-off.)

Oblivious to the upheaval in his wake, the driver of the blue transit van slowed to a halt, parking close to a grey Fiat Uno from which Lambert Ticke emerged with indecent haste.

For a moment, Chuck Grogan wondered if he'd been spotted. If he had, he wouldn't put it past the Commie swine he was tailing to have another car parked nearby and into which he would now leap.

The fat American could hardly have been happier. It had been some time since he had seen action and he had missed it.

Grogan was a man built for action, though not for speed, even he was forced to admit. He had always had a problem with his weight and three months of enforced inactivity, while undergoing what his superiors liked to call 'psychological re-evaluation', had caused him to pile on several more pounds.

His van, 'Gertie' (named after his mother, Gertrude Grogan III – though Chuck himself had dropped the 'III' lest his enemies guess they were related and kill her for revenge), was a veritable arsenal: packed with explosives, guns, detonators, manuals of warfare and three chemical agents outlawed under several Geneva Conventions. He wore a badge on his chest that proclaimed to the world, 'I'm with Trump. Up Yours!' The former President might not be to everyone's taste, but he was most definitely to Chuck Grogan's.

As he climbed from the van and followed Ticke into the service station, Grogan's mind abandoned the prospect of replacement vehicles and embraced instead the likelihood that Ticke was meeting with another agent. Given the speed at which he was travelling, he seemed to be running late. It was fortunate, reflected Grogan, that his quarry was physically disabled, shuffling along like a castrated duck. A war wound, perhaps, picked up in Chechnya, or Iraq, and carelessly omitted from the painfully thin file with which he had been provided. To Grogan's mind, it confirmed what a clever swine he was dealing with. A man who could walk like a bird yet slaughter his enemy at will was a worthy foe.

By now they had reached the restaurant forecourt, with no sign of Ticke making contact with another spy. To Grogan's disappointment, Ticke scurried past all the fast-food eateries, heavy with the stench of flame-grilled burger and onions swimming in fat, and waddled into the gentlemen's toilets.

Toilets and the British traitor had always gone together in Grogan's book, and he felt his stomach tighten. Keeping as close to his quarry as decency allowed, he watched Ticke shuffle up and down the narrow aisle, searching for a vacant urinal. It caught Grogan by surprise when a cubicle opened and Ticke promptly flew inside, bowling past the previous occupant before the poor man had safely navigated his exit.

As the door closed behind him, Grogan's imagination went into overdrive. A vision came to him of Ticke hurtling at speed down a mile-long shaft to a secret control room, and he had all but decided to kick in the door to check his facts when the adjoining cubicle became vacant. A thin old man, more bone than skin, made a valiant, and perfectly fair, bid to enter before Grogan shoved him out of the way and barged inside with as much grace as his bulk allowed.

If Ticke had plunged into a lift shaft, Grogan was ready to smash through the adjoining wall and follow him to hell. But if that were not the case, he reasoned, kicking his way through in order to join another man in the toilet might give others the wrong idea. True, he packed enough weaponry to eliminate every witness in the vicinity, but even he knew the attendant carnage might stretch the CIA's powers of cover-up to breaking point.

From the sounds that drifted through from the far side, it seemed that Ticke had not actually descended into the bowels of the earth. Rather more pertinently, he appeared to be speaking to someone.

As far as Grogan could fathom, Ticke was asking someone to 'Come on, come on, come on!' He imagined the unknown third party must be taking his time to pass over classified information, and it was riling the Russkie. This was more like it, he told himself. With luck, he could seize a stash of secret documents, blast the Commie swine to bits and be home in time for tea.

It was only when he heard the squeal of a zip being yanked

down – he knew that sound as well as any man knows it – and Ticke's voice hit a higher level, that delight turned to doubt and then to something beyond disgust.

'Oh, yes! Oh, yes!' squealed Ticke from next door. 'That's it! That's it! Oh, God, oh, yes! Oh, sweet relief!'

Jesus H Christ! thought Grogan, as the terrible truth dawned. Ticke wasn't exchanging paperwork, he was exchanging bodily fluids. Getting his rocks off in a motorway toilet with one of Putin's Nancy-boys. Grogan was in two minds whether to cut his losses now and simply shoot the perverts through the wall. He couldn't miss at this range and God would surely smile on him, not to mention the late President Trump once he got to hear of it.

On the other hand, even he knew that blasting two Commie swine to kingdom come, followed by something in the region of twenty innocent bystanders to cover his tracks, might be pushing a special relationship into unknown territory.

Instead, he clamped his hands over his ears and waited till Ticke had sated himself inside his lover's body. When he heard the toilet flush – God alone knew what had gone down the pan along with all human decency – and the adjoining cubicle eventually opened, he pulled back the bolt on his own door and peered through the crack. He was in time to see Ticke rinse his hands furiously as if to wash away the sin he'd just committed. Grogan would have liked to catch a glimpse of whatever low-life Ticke had ritually buggered, but whoever the poor sod was, he appeared to have slipped away unnoticed.

The moment Ticke had finished his ablutions and left, Grogan emerged, too, and followed him back to his car. The crafty Russian, he noticed, in a trick to throw pursuers off the scent, was no longer walking like a duck.

ELEVEN

Norah Plank was interviewing. It was a new and curious experience for her, made all the more unusual by the nature of the job on offer. There had only been the one applicant, but then she had only invited one person to apply: Myrtle Fling, a 28-year-old checkout girl from the local supermarket, whose grasp of the real world left much to be desired, a trait which, in the circumstances, Norah considered an advantage.

She had always liked Myrtle, an unfailingly polite girl, whose smile had suggested to Norah an underlying vulnerability. A large, ungainly woman, with prominent teeth and blemished skin, it was, perhaps, hardly surprising. Norah sensed at once a kindred spirit: someone who had been badly treated and deserved revenge on the wider world. Men, in particular, felt Norah, echoing her own feelings.

'Have you ever had a boyfriend?' she inquired gently, not from prurience, but because she wanted to be sure there were no social complications in Myrtle's life. The fewer people involved in this enterprise, the better.

'No, Miss,' answered Myrtle politely. 'Boys don't seem to like me much.' She paused reflectively. 'Do I need a boyfriend to get the job?'

Norah shook her head. There had always been something about Myrtle that had made her feel positively matriarchal. Never having had children herself (Henry's low sperm count had seen to that, not to mention her lack of interest in life below the waist), she couldn't be entirely sure what matriarchal felt like, but she was pretty sure it felt something like this. The girl was soft, hard done by, and needed protecting. She would offer her that. They might go far together.

'What do you think of boys?' asked Norah Plank. This was the crunch question, the one that would determine whether Myrtle was up to the job.

Myrtle's face clouded over. 'I don't like them much,' she replied, rather sadly. 'I wanted to, but they don't like me. They laugh at me. I don't think that's right.'

Norah studied Myrtle closely. She could see why they laughed. Myrtle was big, lumbering and not very bright. She caught a whiff of something stale in the air and wondered if Myrtle washed as often as she should.

'What would you say if I offered you twice as much per hour as the supermarket pays, and a room of your own?'

Myrtle's face was a picture of delight. 'I'd say thank you very much,' she answered, 'though I don't know what I could do to deserve it. I don't have any GCSEs or anything like that.'

Norah smiled. 'GCSEs are not necessary,' she replied. 'But you would be required to hit a man, possibly quite severely. Would you object to that?'

Myrtle squinted, the look of a woman who was sure she'd just misheard.

'Hit him?' she repeated. 'Why would I want to hit him? Is he going to do something to me?'

'He'll want you to hit him,' said Norah Plank. 'And he'll be prepared to pay you good money for the privilege. At least he'll pay me, and I'll pay you. Either way, you'll earn more than as a checkout girl. Does the prospect appeal?'

Myrtle rolled her lower lip. 'I won't go to prison or anything?' she inquired anxiously.

'Not at all,' said Norah Plank, admiring the girl's caution. 'Everything is entirely legal and above-board. I've consulted a solicitor. We can hit whomever we like as long as they pay us.'

'So we don't hit anyone who doesn't pay us?' asked Myrtle, trying to get her limited intellect around the idea. 'If we don't like the look of them, we mustn't bash them up?'

Norah regarded Myrtle with growing warmth. She hadn't heard the expression 'bash them up' for a long time. It had an old-fashioned ring to it. She liked that in Myrtle. She was, like Norah herself, an old-fashioned girl at heart.

'No,' she said, with a touch of reluctance in her voice. 'We mustn't hit them for the sake of it. It has to be a legal transaction, though if we make an innocent mistake I'm sure the law will be on our side.'

To the best of her limited ability, Myrtle considered the facts and tried to make sense of them. She currently lived with her 48-year-old mum in a one-bedroom flat on the rougher side of town. The latter enjoyed an exotic private life that mixed copious amounts of alcohol with equally copious amounts of love-making on the settee that served as Myrtle's bed. The fact that the settee had never been designed to take her weight was bad enough. Add to that the knowledge that it doubled up as a bonking board for half the men above a certain age in Fetherton and it wasn't surprising that she hadn't enjoyed a decent night's sleep since leaving primary school.

Her mother had, on more than one occasion, hinted that her daughter's presence was cramping her style. Not just through a lack of privacy, but because Myrtle herself was a constant reminder to her men-friends that something had once gone horribly wrong inside the older woman's womb and it might not be the safest place to linger.

When all was said and done, even Myrtle, hampered as she was by years of state-funded education designed to turn out half-wits, while suggesting that even Oxford couldn't test their intellectual acumen, was able to put two and two together and reach an answer that would have gained her an A-level in maths had she ever bothered to take one.

'I get my own room?' she inquired, just to make sure she hadn't misunderstood. 'With a bed?' (To be fair, the bed was not a deal-breaker. Myrtle would have happily slept on the floor if that was in the contract.)

'You get a bed,' confirmed Norah, 'and we'll share the

cooking.'

'I can't cook,' said Myrtle honestly.

'When can you start?' inquired Norah, batting the objection aside.

'Straightaway,' said Myrtle, finally making up her mind.

Norah reached out and the two women shook hands.

'Straightaway it is, then,' she said. 'Now .... do you fancy a cup of tea?'

TWELVE

Bernard Lunt had been none too pleased when the idea was first mooted.

'The wife won't like it one bit,' he had protested. 'She barely tolerates me in the house, let alone a stranger.'

Chief Superintendent Troy had hunched his shoulders and clasped his hands as if at prayer. His thin, egg-headed boss was a lay preacher in his spare time and Lunt had steeled himself for a sermon.

'The Lord moves in mysterious ways,' he had begun, confirming Lunt's fears. 'It is not our place to question His motives.'

'That's all very well,' said Lunt, 'but it's not the good Lord who's got to tell my wife she'll have an extra mouth to feed.' He had turned the problem over in his mind and tried another tack. 'She's not much of a cook, either. He'd be better off in a hotel.'

The other man had shaken his head slowly and sucked at the air as if it had a particularly nasty flavour. Now it was his turn to try a different tack.

'This could do your career a lot of good,' said Troy, who, though small of stature, had not achieved his current position without a moderate grasp of the human mind.

Lunt had arched a bushy eyebrow. 'You think?'

'Ticke is a high-ranking government official. He's here on a matter of national importance. Only you, myself and the chief constable know anything about it.'

'How does that affect my career?' asked Lunt, whose interest had finally been piqued. If truth were told, there was only one career move that really concerned him and that was getting the hell out of Fetherton as fast as humanly possible.

'He needs to be kept sweet,' said Troy. 'If we can pull this off, we'll all be looked on favourably.'

'Can I be posted to Leeds?' asked Lunt. It came out quickly, without thought, but he didn't care. He *wanted* to be posted to Leeds. His wife wouldn't like it, but sod her. He hadn't joined the force to help little old ladies across the road. He'd joined it to smash in a few heads, for which, in Fetherton, there was scant opportunity. If he waited much longer, he'd be too old to get out of bed without help, let alone knee a villain where it hurt.

Troy had shrugged. 'Who knows what might happen? Play your cards right. I can't promise anything, but...'

Lunt had leaned forward, eyeball to eyeball. This was too important. This was a chance. It might be his only chance. If this didn't work out, it was Fetherton till he dropped.

'I want your promise,' he had said. 'If this comes off, I get Leeds. And you don't tell my wife. You tell me. You tell me I've no choice, I have to go.'

Troy had looked back at him, his long thin head longer and thinner, it seemed, than ever before. He had taken a deep breath, as if considering the finer points of a particularly awkward mathematical equation.

'You go to Leeds,' he had answered. 'And you will have no say in the matter.'

'I want it on the Bible,' Lunt had insisted, playing his trump card. 'I want you to swear.'

'I really don't think...' began Troy, but Lunt was not to be fobbed off.

'You've got one in your drawer,' he had reminded the other man. 'You've got to swear. I want the Lord in on this, as a witness.'

Troy had dithered briefly. He ought to have pulled rank, told Lunt he'd be back in uniform if he didn't do as he was told. But he didn't, of course, because he hated fuss. Instead he opened the drawer, took out the red-leathered edition of the King James he kept there to give him strength in times of hardship and did as Lunt had asked. He swore he would go to Leeds. Another man might have thrown in a few extra words of swearing, but Ernest Troy was not one of those men. He did offer up a silent prayer, however, and prayed for forgiveness from the people of Leeds for what he was about to do to them.

When it was over, Lunt had punched the air. He would rather have punched a face, but there was no face available, apart from that of Chief Superintendent Ernest Troy, and even Lunt was bright enough to see the obvious drawback.

To his surprise, his wife had not objected. Lunt wanted to put it down to his diplomatic skills and the clever way he had convinced her that this was an honour bestowed on the pair of them, but especially on her. The fact that he had so embellished matters as to make out their guest to be within spitting distance of the Queen and a man who had saved the nation more than once had done his cause no harm, but even he was baffled by his wife's positive response.

'That will be no problem,' she had told him. 'It's the least we can do, and if it's a matter of national security we'd be failing in our civic duty to refuse.'

What she hadn't added, because it would only have made her seem less than noble in his eyes (and who knew when those particular bonus points might be traded in?) was that Mrs Palona had recently told her that suffering – the more miserable the better – was to be heartily embraced because it strengthened the soul. Linda had no doubt that housing a boring old bugger from London fell into that category. Bernard might have made him sound like James Bond on steroids, and a weekly visitor to the Palace, but he would probably turn out to be a dull, middle-aged man with very little hair and even less to say for himself. So she was content to take her punishment and emerge the better woman for it.

All of which brought Bernard back to the here and now, sitting in his office and deeply regretting that he had ever heard the name Lambert Ticke, let alone agreed to have the idiot in his house for the next fortnight.

Lambert Ticke, for his part, was having doubts of his own. He had arrived in Fetherton the previous evening and checked into the Grand Richmond Hotel. Unfortunately, the establishment had failed to live up to its name, lacking both hot water and clean towels and with an 'all you can eat' buffet breakfast that had won him over to the joys of fasting. He had stoically consoled himself with the knowledge that it was only for the one night and that he would shortly be hunkering down with Fetherton's 'finest detective mind' as Roger Caspin (without any evidence to back up the claim) had described Bernard Lunt.

Lunt, Caspin had also assured him, was a man keen do his every bidding. It seemed odd, then, that Lunt gave the impression of being thoroughly disinterested; a fellow, indeed, who would be loath to do any man's bidding. Still, that couldn't be helped. Ticke was here as an agent of the Crown, and the sooner Lunt accepted that the better.

'I've been told you'll be assisting me with my inquiries,' Ticke began pompously.

Lunt curled his upper lip, and made a whistling noise through his nose. Ticke groaned inwardly. The man was clearly a simpleton, a provincial type with nothing much to occupy his days. Not a fellow with much education, he suspected, and wondered whether he should speak slowly.

'My – name – is – Lambert – Ticke,' he announced.

Lunt frowned. Ticke hoped he was getting through. 'I'm looking for a man,' he continued, a little more rapidly.

'Your private life is your own concern,' replied Lunt.

Ticke closed his eyes for a moment. This wasn't going to be easy. Fetherton was the sort of place from which people rarely ventured. The gene pool was undiluted, resulting in travesties of nature like Bernard Lunt.

'His name is Mervyn Ratt, and he lives in Fetherton.'

This time, Lunt's upper lip curled dramatically. 'Then

you've come to the right place,' he said. 'This is Fetherton. Do you have an address?'

Ticke nodded. 'Yes, I do. This is it.' He pushed a piece of paper across the desk.

'Well, then,' said Lunt, pushing it back, 'it's a long shot, but if you pop in later and ring his bell, you might find him at home. It being his house, *the place where he sodding well lives!*'

Ticke's eyes blazed wide. This wasn't the welcome he'd been hoping for. Quite frankly, he'd anticipated more respect.

'You're a public employee,' he said. 'I pay your wages, I expect a cordial response.'

Lunt opened his mouth to reply, then promptly shut it again. Reluctantly, he was forced to remind himself that, despite the fact that the fellow opposite was just the sort of man he'd been put on earth to give a good kicking to, he held his – Lunt's – fate in a pair of soft, manicured hands. Telling the pompous twat he was also a public servant and that he – Lunt – paid his wages, too, and probably twice what Lunt earned, was perhaps not the best approach.

Ticke was a Pretty Boy, decided Lunt, which didn't help his cause in the latter's eyes. Pretty Boys had always wound him up. He looked as if he had softer skin than Mrs Lunt, a woman who spent an obscene amount of money on moisturisers. He dreaded to think what Ticke was getting through. He probably bathed in donkeys' milk.

'Do you have a plan of action?' Lunt inquired, not overly bothered whether the other man did or not. However, he couldn't say two things at once, so asking the question at least kept him from suggesting Ticke commit a sexual act with himself.

'I do,' said Ticke, 'but I can't divulge what it is. It's Top Secret', and he patted the side of his perfectly sculpted nose as if to emphasise the point.

Lunt felt his hackles rise again, and struggled to keep his punching hand under the table.

Ticke eyed him curiously, much as he might a monkey in

a cage. The other man's behaviour appealed to the scientist in him. He had Mervyn Ratt down as a potential threat to the state because of his letters. But what sort of man was Bernard Lunt? What were *his* limits, his propensity for social alienation? He took out a notebook, opened it at a clean page and scribbled something down.

'What are you up to?' asked Lunt, alarmed. He wasn't used to people making notes in his presence. Not unless they were reporters, and not even then, because he had long ago learned that if a reporter was within spitting distance (and he meant that literally), it was best to keep your mouth shut. They'd write their lies without help from you, and you might as well leave them to it.

'I'm making notes,' explained Ticke without looking up.

'I can see you're making notes,' said Lunt, irritably. 'Notes about what, that's what I'm asking.'

'I'm here on behalf of Her Majesty's government,' Ticke reminded him loftily. 'I'll ask the questions.' He was rather enjoying himself now, though he could see the Inspector wasn't. Far from it. Lunt's face had turned a deep shade of puce and a vein was throbbing over his left eye. He looked as if he were in danger of bursting a blood vessel. That wouldn't do, thought Ticke. He wasn't much impressed by the other man, but he would need to keep him onside. His plans depended on it.

'I'm a police officer,' Lunt reminded him, in turn. 'I answer to Her Majesty, not you, and don't forget it.'

Ticke straightened his back, and breathed rhythmically for several seconds. It often helped in moments of stress. It calmed him down, promoted the flow of oxygen to the brain and cleared his mind. What was it Machiavelli had said? You must be devious, convince your enemy that he was your friend. Suck up to him, then strike while his back was turned. Something like that. Lunt was a nincompoop, and would need to be handled accordingly.

'Look, I'm sorry,' Ticke lied. 'We've got off on the wrong

foot. Can we start again?'

Lunt regarded him suspiciously. He had been mesmerised by Ticke's nostrils, which had been flaring in a peculiar manner and squeaking intermittently. He wondered if the other man was about to have a heart attack.

'What do you want with this Ratt bloke?' he asked, sidestepping Ticke's question. 'What's he done? Should we know about him?'

'As of this moment, he's done nothing,' admitted Ticke. 'But it's what he's about to do that concerns us.'

'*About to do*? What the hell's he about to do?' inquired Lunt, hunching forward, more interested now. He wondered if a good kicking might be on the cards.

Ticke leaned forward at the same time, mirroring the other man's movements. He had studied body language and knew it would put him at his ease. It was unfortunate that Lunt appeared to be a man who suffered with his gums, at least if the smell from his mouth was any clue. Ticke glanced sideways as if to confirm they would not be overheard, a superfluous concern as they were alone in a room with its only door closed. It was only then that he realised there were no windows. Good God, it was positively primeval – like a cave, he considered. No wonder Lunt was a barbarian.

'We believe,' said Ticke, deciding that the use of a plural added weight to his words, 'that he is plotting to assassinate the Prime Minister.'

Lunt's eyes narrowed. 'You *are* joking!'

'It's not a joking matter,' said Ticke. 'Why do you think I've been sent down?'

Lunt let that one go. He shook his head. 'We'd have heard of him,' he insisted, 'if he was dangerous. We'd have got wind. Someone would have blabbed, given us the nod. Something. It's not on.'

'We didn't know ourselves until recently,' said Ticke.

Lunt shook his head and succumbed to a deep sigh. 'Good God...' he muttered. 'I can't believe it. Assassination? Here? In

Fetherton?'

'It's the PM's seat,' Ticke reminded him. 'What better place?'

'Yes, but he's never here, is he? I mean, let's face it, he's the Prime Minister, he's got better things to do. We're only handy when it comes to voting for him.'

Ticke sat back in his chair. 'Did you vote for him?'

'That's none of your business,' said Lunt, who had only ever voted once, and never again since the BNP had left town. 'So when's this assassination taking place?'

'We don't know, that's the point. It's why I've been sent. Incognito.'

Lunt looked puzzled. 'You're incognito? Your name's not Ticke?' he snorted loudly. 'I didn't think it was. Bit of a stupid name. I mean, Ticke – sounds like tit!'

'My name *is* Lambert Ticke,' said Lambert Ticke, offended. 'I'm not here in disguise, it's just that I'm not here officially!'

'Not here officially?' Lunt's face clouded over again. 'What do you mean, you're not here officially? I was told–'

'I know what you were told,' said Ticke. In fact, he had no idea what Lunt had been told and he wasn't much bothered either. 'But things are more complicated. I'm here at the request of the Prime Minister himself.'

This was, he knew, a gross distortion of the facts, if not a downright lie, but quite honestly, he no longer cared. Lunt was getting on his nerves. He had expected his mission to be a simple one. A policeman on whom he could rely, some sort of surveillance, a prod or two in the right direction. It was already clear that this would be more complicated than he had hoped. No matter, he had come prepared, he had a plan. All that mattered was that he had official back-up, for when the time came.

'No one must know who I am,' said Ticke. 'My name is unimportant, I'm not known. It doesn't matter.'

'So what do you want *me* to do?' asked Lunt cautiously.

'Nothing for the moment,' said Ticke. 'I'll investigate the suspect on my own. Once I have the proof I need, I'll call you in and you can arrest him.'

'You seem pretty sure of yourself.'

'I am,' said Ticke, though he was anything but. 'That's why I'm here. He leaned forward again. 'You're to do nothing until I authorise action. Do you understand?'

Lunt's eyes narrowed and, beneath the desk, his fists clenched angrily. He'd only been with this idiot for a few minutes and was already wondering how much more he could take.

'I'm a police officer,' he said at last, forcing the words out. 'If he's a danger to the public I should have him in now. For questioning at least.'

'You're to do nothing,' said Ticke, trying to keep the alarm out of his voice. The last thing he needed was for Ratt to be arrested before he could do what he had set out to do. 'I've told you this in confidence. I have the chief constable's backing.'

Lunt chewed his lip so hard it drew blood. He didn't know about the chief constable, but he knew this cretin Ticke had Troy's support. And Troy could swing him Leeds if he followed orders, however much it went against the grain. That was what mattered now.

Another thought struck him, a happier one this time. If Ratt was as dangerous as Ticke claimed, then he might do for the bugger. That would be a result. And Troy couldn't say no to his posting to Leeds, not if he'd done as he'd been asked – even if they found Ticke floating down the canal with his ears in his mouth. Troy had sworn it on the Bible, and that had made things legal. Lunt might not be a God-fearing man, though he liked to put the fear of God into others, but Troy certainly was. He wouldn't tell the Lord he was sending a man to Leeds and then not do it. That would be risking a fork up his arse for all eternity.

'We have to tread carefully,' said Ticke. 'That's how we'll reel our villain in.'

It was a long time since Lunt had heard the word 'villain'. Talking to Ticke was like being transported to another world; a world he hoped Ticke would shortly sod off back to.

'It won't be easy,' said Ticke and flared his nostrils again. It made Lunt start. 'This isn't an exact science.'

'What's science got to do with it?' inquired Lunt, puzzled.

'How familiar are you with Davril's *Law of the Third Brain*?' asked Ticke.

Lunt regarded him coldly. 'Quite frankly,' he replied, 'I'm not that used to most people having the one.'

'Davril postulates – says,' Ticke corrected himself quickly.

Lunt looked as if he was about to erupt, but contented himself by crunching his knuckles one at a time.

'Davril's theory is that we are all three people in one: the conscious, subconscious and a third, combined version of the three. This third state of altered awareness comes about when the first two merge, completing the individual's cross-over to either genius or madness.'

'And this Ratt bloke, he has three brains, does he?'

'In a manner of speaking. I believe he has crossed over, or, if not, is about to.'

'It sounds like gibberish to me,' muttered Lunt.

'Anyway,' said Ticke, ignoring Lunt's objection, 'the chief constable says he's put you at my disposal. While I'm on the case, so to speak.'

The other man's face changed hue. The colour fled for an instant, then returned, like a tide in full flood, his cheeks blood-red, his mouth trembling.

'Is there a problem?' asked Ticke, as if daring the other man to say there was.

Lunt's mouth opened and closed more than once. A vision of Leeds floated through his mind, and new colleagues as thrilled as he was by the prospect of physical violence. How important was it really, he asked himself, to leave Fetherton and put his present life behind him? Was kicking heads in a big city worth the loss of kicking the one currently perched on top of Pretty Boy's shoulders? Could he manage both, perhaps? Was there a win-win solution he'd somehow overlooked?

Sadly, he decided, nothing sprang to mind.

'No problem,' said Lunt, while vowing that if it were at all possible before Ticke cleared off back to London – or ended up in the canal – he would ensure the pompous sod paid for telling him that he was, in any way, shape or form, at anyone's disposal, let alone Lambert twatting Ticke's.

*****

Chuck Grogan was in his element. More precisely, he was in his blue transit van, parked in a side-street two hundred yards north-east of Fetherton Police Station.

Though Lambert Ticke might have been disturbed to learn that his laptop had been hacked, he would have fallen into a dead faint to discover that just about every other aspect of his waking life had been equally violated. Armed with Ticke's details, it had been child's play for Grogan to break into his flat and plant a miniature listening device, no larger than a baby's fingernail and just as thin. Well, several tracking devices, to be on the safe side. He had bugged five pairs of shoes, including slippers, two pairs of silk pyjamas, three suits, an overcoat, jacket, fifteen ties and seventeen assorted pairs of underpants and socks. It had cost the United States Treasury a small fortune but was, Grogan knew, worth every cent. You couldn't put a price on democracy and, fortunately, Grogan didn't have to as he'd failed to tick several small boxes when checking the items out of storage. Each signal operated over a three-mile radius and, as Fetherton, he knew, was only five miles square, tracking the God-forsaken son-of-a-Soviet-bitch should prove simple enough wherever he went.

It was a while since he'd been assigned to a high-profile case and he took it as proof that he was 'back in the loop', the unfortunate episode with the Spanish agents now water under the bridge (along with, it had to be conceded, the two agents themselves). Hapgood and Blag hadn't filled him in on every detail – they didn't need to. Safer that way, for all concerned

– apart from Ticke, of course. Though no one had put it into words, Grogan took it as read that he was authorised to blow the Russkie to buggery and beyond when the time came. (The fact that no one had put it into words because that wasn't the intended outcome was neither here nor there in Grogan's mind.)

Ticke was an experienced Russian hitman, highly decorated and having doubtless seen action in Chechnya, where he'd taken out so many men that the suits in London had pretended he'd taken out no one at all, or had even been there in the first place. They hadn't even said that he *was* an assassin – which showed how serious things were. Should Grogan be captured and tortured for what he knew, before being blasted to buggery and beyond himself, the enemy would get nothing out of him however many toenails they removed. (Not that that would do them any good. In a moment of genius, three years previously, Grogan had had every one of his nails surgically removed and replaced with plastic replicas. He'd had the nerve endings ripped out, too, just to be on the safe side, and half-hoped he *would* be captured and tortured one day so that he could enjoy the look on some sadist's face when he realised he'd wasted a week of his life he'd never get back.)

In the meantime, he was on the trail of a homicidal maniac and he couldn't have been happier.

Grogan was aware, from messages that had passed between Ticke and his handler, Roger Caspinsky, that the man from London was spending his first night in a crappy hotel in Fetherton before moving on to a 'safe house'. (Unlike Ticke, Grogan had checked out the establishment on TripAdvisor, where it had managed to amass a record number of one-star reviews for its lack of anything resembling service, courtesy or basic kitchen hygiene.)

While Ticke had spent half the night swatting bedbugs the size of rodents, Grogan had caught up on his sleep. ('Gertie' was equipped with a small camp bed, as well as enough firepower to take out the centre of Fetherton.) In the morning, suitably refreshed, he had waited for Ticke to emerge (looking considerably more weary than when he had checked in), tumble into his Fiat Uno and drive to the far side of town where he had parked, then marched boldly into Fetherton Police Station.

Though Grogan's recording equipment had remained active overnight, it had picked up nothing more audible than gentle snoring, the occasional burst of flatulence and several 'flipping hells' each time Ticke presumably took a swing at his unwanted bed-mates. To Grogan's dismay, he was currently getting no signal at all and was, as a result, frustratingly unaware of any treacherous conversation Ticke might be having with his Fetherton contact. As it beggared belief that not one item of Ticke's clothing contained a listening device (and malfunction of American military equipment being a firm no-no), Grogan drew the inevitable conclusion: the station was lead-lined and packed with an impenetrable barrier of Russian-made jamming equipment.

That could mean only one thing. The entire cop shop was on Putin's payroll. Were they the 'hundreds of men' he'd been told Caspinsky had boasted about? He wondered if he should bring HQ up to speed, but promptly dismissed the idea. Who knew how far up the sluice pipe the traitors had slithered? No, best keep shtum for the present.

To pass the time, while he waited for Ticke to re-emerge, Grogan busied himself with a run-through of his armoury. It was comforting to know that he possessed sufficient firepower to slug it out with any foe, short of one armed with a medium-sized nuclear device, which, even to Grogan's demented mind, seemed unlikely. Though he might not possess anything in the atomic category, he packed enough weaponry, if push came to shove, to take out an area 50 metres in diameter. Grogan called it his 'Armageddon option' as it involved losing the van, and possibly himself into the bargain. That his superiors in London had no idea he possessed such an arsenal did not trouble him unduly. The men in suits were a nervous bunch at the best of times and the less they knew the better. Besides, there were traitors to be found everywhere these days, even – Goddamnit – in the CIA. It was best to work in secrecy. He could trust himself, that was all that mattered.

FOURTEEN

Colin Crimp had come to a fateful decision. It had occurred quite by chance and, though he had grabbed it with both hands at the time, he was beginning to regret his impulsiveness.

He had asked Karen out for a drink.

Well, to be more precise, Karen had asked him out for a drink and he had said yes.

To be even more precise, Karen had burst into tears, said she didn't know who to turn to, and wished there was someone she could have a chat with after work.

Colin had said he was free and what time suited her best, anything was fine by him. She had asked if he was sure because she knew he was 'taking care of Mr Plank just now,' which made Henry sound as if he might have dementia or couldn't get out of bed to go to the toilet. (The latter perilously close to the mark, reflected Colin glumly.) Colin found himself wishing Henry *did* have dementia, forgot where they lived and had to move into a nursing home on the other side of town. That would suit him down to the ground, however unlikely the prospect.

The outcome was that they had arranged to stop off at *The Hungry Ferret* after work, a pub close by that did meals as well as drink. That suited Colin perfectly, even though he had prepared a rather tasty salmon dish with Waldorf salad and crusty garlic bread which would probably now end up in the bin, but what the hell. (It would have given him no comfort to learn – thanks to Henry's overnight guest sleeping in late – that the meal had not, in fact, gone to waste.)

He wished he could have popped home first and changed.

He wasn't sure into what – or whom. Possibly someone slightly taller, better looking and with a foreign accent as that seemed to be Karen's type. A suit and a fresh pair of Y-fronts might have come in handy, though he suspected the latter were likely to prove academic on a first date. Not that this was a date, first or otherwise, though he liked to think it was. Who knew, perhaps Karen would ply him with alcohol and ask him back to her place for coffee? A man could hope, or at least dream, and both were much the same in Colin's world.

'I've done something I shouldn't have,' said Karen, knocking back a g&t in a single gulp, her face miserably puckered.

'It can't be that bad,' suggested Colin, who wondered if the severity of badness might work in his favour should a lot of understanding be required.

'I took advantage of Bob,' said Karen quickly. 'Yesterday. In the stationery cupboard. After work.' She sighed twice. Once as she said it, and again when she picked up her glass and realised it was empty.

Colin felt his world collapse. 'When you say you took advantage,' he began feebly, and wondered if it was too much to hope that she'd swindled Bob at cards or sold him a time share in Grimsby.

'We made love,' she said bluntly, leaving no room for doubt, which he'd been desperately hoping she would. 'Three times,' she added unnecessarily, and dug a deeper pit in which to bury Colin's body. When she lowered her head and sighed, he wasn't sure if it was because she couldn't bear to look him in the face, or because she regretted emptying her glass so quickly.

'Would you like another one?' he inquired. 'Drink,' I mean, he added swiftly, in case she thought he meant a further round of love-making. Which was silly, because there was no way she would think that, or, if she did, certainly not with him. Henry, possibly; Bob for certain, it seemed; but not Colin. Never Colin.

'Yes, please,' she said quietly, and without lifting her gaze. 'A double, thank you.' For one moment, Colin felt as if he wasn't really there. And, a moment after that, he found himself wishing it were true.

By the time he returned with the top-up (his own half of shandy was still sitting untouched on the table), Karen appeared to have recovered her composure.

'I'm a fool,' she said sadly. 'I'm a sucker for a man who says nice things to me or looks as if he needs a cuddle. I can't say no, even when they don't ask me in the first place.'

'He didn't ask you?' Colin wondered where this was leading.

'No,' said Karen, shaking her head. 'He just looked fed up and I thought it would make him feel better. You know, having a woman do something nice to him.'

What was left of Colin's world exploded. Not for the first time in his life, he wondered what sort of vibes he gave off. He'd been down in the dumps for a long time and Karen had never considered ravishing him in the hope it might help. History, he reflected gloomily, was beginning to repeat itself. And he didn't want it to repeat itself, because it had been pretty rubbish the first time round.

Before he'd had his breakdown, he'd been keen on a fellow-teacher, Maggie Henderson, a quiet young woman who taught French and English literature. He'd gone so far as to ask her out but she'd said no. Well, what she'd actually said was that she was washing her hair that night, which puzzled him as he hadn't, up to that point, mentioned any particular night. Undaunted, he'd suggested another night (just in case she'd misheard him), but it turned out she was washing her hair that night as well. She said it was a hygiene thing as there was an unreported outbreak of lice in the area and you couldn't be too careful.

It was a week later, after she'd been arrested for illegally parking herself on top of an underage boy in the park – someone they both taught – that the full force of his rejection struck home. The boy's name was Wayne Winkley, though his unfortunate nomenclature wasn't his main claim to fame.

Even at the tender age of 15, he was well known to the local police, not to mention the local hospital, where his severe acne and even more severe BO had turned the stomachs of some of the finest doctors in their field.

Romantic rejection, followed by remorseless ribaldry from the amoral and intellectually challenged hell-hounds who made up class 4C, Morton High School, Leeds (even they could see he'd come off second best to someone not quite human), had begun his downward spiral into a pit of mental and physical decay. Barely a month later, he had been carried from his classroom on a stretcher, screaming bawdy limericks that would have embarrassed a rugby squad, while asking two shell-shocked paramedics whether his willy was the smallest one they'd ever seen.

He'd spent a month in hospital, followed by a further year in what his social worker described as a 'care readjustment facility', and which Colin insisted on calling 'a loony bin'. He wasn't going to be patronised by a 20-year-old 'woke warrior' just out of nappies (as he was happy to describe him), especially as he knew he could get away with it, being (as he was also happy to announce) 'not right in the head'.

When he had finally been passed 'fit to return to normal society' (that 'normal society' being the reason he had lost his mind in the first place), he set about finding a less stressful means of employment. As his only qualification in life was a vague mastery of the English language – though English appeared to be evolving with such indecent haste that he doubted anyone could make that claim these days – he had jumped at the chance to work for 'a long-established publisher of quality literature worldwide'. Even more so as the company was just a 20-minute bus-ride from his house and he had already fallen in love with the friendly young woman called Karen who had shown him into Henry's office for his interview.

Henry had hired him on the spot. Colin assumed he had made a remarkable impression on his new employer, who (another bonus!) seemed largely unconcerned about his life up to that point. What he hadn't known just then was that Henry was running late for an appointment with Delia Delightly, a big-bosomed lady in Leeds who liked to bounce up and down on men for a living. Henry was keen to clear the decks for the next few hours and, as Colin was the only applicant and appeared to have no unpleasant habits, he saw no point in prolonging the process.

All of which brought Colin back to the present, sitting in a pub with the girl he loved – or at least fantasised about loving – who had just confessed to ravishing an innocent young man against his will and, even worse, a man who wasn't Colin.

'Why are you telling me all this?' he said finally, having considered the matter for almost a minute and finding no light at the end of life's tunnel. Karen, he noticed in the interval, had emptied her glass for a second time and was regarding it forlornly, much as she might a recently deceased pet she had loved from birth.

'Because he wants to marry me,' she said. 'He said it was only right because we'd – well, you know…'

'Yes, of course,' said Colin miserably, and with no wish to go over the matter again, or in any more detail.

'You're not going to, are you?' he inquired quickly, and hoped the concern in his voice wasn't giving too much away. Or maybe he didn't hope that, he wasn't sure of anything anymore.

Karen shook her head. 'Oh, no!' she squeaked, as if Colin had just pulled down his Y-fronts and exposed himself to the room. 'I wouldn't do that. I couldn't. It wouldn't be fair.'

Colin couldn't imagine any sort of universe – parallel or otherwise – in which being married to Karen was an unfair proposition, but he let it pass.

'That's why I told him you and I were engaged,' she said as calmly as if she'd mentioned that it looked like rain tomorrow. 'I thought it was best, you know, to let him down lightly.'

Colin frowned and tried to process this latest revelation. He couldn't decide if his role in letting Bob down lightly was cause for delight or dismay. On balance, he suspected it was the latter. On the plus side, he was now engaged to Karen, albeit only in that previously mooted parallel universe; the one that existed solely in his imagination.

'What did he say?' asked Colin. 'When you told him?'

'He wasn't best pleased,' said Karen. 'He said I shouldn't have done what I did if I was already engaged to another man. He said I was being unfair to you.'

'That was decent of him,' said Colin, warming to Bob despite the fact that he had done something with Karen that he, Colin, couldn't get away with even in his wildest dreams.

'I asked him not to tell you,' she admitted. 'I said you'd be upset.'

'I should think I would,' agreed Colin.

'I said you might get angry, too, and lose your temper.'

'Very likely,' he conceded, forgetting, for the moment, that none of this was true.

'I told him you'd probably kill him,' said Karen, 'just to be on the safe side.'

'*You said I'd kill him?*' squealed Colin. '*Just to be on the safe side?*' and immediately regretted it. At least three people turned round, including a large, tattooed man at the bar who looked as if he might already have killed someone himself.

'Well, I didn't want him telling you, did I? You know, that we were engaged. I didn't want that coming out.'

Again, Colin withered and waned. Nothing she'd said so far seemed to cast him in a good light. He couldn't see this marriage lasting, even if they got to the altar, which didn't seem to be part of the plan, though he was willing to give it a go if it helped.

'You'll give what a go if it helps?' asked Karen, alerting Colin to the fact that at least part of what he'd just thought had escaped into the real world.

'Marry you,' he said, then blushed and tried to make light of it. 'I mean what are friends for if they're not prepared to marry you for love. I mean, not for love, to help you out of a spot.' In his mind, he added the words, 'And I wouldn't want a shag,' but he managed not to say that out loud, which was just as well because it wouldn't have been true.

Karen smiled, and her entire body seemed to relax, as if the weight of three worlds had fallen from her shoulders.

'Anyway, it doesn't matter now, because I've told you, so we don't have to worry about it,' she giggled girlishly. 'And we don't have to get married, either, what a relief.'

'Yes,' said Colin without enthusiasm. 'What a relief.'

'Shall we have another drink?'

'I think I need one,' said Colin, and took a nervous sip at his shandy.

*****

It was 6.35 pm and Linda Lunt was growing anxious. 'Our guest is late,' she said, tugging back a curtain and squinting into the gloom as if that might conjure him out of the darkness. 'You're sure he knows where we live?'

'I gave him our address,' said Bernard grumpily. 'I think he can read. I'm sure it's one of the skills they expect from a secret agent. That and being able to skin a rabbit in the wild.'

He didn't know why he said that. Having met Lambert Ticke – and been glad to see the back of him – he doubted the man would know how to skin a sausage let alone some diseased beast that loped about at speed and would take some catching. He rather hoped Ticke wasn't going to turn up – that he'd already changed his mind and buggered off back to London – though that might scupper his plans for Leeds. Dinner tonight was going to be a miserable affair. His wife's cooking wasn't up to much at the best of times and they hadn't entertained in years. He trusted she'd kept it simple. Something out of a tin, perhaps, that she just had to heat up and put on a plate. He might not have taken to Lambert Ticke, but even he drew the line at poisoning a guest in his house.

'I haven't cooked rabbit,' said Linda stiffly. 'I hope he's not expecting meat. He'll be disappointed if he is.'

Bernard rather doubted that. Ticke looked like the sort of man who could gorge himself to death on a lettuce leaf. Besides, unless he had a preference for blood-soaked steak or a piece of fish that tasted as if it had just swum ashore and never seen a frying pan in its life, disappointment wouldn't be his first response.

Just then, a flash of headlights brightened their front garden and the sound of crunched gravel announced the arrival of their visitor.

Linda dusted herself down and toyed with her hair in the mirror. She might be putting up with this man for the good of her soul over the next few days, but that was no reason she shouldn't look her best.

Bernard sighed, marched towards the front door and opened it just as Lambert Ticke landed sharply on their doorstep.

'My suitcase is in the car!' he barked, addressing Bernard as if he were a porter on the overnight express. 'Where's your toilet? Quickly! I'm going to have an accident!'

'It's upstairs, second on the right,' began Bernard, who was about to introduce his wife. A moment later, Ticke had vanished, mounting the stairs two at a time before taking the first on the right and crashing unceremoniously into the Lunts' bedroom, where he relieved himself instinctively into the soil of a pot plant conveniently placed at groin level on a narrow, walnut table.

It was not, even Lambert Ticke was forced to admit, the customary way of announcing to a pair of perfect strangers that he had finally arrived in their house.

FIFTEEN

Lambert Ticke's evening had not gone well which, given the manner of his arrival, was hardly surprising. That said, he had escaped lightly. Having emptied his bladder into Linda's favourite house plant (a gift from Mrs Palona, who had assured her it would 'cleanse her soul' as she slept), he had discovered to his relief (no question of a pun entered his practical mind) that his hosts had not followed him upstairs. Realising his mistake, he had quickly located their bathroom, entered, flushed the bowl, washed his hands, and left. Emerging, he nearly bumped into Bernard Lunt, huffing grumpily as he lugged two large suitcases and a rucksack up the stairs.

'You should have left the rucksack in the car,' said Ticke carelessly. 'I always keep it there.' He sighed. 'Not to worry, I won't put you to any trouble. I can return it in the morning.'

'That's very good of you,' said Bernard drily, glad of the fact that both his hands were full as it saved him from deciding which fist he should use to punch Ticke's head in. He dragged himself – and his burden – to a room at the far end of the landing, and paused outside.

'Would it help if I opened the door?' inquired Ticke.

'Well, I'm not going to kick the sodding thing in,' said Bernard sharply. 'It's not a fucking police raid.'

'That would be silly,' said Ticke without a hint of sarcasm. 'It's your house, you'd have to pay for the damage.'

For a second time, Bernard was thankful his hands were occupied. He wasn't sure how much more of this he could take.

Once inside, he had deposited the bags in a heap by the bed, and turned to leave. Ticke reached into his trouser pocket and, for one dreadful moment, Bernard thought he might tip him. Instead, Ticke pulled out a large pink handkerchief and wiped his nose.

'It's a bit musty,' he said. 'The room could do with being aired.'

'We've had no one in here,' said Bernard happily. 'Not since the wife's mother died.' He gestured towards a bright red duvet, garishly decorated with what looked like elves. 'Pegged it in that very bed,' he added with indecent gusto. 'We were on holiday at the time. Torremolinos. Didn't find her for a fortnight. It was hard to get the smell out after that.'

That last piece of the story was only partly true. Linda's mother had actually passed away in a care home, though they *had* been away at the time (Morecambe for the weekend) and the staff hadn't checked up on her for a couple of days. Still, Bernard mused, if it caused Lambert Ticke a few sleepless nights, then it gave belated purpose to the old girl's death.

The meal that followed had almost given purpose to his own demise; it certainly made him appreciate at least one potential benefit of the afterlife: he wouldn't have to put up with any more of his wife's cooking. Baked seaweed (encased in a brick of gluten-free pastry – though it might have been cardboard), floating in a thin vegan cheese sauce and served with turnip chipolatas, washed down with home-made dandelion wine and a selection of beetroot biscuits, had done nothing to take the edge off either his own appetite or his bad mood.

As for Ticke, he found himself reflecting more fondly on his first evening in Fetherton and the gastronomic delights of the Richmond Grand's salmonella-themed buffet. Linda Lunt, meanwhile, and much to her surprise, found herself studying Lambert Ticke and wondering if such a presentable and intellectually gifted young man, who had also, presumably, been trained to kill without compunction should the need arise, was spoken for.

'There's no Mrs Ticke?' she had asked at one point, the

dandelion wine having loosened her tongue.

'On the contrary,' Ticke had responded, and much to Linda's dismay. 'I'm pleased to say she's very much alive and well.'

'You couldn't bring her with you, I suppose?' said Linda, trying to mask her disappointment. 'What with the chance of people getting killed?' She hesitated. 'In your line of work, I mean.' She hoped she hadn't said too much. Not if he was a trained assassin.

Ticke frowned and was glad he'd held back on the dandelion wine. It must be lethal stuff, the woman was clearly drunk.

'Well, she's 72 and has an arthritic hip,' he explained, hoping to put her straight with a few facts, 'so she doesn't get out much.'

'Your mother?' said Linda, her hopes rising again as the penny dropped.

'Of course, my mother,' said Lambert Ticke, who was beginning to think that the Lunts were so perfectly matched as to be an interesting source for study should they die at the same time and donate their brains to science.

Bernard watched as his wife flirted with the enemy and wondered if he dared get his hopes up. Leeds *and* getting shot of his wife was surely a heaven-sent combination that was beyond praying for. It would make Ticke's presence in his house marginally more palatable if there was any chance he might shack up with Linda, but he couldn't see it happening. Ticke, he reminded himself, regardless of his soft, lady-boy looks, was the sort of man who had been put on earth by a kindly God to make other men more desirable, not run off with their wives.

Still, it amused him to see Linda knock back another glass of her dandelion muck and ask Ticke how long he'd been in the secret service and how many men had he killed. It amused him even more when Ticke leapt up, said he was absolutely shattered and could do with an early night. It was clear from the look he gave her that he felt he'd wandered into a lunatic asylum and that Linda was its keeper.

'There's no need to show me to my room,' said Ticke, alarmed, as Linda rose, too. 'I remember where it is.'

'I wasn't going to,' she said. 'I was going to ask if you'd like some pudding. I made dessert.'

The only 'dessert' that interested Lambert Ticke just then was the sort that involved leaving this madhouse at once and never coming back.

'It's seaweed terrine with dandelion sauce,' said Linda, in the mistaken belief the concoction might win his heart, or at least convince him to sit down again.

What the hell was it with this woman and seaweed, thought Lambert Ticke. And dandelions – weren't they a weed, too?

'I couldn't eat another thing,' he confessed and, despite being hungry, he meant every word. 'Thank you for a very...' He hesitated. 'Interesting evening,' he added honestly.

And, having said all he wished to say, Lambert Ticke left the room just as fast as he possibly could.

THIRTEEN

It was mid-afternoon and Henry had still not put in an appearance. At five past three, unable to contain himself any longer, Colin picked up the phone and punched in his home number. It was engaged!

It occurred to him, only briefly, that he might have left the phone off the hook. Or perhaps Henry had done so, as he was so careless. He wanted to believe the latter because it would have given him some comfort, but he knew it wasn't true. Henry was still at home, and he was speaking to a whore. Of course, strictly speaking, Henry could have been speaking to anyone. He might have called Mrs Plank, in the hope of patching things up, or his doctor to make an appointment at the STD Clinic. Both these, and a few other possibilities, passed through one end of Colin's mind and out the other before he reverted to his original conclusion that his lodger was talking to a lady of the night (and/or mid-afternoon).

Even worse, thought Colin, he might be on the phone to one of those expensive 09 numbers, where – he had read in his *Daily Mail* – you could chat to a 70-year-old lady pretending to be an 18-year-old nurse keen to ravish you across the checkout counter at your local Sainsbury's. Sainsbury's regularly offered deals of two for the price of one, a prospect at which, given Henry's depraved proclivities, Colin's mind boggled. He himself might have to take advantage of several two for the price of one offers once the telephone bill came in next month.

Colin put the phone down and considered his next move. Frederick Tipson's novel still sat untouched on his desk. He hadn't had the strength to take pen to paper yet and start correcting it. Not that it mattered as no one would read the fictional monstrosity apart from Tipson himself, and he was under the unshakeable delusion that there was nothing wrong with it in the first place.

Slipping it, unedited, into an envelope, Colin threw it into his out tray where he imagined Karen's soft and scented fingers holding it to her bosom as she carried it to her desk, then addressed it in a slow, sensual manner. After that, she would take it to the post office, ease it across the counter and stroll away without a backward glance. She would tease, fondle and reject it, just the way she had rejected him. He, of course, had not been teased or fondled by her soft, scented hands, which left Frederick Tipson's manuscript – and the gormless young Bob – once more ahead of the game.

Life, he reflected, not for the first time, could be dreadfully unfair.

*****

Henry Plank was naked and fast asleep in Colin's armchair. Amy Horris, his partner for the previous evening, had only stirred at noon. Alcohol, and whatever strong medication she had needed to get her through the night, had combined to plunge her into what Henry feared at one point might be a coma. When, to his relief, she had finally woken (he'd been on the point of phoning 999 to tell them that a friend of Colin's had tragically passed away in his bed), she had proclaimed herself so hungry she could 'eat a hearse'. Though her mispronunciation had seemed quite apposite at the time, it transpired that she had always assumed that was the expression and Henry was too weary to argue the point.

They had enjoyed a fine lunch – smoked salmon with Waldorf salad and crusty garlic bread (all of it lovingly prepared by Colin for his and Henry's meal that evening) – after which they had shagged twice more, and at no extra expense, in return for Henry allowing Amy to phone her mum in Australia.

'The rates is bleedin' criminal,' she had told him bitterly. 'Forty pee a minute, I mean who can afford that?'

'No problem at all,' Henry had insisted, waving away her thanks, while gracefully accepting a rather pointless blowjob for his kindness.

By the time she had staggered through the front door (Henry had generously forked out for a taxi, having come across a jar of loose change in a cupboard under the stairs), he was ready to collapse into an armchair and promptly did so. It had been a long afternoon. After a moment's thought, he stood up, crossed to the French windows and made sure they were properly locked. He didn't want history repeating itself. *Bloody Jehovah's Witnesses,* he muttered. The bastards got everywhere.

*****

On the far side of the road, Lambert Ticke sat in his car and furiously scribbled notes for a new chapter. He had provisionally entitled it, 'The Debauchery of the Alienated Assassin', based largely on what he had seen – and surmised – over the past two hours.

After his mid-morning meeting with Bernard Lunt, Ticke had decided to waste no time in observing his enemy at close quarters. Or at least his house, in the hope it might throw up a few pointers to the way ahead. In truth, he had simply intended to familiarise himself with the lie of the land, then return early next morning and follow his quarry to work – all supposing he was gainfully employed, which a part of him doubted.

What he had not anticipated was to catch a glimpse of Mervyn Ratt in the flesh. Literally, as it turned out, and much to his disgust. The man was much older than he had anticipated. Fifty, sixty, he couldn't be sure, but not a fellow who kept himself in shape. Even so, he seemed remarkably spry, given the fact that he had physically entertained a woman half his age, and with some vigour, over the course of the afternoon.

Ticke's knowledge of Henry's physical accomplishments had been acquired by chance and, though it had appalled his finer senses, the scientist in him had revelled at this fresh input of data.

Having mistakenly assumed that Ratt would not be at home in the middle of the afternoon, Ticke had parked his car nearby, thrown caution to the wind and slipped on his fake beard (the moustache he kept in reserve, for emergencies). Suitably disguised, he had crossed the road, cautiously opened the gate to the narrow drive and made his way to the front door.

He had been on the point of ringing the bell (to confirm the house was empty) when a peal of laughter stayed his hand and he froze. Clearly someone was at home – a woman, by the sound of it – and his wisest move was to get the hell out of there as fast as possible.

Instead, and for reasons which even Ticke couldn't explain, he had darted around to the back of the house, where he had found himself beside an open pair of French windows that looked onto a square and tidy lawn. (By chance, he spotted a shed and filed away the fact for future reference.) As he peered into a clothes-strewn lounge, what he saw turned his blood to ice. Mervyn Ratt – a physical wreck of a man – was sitting naked in an armchair with an equally naked woman on his lap. The pair may have lacked clothes, but what they certainly didn't lack was enthusiasm for the job in hand – some hefty jiggling accompanied by a storm of cursing, squeals and quivering groans. (The woman, Ticke observed, was doing most of the work; Ratt's role appeared to be confined to throwing his head from side to side and doing most of the swearing.)

It was when Ratt opened his eyes, spotted their visitor and said, 'Hello, can we help you?' that Ticke, who had, a moment previously, imagined things couldn't get any worse, realised he'd been a tad optimistic.

The woman turned around and seemed just as unconcerned at having been caught *in flagrante delicto*. Her eyes were vacant, as if she wasn't really there at all.

Dear God!, shuddered Ticke – into what dungeons of depravity had he stumbled?

'Jehovah's Witness!' he had cried without thinking, before adding, 'I'm sorry, I've forgotten my Bible, I'll be back tomorrow.' At which point, he had turned tail, and fled to the sanctuary of his Fiat Uno as fast as his tortured mind and body would allow.

Fortunately, neither of the pair seemed keen to pursue him, which, given their state of undress, was both welcome and, perhaps, unsurprising.

Tearing off his fake beard, Ticke had sat in the passenger seat, quivering for several minutes, his gaze locked on Ratt's front door which remained mercifully closed. Having eventually calmed down, he picked up a small pair of binoculars (an avid bird-watcher in his spare time, he was used to keeping an eye on others while they weren't looking) and trained them on the front of Ratt's house. There appeared to be no sign of life – though he imagined the armchair was still seeing action.

It occurred to him that he should leave, that there was nothing to be gained by his remaining here. But that would mean arriving too early at the Lunts' house, and, after his time with the Inspector that morning, the prospect did not appeal. Mulling things over in his head, it struck him as strangely perverse (in all senses of the word) that the man he had driven north to expose had exposed himself first. Might there be another chapter in that, he wondered, involving a play on words? 'Exposing the Alienated Assassin'? He would have to give it some thought.

In the meantime, he sat and waited, and felt his bladder begin to fill.

SIXTEEN

Sitting upright in bed, Lambert Ticke typed furiously, his fingers flying over the keys of his notebook. It had been a curious few hours, and he had met some unusual specimens of human nature. Though Bernard Lunt was a Neanderthal aberration he had assumed to have been long purged from Her Majesty's Constabulary – if not from the earth itself – his wife seemed equally deranged. Her idea of how to feed herself and her husband, let alone a guest (for whom he imagined she had made some effort), breached all limits of taste and understanding. He would have been dreading the prospect of breakfast, had he not decided on an early start next morning, preferably before the Lunts had risen from their graves.

Then there was Mervyn Ratt. Ticke had spent some time, on his journey north, constructing a mental image of his adversary, but the man he had met this afternoon was nothing like the one he had envisaged. That he was irretrievably debauched, and had thrown off any semblance of a moral code, confirmed Ticke's conclusions in Chapter 42, 'The Mind of The Alienated Assassin', and he basked in the satisfied glow of having another of his theories vindicated.

Earlier that afternoon, while sitting in his car, recovering from the shock of a first meeting with Mervyn Ratt, Lambert Ticke had realised there was no time to waste. The sooner he could unmask his enemy, and return to London, the better. Now, just a single evening with the Lunts had encouraged him to speed up his already accelerated schedule. He would need to gain access to Ratt's house, and as fast as possible. How he might manage that, he wasn't yet sure, but he would watch, wait, and hope that an opportunity presented itself. Fortune might favour the brave, as the Roman playwright Terence had once remarked, but it also favoured the prepared mind and Lambert Ticke was nothing if not prepared.

Having set his alarm for 6.30 and settled down, he switched the light back on and set it again – 5.30 just in case – then he thought a bit more and altered it a second time. It was one thing to be prepared, but it was even better to be out of this house before breakfast.

*****

Linda Lunt, by contrast, had not been prepared for what the evening had brought. She was in love, and was pretty sure Lambert Ticke felt the same way. The chemistry between them was impossible to deny. A woman knew these things instinctively and, even if she were wrong, a woman also knew how to bring about the desired result.

She had seen the way Ticke had picked at his food, unable to eat. That was always a good sign. He was a handsome young man, with flawless skin and firm cheekbones, an angular, Romanesque nose and a solid chin. True, he lacked both height and the taut, muscular physique she had imagined a ruthless killing machine to possess, but doubtless what he lacked in size, he made up for in other areas. At 38 years of age, she wasn't yet past her child-bearing potential, though time, she knew, was running short. Bernard had never wanted a family, and his job had always claimed first place in their marriage. Perhaps she was clutching at straws, but she didn't care. Mrs Palona had told her (among so many other things that she was in danger of losing track) that the universe had her back covered and would show her the way ahead as and when. Well, if Lambert Ticke, a high-ranking official, undercover – and blessedly single – young man turning up on her doorstep like this wasn't the universe answering her prayers for a way out of her current misery (and she'd been praying a lot lately), then she didn't know what was.

While Bernard snored heavily beside her, and occasionally broke wind, Linda closed her eyes, took several deep breaths (through her mouth, to be on the safe side), and thought happily about the three children she and Lambert Ticke would have – triplets with luck, to speed things up – and the curtains she had already picked out for their living room window.

*****

Three hundred yards away (it being the closest he could park – and even then, on double yellow lines), Chuck Grogan cursed the fact that modern technology wasn't all it was cracked up to be. None of the listening devices he had so carefully planted in and around Lambert Ticke's clothing appeared to be working properly. He'd caught something about Ticke having killed lots of men, but that was all – and hardly news that surprised him. It was the woman who had spoken and she seemed to be quite excited about it. Grogan hoped the two of them wouldn't end up shagging throughout the night while she quizzed him about his favourite methods of despatch. The sound had cut out after that, and made him think they were using some kind of jamming device for which, on this occasion, he was grateful. The tracker in Ticke's pyjamas kept switching on intermittently, though it wasn't proving any use, especially as he seemed to have gone to bed alone. Brits often talked through their arses, but it wasn't likely to be much help on this occasion and, admitting defeat for the time being, he finally switched off the receiver.

Fortunately, the day had not been a total loss. He had at least been able to monitor Lambert Ticke's visit to a house in Fetherton where, it seemed, he had met – albeit briefly – with a co-conspirator. The fact that he had worn an elaborate disguise, so as not to be recognised, had confirmed Grogan's worst fears. The terrorist gang was everywhere. God knew how many of them there were, but that they were planning something big was certain. Why Ticke had sat in his car for almost two hours after the brief meeting had puzzled him. Had he realised he was being monitored? Or was he waiting for further instructions – possibly from someone even higher up the command chain?

When Ticke finally started up his motor and headed for the policeman's house, Grogan felt his senses tingle. He'd evidently received a message (Grogan bemoaned, again, the fact that his listening devices were proving so ineffective) and, from the way he raced into the Lunts' house, two things were immediately apparent. One, something 'big' had happened, and two, Ticke was the head man here. Not only did he heave both Lunts aside as he stormed in, but the policeman even came out to collect his luggage. There was no doubt about the pecking order in this gang.

Of course, travelling behind him in 'Gertie', Grogan had seen nothing of Ticke's arrival at the time. It was only later, when, as was his custom, he had, without official sanction (and unknown even to Blag and Hapgood back in London), hacked into the Pentagon's 'Spy in the Sky' satellite monitoring system and downloaded the footage over the Lunts' house, that he saw enough to confirm what he had already surmised.

He looked at his watch. It was 11.30 and all the lights had gone out in the Lunt household. The terrorist trio had turned in for the night, though it might be a ruse, he'd put nothing past them. He couldn't sleep, not yet, he needed to remain alert. The balloon was going up. He didn't know where or when, but it was going up for sure – and, when it did, he would be there to blast it back to earth with a vengeance.

Oh, yes, sirree!

SEVENTEEN

Linda Lunt had slept like a log and awoken with a song in her heart. Life, she knew, as she opened her eyes on a brand-new day, held hope, it held opportunities, and, more importantly, it now held Lambert Ticke. She had mulled things over before dropping off and had made up her mind. True, Ticke wasn't her ideal man, though the dandelion wine had done its best to convince her otherwise. Her ideal man was George Clooney, but he was spoken for and had probably never heard of Fetherton, let alone put it on his bucket list of places to visit before he died.

Bernard wouldn't care if she ran off. Linda might have preferred it if he had. Then again, their marriage had long been a sham. They had been together for almost nine years and it saddened her to realise what a waste of their lives that had been.

Knocking back a stiff g&t (she was out of dandelion wine by now, and forced to make do), Linda mused on what it would feel like to have Lambert Ticke seize her in his strong, manly arms and make wild, passionate love. The man was a secret agent, and trained to kill, so he probably knew a few moves she had never heard of. Doubtless, he had a string of girlfriends around the world with exotic names like Clitty Galore and Randy Buttock, but that would be just for show. Deep down, he probably yearned for domestic bliss and a wife to come home to after a hard day's work killing Russians – or whoever the enemy were that week.

In bed last night, she had asked Bernard if he knew how many men Ticke had actually slaughtered, but he seemed keen to change the subject. It occurred to her that he had probably told her more than he ought to have and was belatedly trying to backtrack.

'He's not a secret agent at all,' he had insisted. 'He's a pillock, sent to punish us for our sins.'

'Yes, well you would say that, wouldn't you?' sighed Linda before closing her eyes, putting in her ear-plugs and imagining their virile house guest climbing in on top of her.

It was a disappointment, on rising early, to discover that Ticke had risen even earlier and gone. A short note, propped up against the toaster, revealed that he would be 'out all day, back later this evening'.

That was a pity, thought Linda. Seaweed might save the world, but even she had the sense to realise that people who killed for a living required something more substantial in their tummies. To be honest, though these were early days and she hoped to overcome her weakness, she felt very much the same way herself.

Having come to that decision (among others), she had hoped to wave Ticke off with a bacon fry-up, all the trimmings and as much tea as he could swallow. That would set him up for the day ahead and ensure he regarded her fondly.

Linda comforted herself with the thought that leaving at the crack of dawn without breakfast was the way a top man worked. She wished Bernard would leave at the crack of dawn without breakfast. Indeed, with increasing frequency these days, she wished he would leave without breakfast and not return for his dinner, either. Or, indeed, anything else.

'You haven't forgotten it's my darts' night tonight, have you?' he inquired cautiously, shovelling toast into his mouth – the least lethal cooked item he could stomach (literally) this morning.

Linda *had* forgotten, and experienced a rapid helter-skelter of emotions for almost half a minute while Bernard chewed noisily, and swigged tea from a cracked mug (half the contents of which went down the front of the same shirt he had worn yesterday). Finally, with a loud belch, he announced that she would have to put up with Ticke in his absence, because it was the quarter finals and they were up against 'a bunch of Nancy-boys from the local chippy'.

She had said that would be no problem at all and he mustn't hurry home on her account. He told her that he wouldn't and left with a spring in his step that hadn't been there since a riot in Bristol the previous year that had left three protestors dead and fifteen more in traction.

Two hours after he had gone, Linda took a last sip of her g&t, draining the glass. She didn't normally drink this early in the day, but these were unusual times, and the alcohol helped to focus her mind.

She had been doing a lot of thinking, and a lot of reading, too. *Seize the Moment!* lay dog-eared and open on her lap. The book had been recommended to her by Mrs Palona as a 'Bible for the modern woman keen to make her way in the world'. The fact that it had been written – and (admittedly) self-published – by Mrs Palona herself was neither here nor there. The book's curious, and at times old-fashioned, take on the English language was its strength in Linda's opinion, because it spoke to her (as it was meant to speak to any reader of limited intelligence) in a plain and straightforward manner.

Chapter Six – 'Achieving your Goals' – was currently speaking to her, and she liked what she had heard. As Mrs Palona had astutely observed, 'We are but flotsam on the ocean of life, and destined to sink or swim by the decisions we take.' Life, Mrs Palona had wisely pointed out, was for living. We would be dead soon enough and with no God to punish us in the hereafter (Mrs Palona was a staunch atheist), a woman owed it to herself (Mrs Palona was also a staunch feminist) to enjoy life to the full.

'All or nothing' was the rule by which life should be lived (that, and 'Seize the moment' – while not forgetting 'When you're dead, you're dead'). If truth were told, Mrs Palona had a lot of rules by which life must be led in order to achieve happiness. You were allowed to lie, cheat and threaten your way to glory, and Linda – having read the book several times and finding nothing in it with which she disagreed – was ready to do whatever was necessary to land the man destined to save her from a miserable marriage. And that man – whether he liked it or not (and he most certainly didn't) – was Lambert Ticke.

Washing her glass under the cold water tap, drying it and returning it to the cupboard in case Bernard, unlikely though it was, came home early and caught her out, Linda put *Seize the Moment!* to one side, reached for a large cookery book and began her search for something special for tonight's meal. With Bernard hopefully getting drunk with his mates, she could throw herself into the pleasurable task of preparing a feast for the new man in her life.

*****

Just then, and blissfully unaware of his fate, the new man in Linda Lunt's life was sitting in his car, keeping a watchful – if jaded – eye on Number 78 Arcadia Avenue, Fetherton. He had been sitting there since 7 am and had started to grow fidgety. In a break from his usual routine, Lambert Ticke had eschewed food and drink of any kind before leaving the Lunts' house this morning, fearful that even turning on a tap might wake one or other of his hosts. As a result, his bladder had held reasonably firm, though thirst and whatever poisonous muck had lived inside the seaweed was finally beginning to make its presence felt.

He had dressed quickly in the dark, gathered what he needed in his rucksack and tiptoed outside with as much speed as was possible for a man who had no wish to be spotted.

One man had spotted him, of course. Three hundred yards away, Chuck Grogan had stirred just a moment after Ticke himself. Grogan regarded sleep as the devil's handmaiden; a weakness sent from the bowels of Russian Hell to test the resolve of the American patriot. Fuelled up on coffee, and some experimental tablets he had 'borrowed' from the doctors who had treated him during his time off, Grogan had remained dressed and at his post for some time after Ticke had retired. Though the Russkie seemed to have nodded off (if the faint, whistling noises that emerged from inside his pyjamas were anything to go by), it was only at 3 am, when the tracker over Ticke's groin had not moved for almost four hours, that Grogan allowed himself some rest. But even that required surgical intervention: an infusion into his arm of something unpronounceable that nullified the effects of the tablets and coffee. It sent him to sleep at once. His computer, for its part, had been programmed so that the moment Ticke's tracker indicated he had risen and moved around, an electric current would surge down a wire connected to an external hard drive and into a bracelet around Grogan's left thigh. This was more experimental technology. Possibly fatal and likely to be discontinued, the boffins had told him. Only a lunatic would be stupid enough to use it, they had said, which was all Grogan asked of any equipment before signing it out. Danger had never bothered him; danger he thrived on.

As a surge of electricity hit his leg, then shot up through his stomach to his brain and warned the rest of his body that it was under attack, Grogan screamed, jerked upright on his camp-bed and praised the late President Trump for having come down to earth to save mankind. As the pain gradually subsided, he ignored the smell of burning flesh and peered at a bank of TV screens that lined the upper reaches of his portable HQ. Each one remained logged into the hundreds of CIA spy-cams circling the world. God bless America, he muttered, for keeping an eye on everyone while they slept.

When, some ten minutes later, Grogan saw a slim, distorted figure emerge from the gloom of the Lunts' house into the equally murky world beyond, he knew that something was up – and it wasn't just Lambert Ticke. Did the Russkie know he was being tailed, or was he just being cautious? Either way, he hadn't reckoned on the might of the US secret service working through the night without sleep or fear to ensure that freedom-loving people everywhere continued to speak English with an American accent.

Ticke's dread of alerting his hosts to his departure had taken no account of the fact that Bernard Lunt could sleep through the Last Judgment, while his long-suffering wife was compelled to wear industrial-strength earplugs to block out the sound of her husband's industrial-strength snoring. As he crawled left into the Avenue, convinced that one or other of the Lunts would rush out and head him off before he engaged the safety of second gear, Lambert Ticke was blissfully unaware of the blue transit van easing out into the road behind him.

*****

Some five hours later, and Grogan was none the wiser as to what the hell was going on. He began to worry that this might, perhaps, be an elaborate set-up. Had Ticke pulled a fast one? Had he realised he was being tailed and, turning the tables, lured Grogan away from the main action? It was a disturbing thought and one that Grogan's limited intellect struggled to process. He was debating his best approach – which had come down to either sitting tight and awaiting developments, or pressing a small red button that would launch a heat-seeking missile thirty yards down the road and blow Lambert Russkie Ticke to kingdom come – when the problem was mercifully resolved.

Ticke's car stuttered into life and drew out into the main road. Freed from the dilemma of determining how many British houses he could lawfully demolish without causing a diplomatic incident, Chuck Grogan slid back the communicating panel that masked his less-than-legal activities from the rest of the world, and eased himself into the driver's seat. A minute later, he was once more in pursuit of his quarry.

EIGHTEEN

Colin Crimp's life had taken an unexpected turn, and one he could never have envisaged. After his meeting with Karen in *The Hungry Ferret,* he had returned home to find Henry busily hoovering the front room. His favourite armchair had been given a good going-over, as had every visible inch of carpet, and even, from the occasional track lines, those parts that generally never saw the light of day. The room had a fresh smell, as if it had been thoroughly aired, and Henry promptly heated up a cafetiere of coffee, while insisting Colin 'take the weight off your feet and relax'.

'You've done a lot for me,' said Henry graciously. 'Only fair I do my bit around the place.'

Colin wasn't sure whether to be grateful for the offer, or fear that Henry had sold the house while he'd been out. In the end, he decided he was so tired, and his mind in such a whirl, that falling into bed, and as quickly as possible, was all that concerned him. He had planned to tackle Henry about his habit of trying to squeeze loud and unsavoury women into his life while he was trying to sleep. Henry's recently acquired knowledge of his medical records was another source of concern, suggesting, as it did, that Henry had been rifling through his bedroom cupboards (which was where, since Henry's arrival, he had kept his medication). But it was all too much so late at night. Then again, Colin wondered if it might be best to let the whole thing drop. Henry hadn't known he was awake, and perhaps he should let sleeping dogs lie. He was a coward by nature, and there were times when he felt that nature had made him that way for a reason – that reason being the quietest life possible.

When, the following morning, Colin had gone to the fridge for milk, he had discovered, to his surprise, that the smoked salmon with Waldorf salad and crusty garlic bread he had expected to find there from the day before were noticeable by their absence.

'You ate the lot?' asked Colin, not troubling to hide his disbelief at Henry's prompt confession.

'Well, when you weren't back at your usual time,' said Henry, who had had time to make up a story and was ready to use it, 'I just got stuck in and, to my shame, the food was so delicious I just kept going. Couldn't help myself. What you can do with a walnut is beyond belief.' He kissed his fingers in an extravagant show of approval, and promptly regretted it as Colin frowned. Even Henry knew he was at risk of over-gilding that particular lily.

Colin shook his head doubtfully. His short time with Henry Plank – not that, sadly, it seemed that short – had convinced him the man was a barbarian for whom neither manners nor walnuts held much appeal. He'd probably fed the salmon to a neighbour's cat and chucked the walnuts at a passing pigeon. As for the bread, Colin made a mental note to check his bins before the next collection.

On the other hand, what did it matter? He was in love, and, even better than that, engaged to the girl of his dreams. True, the whole thing was a sham and likely to remain that way, but as it was the closest he was ever likely to get to a real-life wife, he was determined to enjoy it while he could.

What might have concerned him, as he left for work that morning (Henry remained behind, explaining that he had 'business in town' and would see him later in the day), was the fact that, on the far side of the road, a short, arrogant-looking man, with smooth skin and an angular nose, was busy scribbling notes for what he planned to entitle, 'Chapter 104, Sodomy and the Alienated Assassin'. The violent doorstep hug that Henry insisted on giving Colin, while telling him that 'you're a pal, and no mistake,' was proof positive, to Lambert Ticke's analytical mind, that Mervyn Ratt's sexual leanings were painted across a broad, and possibly limitless, canvas.

Though Colin had been loath to take the bus into work alone, he realised, looking on the bright side, that it gave him more time with Karen, away from Henry's lustful eye. That was time he did not intend to waste, even more so now that they were engaged.

The building out of which Henry Plank (Publishers) Ltd operated comprised a modest collection of rooms: Henry's office was the largest, and opened out into a smaller cubbyhole where Colin carried on his editing work. Karen's room – on the far side of a narrow passageway – was smaller than Henry's but larger than Colin's. As well as her desk, which also served as the reception area, it housed a photocopier and kitchenette. A second door opened out into the stationery cupboard which, in the building's earlier incarnation, had provided storage for linen, although these days, as Colin had recently learned, it doubled up as a place to make Bob happy.

First into work that morning, Colin found himself drawn – with perverse curiosity – into searching for envelopes, pens and other items he didn't require, while trying to envisage how two enthusiastic adults could hold a conversation, let alone each other's private parts, in such a confined space. He moved about carelessly, bending his body into a variety of uncomfortable shapes, all of which left him bewildered as to how Bob had derived any pleasure from the experience, even if Karen was the other party involved.

He was straightening himself up, and hoping to God he hadn't pulled a muscle in his back, when Bob wandered into the office, whistling a discordant tune. Bob often whistled and, as far as Colin could make out, rarely to any purpose.

'Good morning, sir,' he said as Colin emerged from the cupboard. Colin knew he was blushing and hoped it wasn't obvious.

Bob had addressed Colin as 'sir' from day one. Though the latter had told him on several occasions that 'Colin' was perfectly OK, the young lad had insisted on showing him undue respect. Until now, that is, reflected Colin, the other man having rogered his fiancée senseless for no better reason than that he was feeling a bit low and had been unable to fight her off.

'Would you like a cup of coffee, sir?' asked Bob cheerfully, and began to fill the kettle.

Aware of what was coming next, Colin said, 'Yes, that would be lovely, thank you,' and retreated to the sanctuary of his office.

'Congratulations, sir,' said Bob, arriving, three minutes later, with a mug of luke-warm tea. Bob always brought tea when coffee was asked for and tea when it wasn't. It was invariably on the tepid side, too, as Bob had an incomplete grasp of how kettles worked.

'Thank you,' said Colin, only vaguely convinced that Bob meant his imaginary pending nuptials. With Bob, one could never be sure. He might have been applauding Colin's choice of shirt, or the fact that he had made it into work without being flattened by a whale.

'Will you be having a quiet wedding, sir? Or will it be a big affair?'

'Oh, quiet, I should think,' said Colin, trying not to dwell on the thought that – unless his luck took an unexpected turn for the better – not even Karen would be present.

'I'm very sorry, sir, about, well – you know,' said Bob and heaved his shoulders as if he'd been gripped by a spasm.

'Shagging my fiancée?' was what Colin wanted to say in high dudgeon, except that he knew it wasn't true, so he kept his mouth shut.

'Letting your wife have her way with me,' said Bob, both jumping the gun and at the same time reminding Colin that he hadn't so much been left out of the team as not told there'd been a match in the first place.

'Least said,' muttered Colin, pressing his computer's 'on' switch and hoping Bob would go away.

'I was very tired afterwards,' said Bob innocently, and failing to get the message as usual. 'My mother thought I'd missed the bus and run home.'

Colin looked up, alarmed. 'You didn't tell your mother?' he inquired fearfully. He wasn't convinced that Karen's ravishment of the young man had been entirely legal. Though Bob's limited grasp of the real world didn't make him any less of a man in the eyes of a warm-hearted woman, a judge, he knew, with no sense of justice unless it involved letting killers off with a cuddle, might see things differently.

'Oh, no,' said Bob. 'I promised I wouldn't mention it. Karen said my mother would tell her off and that would make her cry. I couldn't do that to Karen, it wouldn't be right.'

'Good lad!' said Colin, as if, for one peculiar moment, he were a father praising a well-mannered son and patting him on the head for good measure.

'I wish it was me marrying her, though,' said Bob, dragging their conversation back into muddied waters. 'She's soft and pretty and she's got these–'

'Yes, well I think that's all for now,' said Colin, keen to end their awkward chit-chat.

'You're not going to kill me, are you, sir?' said Bob, in much the same tone he might have used had he been asking Colin for the loan of a fiver to buy some socks.

'Good lord, no!' said Colin. 'No one's going to kill anyone, and you mustn't say they are. It's what Karen would want. You not being killed, I mean. And definitely not talking about it, either.'

'That's a relief,' said Bob, visibly relaxing. 'I was worried you might be jealous.'

'Not me,' lied Colin. 'Not jealous at all. Now, I really must get on. You know – work and all that – the reason we're here.'

'My mother says the reason we're here is to make God happy,' said Bob.

'Yes, but he doesn't pay our wages, does he?' said Colin, grasping at straws.

Bob nodded thoughtfully, as if filing the remark away for later consideration.

'I'll make some more tea,' he said happily, picked up Colin's mug and returned to the kitchen. A moment later, Colin heard the kettle sizzle briefly into life, then fade again.

NINETEEN

Fetherton Agricultural Centre was a grey, slated building on the far side of town. Built over two acres, it comprised a sprawling mix of farm supplies, plants and other gardening products, squeezed around a cramped clothing section and high, open-roofed restaurant to relax in at the end of a hard day's shopping.

Lambert Ticke had arrived on a particularly crowded afternoon and had taken some time to find a parking space. Chuck Grogan took even longer, eventually forcing his van into a narrow gap that prevented ingress and egress for both him and the driver of the Nissan Micra next to which he had parked. He wasn't much bothered. His vehicle's rear door allowed for exit if necessary and the other guy could always climb in over the passenger seat. If he drove a Nissan Micra, considered Grogan, as he slid back the security panel and hauled himself into his control room, he was probably small enough to squeeze in through the window.

To his delight, the trackers attached to Ticke's clothing appeared to be working again, allowing him to both monitor the latter's progress and eavesdrop on any conversations he might have en route. This was more like it, he thought happily, while making a mental note to strike the FAC off his list of Russian lead-lined buildings in the area.

Ticke's first port of call, from what he could hear (a little too well for his liking), was the restaurant's toilets. The fat American flinched as a loud hiss of urine struck the porcelain bowl and Ticke released a lurid moan. He thought he heard a muffled shriek and someone close by telling someone else to 'mind the fuck what you're doing!', but it was hard to be sure, there was a lot of static. Even so, Grogan shuddered. What was it with this guy and toilets, he wondered, though grateful, on this occasion, to be spared the groans of eager love-making.

By the time Ticke had successfully relieved himself, Grogan had hacked into the FAC's administrative database and pulled up a plan of the building. Patching the tracker's signal into the system, he was able to superimpose a large red dot (for commie bastard, naturally) and follow Ticke's progress as he wandered around the store.

Having zig-zagged his way past Grow Bags, Pot Plants, Gardening Tools and Lawnmowers, Lambert Ticke's bright red dot came to a halt in an aisle labelled, 'Pesticides, Agrochemicals, Fertilisers and Grass Seeds'. Grogan's eyes narrowed and he felt a rush of excitement. Ticke didn't move for almost a minute. He had either reached his destination and was weighing up his options, or he'd dropped dead. Grogan didn't know whether to be pleased or disappointed when the dot began moving again. This time it travelled only to the end of the aisle, before returning to the spot it had just left.

There was a lot of background noise, which didn't help, but Ticke appeared to be speaking, though his voice was heavily muffled. Grogan couldn't make out a single word and wondered, for a moment, if Ticke had reverted to his native Russian. Someone else was speaking, now. The other voice was thin, shrill, and only vaguely human. It occurred to Grogan – though only for a moment – that Ticke might be torturing someone, though to do so in public seemed remarkably daring even for a trained assassin.

It was only when he heard the words, 'I'm sorry, Mister, I can't understand a word you're saying' – in the same tormented voice – that Grogan realised Ticke was talking to a sales assistant. He didn't need spy cam visual to know the lad was straight out of school with acne, bad breath and less chance of pulling a woman than he, Grogan, had of winning the high jump any time soon. The sound broke up after that, but it didn't bother him unduly. He knew what Ticke was up to, and he knew the reason why. Patience was the order of the day. With luck, it wouldn't be long before the other man made his move and, when he did… Grogan licked his lips eagerly and hoped he'd have a clear view of Ticke's astonished face before he pulled the trigger and blew the commie scum into the next world.

TWENTY

Now that it was time to put his scheme into action, Lambert Ticke wondered if he wasn't, perhaps, being a tad over-zealous. It was one thing to plan an enemy's downfall from the safety of his laptop in London, quite another to cross what had, until then, been a theoretical Rubicon – existing only in his head – and set about breaking the law.

It took a huge effort of will to remind himself that his cause was just, and its purpose sound. Not only that, but his mission had been authorised at the highest level. (Whether Roger Caspin, even at his most conceited, would have accorded himself that accolade was another matter.)

Having taken the precaution of donning his beard, moustache, and – to be on the safe side and despite the drabness of the day – a large pair of sunglasses, Lambert Ticke had discovered that his progress around the store was not without its problems. He had twice walked into a wall, and, during his time in the toilet, the man at the next urinal had refrained from thumping him only because he realised that the idiot spraying the walls, not the bowl, was blind.

Armed with a list of what he hoped were the appropriate fertilisers (not that it mattered unduly – he had a back-up plan), Ticke had located the relevant aisle and the necessary items. The stuff was sealed in large green bags and wasn't on the light side. He'd struggle to carry one of them to his car, let alone the twenty he intended to buy. He baulked a little at the price – two hundred pounds for something he'd never use himself – but it would be money well spent if it brought Ratt to justice, and hopefully he'd be reimbursed for sundry expenses once this was over and he was hailed as a hero for what he had done.

His immediate problem was getting the bags from the shelf to the checkout and from there to his car without giving himself a hernia. The lad with whom he was presently attempting to converse appeared to be from the same gene pool as Bernard Lunt, unable to understand the Queen's English however short the words.

'Can – you – help – me – with – bags?' said Ticke, resorting to the simplest English he could put together.

The young lad scratched one of his boils and rocked his head anxiously.

'I'm sorry, Mister,' he said, having given the matter some thought. 'Are you French? Are you from Franceland?'

'Of course I'm not French!' yelled Lambert Ticke. 'Why the hell would you think I was bloody French?'

The lad shook his head a second time. He had another idea, as equally annoying.

'Do – you – speak – English?' he inquired, taking a leaf out of Ticke's book.

'English?' squealed Lambert Ticke. 'What the hell do you think I'm speaking? *Russian?*'

It was unfortunate, just then, that the one word the lad was able to make out, from the muffled squeals emerging from behind Ticke's beard, was 'Russian'. Out in the car park, Grogan heard it, too, and was forced to make a huge effort not to press any buttons.

'You're Russian?' said the lad, and jerked his head sharply as if that explained everything. Out in the car park, Grogan's fingers twitched again.

'No, of course I'm not Russian!' shrieked Ticke though to both the lad and Grogan, whatever he was trying to say sounded suspiciously foreign.

In desperation – and to give himself a little more air because it was horribly warm behind his disguise – Lambert Ticke reached under the beard, pulled it away from his mouth and tried again.

'Can you hear me now?' he inquired in a low voice, which he hoped would carry a few feet without giving too much away.

'Yes!' said the lad, with all the delight of someone who had just phoned a friend and been told he had won him a million pounds for knowing the capital of Burundi.

Ticke felt a wave of relief. 'I want to buy twenty bags of fertiliser,' he said, striking while the iron was hot.

'For your garden?' asked the lad.

'Does it matter?' asked Ticke and immediately regretted it.

'It depends on the soil,' said the lad, repeating what his supervisor had told him to say, in the hope of selling a few bags of compost on top.

'Can you have them carried to my car?' asked Ticke, not wishing to embroil himself in a horticultural debate.

'That's a lot of bags,' said the lad, as if the task might prove beyond him.

'That's why I need help,' said Ticke, releasing the beard.

'You need some kelp?' said the lad, fearing he was back to square one. 'I don't think we sell that. I can always ask the manager–'

'I don't want any bloody kelp!' yelled Ticke, who, in his short time in Fetherton, had eaten enough seaweed to last him a lifetime.

The lad shook his head and Ticke's spirits slumped. He lifted the beard again.

'Twenty bags of fertiliser. I'll pay you in cash.'

Out in the car park, Grogan heard the words, 'Pay you in cash' and chewed his lip till it bled. Weapons were being traded now, on top of the fertiliser needed to build a bomb. He thought he'd heard the word 'Howitzer,' and possibly twenty of them. Ticke must be planning to take the town apart. Grogan was forced to suppress a sneaking admiration for his enemy's homicidal extravagance.

'No problem,' said the lad. 'I can do that for you,' and he promptly walked away.

Ticke slumped and wondered if he shouldn't just cut his losses and buy a bomb on eBay. He was still mulling over his options when the lad returned with a low, wheeled cart and began shovelling in the bags one on top of the other.

'Did you say twenty?' he asked, not wanting to do his back in for nothing.

'Yes, twenty,' said Ticke, relieved at his sudden change of fortune. A couple of minutes later, they were at the counter and he was handing over the cash in crisp £20 notes, withdrawn the day before he'd left London.

'My name is Mervyn Ratt,' he said, remembering to lift the beard before he spoke. Clarity, at this point, was vital. He didn't want the lad to think he was in the market for a rodent, and start another conversation. 'With two "t's", he added, for good measure. 'If you need to make a note of it.'

'No, that's OK,' said the lad, much to Ticke's dismay.

'Are you sure?' asked Ticke, hoping to sway the youngster. 'It's a lot of fertiliser. Twenty bags. If anyone should ask. Best to keep a record, surely?'

'No one ever asks,' said the lad lifelessly. He didn't even count the money, Ticke noticed, as he dropped it into the till. He could have saved himself sixty quid.

'Well, the name's Ratt, anyway,' said Ticke, with one last, pointless throw of the dice. 'Mervyn Ratt.' He tapped the side of his nose. 'But keep it to yourself, OK?'

The lad returned his gaze with all the gormless emptiness of someone who had already forgotten the name and would be unlikely to recall it even under torture.

Out in the car park, Grogan was still gnawing on his lip. He, by contrast, *had* registered the name 'Mervyn Ratt', though little else. Ticke's disguise, and the inconsistent performance of his tracking devices, had combined to render most of the conversation a mystery that would never be solved.

It didn't matter. Ticke had mentioned Mervyn Ratt, the man he'd come north to meet up with; the man with whom he was planning the assassination of the British Prime Minister.

Why he had mentioned him – and so many times – Grogan couldn't fathom, but the mention was enough. London had told him to keep an eye out for Ratt, to see if he and Ticke met up, and find out what they were planning. He was clearly a vital cog in the set-up, a man perhaps even more senior and ruthless than Ticke himself. Grogan felt a tingle in his stomach. The chase was on and he had the enemy in his sights. Not for the first time, his finger strayed towards a row of buttons before reluctantly retreating.

*****

Lambert Ticke turned cautiously out of the FAC car park, then left onto the main road into Fetherton. The Fiat's boot was piled high with fertiliser, rendering his rear-view mirror a pointless luxury. Had his vision been clearer, he might have noticed the blue transit van weaving in and out of the traffic behind him and wondered if he'd seen it before. The drivers of the cars in its way wished fervently that they had never seen it at all. If its owner's approach to navigation was anything to go by, it seemed likely he had died at the wheel and was doing his best to take others with him.

By the time Ticke had reached the relative safety of Arcadia Avenue and parked in his usual spot opposite Number 78, at least three women, a priest and a lorry driver from Romania had vowed to take taxis in future or, better still, phone up the Army and ask what the going price was for a tank.

Grogan parked in his usual spot, too, further down the road, but with visual access for his recording equipment and, if necessary, his onboard guided missile system. A further three hours passed, during which time nothing of any note occurred until, at a few minutes after six o'clock, a taxi pulled up outside Number 78 and a rough-looking, middle-aged man whom Grogan recognised as the pervert he had seen hugging a younger man on his doorstep that morning (and whom Lambert Ticke recognised as the homicidally inclined and libidinous Mervyn Ratt) got out and went into the house alone.

Ticke waited another ten minutes before restarting his car, drifting out into the road and heading back, with a heavy heart, to dinner with the Lunts. Satisfied that, for the time being at least, his tracking devices seemed to be functioning again, Grogan waited a couple of minutes – to be on the safe side – and followed the other man home.

TWENTY ONE

Retirement, thought Ernest Cupperby, had much to recommend it. The prospect had weighed heavily ever since Norah Plank had barged into his office and sought out his legal views on the rights and wrongs of beating men senseless with a frying pan. Men who had done nothing more than help out around the house – a kindness for which the dreadful woman was planning to charge them on top of their suffering. The world, he concluded, was going to hell in a handcart and Norah Plank was giving it a generous push.

Just now, Henry Plank was sitting opposite – on the same chair once occupied by his wife. Though no fulsome breasts heaved disturbingly beneath a thin cotton blouse, and Henry, to date, had made no attempt to discuss the merits of thrashing the mentally incompetent to within an inch of their lives, his presence – and purpose – was equally unsettling.

'You want to make a new will?' said the old lawyer. 'Leaving everything you own to, erm–' and here he glanced at the rough handwritten notes Henry had slid across the table, 'one Colin Crimp?'

'That's the fellow,' said Henry. 'Like a son to me,' he added dutifully, though the way he looked away as he spoke suggested otherwise to the jaded Ernest Cupperby. 'Salt of the earth. Deserves all that's coming to him.'

'I'm sure he does,' said the other man. It crossed his mind, fleetingly, that, given his recent experience of Norah Plank, the phrase carried a dreadful unspoken threat. She wouldn't like what her husband had in mind and might not be beyond showing her disapproval in ways that didn't bear thinking about.

'Might I ask who–' and here Ernest Cupperby paused, fearful of the path he was about to tread. 'Who the gentleman in question is?'

'My landlord,' explained Henry happily. 'In a manner of speaking. Putting me up, at any rate. Fine chap.' He tapped his head lightly. 'Not fully functioning on the top floor, but wouldn't hurt a fly, so good enough for me.'

Ernest Cupperby shifted awkwardly. He wasn't sure how flies fitted into the arrangement, nor, for that matter, landlords. It was, he considered, all most unusual. He thought about inquiring further, but decided against it. It was, thankfully, none of his business. There was, he felt certain, more to this matter than met the eye. It might account for Mrs Plank's unusual behaviour if her husband had run off with a man of property, to whom he now wished to leave his worldly goods. Even so, the lawyer in him felt compelled to cross at least one more 't' before retiring hurt.

'Have you spoken to Mrs Plank,' he inquired cautiously, 'about your – erm – testamentary intentions?' His tone was almost apologetic, and, had he been standing, he might have bowed politely and taken a step back. It was best not to run any risks, he told himself. For all he knew, Henry Plank approved of his wife's career change and was no stranger to the frying pan himself, whether on the receiving end or otherwise.

Henry's face briefly went blank, before his brain caught up and hauled itself back onto the bus. He had imagined he had heard the word 'testicular' and couldn't see what business his medical health was to an elderly lawyer. His mind, he conceded, had been elsewhere just then, wandering crudely around the shapely Amy Horris's bottom.

'It's none of the bloody woman's business,' he responded with feeling. 'What's mine is mine and I'll do what I like with it.'

'Even so,' said Ernest Cupperby, 'she may contest your wishes, should you predecease her.'

'I've no intention of predeceasing her,' said Henry, with all the confidence he could muster. 'The woman takes no pleasure from life. For me to go first would be a crime against nature.'

Ernest Cupperby was on the point of raising the question of Norah Plank's new profession when it occurred to him that Henry – from his response – was almost certainly *not* aware of her changed lifestyle. Best, in the circumstances, he decided, to let sleeping dogs lie.

'It might be as well,' he continued, succumbing to the lawyer within, 'to add a qualification or two – something along the lines of–'

'No qualifications!' said Henry sharply. 'This is my will, and this is what I want it to say. Word for word, nothing changed. It's simple enough, the lad inherits everything. House, firm, anything else he takes a fancy to, it's all his.'

'But if *he* should predecease you,' attempted Ernest Cupperby, determined to be heard.

Henry huffed. 'I've told you already. No one's predeceasing anyone. Now, can the will be drawn up or not? I can go to WH Smiths if you prefer. It'll only cost me £19.99.'

Ernest Cupperby shivered. The document would take no time at all to run up and it went against his lawyer's nature to turn down a hundred pounds plus VAT.

'I'll need it by tomorrow,' said Henry, heaving himself upright. He was booked in for an afternoon session with Amy and might have to put his foot down not to be late. She charged by the hour whether he arrived on time or not. He wasn't made of money, whatever impression he had given her.

'Expedited? Of course,' said Ernest Cupperby, finally admitting defeat, but with the comforting thought that he could add another fifty pounds to the bill. Plus VAT. 'Call in at eleven tomorrow morning, and Miss Perkins, my secretary, will witness it.'

The Planks, he concluded wearily, were both as mad as hatters. The sooner he was shot of them, the better.

TWENTY TWO

Colin Crimp had had the best day of his life, and it wasn't over yet. Henry Plank had been conspicuous by his absence and, though it had crossed Colin's mind more than once that his employer might be rifling through his underpants drawer or entertaining strange women in the guest room at Number 78 Arcadia Avenue, he didn't care.

Karen had strolled into the office at 9.30 am, hung up her coat and kissed him on the mouth. That hadn't been her plan. Her plan had been to kiss him on the cheek – as a show of mild affection designed to convince Bob his cause was lost and Colin had won first prize in life's lottery. Colin's unaccountable decision – in her mind at least – to turn at the last moment and mash lips, had thrown her off her stride. When his arms flew around her waist, held her tight and refused to let go, she clung on, too, fearful he might have had a seizure and was about to fall over.

'Bob says he doesn't think we're getting married,' Colin explained sheepishly, after the other man had run off to seek sanctuary in the toilet. It wasn't true, of course, but he couldn't help himself. Last night had changed his life forever. He might not have laid Maggie Henderson – beaten to the punch by a pimply 15-year-old schoolboy – but he sure as hell had done the business with her ghost.

'He thinks we're just pretending,' said Colin, throwing himself into the lie headfirst. 'I mean, I know we are,' he went on, because the bits that were true made it easier to fib. 'But – well – I thought if we put on a show, make him see that he's wrong.' He hesitated. 'I mean, I know he's right, but if he sees us – well…' At which point, Colin ran out of steam, and would have probably fled to the toilet, too, if it wasn't already occupied.

'Of course, I see your point,' said Karen, mulling things over. 'We should act like we're really engaged so Bob doesn't get the wrong idea and think–'

'Exactly!' said Colin, leaping in. 'The wrong idea, I mean. We wouldn't want that. Not until he forgets it ever happened. You and him, I mean, in the–'

'No, that would be terrible,' agreed Karen, leaping in herself this time. 'Not that it was terrible, I mean it was actually quite nice, really–'

'Good, then that's settled!' said Colin, anxious to head her off at the pass. There were some roads he never wanted to head down again – and one cupboard he certainly didn't want to enter.

After that, they had cuddled at regular intervals and, much to Bob's discomfort, taken to patting each other on the bottom. Well, Colin had done most of the patting while Karen had provided most of the bottom. He had enjoyed it so much that she had to remind him it wasn't always necessary, in particular on one occasion when Bob had nipped out to the post office and Karen had bent down to retrieve a biro. (One Colin had 'accidentally' knocked off the table a moment before.) Colin said they should take no chances, in case Bob came back unexpectedly; that would be a real clincher, he insisted, and she mustn't worry she was putting him to any trouble.

Everything considered, thought Colin, as the day wore on, life wasn't the miserable dead-end hole he'd imagined it to be. True, his unwanted house guest remained *in situ* almost three weeks after moving in, and only this morning he'd found a pair of knickers in the washing machine. (What the hell he was expected to do with those defeated him.) But, on the plus side, he was engaged to be married – and to Karen of all people. If everything went well, they'd have tied the knot by the end of the year, bought a cottage in the country and be living happily ever after. It was all Colin had ever wanted from life.

Of course, the one fly in the ointment was the fact that none of the last was actually true, or, in any way, remotely probable. However, just now, that didn't really bother him. He had followed Hugo Lake's advice and taken a leaf out of Henry Plank's book – life was meant to be lived, even if it didn't always make sense or accord with other people's view of what was proper.

'Anything is possible,' Lake had once told him (or he might have read it on the internet), and, in the swirling ocean of life, that was the piece of wreckage he intended to cling to. Of course, more often than not, you had to make your anything possible, which was where lying came in. Colin had never approved of lying in the past, but since Henry Plank had parked his suitcase on the lawn, he had begun to see he'd underestimated the value of a good fib. Sitting quietly at his desk, while Karen did whatever it was she did at hers, and Bob continued to skulk in the toilet, Colin's face broadened into a triumphant grin.

He'd just come up with a screamer.

*****

'You've told him he can be best man?'

Karen folded her arms as if, in Colin's excitable imagination, she were trying to hold back her angry bosom. It occurred to him that there were worse ways for a man to be assaulted, though he suspected, sadly, that he was in no immediate danger.

'I couldn't help it,' lied Colin, to whom falsehoods were fast becoming second nature. 'He looked so miserable, I said it without thinking.'

Karen shook her head gloomily, and her breasts wobbled. Colin averted his gaze. There was no point getting his hopes up.

'I think this is getting out of hand,' said Karen. 'Perhaps we should own up. Admit we were just pretending.'

'He threatened to tell his mother,' lied Colin quickly, swinging his axe at the truth and leaving it for dead. 'If she goes to the police–'

'Why would she go to the police?' asked Karen, though she knew the answer already.

'You said so yourself,' Colin reminded her cruelly. 'Bob's not – well – not like other men.'

That bit was true, remembered Karen fondly. None of her previous boyfriends had been so well-endowed. She wished she'd never seen what she had seen – and then enjoyed it into the bargain – it had ruined the future for her.

'They'd say you were taking advantage,' continued Colin, recalling the unfortunate Maggie Henderson. He'd only learned some time later – after he'd been released back into the community – how that had all worked out. There were those who would have argued that having a pimply youth wriggling beneath her on the grass was punishment enough for any self-respecting woman. Being locked up for three years on top, for what others might have viewed as an act of kindness, seemed unduly excessive. Maggie would have got off more lightly, thought Colin bitterly, if she'd knocked back three vodkas, jumped in her car and run Wayne over on the pavement. There was no justice in the world. Not if a judge had anything to do with it.

'I still don't see how it helps,' said Karen. 'Making Bob best man, I mean.' She hesitated. 'For a wedding that's never going to happen.'

Colin pushed any hurt to one side and considered his next move. Though he knew what he planned to say, he wanted to be sure his words came out in the right order.

'I told him the best man is sworn to secrecy,' he announced. 'Now and forever.'

What had actually happened had been very different.
The moment Karen had nipped to the post office, Colin had cornered Bob in the kitchen.

'So you're definitely not planning to tell your mother?' he asked, a part of him still fearing the worst. 'About you and Karen?'

'Oh, heavens, no!' Bob had assured him. 'It's private. I wouldn't tell anyone.' Then he had shaken his head and said, 'I'm not even sure I know what did happen. It hasn't happened before. Not even at the doctor's.'

'Excellent,' Colin had responded happily, and with no interest in exploring Bob's medical issues. 'And you don't mind us getting married?'

'I'm not sure,' said Bob. 'Is it legal for two men to get married? I think I saw something on the telly, but–'

'Not you and me!' said Colin quickly. 'Me and Karen!'

Bob shrugged. 'Oh, no, sir,' he said. 'Not now you've explained everything.' He shrugged again. 'Besides, I've got mother, so it doesn't really matter.'

'Then I'd like you to be my best man,' said Colin sharpish. 'And give me away at the wedding.'

He knew he'd got that last bit wrong, but he was excited and he didn't care. Asking Bob to be his best man was a step in the right direction, that direction being an altar in a small church, or perhaps just a registrar's office, it didn't matter. Nothing mattered so long as Karen was there, too, and she said, 'Yes'.

Which brought him back to the present.

'I suggested we all have a drink after work, to celebrate,' said Colin, who was keen for this day to never end and, if possible, to go home with Karen and hope she had a stationery cupboard. It wasn't going to happen, of course, but that was no reason not to enjoy the prospect, however unlikely.

'But Bob doesn't drink,' said Karen, who remembered their Christmas office party two years ago. Henry had topped up Bob's orange juice with gin and they'd had to talk him down from a ledge. That was before Colin's time, and, fortunately, the ledge had only been on the ground floor, but that wasn't the point. The point was: Bob didn't drink. Still, she reflected, lemonade wouldn't do any harm, and as Henry wasn't invited, they should be safe enough.

Colin reached into his pocket, removed a square, mahogany box and flicked it open. Inside was a ring, white gold with a small diamond cluster that sparkled as it caught the glare from his angle-poise lamp.

'Jesus Christ!' squealed Karen. 'What the hell's that?'

'It's an engagement ring,' said Colin, trying to ignore the terror in her face. 'I thought if we were going the whole hog, we might as well do it right.'

'We're not going the whole hog!' Karen reminded him jumpily, though her gaze never left the ring as she spoke. 'It must have cost you a bloody fortune!'

Karen rarely swore and it struck him, rather late in the day, that he might have gone too far.

'It belonged to my mother,' he said, trying to dig himself free. 'I didn't have to buy it. It didn't cost me anything.'

He wasn't sure if that made things worse. He didn't want Karen to think he was a cheapskate.

'Your mother?' she repeated, her gaze still focused on the ring. No one had ever asked to marry her before and, despite her misgivings, she found herself wondering if the ring would fit.

'Yes,' said Colin, adding another lie to his account. He was getting rather good at this, he realised, though he wasn't sure it merited praise. It was all Henry Plank's fault, making him feel awkward in his own home, and keen for any reason not to be there. Maybe this *was* getting out of hand, maybe he should stop right now, while he still could.

'I could always try it on, I suppose,' said Karen, putting paid to any chance there had been of Colin doing the right thing. 'See if it fits.'

'Right!' said Colin, though he didn't know what he was saying 'right' to as his eyes had glazed over and his brain had gone into meltdown. He fumbled with the ring, then gave up altogether as Karen leaned in and took the box from him. Their hands brushed for a moment and Colin felt his tummy wobble.

To his great surprise – and Karen's, too – the ring slipped easily onto her finger and remained there.

'Almost as if it was made for me,' she said, turning her hand first one way, then the other. When the pale lamplight played over the stones and dazzled them into life, Colin's stomach wobbled again.

'So your dad gave this to your mum, then?' she inquired. 'And his dad before him?' she added with no proof, but already keen to embellish its history.

'Oh, yes,' said Colin. 'And his dad again. It goes back hundreds of years.'

Karen frowned. 'Are you sure?' she said, wanting history not fiction. 'It doesn't look *that* old.'

'It's been well looked after,' said Colin, who had no idea whether it had been or not. The fact was, he knew very little about it. True, it belonged to his mother, but only because her sister – his Aunty Edna – had found it on a beach and given it to her in settlement of a gambling debt. The debt was for £5, but the ring turned out to be of no value and the stones paste. It looked like the real thing, though, and that was all that mattered. His mother had kept it in the hope of one day passing it on to some other mug, but after his father had nipped to the pub one evening and not returned, and his mother had run off with a travelling salesman, Colin found himself the unexpected guardian of a worthless piece of costume jewellery.

Worthless, that is, until now. Now, finally, it was coming into its own. Even he had to admit that, not only did it look good in the real world, it looked even better on Karen's finger. Karen, just then, was having much the same thought.

*****

The evening itself had passed off tolerably well, given the utter pointlessness of the occasion: a few drinks to celebrate a non-existent engagement, and a thank you to Bob for being best man at a wedding that would never take place. Colin might have suffered further pangs of remorse had he known that, on this particular night, Bob was one of several men in the pub who had actually had sex with Karen at one time or another, while he – her imaginary intended – was one of the few men who hadn't.

When, after half an hour, Bob said he'd have to go because it was his bath night and his mother would have started running the water, Colin's hopes lifted. They plunged back to earth when Karen said she'd call a taxi and drop Bob off en route as it was on her way home so it was no trouble.

Colin said he'd be happy to come, too, but Karen said there was no need. She was washing her hair and having an early night, but she'd see him in the morning and they could talk about what she called 'the arrangements'. The way she lowered her voice as she spoke made it sound as if they might be taking someone for a drive and not bringing them back. More than likely, thought Colin, it would be his hopes for a future with Karen that would be given a lift to the local quarry, hit over the head and chucked in with both feet tied together. His thoughts drifted back to Morton High School, Leeds and the night Maggie Henderson had washed her hair. She'd ended up giving mouth to mouth to an acne-ridden yob with bad breath. Bob might be marginally more presentable than Wayne Winkley (and probably brighter, too), but the thought of him and Karen snuggled together in a warm taxi did nothing to lift his spirits.

Back home, at Number 78 Arcadia Avenue, Fetherton, however, he would count himself grateful for the light-hearted mood in which he had left the pub.

TWENTY THREE

Linda Lunt had abandoned all hope. It wasn't that her vast collection of cookery books were bereft of culinary inspiration, it was that she was. Try as she might, she could find nothing that filled her with confidence; nothing she could be certain was good enough to win the heart of a ruthless London assassin. Nothing, if she were forced to admit it, that she *could* cook. In the end, she threw all her books to one side and telephoned the local Indian. *The Ali Tandoori* wouldn't let her down, they wouldn't dare. Bernard ate there all the time and knew every waiter by name. True, most of the names he knew them by weren't the ones they'd been given at birth and wouldn't bear repeating in church, but that wasn't the point. Bernard didn't eat there alone, he ate there with his mates. Mates from the station who were as equally loud and foul-mouthed as he was, and weren't to be asked to leave even if they never tipped and occasionally threw up over the chef.

To be on the safe side, she ordered twice as many dishes as she thought she'd need – starters, mains and sides – and half a dozen sugary puddings. Twenty poppadums, three pickle trays, five naans and six different types of rice would, she decided, be more than enough, then rang back five minutes later to add three chapattis and a raita, just in case.

The Ali Tandoori was only open in the evening, but, when Linda told them it was for Bernard and his friends and could they get it round to her by no later than the middle of the afternoon, they said they were happy to oblige. The chef himself – thrilled at the prospect of a vomit-free evening – delivered the meals in person and refused to take a tip for fear he was being tested or that Bernard was hiding in the bushes waiting to be sick on him.

It took Linda some time to decant all the food into pots, pans and assorted trays and dishes. After dumping all the containers into an outside bin, she put three curries on to simmer, and switched on a couple of fans to spread the smell around the house. She had no idea when Lambert would be home, but it would surely please him to know that she'd been hard at work all day on his behalf. (Even if most of that time had been spent on the phone to Javid at *The Ali Tandoori*.)

Linda looked at her watch and saw that it was 5.15. It was normally at this time that she would crack open a bottle of dandelion wine and squeeze in an hour's yoga before Bernard rolled home in a bad mood. But tonight, she knew, was no time for restraint. Tonight was made for love. Or at least a valiant attempt at the same. She opened the drinks cabinet – generally Bernard's sole preserve – selected a cheap supermarket red, unscrewed the cap and poured herself a generous measure. Having downed half the glass in one, she refilled it and this time took a more leisurely sip. Relaxed but not rolling, that was the plan. She took another sip and surrendered to a long, decadent sigh. Linda Ticke, she murmured out loud, and repeated it again just to be sure. It had a satisfying ring to it. Belatedly, it occurred to her that she was hideously over-dressed, and should slip into something more simple. Something it would be equally simple to slip out of should the opportunity arise...

*****

Colin Crimp was sitting at his desk typing furiously. After leaving *The Hungry Ferret*, he had caught a taxi back to Arcadia Avenue, prepared to endure further misery this evening in the company of Henry Plank. To his surprise, Henry was not at home, though, from the mess in the kitchen, he had clearly been there at some point. Perhaps he had gone for a walk, thought Colin. Perhaps he had gone to the pub, perhaps – and though the idea appealed very much, Colin doubted his luck would stretch to it – he had gone down to the river and thrown himself in.

Unexpectedly alone for the evening, and keen to vent his anger with the fates, Colin made himself a ham sandwich, boiled up a cup of tea and switched on his desktop, ready to tackle the world and everything that was wrong with it. The Prime Minister had got his back up again, claiming – to show that he was a 'man of the people' – to have watched Sir Stanley Matthews score a hat-trick for Blackpool when he, Sir Edward St John Stark, former DPP and proud Blackpudlian, 'were just a lad'. Colin had checked the great man's details on Wikipedia (Matthews not Stark!) and discovered that Sir Stanley played his last game for Blackpool in October 1961. As Sir Edward St John Stark had not graced the world with his presence until September 1962, he could only assume the nation's leader had built himself a time machine about which he had modestly kept quiet. That wasn't on and he mustn't be so shy. He might want to hide his magnificent light under an equally magnificent bushel, but Mervyn Ratt had other ideas.

Colin was still editing the letter which, however hard he tried, just wasn't going well tonight, when his train of thought (half-hearted though it was) was derailed by the front door slamming. Henry was home and it was only 8.30. At least he hoped it was Henry, or at least just Henry. He wasn't in the mood to hear a woman's voice tonight, especially one who was likely to start screaming at Henry to 'give her one'.

He heard a thud of footsteps on the staircase, and realised, to his despair, that they had not veered off towards Henry's bedroom. A moment later, his door was flung open and Henry stormed in.

'The fucking bitch!' cried his unwanted intruder. 'The whore of fucking Babylon!'

Colin tightened. Aware by now that Henry knew some peculiar women, he couldn't be sure if his lodger was expressing outrage at some perceived sleight or simply bringing him up to date with his contorted love life.

While Colin was still pondering the matter, Henry threw himself onto his bed with indecent force. It didn't seem to bother him that he was overstepping another boundary. Boundaries didn't seem to matter to Henry.

Colin shut down his computer. So much for his plans for a quiet evening. This invasion of his bedroom for the second time in 24 hours made his stomach churn. He wondered how keen Hugo Lake would be now to encourage him to 'learn from an older man'.

'Do you mind if we go downstairs?' asked Colin, standing up.

Henry did seem to mind and stayed where he was. In fact, even worse, he progressed from sitting on the edge of Colin's bed to falling back, stretching his legs and staring at the ceiling.

'In God's name, Colin!' he cried. 'Can it get any worse?'

From his perspective, Colin doubted it. He crossed to the door, hoping that Henry would get the message. Henry didn't. The latter passed a hand across his face and released a long, withering growl. 'Women!' he bellowed. 'I'd like to fuck the lot of them!'

Colin paused with his fingers around the handle of the door. He didn't know if Henry's cry was one of hope or anger. He suspected it was a little of both.

'Shall I make us a cup of tea?' he inquired miserably. It seemed a feeble response in the circumstances, but anything, he thought, to get Henry out of his room.

'I need something stronger than tea!' cried Henry, but at least he now propelled himself upright, a blotchy face regarding Colin wearily. Henry fumbled in his jacket pocket and withdrew a small flask which he held high. 'There's more where this came from!' he cried, as if it were a hard-won trophy and he was about to embark on an open-top bus tour to celebrate. Before Colin could respond, Henry heaved himself from the bed and staggered over to the door. Colin seized his luck with both hands and rushed ahead of him, with the other man in hot pursuit.

*****

On reaching 33 Felicia Drive, a hundred yards or so from the Lunts' house, Lambert Ticke parked in the first available space, switched off the engine, climbed out and considered his next move. The bags of fertiliser were currently piled illegally high in the boot, which wouldn't do at all. Bernard Lunt might be a cretin of the highest order, but even he couldn't fail to notice the potential offence for which Lambert Ticke had no wish to be pulled over.

Fifteen minutes later, with a great deal of huffing, puffing and the occasional yelp of discomfort as something threatened to go in his back, Ticke – a man, even he would be happy to concede, built for intellectual rigour not humping great weights around – had rearranged the load, shifting several bags from the boot onto the back seat, before covering everything with a rug he kept for frosty winter mornings. (The heating system in his car was unreliable at the best of times, and Ticke's internal thermostat was always set to low.)

Satisfied that his secret was as safe as it could be, Lambert Ticke got back into the car and, without enthusiasm, completed the remaining few yards into the Lunts' driveway, parked and rang the front bell with a heavy heart.

He had not expected the effusive welcome he received when the door opened and a hideous vision in red flung herself into his arms, said how lovely it was to see him again, and then dragged him inside.

And that was just the start of a long, bewildering evening he would soon want to forget in a hurry.

TWENTY FOUR

Lambert Ticke, as it transpired, was not alone in suffering that evening in Fetherton.

At Number 78 Arcadia Avenue, Colin Crimp was having an equally torrid time.

Having reached the relative safety of the lounge (anything was better than having Henry in his bedroom), the older man shoved an opened copy of a thin, glossy magazine under Colin's nose.

'What do you make of that?' he cried, throwing himself into Colin's favourite armchair and staring at the ceiling, his face blood-red, hands beating a fierce tattoo against the arms of the seat.

Colin slunk into the settee opposite.

'What am I supposed to be looking at?' he inquired, before stiffening as he spotted the words *Thrasher's Weekly* printed in big red letters across the top of the page. He wasn't sure he wanted to read any further.

'Personal columns, four down, one across.'

Colin had never excelled at crosswords and found himself struggling to locate the relevant section. What he was able to discern, at a first, cursory glance, was that he had stumbled into a sordid *demimonde* – a twilight world of masseurs/masseuses and other purveyors of hedonistic relief.

'I'm sorry,' he said, 'I don't know what you're getting at.'

'Do you need taking in hand?' cried Henry, addressing the question to the left-hand corner of Colin's sitting room ceiling.

'I beg your pardon?' said Colin.

'The advert!' cried Henry, stabbing a fat finger in the vague direction of the magazine. '"Do you need taking in hand?" Phone – and then the number. It's there, as plain as a bishop's prick! *My* number! My bloody number!'

Colin scanned the columns again, and more closely this time. An advert had been ringed in blue, several times, the biro scored so deeply it had torn through to the next page. Colin read it quietly to himself, and was glad that he did. This wasn't the sort of thing to read out loud. He hadn't met Mrs Plank, so couldn't imagine what sort of creature could sink this low, and for that he was grateful. It wouldn't have done him any good to have a mental image of the woman, he wouldn't sleep at nights. Mind you, a lifetime spent under the same roof as Henry Plank would surely wreck the soundest constitution. He had only been with Henry three weeks and was feeling the strain.

'Read it out loud!' said Henry. 'Don't be embarrassed.'

'I'd rather not,' replied Colin, for whom embarrassment was a ship that had left port several days ago and sunk somewhere out in the Atlantic. 'It's not really my sort of thing. Possibly it's a mistake. They've printed it with her name in error. For someone else.'

'For someone else?!' cried Henry. 'Dear God! Listen!' He jumped up, snatched the magazine back, flourished it wildly and intoned in a loud voice, quivering with rage:

'Men! Do you need taking in hand? A damn good thrashing is to be had at Madam Norah's. Please call to make an appointment. Bring a scrubbing brush!'

'Possibly she's simply advertising for help around the house,' suggested Colin desperately.

'Help around the house?' roared Henry. 'The bitch says she'll thrash them senseless. What sort of thanks is that to give a man who's helped you out?'

'She doesn't actually say "senseless",' began Colin, and immediately regretted it. If he didn't want to get involved, he realised too late, passing a remark was not the best way to go about it.

'The severity of the beating is academic,' continued Henry. 'The woman's given my name, address and telephone number!'

Colin bit his tongue. He had been about to say that she had not given Henry's name. Not unless his middle name was Norah which, he prayed to God, it wasn't. But that she had given his home address and telephone number seemed clear enough. He wondered whether it was worth reminding Henry that he no longer lived at home, but saw no point in complicating matters. Besides, it might imply that this was his home now and that was the last thing Colin wanted.

Another thought crossed his mind. 'How did you find out about this? I mean how did you know she…? I mean…' At which point he lapsed into silence. He wasn't sure he wanted to know the answer.

'The bitch sent me a text!' yelled Henry, and Colin instantly regretted opening his mouth. 'Said I should nip into Leeds and ask one of my whores if she had a copy.'

'And did she?' was on the tip of Colin's tongue, but he bit it again.

'That's where I've been all day,' lied Henry, who saw no reason to admit that he'd been fiddling with Amy Horris at the time. It had ruined his mood and no mistake, which had been a hundred pounds down the drain. 'Tried phoning her as soon as I got back. No answer.'

Colin felt his shoulders tighten.

"S'all right, didn't use your phone, didn't want her knowing where I was, calling me at all hours.'

Colin relaxed a little. That was something, at any rate. It was bad enough having Henry in the house without his wife joining them for tea.

'Couldn't get a signal, mind,' said Henry, pulling out his mobile now and waving it with the other hand. He shrugged, and looked as if he might have run out of steam. 'Went for a walk. Calm down. Work out what to do for the best.' He sagged and collapsed into the chair, utterly spent.

Colin breathed slowly and tried to recall what Hugo Lake

had advised about letting the problems of the world wash over him.

'Anyhow, managed to get a signal finally,' said Henry. 'Inside the pub.' That didn't surprise him, thought Colin. The pub, that is, not the signal. What did surprise him was that Henry seemed quite sober, albeit agitated.

'Got through to some girl. Didn't sound right in the head. God knows what's going on. Put me through to the wife like some bloody secretary. Woman's getting airs and graces.' He puffed out his cheeks. 'I said we needed to talk. Meet up. Thrash things out.'

Colin tightened again. All this talk of thrashing was wearing him down.

'Do you know what the bitch said?'

Colin said that he didn't, but he knew he was about to find out.

'Said I must book an appointment like any other punter. She couldn't give me preference just because I was family. Family? I wouldn't be part of her family now if she paid me in whores!'

Colin frowned. He wasn't sure where Henry was coming from with this one. He was fast losing track of the other man's train of thought. Indeed, he rather thought Henry might be losing track of his own train of thought, for he was surely just the kind of man who would find payment in whores perfectly acceptable.

'Asked me to give her regards to the vicar next time I see him,' grumbled Henry, who clearly hadn't finished. 'Woman has lost all respect for the church.'

Colin regarded him curiously. Henry had never struck him as a man with much time for the church. Not its moral teachings, at any rate. Then again, the church was very liberal these days. Perhaps it no longer frowned on brothels.

'Must have been planning this for weeks!' said Henry, getting into his stride now. 'Woman's off her head!'

'But I thought you said she wasn't into – well – that sort of thing. It doesn't make sense,' countered Colin, then wished he hadn't. It would only prolong the conversation.

"Course it doesn't make sense,' agreed Henry, 'but what does? Mrs P has chucked me out and become a Madam, all in the space of three weeks. It's a queer old world, and that's a fact.'

'Do you think she could be unwell?' suggested Colin, trying to feel his way through the minefield. 'I mean...' He hesitated. This was a little too close to home. 'In the head? Perhaps she's depressed?' he added rapidly, in case he'd overstepped the mark.

'Depressed?' huffed Henry. 'Woman sounded brighter than she has for years.' He pinched his mouth thoughtfully. 'But I take your point. She may have gone whacko, need to see someone, yes...' He considered the matter for a few moments, then said, 'What about your bloke, the nut-doctor? Might he be the man for the job? We don't want this going public. Not on top of her being a Madam.'

'He's not a nut-doctor,' protested Colin quickly, then drew up short. 'How do you know about that anyway? That's my private business.'

'Can't hide that sort of thing,' said Henry. 'Besides, he phoned me a while back, when you were out. To cancel an appointment.'

'You never mentioned it.'

'Didn't have to. He rang back 20 minutes later and said he'd made a mistake. Didn't see the need to bother you. Said you weren't dangerous, just lacking in social skills.'

'He's not supposed to talk about me!' protested Colin. 'That's confidential!'

'Not his fault. I told him I was your father, that I was concerned.'

'What?'

'Did it for your own good. I *was* concerned. Had to be sure you weren't going to come at me with a carving knife. Anyhow, he said you were harmless and that was good enough for me.'

Colin felt his left arm begin to twitch. His arm often twitched when he was under stress. He wondered if he should take one of his tablets, to calm himself down. He could ask Henry to bring him one as the swine knew where he kept them.

'Wondered if you could do me a favour, Colin,' said Henry.

Colin glared back. He didn't feel like doing Henry any favours right now. What he felt like doing was throwing him out of his house. But that would cause upset, and he might lose his job. He didn't want to lose his job. Hugo Lake had told him that what he needed most at present was a settled existence. Nothing must excite him. Besides, how long would his engagement to Karen last if he couldn't see her on a daily basis?

'What sort of favour?' he asked in a subdued voice.

Henry looked suddenly sheepish.

'Thought you might be able to go round in the morning and sort her out,' he said hopefully.

'I couldn't do that,' protested Colin. 'I'm the wrong man for that sort of job, the wrong man altogether.'

'Well, she won't speak to me,' said Henry. 'She's made that clear.'

'That was in the heat of the moment,' countered Colin. 'I'm sure by now–'

Henry shook his head. 'No, never. The woman's addled. But you'd be perfect. You have a glib tongue.'

Colin stared at him. Now he knew Henry had lost touch with reality. He might be many things, and, sadly, there were probably more things that he was not. But one thing not even he was prepared to lay claim to, was having a glib tongue.

'I'd go to pieces, I wouldn't know what to say.' Colin knew he might not be covering himself in glory, but the time had come to be honest. One of them had to face reality, and it was clear that Henry wasn't much bothered.

'Nonsense,' said the other man. 'You have a placid manner, it's always impressed me. What do you say? You may be able to talk some sense into her.'

'Talk some sense into her? She's a dominatrix! She'll probably beat the living daylights out of me.'

'Not unless you pay her in ready cash. It's the way they work. Mind you, she's new at the game and may not have mastered the finer points. Still, I can't see it happening. She'll be civil enough, I'm sure, once she knows you're on an errand of mercy.'

'Why don't you go?' suggested Colin, hopefully. 'If I turn up, she may think you don't care. You need to show her you're still interested.'

'I don't know that I am. Not if she's into sado-masochism.'

'Surely not? It just says she wants you to take orders. That doesn't sound too bad.'

Henry shrugged. 'You'll be safe, then. She won't hit you. What do you say? It would be a great kindness.'

'I've already told you, I wouldn't know what to do.'

'Just ask her what the hell she's playing at, and how long she means to keep it up. No need to be that blunt, of course. You'll want to put it more tactfully. I can leave it up to you. Just make it up as you go along.'

'I don't know,' muttered Colin lamely. He was fighting a losing battle, and he knew it.

'Fact is,' said Henry, returning to his theme, 'the woman won't see sense. She needs to communicate with a third party, someone we both trust.'

'I've never met your wife,' said Colin, grasping at the straw for dear life. 'There's no reason she would trust me.'

'Course she would,' said Henry, dismissing Colin's objection with a wave of his phone. 'She'll only have to see your honest face and she'll be putty in your hands.'

Colin sighed. No woman had ever been putty in his hands, not even Karen, and he was engaged to her. Well, sort of. No woman had been anything in his hands, nor, to his intense regret, even in his hands. (An image of Karen floated through his mind again, being chased around the office by Bob.) He hardly thought that a woman who was prepared to knock seven bells out of a man with a scrubbing brush would listen to him.

'It's up to you,' said Henry. 'I won't force you, of course. Besides,' and here he paused, as if to let the impact of his words sink in, 'I've rather got used to the single life. You and me, men about town. Who needs the women, eh? Well, not one to come home to, if you get my drift.' He puffed out his cheeks 'Maybe you're right. Maybe it's time to call it a day.'

Colin blanched. 'I never said it was time to call it a day,' he responded quickly, struggling to keep the panic out of his voice. 'I just said–' And then he ran out of steam. He knew what he wanted to say, he just couldn't think of the best way to put it; a way that would steer Henry in the right direction; away from his house and his private life as fast as humanly possible.

'What do you want me to do?' he said in a defeated voice. There was no point in fighting a lost cause. The sooner he got Henry out of his home the better. He must do whatever it took and hang the consequences.

He would not have been so keen had he foreseen those consequences. But possibly it was as well that he couldn't. He wouldn't have slept that night.

Not that he slept much in any event. Nor did Henry.

TWENTY FIVE

At roughly the same time that Henry Plank was thrusting a copy of *Thrasher's Weekly* into the reluctant hands of Colin Crimp, Lambert Ticke was swaying awkwardly on the edge of a settee, and wondering what twilight world of madness he had stumbled into.

When Linda Lunt had greeted him at the door, clad only in a scarlet negligee (though she insisted it was 'just an old dress' she'd thrown on), he ought to have turned and fled. He might have done so were it not for the fact that there was nowhere for him to flee and, more urgently – his bladder having had no relief since his visit to the Fetherton Agricultural Centre – he was in need of the toilet.

'I'll show you where it is,' said Linda, staggering towards the foot of the stairs as if she'd been drinking all afternoon.

'There's no need!' said Lambert Ticke, ready to wet himself there and then sooner than have this nightmare in red stand over him while he peed.

'No need to be shy,' she giggled, as he tried to ease past. Her hand came up as if to stroke his face but he dodged it nimbly. 'We're all women here.' She giggled again. 'Well, I'm all woman – but I think you've noticed that, haven't you?'

Though Lambert Ticke was trying his hardest not to notice anything of the sort, what he *had* spotted was that one of her breasts, inadequately squeezed into whatever scrap of hanky she was wearing – and seemingly lacking a bra to hold it back – appeared to making a bid for freedom. Leaping up the stairs two at a time, he prayed to a God he didn't believe in that the thing wasn't giving chase on its own. In this hell house, he considered morbidly, anything was possible.

*****

Having relieved himself, and conscious – unless the woman was creeping around the house like some demented huntress – that Linda Lunt had not followed him upstairs, Lambert Ticke was faced with a fresh dilemma. On the one hand, it had been a long day, and he was hungry. On the other, an evening in the company of the Neanderthal Lunts held little appeal, other than from an anthropological point of view. Then again, could he stomach another bowl of seaweed? He rather doubted that and was still debating whether to slip away unnoticed and find himself a halfway decent restaurant when he became aware – belatedly – of a strong, exotic smell in the air. Curry.

Lambert Ticke enjoyed a good curry. As a man who prided himself on having no weaknesses (he was the only one who viewed himself in this light), this was his Achilles' heel. He sniffed again, and with approval. Of course, it might be that what he sniffing was some vile seaweed concoction spiced up with tamarind. He doubted that would bode well and, from what he had experienced last night, Linda Lunt was no chef. Then again...

Venturing cautiously downstairs, he savoured the air with growing interest and a gnawing hunger. He was close to the kitchen door when it swung open and nearly sent him flying. Linda Lunt emerged and, to his relief, she was – for the present at least – less mischievously dressed, having thrown on a bright, checked apron, at least a size too large but which mercifully covered the bits that had been so flagrantly exposed a few minutes earlier.

'Would you like an aperitif?' she inquired giddily. 'You must be exhausted after a hard day's work. Killing people and that sort of thing.'

'A cup of tea would be nice,' said Lambert Ticke, who rarely touched alcohol whatever the provocation – even in the form of an unhinged harpy who seemed to think he slaughtered strangers for a living.

'I hope you like curry,' said Linda, waving airily over her shoulder. There were pots and pans sizzling on the stove behind and half a dozen cook books thrown carelessly across the worktops and table. She'd used none of them, of course, but hoped they added a touch of veracity to the proceedings.

'Yes, I do,' said Ticke cautiously. 'Might I ask what – erm – what sort of curry it might be?'

'Oh, all sorts,' said Linda, sending Ticke's mind off in a new direction. He hoped to God she'd not been frying liquorice all afternoon, and spicing it up with fenugreek.

'I'm vegetarian,' he said quickly. He wasn't but, having endured one evening of the woman's cooking, he felt it was the safest approach. Food poisoning might still be a possibility, but less chance, he told himself, of it being lethal.

'There's biryani, she said, 'and lots of other stuff you can have. I'm vegetarian, too. It's only Bernard eats meat, the beast. You and I are like-minded souls. Creatures of the earth, I knew it from the first.'

Lambert Ticke bobbed his head but said nothing. He had no idea what a creature of the earth was but thought it best not to deny the charge. Besides, he *was* hungry, the food smelt good and, from what he had gathered, seaweed was off the menu.

Two hours later, Lambert Ticke did his best to stand up and failed for the third time in a row. Something, he told himself, was not quite right. The woman beside him for a start. She was definitely lacking something. A husband, that was it. It had come as an unnerving surprise when she had told him that Bernard wouldn't be joining them for dinner.

'More for us!' she had cackled gleefully and performed a spectacular twirl that had left her needing to sit down for a couple of minutes in order to recover.

The prospect of an absent Bernard Lunt ought to have cheered him. The man was a brute, not fit for civilised company. But an evening in the company of his unbalanced – and scantily clad – wife was just as bad.

Though he had refused all offers of alcohol, the water she had fed him was foul.

'It's hard,' she explained, and he had to agree that it was definitely that. It left a peculiar aftertaste on the tongue, like nothing he had ever experienced. It occurred to him that the water was off, though he doubted such a thing was possible.

He wouldn't have drunk any of the muck but the food was oppressively hot and salty, so much so that, despite his reluctance, he continued to knock back water long into the evening until, stuffed to the gills in every respect, he collapsed onto the settee, closed his eyes and wondered why his world was spinning round.

Looking down at him, and feeling almost as dazed, Linda Lunt hoped she hadn't overdone the vodka in his drink. He had knocked back several glasses, and eaten enough for two which she took as a good sign. More than once he had complimented her on her cooking and said she should take it up for a living, she was a wasted talent.

Halfway through a sickly sweet dessert of gulab jamun, she had giggled loudly and asked if he'd killed anyone today. He had giggled back and said, 'No, but maybe tomorrow with a bit of luck.' Then he had tapped the side of his nose and said she must keep that to herself or he'd have to kill *her*, which would be a shame as she 'made a damn good curry'. Then he had replenished his glass, stood up, and toasted the Queen.

Linda Lunt sank into the sofa beside him and felt curiously happy. She never got drunk with Bernard, there was no point. Bernard was a pig and much preferred to get drunk with his mates, swear at an Indian waiter and beat up a tramp on the way home.

It was only when she leaned in close and breathed the remnants of a rich masala into his face that Lambert Ticke first sat up, then almost threw up.

'I don't feel well,' he moaned, the vodka and spices merging like napalm in his stomach.

Linda reached out and made a valiant attempt to undo the top of his shirt.

'Let me loosen your clothing,' she whispered huskily. 'I used to be a nurse, I know what I'm doing.'

Lambert Ticke knew what she was doing and it didn't meet with his approval.

*****

The ensuing grunts, groans and muffled squeals didn't meet with Chuck Grogan's approval, either, though it was marginally more acceptable than listening to Ticke bugger a Russian spy senseless in a motorway toilet. From what Grogan could gather – in the relative sanctuary of his van – Ticke had moved on from screwing his fellow man to screwing his fellow woman, in this case Inspector Lunt's wife while her husband was conveniently absent. The listening device continued to break up from time to time, for which he was grateful. In between bursts of static, it seemed that Ticke was struggling to keep his trousers on. As for the woman, she was either in the throes of debauched ecstasy, or being horribly tortured to death, it was hard to be sure which.

*****

Back in the Lunts' sitting room, Ticke was of the unshakeable opinion that his time on earth was up. His head was swimming, his stomach heaved, and a half-naked woman was trying her best to pull down his underpants while asking him to remind her again how many men he had recently strangled.

*****

Out in the van, Grogan caught that part, too, and pondered on the enormity of the task he had undertaken. He had caught something during dinner about Ticke planning to kill someone tomorrow and wondered what poor bastard he had in his sights.

Just then, he heard a deep, guttural roar and promptly pressed the 'off' switch on his listening equipment. There was only so much degenerate fornication a good Christian man could be privy to before going to Hell and Grogan had reached his limit.

*****

Back in the Lunts' sitting room, the unfortunate Lambert Ticke had reached his, too. The animal-like cry that had proved to be Grogan's breaking point had been a very different bodily need to the one that the fat American had envisaged. It had, in fact, been Lambert Ticke's stomach abandoning the fight to keep itself to itself and evicting its unwanted guests. As waves of curry and vodka exited with more speed than they had originally entered, Linda Lunt was the first to regret her unorthodox approach to wooing a trained assassin.

The man she had set her sights on seemed intent now on adding her to his list of victims. Regurgitated naans, poppadums, gulab jamuns, and assorted vegetarian delights struck her from every angle as she struggled to save herself from drowning in curry. The hand she had down his pants restricted her movements somewhat and, as Lambert Ticke yo-yoed giddily on the sofa, she felt the bones in her wrist come close to cracking.

When he stood up without warning, the laws of physics ensured that she was propelled in the opposite direction, hitting the carpet at speed as she prayed – for one delirious moment – to wake up and find this was all a dream.

For Lambert Ticke, the word 'nightmare' felt more appropriate. Without a backward glance, like a tethered goat breaking free just before the lion strikes, he ran into the hallway, and up the stairs before flinging himself into the bathroom. His stomach might now be empty but his bladder was ready to burst. Having relieved himself furiously and without thought, he exited at speed and fled to his room. With a strength born from terror, he took hold of a small chest of drawers and heaved it behind the door. Satisfied that he was safe for the time being, he took a final breath to steady himself, then promptly passed out on the floor.

In the sitting room downstairs, Linda Lunt surveyed the damage, both to the carpet and to herself. It struck her as faintly ironic that it was she, not the chef at *The Ali Tandoori*, who had been the recipient of his regurgitated specials tonight. Her wrist ached badly, and, when she tried to move her hand, a searing pain shot up her arm. Her dress was ruined, the carpet was ruined and, more importantly, her life was ruined. She took a few moments to consider this unfortunate turn of events, then burst into tears.

TWENTY SIX

Lambert Ticke slept soundly on the carpet till just gone 1.30 in the morning. When he finally stirred, he wondered what the hell had hit him. His body ached from top to toe, with the exception of his right arm, which seemed to have lost all feeling. As he eased himself awkwardly into a sitting position, his muddled thoughts began to clear.

Something didn't smell right and it took him a few moments to realise it was him. He pressed a hand to his face and sniffed the unmistakeable aroma of stale vomit. A vision forged in the bowels of Hell crawled out from somewhere inside his head. With a shudder, he recalled Linda Lunt's lipsticked mouth leaning in close, one breast swinging freely as she fiddled with his trousers. He remembered his stomach heaving – whether from the vile concoction in his belly or the dreadful sight of Linda Lunt bearing down on him, it was hard to say. After that, things were something of a blur. Linda Lunt had screamed and so, he recalled, had he. He had a vague memory of running upstairs and wanting to throw himself out of a window – preferably one high enough to end his misery – and then nothing.

Lambert Ticke stretched out his arm, as the feeling began to return, and considered his next move. A shower would be nice, but a glance at his watch told him that the timing wasn't good. He was thirsty, too, unbelievably so, and his head hurt. The longer he mulled things over, the more convinced he became that the woman had doctored his water. Dear God! Who the hell doctored water – and how? Alcohol, of course, that had to be it. She had spiked his drink with methylated spirits or something equally lethal in order to ... what? Kill him? Or, to his mind, something far worse. He had read about nymphomaniacs but never imagined he would meet one in Fetherton, still less the wife of a policeman charged with assisting his inquiries. Lambert Ticke shuddered again. He had had a narrow escape.

More pressing, just then, was the fact that his mouth was as dry as the Gobi desert. (And tasted like a camel's armpit passing through.) He might have woken to find himself mercifully alive, and his stomach pumped of whatever toxic brew had laid him low, but he was in desperate need of liquid. Water, preferably and – even more preferably – this time unadulterated.

Struggling to his feet, Ticke switched on the bedroom light and surveyed the makeshift barrier he had erected to keep out his unwanted admirer. With some difficulty – he wondered how the hell he had ever managed to position it there in the first place – he dragged the chest of drawers away from the door. Then, switching off the light, he cautiously opened it a fraction and peered out onto the landing.

All seemed quiet enough. By now, Linda Lunt had surely gone to bed. Either that, Ticke imagined, or into whatever box of her native soil she kept hidden in the basement. Her husband must have returned, too, he assumed, and be sleeping off whatever Bacchanalian revelry he had indulged himself in. Ticke needed water and the bathroom was closest, but he had no wish to make any noise that might disturb the Lunts. The kitchen would be the safest option, though he would have to be careful. Closing the door, he turned the light back on, crossed over to the bed, and rifled through his suitcase. Having found one of three small torches he kept for emergencies, he flicked it on, then crossed back, switched off the main light, opened the door and stepped out onto the landing.

Moving slowly, he crept downstairs with all the caution of a man expecting Death itself to leap out at him at every step. And not a pleasant death, if his time in this house had taught him anything. After what seemed like an age, he tiptoed into the kitchen. Having opened three cupboards, he eventually found himself a glass which he rinsed five times before filling it with water and drinking greedily as if his life depended on it.

By the time the sixth glass of liquid cascaded into his stomach, Ticke's head had begun to spin and he feared, for one awful moment, that he was about to be sick all over again. The kitchen was sited at the rear of the house, with an outside door leading into the garden. Spotting keys in the lock, and hopeful that fresh air might revive him, Ticke turned them, opened the door and breathed deeply. He stood there for a full minute, inhaling as much fresh air as his body could take. It was a cold night and, though the chill helped to clear his head, it quickly encouraged him to return to the sanctuary of the house. Closing the door behind, he walked forward a few steps and then screamed.

The reason he screamed was that a hideous apparition had emerged from the shadows, flung itself forward and hurled him to the ground. In the darkness, illuminated only feebly by the light from the torch he had left on a worktop, Ticke caught sight of a face like the devil, with breath from the sewer, and arms that rightly belonged to an adult gorilla that had been working out to improve its fitness.

'I've got you now!' it screamed. 'Thinking you could fuck with me in my own kitchen! I'll have you! Up yours, you bastard!'

'Oh, for God's sake!' cried Ticke! 'Get off me, please! Get off me!'

'I'm not getting off!' yelled his unknown assailant. 'I'm gonna have you, you bastard! You're going down, big time!'

Somewhere, in his delirium, Ticke thought he recognised his attacker's voice, but his mind was in a whirl and nothing made sense any more.

*****

A few hundred yards away, Chuck Grogan had no doubt about what was happening. Ever since Ticke had woken in a pool of his own vomit and a surge of electricity had swept through the fat American's leg, en route to his brain, he had been steeling himself for further debauchery. It had not been long in coming and his mind revolted at this fresh turn of events. It was bad enough that Ticke found pleasure not only in public toilets but also with the wife of a fellow gang-member. Now it seemed the gang-member was taking his pleasure with Ticke, and screwing him senseless on the kitchen floor. It was hard to tell whether Ticke approved, though being a Russian, Grogan decided, he probably did.

Mercifully, the listening device was acting up again, and not every joyful scream made it through to Grogan's recording equipment. He caught a few 'Oh, Gods!', a couple of 'Get off me's' and an 'Up yours!' (which particularly upset him). When his lover told Ticke it was time to go down on him big time, Grogan almost reached for his gun. Other than that, he was forced to endure a volley of grunts, groans and shrill squeals as, he assumed, Ticke found depraved but blissful joy in the other man's arms.

Had the equipment not shut down completely for several minutes, he might have gained a rather different picture of what was happening in the Lunts' kitchen. The last words Grogan heard were, 'I'm going to handcuff you now, you bastard, and then we'll see how hard you are!'

The fat American was a devout church-goer and would have pressed the 'off' button himself had a poor signal not done the job for him. Homosexual degeneracy was already a hanging offence in his view, but one man handcuffing another just to see how excited it left him took sexual deviancy to a whole new level.

*****

Back in the kitchen, Lambert Ticke would have been the first to agree. When the brute who had secured his arms behind his back, then kneed him in the arse for good measure, stood up and switched on the light, he shut his eyes tightly and wondered what further misery was coming his way.

There had been something familiar about his assailant's voice. Fear that his last moments had come at the hands of a passing madman had clouded his reason and it was only when he was rolled sharply onto his front and suffered another kick to the groin, that enlightenment dawned. A voice in the darkness (Ticke still had his eyes firmly closed) confirmed his worst fears.

'What the fuck are you doing sneaking around my house in the dark?' yelled Bernard Lunt, thrilled and dismayed in equal measure to discover that it was Lambert Ticke squealing like a stuck pig on his kitchen floor.

Just for the moment, Ticke was unable to respond. There were tears in his eyes, his stomach was again threatening to heave, and his balls were on fire. When he did finally open his mouth to speak, all that emerged was a child-like squeal of despair.

'You're lucky I didn't hurt you,' said Lunt, rolling Ticke onto his back, then leaving the room in search of his keys. When he finally returned about five minutes later, Ticke had not moved. He felt he didn't dare, though he did his best to keep his legs together in case Lunt took another swing at him for old times' sake.

Dragging himself upright, or as upright as he possibly could, given his weakened condition, Ticke flared his nostrils indignantly and tried to speak again.

'You almost killed me!' he complained in a shrill voice.

'Well you shouldn't be sneaking round like a thief in the night,' said Lunt with equal vigour. 'How was I to know you weren't a burglar? You might have been planning to ravish my wife.'

Ticke bridled at both suggestions, but especially the latter. It would take a brave man or a lunatic, he told himself bitterly, to come here looking for Mrs Lunt. He'd have liked to have said that out loud, but he was struggling to stand upright and had no wish to provoke the insult-to-nature who had almost emasculated him.

'You woke me up,' said Lunt, as if Ticke was to blame. 'I was kipping on the settee.' He poked his thumb at the ceiling. 'Back late, didn't want to wake the wife. She can take things the wrong way this time of night.'

Ticke didn't doubt it in the slightest but wasn't about to give his host support.

'I only wanted a glass of water,' he said feebly.

'I could have killed you,' said Lunt, as he reluctantly uncuffed him.

'That's what I said,' muttered Ticke, rubbing both wrists as if he were creaming his skin.

'You're a lucky man.'

'What?' squealed Ticke, then promptly shut up. He'd been poisoned and nearly raped by a drunken nymphomaniac, then beaten up and kicked in the groin by her thuggish husband. 'Lucky' wasn't how he'd describe his evening.

Lunt wrinkled his nose and sniffed the air. 'Was it you that threw up on my carpet?'

'I don't recall,' said Ticke guardedly. In his defence, his memory of the occasion wasn't that clear, though he knew that would cut no ice with Lunt.

The policeman regarded him sourly. 'You smell like a horse's arse,' he said, breathing rancid beer fumes into Ticke's face. It was touch and go, thought Ticke, as to whether he threw up again. 'You should have a shower. You're ponging out the house.'

'I didn't want to wake you up,' said Ticke wearily. 'Or your–' He hesitated. 'Mrs Lunt,' he added quickly before his anger made him say something worse.

Bernard snorted. 'I wouldn't let that stop you. The house

could fall down, she wouldn't hear.'

'I thought you said you didn't want to wake–,' began Ticke, then shut his mouth again. He shrugged his shoulders. He could do with a good wash. It would be a long day tomorrow and he didn't want to stink the car out. 'Thank you,' he said. 'Could I take up a glass of water? I'm thirsty.'

'Take what you like,' said Bernard. He cackled gleefully. 'Take my wife if you want,' and he snorted again.

'The glass will be more than enough, thank you,' said Ticke with as much politeness as he could muster. Grabbing a tumbler from the worktop, he waddled up the stairs as fast as his swollen testicles allowed.

TWENTY SEVEN

Lambert Ticke rose early the next morning, though not at all refreshed and ready for the day ahead. Unsurprisingly, he had struggled to sleep after his successive treatment at the hands (and, in Bernard's case, feet) of both Lunts. Though his shower had revived him a little, he was a worn-out shell and had lacked the strength to heave the chest of drawers behind the door, ensuring a semblance of safety overnight. Even if had managed the feat, he knew he would not have had the strength to shift them back again in the morning. As a result, anxious and aching, he dozed fitfully and, woken all too soon by the shrill clatter of his alarm (and just five minutes after he had finally nodded off), he crawled from his bed, exhausted.

At least he no longer smelt of vomit – or Linda Lunt. The shower had washed away the physical evidence of that ordeal, though the memories, he feared, might never fade. His mouth remained horribly dry, despite the many glasses of water he had swallowed in the bathroom.

Creeping downstairs, guided only by his torch and fearful that at any moment a monstrous figure might emerge from the shadows and haul him to the carpet for another sound beating, Ticke found, to his relief, that Bernard had vacated the area, presumably for the more comfortable warmth of his bed, albeit one shared with his sexually voracious wife.

Filling a fresh glass from the kitchen tap, Ticke downed first one pint of water, then another. His mouth was still dry and, after allowing a minute or two for the liquid to settle, he drank a further three glasses, still failing to quench his thirst. By now his stomach had stretched to breaking point and the skin around his abdomen felt like steel.

With some difficulty, he waddled into the hallway, and over to the front door. Turning the key in the lock and opening it as quietly as he could, he was swamped with a sense of gloom. Today was the day he hoped to put his masterplan into operation; the day he lured Mervyn Ratt from out of the shadows and saved the life of the Prime Minister, Sir Edward St John Stark. But once it was over, he would have to return here, to this house of torment. It occurred to him that he could always check back into the Grand Richmond Hotel. What it lacked in bug-free bedding and edible food, it more than made up for in not being the Lunts' home. Then again, he had no wish to antagonise his lunatic hosts. To his knowledge, he had done nothing to offend Bernard Lunt, yet had been almost crippled for his pains, not to mention very nearly raped by the man's wife. Though convinced his plan was fool-proof, he needed the police onside as back-up. He might need to stay here a while longer, though he would have to tread carefully if he were to escape in one piece. It was Ratt he hoped to snare in a trap, not himself.

As he had done on the previous morning, he left the house as quietly and as cautiously as ever.

And, as he had also done on the previous morning, Chuck Grogan, having recovered from a further blast of voltage to his legs and head, had slithered unshaven and unwashed into the driver's seat, waited for Ticke's car to crawl slowly out of the Lunts' drive, then set off in pursuit.

Grogan was not a patient man by nature and things were moving too slowly for his liking. The day before, he had watched Ticke's accomplice load several bags of bomb-making fertiliser into his car and, to his knowledge, they were still there. His handlers in London had told him very little – just to follow Ticke and report back with his findings. He had done as they had asked and his orders hadn't changed – even after last night. He was still to 'observe and evaluate' – which, in his book, meant pussyfoot around. Well, bugger them, as the

Brits liked to say – especially Ticke who seemed to be doing a lot of that lately. From now on, he would do things his way.

As he followed his quarry from a safe distance, Grogan went over everything he had learned so far. Ticke was an insatiable sex maniac, who pedalled his bike down both sides of the street. When he wasn't debauching himself in motorway toilets, he was happy to be handcuffed and rogered rigid on the kitchen floor by homosexual policemen. (And that after screwing the other fellow's wife till she screamed.) Ticke had also made brief contact with a man who lived at Number 78 Arcadia Avenue, and who was almost certainly a member of his terrorist cell. Grogan had hacked into the electoral roll and learned that the man's name was Colin Crimp. He had seen two male suspects leave the house, but had no idea which one was Crimp. For the moment, that didn't matter. Given how the pair had behaved on the doorstep, fondling each other shamelessly, he imagined it likely that Crimp was the older of the two, and the younger man some sort of rent boy, hired for his sexual favours. It certainly wasn't his looks.

Which brought his mind back to the deviant Ticke, who appeared to make a habit of getting up early in the morning, but for no particular purpose. Prior to his trip to the agricultural store, all Ticke had done yesterday was to sit outside an empty house for several hours, probably playing with himself, though Grogan had no wish to dwell on the image. From all he now knew about the man, he could imagine no other reason for wasting all that time.

He hoped that whatever Ticke had in mind for today, it involved more than sitting in a car for hours on end, while fiddling with his private parts.

*****

By 10 am, some five hours after he had slipped out of the Lunts' driveway, Ticke had shown no sign of deviating from his behaviour of the previous day. As before, a couple of men had left the house – the same two perverts, Grogan observed grimly, as yesterday morning, confirming, in his jaded view, the moral turpitude of those degenerate forces currently ranged against the free world. The rent boy had left first, followed, some thirty minutes later, by the second, older man – Colin Crimp (Grogan muttered through clenched teeth), the libertine Russian spy (he saw no reason to think otherwise) who owned the house. The first man had walked away, the second had got into a taxi.

Another half hour had passed, during which time Ticke, much to Grogan's renewed disgust, had begun fiddling with himself again. For the past ten minutes, he had been swaying awkwardly, wriggling his buttocks and pulling faces. Grogan cursed the excellent quality of his Japanese state-of-the art visual monitoring equipment; it gave him an all-too revealing insight into the sordid goings-on inside the Fiat Uno. Worse still, whatever tracking devices Ticke was currently wearing were currently functioning properly, and in quadrophonic, too, which only added to Grogan's misery. The squeals, moans and lingering sighs were almost too much for him to stomach. More than once, it crossed his mind that he had learned as much – if not more – as he needed to know about Ticke, and was perfectly within his rights to kill the swine. He could always report back to London that Ticke had pulled a gun and forced him to respond with lethal force. No one could blame him. Not after what he'd seen and heard these past few days. Lambert Ticke was an abomination who deserved to be put down, and as painfully as possible. His contacts in Arcadia Avenue – and those sex-obsessed deviants in Felicia Drive he'd been humping for the past two days – could be hauled in for questioning, or, better still, tortured. In Grogan's experience, torture always produced swifter and more encouraging results than formal interrogation, though he often found he had to nip in quick and twist a few nipples himself. Most of his colleagues lacked his work ethic, preferring to pussyfoot around, and offer the occasional cup of tea or cigarette. That wasn't the way to keep democracy alive in his view. You couldn't bake a do-nut without breaking eggs and you couldn't save the free world without doing the same to a Russkie's wedding tackle. Ticke might not be a Russkie by birth (though Grogan had his doubts), but he was as close as dammit, and that was good enough for him.

Lambert Ticke, meanwhile – unaware that he was under close surveillance – had begun to regret having drunk so much water before setting out on what he hoped was the final phase of his plan to bring Mervyn Ratt to justice. His bladder was painfully tight and, with no immediate way of relieving the pressure, he shifted painfully in his seat, stifling the occasional squeal of discomfort and trying not to think about toilets.

It was no good, he decided finally, he couldn't restrain himself much longer. Ratt had left the house a good thirty minutes ago and it seemed unlikely he would return any time soon. Every minute counted. Ticke had to get into the house – or the garden at least – and do what he planned to do as fast as possible. Further delay was out of the question – for physical as much as tactical reasons.

Taking a deep breath and doing his best to avoid sudden movements, Ticke opened the driver's door and eased himself out onto the pavement. With his bladder at bursting point, he was unable to straighten his back, and waddled across the empty road, one hand clutched to his belly, fearful that his body might let him down at any time.

From his mobile command centre fifty yards away, Grogan watched, open-mouthed, as Ticke approached the house. He could hardly believe his eyes (or ears for that matter). From the way the man hunched, groaned and clutched his lower regions, it was horribly clear that Ticke had advanced from fiddling with himself in private to full-blown public masturbation and to hell with whoever saw him. Jesus! The man had no shame!

Grogan felt a wave of relief as Ticke shuffled down the side of the house and disappeared from view. To his distress, he could still hear the other man whimpering with delight, and doubted he could take much more. When, a few moments later, he heard Ticke pull down his zipper and release a squeal of joy, Grogan finally cracked and switched off his listening equipment. Even he had his limits and he wasn't ashamed to admit that he'd reached them again. He'd gone through the fires of hell being forced to eavesdrop on Ticke's perversions in the name of liberty, but he was damned if he was going to listen to the deviant ejaculating into a rose bush. Rolling his chair back, Grogan opened the door to a large fridge, removed a frozen Alabama Burger ('The One Mom Always Fried Up For Breakfast'), and popped it into the microwave. He needed something to take his mind off Ticke's willy and nothing, he knew, would do that better than a slab of processed beef, from a cow fed on a pig's innards, topped with chemically enhanced pickle and served in a sesame seed bun made from American wheat grown in a pesticide-drenched field just outside Las Vegas and previously used for nuclear testing in the 1950s. He licked his lips and began to count down the five minutes – including waiting time – it would take the tiny oven to bombard his nourishing snack with the necessary amount of radiation to bring out its full flavours.

As for Ticke, just then, he was as relieved – quite literally – as he had ever been, urinating freely into a patch of earth behind the garden shed. Another few seconds, he was sure, and he would have done himself irreparable damage. A plentiful intake of water might ensure a healthy mind and body, but a ruptured bladder was too high a price to pay even for a man of his intellect. The curry hadn't helped, nor had Linda Lunt's attempt to seduce him with vodka pretending to be something innocent out of a tap. Someone had once said that having the urge to pee sharpened the mind at times of crisis. If that were true, he considered sourly, zipping himself up and feeling relaxed for the first time in hours, his could saw through an elephant's penis.

Returning to the problem in hand, his current concern was

how to gain entry to the garden shed. It was locked, which was not something he had anticipated, and he cursed his lack of foresight. From the cobwebs and grime coating the large, rusty Chubb, he guessed it had not been opened in a while. That suggested Ratt was unlikely to examine the interior any time soon, which raised his spirits a little. They lifted even more when, noticing a large face-down pot nearby, he threw caution to the wind and prised it up a fraction. Peering underneath, he could hardly believe his luck. He had heard of people, lacking all common sense, who kept a spare set of household keys under the mat. But he had always imagined such people did not exist – outside of a home for the criminally insane. Yet here was concrete proof that, for all his evil intent and schemes to topple civilised society (or what little remained of it), Mervyn Ratt was a moron. He made a mental note to pen an additional chapter on the mental deficiencies of the Alienated Assassin, then picked up the keys and examined them carefully. There were three in all, and, from his limited knowledge of Ratt's house, he guessed (and, as it turned out, he was correct in every detail) that they opened the front door, French windows and, of particular interest to him just now, the garden shed.

Lambert Ticke was an atheist. No other way of looking at life made sense in his experience. Given the vile nature of both the natural and the human world, the prospect of a God of any description, let alone the vengeful Deity of mainstream faiths, seemed a more terrifying prospect than believing in no God at all. But there were times – as now – when he felt a primeval urge to fall to his knees and thank a benevolent cosmos for keeping an eye out for him.

There were two small keys and one very long, battered piece of metal which had 'shed' written all over it; literally, as it turned out, because the letters 'S H E D' had been marked in a fading felt pen across a strip of tape that had been wound around the longer key. He could fathom no reason why anyone would need to do that, and made another mental note to include something about 'anxiety syndrome' in the as-yet unwritten chapter he had recently decided to pen.

Inserting the key into the rusty old Chubb, he twisted it gently. The lock remained stubbornly closed so he tried a little harder, pulling it this way and that until it finally clicked open. Pushing at the door, he peered inside and saw, to his delight, that, apart from a few discarded paint tins and a small wheelbarrow, the shed was empty. The wheelbarrow was an unexpected bonus. He hadn't fancied lugging all that fertiliser across the road on his own. Indeed, the more he thought about it, the more sense it made to park his car in Ratt's drive and lighten his workload further.

His mind made up, he rolled the wheelbarrow out of the shed, up the side of the house and around to the front. The avenue remained as quiet as ever, which suited him perfectly. He didn't want any nosy neighbours popping out to ask awkward questions. Whatever misconceptions the lunatic Linda Lunt might harbour, he was neither authorised nor especially keen to kill a local busybody just because they wanted to know what he was up to.

Hurrying back to his car, he started up the engine and reversed neatly into Ratt's driveway. A hundred yards away, Grogan watched with interest. Relieved to see, for the moment at least, that Ticke appeared to have sated his carnal urges, the fat American switched the trackers back on. They might not be of much use for the present, but it was as well to be prepared. He assumed the house was empty, but Ticke was a devious sort and he could take nothing for granted.

When the other man unloaded two bags of fertiliser into the wheelbarrow and trundled them around the corner, Grogan shook his head and took another bite from his Alabama Burger, regretting his lack of foresight in not warming up two of the beauties. Chewing thoughtfully, he mulled over the prospect that whatever Ticke was up to, it presented a threat to life and limb – one sufficiently grave enough to warrant the use of lethal force. For the present, however, he would watch, wait, and keep his finger close to the comforting array of trigger buttons on the control panel in front of him.

This day wasn't over yet. No, siree. Not by a long way.

*****

It took Lambert Ticke almost an hour to load, move and finally unload the twenty bags of fertiliser. By the time he had finished, Ratt's shed was piled high to the roof. Rolling the wheelbarrow back inside, he refastened the lock, and sat on the large pot to recover his breath. It had been back-breaking work, and Ticke was not a man built for physical labour. Extracting his pink cotton handkerchief from a jacket pocket (not removing the jacket hadn't helped his endeavours), he wiped the perspiration from his forehead. He had no idea if twenty bags of fertiliser was sufficient to build a bomb capable of taking out the Prime Minister, and however many bodyguards were unlucky enough to be travelling with him at the time, but he didn't care, the point was academic. Without a detonator – which both Google and several ISIS-friendly websites had assured Ticke was essential to success – there would never be a bomb in the first place, however many bags of this muck he could lay his hands on. All that mattered was that it *looked* as if Ratt was planning to build a bomb.

It was time, he knew, to focus on the next stage of his plan. He had hoped against hope that he might somehow gain access to Ratt's house. It was one thing to plant incriminating evidence in his shed, quite another – and even more damning – to infiltrate his inner sanctum. He had come prepared to do so, but more in hope than expectation. Turning the keys on his palm, he knew that fate had, quite literally, dropped the means of Ratt's undoing into his hands.

Taking a deep breath, Ticke crossed to the French windows and selected a second key – one that looked unlikely to fit the main entrance. He pushed it into the lock, turned it twice and felt a thrill of excitement when the door swung open.

A moment later, he had stepped into the enemy's sitting room, his heart pounding loudly in his chest.

TWENTY EIGHT

Colin Crimp was in a quandary. He was also, just then, standing across the road from a detached bungalow on the outskirts of Fetherton – that bungalow being the source of his current concern. A thick wooden board, carved in the shape of a squirrel, proclaimed the property to be 'Shangri-La', though Colin suspected it was anything but. The 'Abyss' might have been a more appropriate description, given his promise to Henry and how he feared today might turn out.

He had left Arcadia Avenue first thing and headed for the office. Henry had remained behind, muttering something about a mid-morning meeting with his solicitor, to 'sort out a few pressing matters'. Colin suspected that if his employer had a meeting, it was more likely to be with one of his trollops, and a different form of soliciting altogether. Be that as it may, his own course of action was inevitable. He wanted Henry out of his house, and if that meant enduring a face-to-face meeting with Norah Plank, it was a price he would have to pay.

Henry had told him to take the cost of a taxi out of petty cash and drop in on his wife at 11.15. Apparently, she enjoyed listening to Ken Bruce on Radio 2, and it always put her in a good mood. She would be sufficiently relaxed by then, which would make her more amenable to what he insisted on referring to as Colin's 'voice of reason'. Colin wasn't convinced on either front but, lacking alternatives, and keen to get the job done quickly, he had told Karen he was off to the dentist and might be some time. Having received her assurance that she wouldn't break off their engagement and elope with Bob while he was having his gums syringed, he had taken a cab to the outskirts of Fetherton, made a note of the firm's number for the return journey, and walked up and down the road several times rather than ring the front doorbell.

He had set out in good time, though not in a good mood. The petty cash box had proved to be empty which, in hindsight, was hardly surprising. Henry had expensive tastes and was already two weeks behind with his rent. At this rate, Colin had reasoned sourly, he would be bankrupt by the end of the month – unless he could shift the problem of Henry Plank back to where it belonged. Having put up with his boss for the past three weeks, however, he struggled to see why Norah Plank would want him home on any terms. The situation was grim, and that was even before he rang their wretched doorbell.

Reaching the end of the road for the thirteenth time (he had kept an accurate tally – much like he might have counted sheep – in the hope it would calm him down), Colin briefly considered continuing on his way and walking the five miles back into town. At that moment, it was an appealing idea. More appealing, certainly, than the alternative. But then he might be stuck with Henry Plank for good, and that was too dreadful a prospect whatever torments he might otherwise avoid.

Turning around slowly, Colin took a deep breath, like an athlete preparing to burst from the blocks in one last bid for fame and glory. It was all or nothing now, he knew, while trying hard to dismiss the thought that, if he were a betting man, 'nothing' seemed the runaway favourite in today's mid-morning race.

*****

While Colin had been pacing up and down the road, in a pointless bid to delay the inevitable, Norah Plank had been peering out of her sitting-room window, baffled by the behaviour of fee-paying clients eager to give her home a good tidying-up in return for being soundly beaten on the bottom.

'He's passed the house about ten times,' said Norah, addressing an equally perplexed Myrtle Fling. 'You'd think he didn't want to be thrashed senseless.' She shook her head and dropped the curtain.

'Perhaps he's nervous?' suggested Myrtle, focusing her limited brain power on the problem at hand. 'I'd be nervous, too, if someone was going to beat me up.'

Norah huffed loudly and did some pacing of her own. If truth be told – not that she was ready to admit it to Myrtle – she was a little anxious herself. Though officially due to launch her new business in three days' time, she had received a phone call late the previous evening from a man called Cyril (though she suspected it might be a pseudonym). He said he'd seen her advert in *Thrasher's Weekly* and wondered if she could fit him in early. He was only in town till tomorrow evening and mightn't be back for months.

She'd had a couple of drinks (the alcohol flowed more freely since Henry had left) and it had gone to her head. Three glasses of a rather fruity Cabernet had loosened both her tongue and what little remained of any morals she'd been gamely clinging on to till opening day.

Her terms had been simple enough – albeit fuelled in part by drink and the rest by the sincere belief he would baulk at the price and leave her in peace.

'Two hundred pounds, you clean the bathroom and I beat you on the arse with a stick for being a worthless piece of scum,' she had announced, while flicking through a copy of the *Radio Times* and wondering if there was anything good on the telly.

He had surprised her by replying – in a curiously shrill voice – 'That sounds very reasonable', and even more so when he suggested she gag him with a used tea towel before whipping him so he wouldn't disturb the neighbours with his screams. Her escape route blocked off, she had thanked him for his thoughtfulness and said she looked forward to making his life hell at 11.30 the following morning.

'Now sod off, you pillock,' she had concluded, in the hope it might yet save her at the death. He had merely responded with a curious, lingering moan, and a squealed cry to the Almighty, after which he had put the phone down, just in time for her to catch a repeat of *Fawlty Towers.*

'He said he'd ring the bell and pretend to be from the council,' explained Norah. 'Or it might have been a door-to-door-salesman, I wasn't really listening.' She shrugged her shoulders. 'Anyhow, we're to invite him in for a chat, then tie him up and tickle him with feathers until he agrees to clean out the toilet. Something like that. We can make it up as we go along. The main thing is, he gives us two hundred pounds and does a bit of hoovering before we throw him out.'

'Do you think he's changed his mind?' asked Myrtle, lifting the curtain herself and peering towards the top of the drive.

'Who knows?' said Norah, who was rather hoping that he had. Now that push came to shove, she wasn't entirely convinced she was suited to her new role. It had all seemed so simple several weeks ago, following her alcoholic-fuelled epiphany. Tart up the house to embarrass Henry and two fingers to the vicar (among others). Drink had given her courage, no doubt about it, and had become a best friend on whom she was happy to rely. She'd wanted to beat Henry at the time. Physically and as hard as possible. Any man, come to that, because they were all cut from the same cloth. Even the vicar was married – to a softly spoken, middle-aged lady who ran the local WI. He probably did things to her that weren't allowed in the Bible, and forgave himself because God had given him authority to ravish a woman with impunity. Which was men all over, of course, even if they prayed a lot.

Even so, she wasn't a violent woman, not really. In her imagination, perhaps, but not in the real world. Myrtle wasn't much better though she carried extra weight and could probably knock a man down without meaning to. Hopefully, she could handle the more physical side of things, that's why she'd taken her on, after all.

'Perhaps we should go out and ask him in?' suggested Myrtle.

'Not dressed like that, you won't,' said Norah, alarmed. Though she had opted to embrace her new life still clad in her favourite grey skirt, cream blouse, tights and sensible shoes, she had been persuaded – by the company who had sold her a terrifying medley of whips, a rack, St Andrew's Cross, ball-gags, blindfolds and tickling sticks – to splash out £129.99 on what they called the 'deluxe dominatrix model'. This comprised a rubber basque (cut obscenely low at the breast), a studded neck choker with matching wristbands, fishnet stockings, a whip and a pair of dangerously high-heeled leather boots. Though the outfit came in Extra Large, Myrtle herself was Extra Extra Large, with the result that once squeezed into the revolting ensemble, she ran a grave risk of exploding out of it should she move in any direction too quickly.

Given that Myrtle was currently garbed and ready for action, even Norah – despite her wish to heap embarrassment on her cheating husband – was loath for the younger woman to waddle into the street half-naked and almost certainly return to the house with the job properly done.

It was at that moment, however, that the argument became academic. The rather gormless-looking young man, who had been striding up and down the road for the past ten minutes, came slowly back into view. But this time, instead of marching on and disappearing once again, he turned sharp left and walked anxiously towards the front door.

THIRTY

Norah Plank gazed through the spyhole at the young man standing outside her front door. She had always wondered what a pervert looked like, and now she was studying one close up. Of course, Henry was a pervert and she had seen him – often more intimately than she might have preferred – but he was *her* pervert; this man belonged to someone else, and they were probably glad to be shot of him. He looked anxious, reminding her of a monkey who had attempted an evolutionary leap but hadn't quite made it. Nondescript, too, despite his simian features. That was probably how he got away with being a pervert. No one he knew, not even his mother, wife or favourite aunt, had the slightest idea he was happy to be thrashed senseless in return for tidying up a stranger's house.

She glanced at her watch. Despite the fact that he had been marching up and down the road like a demented guardsman for the past twenty minutes, he was still a quarter of an hour early. Still, that was all to the good. She had neglected her household duties of late and Myrtle, whose hygiene left much to be desired, was no great shakes when it came to cleaning. There had seemed little point in making any fuss when a regiment of willing men was waiting to beat its path to her door, though possibly 'beat' was an ironic word in the circumstances.

Myrtle took her turn to look through the spyhole and study the young man who, it was hard to believe, was about to earn her twice as much per hour as any job she'd previously had, in return for which all she had to do was beat him harshly with a stick. It was a funny old world, and no mistake.

'Best you make yourself scarce,' said Norah. 'I'll get him into position, then you do what we agreed. After that we'll take it as it comes. I'm new to this myself, so we'll learn together.'

With that, Myrtle scurried into the front room and out of sight. Satisfied that everything was as it should be, Norah took a deep breath, adjusted her blouse, and opened her front door to the first – and as fate would have it, the last – client of her new career.

*****

Several miles away, on the far side of Fetherton, Lambert Ticke trembled behind a shower curtain, his feet immersed in two inches of filthy bath water. With one hand he fought gamely to pull up his trousers. Curled around his ankles as he leapt from the toilet to the bath, they were almost as sodden as his feet. The other hand clung protectively to a part of him which, all too recently, Linda Lunt had sought to claim as her own.

Just a short time previously, his victory had seemed assured. He had gained access to Ratt's house and planted sufficient evidence to ensure the other man's downfall. The contents of the CD – now lodged incriminatingly on Ratt's computer – allied to enough fertiliser in his shed to build a bomb with the help of Google (motto: 'We're here for you, whoever you are'), would convince any court in the land, whatever the jurors' collective IQ, that Ratt was a dangerous psychopath who planned to murder Sir Edward St John Stark, Prime Minister of the United Kingdom of Great Britain, Northern Ireland and All Her Colonies Beyond the Sea. The fact that Ratt himself had not gone so far as to plot the PM's murder was irrelevant. This was pre-emptive action, designed to forestall any attempt by a man programmed – possibly from birth, and certainly from his letters – to bring society to its knees.

And now here he was, Lambert Ticke, the nation's saviour,

skulking in a bath, trousers drenched, legs crossed and still desperate for a pee. His moment of relief had lasted one full second. Who the hell 'Henry' was, he had no idea – the young man, possibly – but the instant he had heard that dreadful squeal on the stairs, his penis had locked up. His bladder still ached like buggery – even more so now – and it was all he could do to hold himself in check. This isn't right, he thought miserably. *Life isn't fair!*

Unfortunately, for Lambert Ticke, life was about to get less fair still.

'*You in there, babe?*' called a voice at the bathroom door. Ticke felt his bladder tighten and, unable to contain himself, he released a mournful groan.

'Naughty, naughty!' giggled the voice, as a pair of stilettoed heels clacked ever closer.

When two painted fingernails curled around the edge of the shower curtain and pulled, Lambert Ticke panicked. The hand with which he had been gripping his trousers abandoned the cause and fought hard, instead, to yank back the curtain. It was an uneven contest, made even more so when Ticke's trousers slid down into the soapy water lapping around his feet. In a last bid to save himself, he released the curtain briefly and, in that instant, Amy Horris, escort from Leeds and long-time purveyor of sexual favours to Henry Plank (none of which, in fairness, involved thrashing), tugged the curtain so hard that she tore it from its runners.

As the two of them finally came face to face, Lambert Ticke screamed. Amy Horris screamed, too, and twice as loudly which, allowing for the shrillness of Ticke's cries, was some achievement. A couple of hundred yards away, from what he had imagined to be the safety of his mobile command centre, Chuck Grogan also screamed, though largely from a belief that he might have suffered permanent damage to his eardrums. Having seen a blonde, pneumatically enhanced woman enter the house about a minute earlier, and keen not to miss any subsequent chat which he hoped might furnish useful information, it occurred to him that the volume on Ticke's tracking devices might need to be increased. He had just ratcheted up the sound system to double its previous level when first Ticke, then the woman, yelled.

In Grogan's experience, one high-pitched cry signalled a threat to life and limb. Two generally hinted at something more sordid which, given Ticke's proclivities, seemed the most likely scenario here.

He was forced to hand it to Ticke, however reluctantly, his sexual prowess was second to none. The woman had been in the house for under two minutes, and already the pervert had got her pants down. The man's powers of recovery, given his recent activity in both the car and the garden, were phenomenal. How he found time to plot the downfall of the western world in between screwing anything that moved (and sometimes didn't) was beyond his understanding.

Back in the bathroom at 78 Arcadia Avenue, Lambert Ticke gazed directly into Amy Horris's eyes and finally knew the meaning of fear. Amy, for her part, felt much the same way. She had only dropped in on the off-chance, having – by happy coincidence – recently rogered a nervous first-time librarian half a mile away. It occurred to her that she might get another chance to speak to her mum in Australia at favourable rates (and possibly another salmon salad as Henry was a surprisingly good cook). She hadn't rung the doorbell, thinking it might be fun to surprise Henry, and had, instead, used the spare key he had been kind enough to have had made for her. Though she hadn't expected to find the randy old devil fired up and ready to go, what she had definitely *not* anticipated was finding herself face to face with a sex-crazed maniac, hiding in the bathroom with his trousers down and his thingie out.

But how did he know she would be here? And then a second, more dreadful question crossed her mind. *Where was Henry?* Dear God! What had the monster done to him?

Several notions chased each other through her head, and

none of them gave her any comfort. When Lambert Ticke, losing his balance as he tugged on his trousers, tottered forward, Amy's first thought was to turn and run. Her second was that as soon as she had her back to him, the pervert would be on her like a limpet. Even if he wasn't, he'd catch her on the stairs for sure. He'd killed Henry Plank, she was certain of that, probably chopped him up and put him in the fridge. That was what these people did, she'd read it in *The Sun*. It was him or her now, no two ways about it.

As Amy stepped back, she felt the searing warmth of the bar heater scald her bare leg. Moving quickly, she flung out both arms and seized the appliance, holding it like a shield across her bulging breasts.

'Come any closer, you weirdo!' she yelled, 'and I'll burn off your goolies!'

Lambert Ticke had no wish to have anything burned off and gave a fearful yelp. It was the last straw. For almost two minutes he had strained every nerve to keep himself in check. Fear had built a wall around his bladder and now fear tore it down and threw away the bricks. Instinctively, he tightened his hand around his penis, pointing it revolver-like at the woman trembling in front of him. A moment later, a thick arc of pee streamed from his body, and – even more dreadfully – in the general direction of Amy Horris.

Aware that she was under attack, and in the most appalling manner, Amy jiggled the heater from side to side, in a vain attempt to repel the assault. She was vaguely aware of a puddle of urine forming around her feet, a moment before a fresh stream of hot pee drenched her bosom. Amy screamed and dropped the heater. As it struck the floor, her fate was sealed. There was a blinding flash, followed by a bang and then another flash. A faint smell of burning flesh filled the air, and Lambert Ticke almost fainted. Amy Horris screamed, he screamed and then she screamed again. Or it might have been him, he couldn't be sure.

Seated at the control panel in his mobile command centre,

Chuck Grogan also screamed, then cursed obscenely as he ripped off his headphones and flung them to the floor.

'*Jesus H Christ!*' he yelled. It had taken him all this time to recover from the first assault on his eardrums. He had only just put the headphones back on, and now the bastards had deafened him again.

Back in the house, Amy Horris was no longer screaming, though that was of little concern to Chuck Grogan, who had had enough of Lambert Ticke's sexual exploits to last him a lifetime. Amy – having jack-knifed onto her back – lay sizzling on the bathroom floor, marinating in a puddle of someone else's urine, now shot through with a little of her own.

Lambert Ticke fell back against the wall, trying his damndest not to breathe, and failing abysmally. His heart – unlike that of the late Amy Horris – was beating twenty to the dozen, though his bladder was feeling a tad more comfortable than it had been. With some difficulty, he was able to reach down and pull up his pants. By now they were sopping wet and it seemed hardly worth the effort.

He couldn't believe what had happened. God in heaven! he thought miserably – what *had* happened? A woman he had only just met was lying on her back, arms thrust out at impossible angles and her legs dangling wide over the rim of the bath. Even to his untrained eye, a quick glance confirmed that she had forgotten to put on her pants when leaving home that morning. Just now, however, that seemed to be the least of her concerns. Her backside was on fire, though the puddle in which she lay was doing its bit to keep the flames under control. He had only come in for a pee. This couldn't be happening. Not to him. In heaven's name, this sort of thing didn't happen to anyone. It was beyond all reason.

And just then, so was Lambert Ticke. With some difficulty, he eased first one leg, then the other out of the bath and onto the urine-drenched floor. Carefully, he squelched his way around the late Amy Horris, considering, then promptly dismissing, any attempt to put her out. There was no point.

The flames were slowly dying, following the now lifeless woman into the great beyond. In truth, he had no wish to touch any part of her, dead or alive. A woman who entered a house without knickers, while inquiring as to the whereabouts of a 'randy bastard', wasn't to be approached by anyone decent. He had imagined the Lunt household to be the foulest place on earth, but now he knew better. Ratt was not simply an alienated terrorist in embryo, he was, without doubt, a deviant of the grossest kind. Gathering himself briefly, the scientist within came to the fore and Ticke made a mental note to include an additional chapter on the 'Carnal Alienation of the Lone Gunman'. He had often wondered if sexual perversion went hand in hand with social disaffection, and now he had his answer.

His work here was done, along with the unknown (to him at least) woman currently smouldering on Ratt's bathroom floor. He couldn't wait to get out of this pit of misery, and as fast as possible.

*****

Outside in the road, Chuck Grogan had come to a fateful decision. He had – with perfect timing – just received an update from London. The Prime Minister was planning an impromptu – and secret – visit to his home constituency. It wouldn't be till next week, but it served to concentrate his mind.

'Any word on Tit?' Blag had inquired, after imparting the news. 'Has he done anything we should know about? Do we need to send in back-up?'

Send in back-up? Grogan knew what that meant. It meant he would have done all the donkey work, while others reaped the glory. *His* glory! That wasn't on. He hadn't spent the last few days trailing a depraved Russian mastermind bent on sexual conquest and world domination only to have another man put a bullet in the enemy's head the moment his back was turned. They'd have had their feet up in some cosy billet playing poker all this time, while he, Grogan, a God-fearing Christian, had been forced to sit by and listen to a deviant shagging himself comatose with anything or anyone – man, woman or bush – he could lay his filthy hands on. Grogan had scarcely any time to make up his mind, but make it up he now did.

Twiddling a frequency dial first one way, then the other, he allowed himself a mischievous smirk as waves of static turned the broadcast from London into nonsense and removed, along with it, any need for his reply. The last words he heard, before the message was rendered incomprehensible, were 'The idiot's breaking up!', after which he took the precaution of shutting down completely in case they tried another channel.

It was time to take the Russkie out. London could go to hell. If the British PM was on his way north, you could bet your last dollar that the enemy knew his itinerary inside out. Ticke had bought enough manure to build a bomb the size of a nurse's arse and carried it into another Russkie's house. The police were involved, the sex-crazed Lunts and God knows who else, too. He couldn't afford to pussyfoot around any longer. Ticke had to be terminated, and the sooner the better – before he did whatever it was he'd been planning to do since he left his mother's womb.

Opening up Google Earth on his ballistics control panel (made in Japan but lovingly assembled in the USA), Grogan programmed in the coordinates for 78 Arcadia Avenue, Fetherton. Without looking up to see if any of the neighbours had been foolish enough to wander into the road unannounced, he armed one of three small warheads capable of taking out an average semi-detached house with a maximum of four bedrooms and a medium-sized garden. Then he stood, turned to face a large silver-framed portrait of Donald Trump, draped in the American flag, and placed a hand over his heart.

'For God and America!' he announced patriotically, before

pressing a large red button marked 'Fire', and raining down hell on 78 Arcadia Avenue, Fetherton.

TWENTY NINE

Lambert Ticke could hardly believe his luck. At the same time, he could hardly believe that that very same luck would not shortly run out, and as rapidly as it had run in. Though he had breached his enemy's lair, he was not a man to whom danger came without a second's thought. Indeed, as the first flush of excitement faded, he felt a sickening chill in his tummy. What if Ratt were to return now and find him *in situ*? The fellow might not be a Latin scholar and fully understand the term, but, if Ticke's own analysis was correct – and he saw no reason to doubt himself – Ratt was every bit as capable of 'taking a man out' as the gruesome Linda Lunt erroneously imagined Ticke himself to be.

He hesitated briefly, torn between fleeing the scene, his work done, and pressing on to further glory. It was madness, he knew, to linger, but, as a wave of adrenaline swept through his body, he knew, also, that this was a once-in-a-lifetime chance to make a difference. Gathering all of his courage in his small, manicured hands, Lambert Ticke strode out, through the sitting room door, and hurried up the stairs. With every step, his assurance redoubled until, by the time he had reached the landing, and registered three rooms leading off, he felt he could conquer the world.

The first room was an absolute mess, with a single unmade bed, and clothes discarded on the carpet. He guessed this was the younger man's room, the one with whom Ratt shared a home, though to what degree and for what reason, he had no wish to speculate. The man was a pig, that was clear. Moving on, he came to the bathroom, where he stalled as a blast of heat struck his face. To his astonishment, he saw that a three-bar electric heater had been placed on the closed toilet seat and not switched off, its long cord trailing around the doorway and out onto the landing. A further glance revealed an inch or two of water in the bathtub-cum-shower where, it seemed, someone – Ratt, presumably – had recently washed and not bothered to pull out the plug. The man appeared to have no standards whatsoever. As for using a heater in the bathroom, that was criminally insane, and every fibre of him yearned to rectify the matter. The house could easily burn down, what on earth was Ratt thinking? Then again, it was none of his business, and what if the other man had left it on deliberately? Ticke had no wish to do anything that suggested he had been there, however great the urge to put things right.

Another thought struck him – almost as forcibly as the heat from the three glowing bars. His bladder had begun to fill again, as more water worked its way through his system. He was anxious, too, and that always made him want to pee. He could do with going to the toilet, though that would involve removing the heater and he wasn't sure he wanted to touch the thing. With an effort of will, he resisted the impulse. If he had time before he left, perhaps he might take a chance. But it could be risky; the last thing he wanted was for Ratt to return, find him with his trousers down and no way out.

Turning away – albeit with some reluctance – he opened the final door on the landing and found himself in what he knew at once to be Ratt's bedroom. To his surprise, it was airy, neat and orderly – three factors of which he instantly approved. More importantly, as well as a smartly-made double bed, the room boasted a broad mahogany desk, on top of which was perched a black, wide-screen computer. Next to it sat a low, silvery-grey printer.

Barely able to contain his excitement, Ticke crossed to a chair in front of the keyboard and sat down. A little nervously, he stretched out a finger and pressed the tower's 'on' button. As the machine whirred into life, Ticke reached into his jacket pocket and removed two CDs which he placed on the desk.

His next move would depend entirely on whether Ratt used a password to access his computer. Better for Ticke's scheme if he didn't, but, like all good strategists, he had come prepared. His spirits sank a little when a white rectangle popped up, confirming that a password was indeed required. He thought for a moment, threw caution to the wind and typed in the four letters, 'R-A-T-T'. He could hardly believe that Ratt would be that stupid, but it was worth a shot. When the blue screen gave way to the home page, littered with files and icons, Ticke resisted a temptation to fall to his knees and acknowledge that, for the second time today, a benevolent Deity appeared to be challenging him to defy His existence.

Opening up a new text file, Ticke cast around for a CD burner. Delighted to see that Ratt's machine was equipped with one, he promptly popped in one of the CDs. An age seemed to pass before its contents became visible onscreen. Fingers trembling, he hurriedly copied its text, then pasted it into the new document, before closing down his original folder. Ejecting the CD, he dropped it back into his pocket.

Ticke read over the material as quickly as he could to ensure all was as it should be. He knew the wording backwards, of course, having written and rewritten it several times over the past few weeks. All that remained was for him to convince the rest of the world – and the police in particular – that Ratt himself was the author.

Having satisfied himself that everything was in order, he saved the file as 'Top Secret' and placed it in a crowded Documents folder. He knew that Ratt was a prodigious correspondent, but, even so, it staggered him to see how many letters the man had churned out over the past few months. As each was headed with a laboriously long title reflecting its content, Ticke felt confident that this latest addition to the collection would pass unnoticed in the short time Ratt had left to save himself.

The file conveniently hidden, all that remained was for him

to save it to the empty spare CD he had brought along. Slotting it into the burner, he fired up the relevant program, made the copy and ejected it. His heart racing, he slid back the bottom drawer of Ratt's desk. It was chock-a-block with pens, pencils, paper and notebooks. How he longed to examine everything carefully, both the contents of the desk and the computer. But he knew, reluctantly, that time was not on his side.

Extracting several items, he pushed the CD to the back of the drawer, then returned a pile of paperwork and pens on top, hiding the CD where it would never be found. Not by Ratt, at any rate.

His work here was done. Or would have been if his bladder had not reached bursting point again. He thought of Ratt's toilet, so conveniently close, even if it *was* guarded by a three-bar heater that might incinerate the house at any moment.

Oh, what the hell, he decided. He had no idea where the nearest public loos were, and no wish to have an accident in his car which, in the circumstances, seemed increasingly likely.

Checking that he had left nothing behind, Ticke slipped out of Ratt's bedroom and into the bathroom. Gingerly, he picked up the heater and set it down on the floor. Lifting the toilet seat by his fingertips, he unzipped himself and sighed with relief.

It was at that moment, when everything had gone as well as it possibly could and he was ready to allow himself a congratulatory pat on the back for all he had achieved, that the downstairs door first opened then closed very loudly. A moment later, he heard footsteps on the stairs and a shrill, harshly female voice call out, '*Henry! Are you at home, you randy bastard?*'

THIRTY ONE

Colin Crimp was sitting on an armchair in a low-lit, scented room, and feeling less than happy with his lot. Had he been aware of events unfolding at his house a few miles away, his anguish would have been indescribable. Fortunately for him, he was not. Ignorance may not always be bliss, but on this occasion it was close enough to make no difference.

Never at his most relaxed in the presence of an attractive woman, Colin felt uneasier still in the presence of Norah Plank who, it had to be conceded, was one of the ugliest women Colin had ever met. She looked at least ten years older than her husband and the blood-red lipstick she had plastered across her thin, wrinkled lips served only to accentuate the severe nature of her long, haggard face. He couldn't imagine what Henry had ever seen in her and wondered if she had money. He could hazard no other guess, just then, as to why his employer would be so keen to have her take him back.

Colin had been surprised when she had greeted him at the door with a brisk, 'I've been expecting you,' and assumed that Henry had warned her after all. As she ushered him in, and through to what he assumed was her sitting room, he caught a whiff of whisky in the air. She was, he considered glumly, cut from the same cloth as her husband. His spirits lifted. Perhaps it wouldn't be so difficult to get them back together, after all. Not if Henry was keen and his wife was slightly tipsy.

'I've come about,' he began, then faltered, as a fresh sense of unease washed over him. 'I've come about – well, I think you know what I've come about.' And then he lapsed into silence, fervently hoping she would carry the rest of the conversation for him.

'Yes, I think I do,' she replied. 'You're here to read my meter, aren't you? So you can report back to head office and have me put in my place.' As Norah had admitted to Myrtle, she could no longer remember the precise reason Cyril the Creep (as she unfairly thought of him) had settled on for being here, but she wasn't much bothered and she doubted he was, either. What puzzled her just then was why he appeared to be so anxious. He didn't look like a man who had travelled far in search of a good hiding. If anything, he looked more like a man who *had* come to read her meter.

Colin slumped. The woman was rambling already, talking gibberish. Having got his hopes up, he felt them plunge again. It wasn't yet mid-day and Norah Plank was as drunk as a skunk. Even Henry did his best to remain sober until mid-afternoon. She also smelt horribly over-scented – she must have bathed in some dreadful muck. Perhaps that was common among women who thrashed men for a living. Henry could have told him if he were not safely somewhere else. The overpowering stench wasn't helped by heavy incense drifting up from a bank of candles placed higgledy-piggledy across the oak credenza just behind her. It almost turned his stomach and his chest began to hurt.

He flinched as Norah edged a little closer, and he caught another whiff of her whisky-soaked breath. As if noticing his reaction, Norah said, 'It's all right, dearie, drinking is the only way I can stomach being near you.'

Though Colin took this to be a gratuitous insult, and not one he could shrug off lightly, it was, as Norah Plank reflected, perfectly true. Whatever her original intentions may have been – to embarrass Henry and revenge herself on men in general – she often did need a drink these days to keep her on the path she'd chosen to pursue.

It caught her by surprise when she found herself thinking, just then, that if Henry were to apologise for his behaviour and throw himself on her mercy, begging forgiveness for his sins, she would probably take him back. God knows why, but she would. Indeed, if he baulked at the thought of seeing her in person and sent an intermediary to do the dirty work on his behalf, that would have been perfectly acceptable.

It wasn't going to happen, of course, and maybe she didn't want that, after all. She felt confused, and the three whiskies she had knocked back with her breakfast hadn't helped. Norah Plank wasn't drunk – she had built up some staying power these past few weeks – but she wasn't completely sober, either. Not able to think straight, certainly.

Had she realised that the anxious young man sitting in front of her was, indeed, an intermediary, and not the client she thought of as Cyril the Creep, things might have turned out differently. It was all Herbert Hutchinson's fault, though she had no idea, of course, and never would. Herbert, a retired housing officer from Fetherton County Council who – both from timidity and a wish not to give too much away – had pretended to live elsewhere, had abandoned his plan to be soundly thrashed after ejaculating at the end of his telephone call the previous day. The moment his interest in being beaten for pleasure had passed, he saw no point in wasting good money when he could clean his own bathroom for free. There was also more fun to be had, he decided, in making rude phone calls to the secretary of a girls' school in Chichester, while taking the precaution of withholding his number so as not to be subsequently bothered by the police. And so, his eagerness having waned, he put Norah Plank out of his mind completely.

Meanwhile, under the mistaken impression that Colin *was* Herbert (or, in her mind, Cyril the Creep), Norah determined, however reluctantly, to press on and see how things panned out. Myrtle could take care of the details. The girl was primed and ready for action. She had a vague recollection – though drink had muddied the waters a little – that, whatever pretended reason the young man had for being here, he had asked, quite specifically, to be taken by surprise, overpowered and held against his will. Having been forced to clean her bathroom, she was at liberty to punish him as no man had been punished before. (Whatever the hell that meant.)

It was at that point that Myrtle, entering the room as quietly as she could (which, to Norah's surprise, given the girl's size and awkward way of walking due to the skin-tight basque into which she had been shovelled, was very quiet indeed), threw a large hessian sack over Cyril the Creep's shoulders, dragged him from his chair onto the floor and proceeded to perch her huge backside on the rear of his hooded head. While he swore incomprehensibly in the darkness, in the mistaken belief he had been viciously assaulted by a passing buffalo, Norah stood up, took a pair of handcuffs from the credenza and, with some difficulty because Cyril the Creep was – in her view – struggling with unnecessary vigour for a man who wanted to be subdued, secured both of Colin's hands behind his back.

There, she thought – stepping away quickly before one of his madly kicking legs did her permanent damage – let the filthy sod get out of that one.

THIRTY TWO

By the greatest good fortune, Lambert Ticke, having rushed downstairs in a bid to put a safe distance between himself and the late Amy Horris, broke the habits of a lifetime and, for once, acted on instinct not logic. Instead of leaving through the front door – the fastest way to make his escape – Lambert Ticke turned left and ran back into the sitting room, towards the French windows through which he had originally entered. This error, for which, having reached the windows, he briefly admonished himself, had the unexpected – but not altogether unwelcome – bonus of saving his life.

Lambert Ticke had barely flung himself into the garden when an American-owned, albeit (fortunately, for his peace of mind, unknown to Chuck Grogan) made-in-China heat-seeking missile struck first his Fiat Uno, and then the front door of the house he had just exited. The rocket was designed to explode on impact, which it did the moment it hit his car. Though parts of it continued on their way, reducing Colin Crimp's home to a smouldering heap of rubble, the resulting fireball first dried, then seared off, most of Lambert Ticke's trousers, his jacket and one of his shoes.

The impact blast propelled Lambert Ticke forward at a getaway speed of which he would never have normally been capable, even at his terrified best. Arms and legs whirling like a clockwork dervish, Ticke flew through the air and also through the reinforced glass window of the shed he had recently secured. A moment later, the shed itself collapsed, showering him in splinters and enough fertiliser to raise a record crop of tomatoes in a good year.

He passed out, woke, then passed out again as the explosive heat of a twenty-pound guided javelin of death left bits of itself almost everywhere except, thanks to the protective cover of the shed, on or in Lambert Ticke himself.

As the blast waves faded, Ticke came round again and prayed to a non-existent God (who was having an unusually busy day) that he might wake up a second time to discover this was all a dream. Just then, he had no idea what had happened, other than that perhaps the end of the world had arrived marginally sooner than science had predicted.

Scrambling through an overcoat of broken glass and wood, he surveyed the devastation. His backside had taken the brunt of the damage and stung like hell, splinters of glass embedded in his delicate white skin. On top of that, he bled and burned in several different places and was aware that, whilst not naked, he was no longer fit for decent company. (Not that he had seen much of that in Fetherton!) The house from which he had just fled was a heap of smoking bricks and rubble and it occurred to him, with all the miserable benefit of hindsight, that it had been a dreadful error not to switch off the heater. He tried to reassure himself that it wasn't his fault. This was Mervyn Ratt's responsibility – and possibly that of the woman who had chosen that day to expire on his bathroom floor.

One thing was certain, though. Whichever way he looked at it (and looking at it caused him some distress just then), this had ruined his plans. Or had it, he wondered, in the desperate hope of salvaging something from the burning wreckage of 78 Arcadia Avenue, Fetherton. He had hoped to convey the impression – to even a policeman as intellectually dim-witted as Inspector Bernard Lunt – that Ratt was building a bomb. Who was to say this wasn't a bomb that had gone off prematurely? Perhaps the explosion might have benefits, after all. There was enough fertiliser here to sink a battleship, far more than was decently required for such a small, and now rather pointless garden. If the computer's hard drive had survived intact – which, surveying the destruction all around him, might be a large 'if' – then maybe all was not yet lost.

Still, that was not his immediate concern. His immediate concern, he decided, as his wits slowly returned, was to jump into his car and get the hell out of here as fast as possible. His recent surveillance had convinced him that people in Arcadia Avenue tended to mind their own business and keep out of each other's way. That said, it seemed unlikely that even the most disinterested observer would overlook his neighbour's house spontaneously combusting on an otherwise quiet afternoon.

It would not be long before someone – police, ambulance, fire brigade (probably all three!) – turned up, and he didn't want to be there when they did. It was only on staggering around to the front of the burning wreckage that had so recently been Number 78 Arcadia Avenue, that Lambert Ticke realised his car had suffered a certain amount of collateral damage. More accurately, there was no sign of it at all.

Unaware that, having borne the brunt of an American-owned, made-in-China heat-seeking rocket of death launched by an irate Chuck Grogan in a failed attempt to remove all trace of him from the earth, his Fiat Uno had been vaporised in an instant, Lambert Ticke cast around for where he might have parked it by mistake. When it finally dawned on him that he would never again see it in this world and, unless the God he didn't believe in numbered Fiat Unos among those He planned to resurrect on the Day of Judgment, he would not see it in the next one, either, Lambert Ticke felt his knees buckle. He threw back his head and released a mournful peal of despair, before pulling himself together as the familiar clatter of a fire brigade engine caught his ears.

As Lambert Ticke turned on his heel and hobbled off blindly in the opposite direction, Chuck Grogan could scarcely believe his eyes. Having rained down hell on the Russkie and his stupid Fiat Uno, his enemy was still in one piece! Too shocked to fire up and launch a second missile in time, he was forced to watch miserably as Lambert Ticke skidded around the first available corner and disappeared from sight.

*****

Lambert Ticke was lost, both geographically and, he felt, in the wider metaphysical sense. He had plotted Ratt's downfall in meticulous detail; hours spent combing the internet for bomb-making ingredients, then purchasing the damn stuff and lugging it into the other man's shed. On top of that was all the time he had spent putting together incriminating evidence to plant on Ratt's computer and, as a back-up, in his desk. A word in Lunt's ear and he had reckoned on a search of Ratt's house and his prompt arrest. If his theories were correct – and he had no reason to doubt them – Ratt would happily admit his guilt and even claim belated credit for everything of which he was subsequently accused. (Chapter 147, 'The Confession of the Alienated Assassin'.)

What he had not anticipated was setting fire to an underwear-free prostitute, before razing Ratt's house to the ground. Even worse, all but obliterating it from the face of the earth – along with his Fiat Uno – in some freak accident that must have shattered a gas pipe and triggered a fireball in Arcadia Avenue.

What the hell was he to do now? Battered, bloodied and barely decent, his troubled brain sought for a way out – both physical and practical. He could hardly trek all the way home in his present condition. Not that he liked to think of the Lunts' house as home but, for the moment, it was all he had.

By some miracle, he still had his mobile phone, lodged in the only remaining pocket of his torn and flame-damaged jacket. But he could hardly call the barbarian Lunt and bring him up to date. The man had assaulted him once already, and very nearly castrated him into the bargain. Contacting him now, to tell him he'd blown up a house, would be asking for trouble.

It was a miracle no one had yet spotted him and he

breathed another prayer of thanks to the non-existent God who had encouraged Ratt to live in an area where the neighbours were either out at work all day or mindless fans of afternoon TV. But he knew his luck couldn't hold for ever.

And that was when he saw it. A car. A parked car. A car with its engine running, and its driver's door invitingly open. He noticed the door to a nearby house was also ajar, and guessed, correctly, that the owner had nipped out, then realised he'd forgotten something and popped back in again.

Ticke steeled himself. He was, he reminded himself, an agent of the Crown and thus authorised – perhaps not technically, but morally for certain – to take whatever steps necessary for the defence of the realm. And if defending one's country required him to commandeer a civilian's vehicle, then so be it.

His decision made, Ticke hobbled round to the driver's side – as fast as his tortured body would allow – and climbed in. It was only then that he realised life was rarely as simple as one hoped. The moment his almost bare bottom – embedded with shards of glass – touched the chair, he squealed, shot up and hit his head on the car roof. The driver had covered the seat with a horrible bead-like contraption – ostensibly for comfort, but in this case having just the reverse effect.

Lambert Ticke lowered himself a second time, but it made no difference to his raw backside. He studied the bead-like arrangement but it was firmly fixed and, though doubtless he could remove it given time, time, he knew, was not a luxury he enjoyed. His mind raced. He had to get away fast, and this was his best means of doing so. Walking home was out of the question, not with his clothes in tatters, and his bloodied arse exposed for all the world to see.

Nor must he be caught in this neck of the woods, so close to Ratt's demolished home. At least not until he had time to think up a reasonable excuse, which, he feared, might not exist this side of sanity.

There was nothing else for it. Readjusting himself

carefully, he kicked off his one remaining shoe, raised both legs, and lowered himself into a kneeling position on the seat, easing the pressure on his damaged behind.

His luck was in. A glance showed the car to be an automatic. Ticke was only licensed to drive an automatic. Theft was one thing, illegal driving quite another.

Even better, the seat was deep and pushed far back. The owner was clearly a large man, which was fortunate as it gave Ticke more room for manoeuvre. Resting both heels against the edges of his buttocks, he found the pain just about bearable. As long as he made no contact with the beads he was safe.

Next, he reached up and pulled at the seat belt. No reason to ignore road safety laws. He didn't want to kill himself for the sake of added comfort, not after everything he had been through. It wasn't easy, locking the belt around his body, but then, he realised, it couldn't have been easy for the car's clinically obese owner and he had clearly managed it.

Reassured that all was as it should be, Lambert Ticke turned the ignition key, and then, for the first time, became aware of the flaw in his plan. He could reach neither of the pedals! Sitting down, as he already knew, was out of the question, but possibly – he wondered – could it be done? He eased his right leg from under his bottom and winced as a buttock made contact with the beads. Shifting his weight to the left, he lifted his injured rump a fraction, and all, though not well, was at least a little better. He jiggled his foot around, touching the pedals lightly, accustoming himself to their feel. It wasn't ideal, but he had no choice.

Checking in his rear-view mirror – driving on one knee didn't mean he must ignore all the rules of the road – he eased the car into life and moved off. He took it carefully for the first hundred yards, before glancing at the mirror and spotting the car's owner, who had evidently caught on to what was happening, lumbering up the road behind him, waving both arms and – if his ears were any judge, even at this distance –

yelling something obscene. It was fortunate he was a big man, thought Ticke. Anyone of normal size might have caught him by now.

Even so, there was no time to hang around. Slamming his only working foot against the accelerator, he was off like a shot, leaving the fat man flailing in his wake. He reached the end of the road, turned left and was gone.

It was at the end of this particular stretch that trouble reared its head again. The main road crossed at that point and traffic was filtering out slowly. There were two cars ahead and neither looked set to go. Glancing into his rear-view mirror, Ticke uttered a squeal of despair as the car's owner, slow, panting, but still giving chase, turned the corner. The fellow might be morbidly obese, but his eyes were sharp enough and, though forced to rest on a lamp-post to get his breath back, it was clear that he had spotted Ticke and it had given him fresh hope. He set off again, huffing and puffing, but in the certain belief that the thief could be caught.

Ticke twisted his head sharply, taking in first the road ahead, then the danger from behind. At his current pace, the man would reach him in – what – 10 to 20 seconds, no longer, surely? The road ahead was blocked. Ticke toyed with forcing his way through and on to the main road, but that would attract attention and, given his current state of undress and damage, it was the last thing he needed.

If he couldn't go forward, then only one option remained. He must go back. Which was when the white van emerged from a side road and slotted in behind him. Bugger and damnation, he was trapped! Ticke's mind whirled. What could he do? There must be something! He was still pondering his dilemma when a large, ungainly figure staggered into view.

Quick as a flash, he locked both doors, and not a moment too soon. The car's owner had finally arrived and was hammering on the window, cursing him to buggery and beyond. Ticke knew his options had narrowed considerably. He racked his brain for a way out, not only from his current predicament but also from the wider one into which fate had thrown him.

And then it happened. A spark of genius – or possibly madness, he considered later. The idea arrived almost fully formed as if it had been lurking in the shadows, knowing its time would come. Some of it, he knew, would have to be made up as he went along, but that was unimportant. He would have to think quickly and throw caution to the wind. That wasn't his preferred approach but desperate days called for desperate measures and it helped that he was dealing with halfwits.

His mind made up, he whipped out his mobile phone, stabbed in '999' and waited.

'Come on, come on!' he yelled as the drumming grew ever more urgent. It was an old car and he doubted it could take much more. He knew what he wanted to say, and the sooner he got it out the better.

At last, he heard a voice at the other end, faint, female and rather too sure of itself for his liking.

'Which service do you require?' she asked melodiously.

'Pleece!' yelled Ticke, in what he hoped was a distinctly Russian accent.

'I'm sorry, I didn't catch that,' said the melodious, disembodied voice. 'Please state the nature of your emergency.'

'I vont Lunt!' yelled Ticke, lapsing into German. 'Git me Lunt!'

'You want lunch?' queried the voice. 'I'm sorry, sir, I don't think I heard you correctly. Would you mind repeating that?'

The man had moved round to the front of the car now, clambering onto the bonnet and hammering at the windscreen. Ignoring the girl's response, Ticke yelled again, 'I don't vont fucking lunch! I vont Inspector Lunt!'

'You want to inspect my what?' repeated the girl, her voice no longer melodious nor calm. 'You filthy swine! I'm authorising a trace on your number. You won't get away with this!' And then, suddenly and inexplicably, she began to cry.

Before Ticke had a chance to fashion a response, a male

voice came through, loud, firm and angry. 'Who am I speaking to?' it asked. 'You might as well give yourself up now, sunshine. We'll have your name soon enough.'

'Gif myself up?' squealed Ticke, struggling to hold on to some sort of accent. This thing was harder in real life than it was on the telly. 'Why – vye – should I vont to give myself up? No, forget zat!' At which point he realised he'd also forgotten what he wanted to say next. It didn't help that the man on the bonnet had pressed his face to the windscreen and, from one angle, he appeared to be melting.

Ticke's jaw dropped, then he threw back his head and yelled into the car roof. The combination of his feral scream and the fact that just then the owner noticed, for the first time, that his pride and joy had been stolen by a bare-bottomed lunatic who was currently squatting on his beloved beaded seat, caused the other man to scream, too. His cry coincided with the arrival of the white van driver, who, under the impression that the owner of the car in front was under assault from a drug-addled mugger, possibly intent on murder, had gallantly leapt from his vehicle determined to do his civic duty and prove, in passing, that not all white van drivers were anti-social morons.

Unfortunately for him, it was at that moment that the man on the bonnet, tormented beyond endurance, and carrying far too much weight for someone of his age, felt a sharp pain in the chest, clutched at his heart and rolled backwards.

Ticke had only seconds to act but he wasted none of them. Flicking up the lock on his door, he pushed it open and staggered out. By now, the white van driver was on his knees, administering mouth to mouth to the fat man, and cursing himself for ever getting involved.

For his part, Ticke saw a fresh avenue of escape open up. It was madness, he knew, but it was a mad day and he hardly cared any more. Hobbling over to the white van, he heaved himself inside. The key was still in the ignition, as he knew it would be from the dull throb of the van's engine. He no longer cared about his ravaged arse, or whether the van was an automatic; all he cared about was getting the hell out of here as fast as he possibly could.

One more thing to do first, though. 'Are you still zere?' he yelled into the mobile.

'Give yourself up!' said a voice he had not heard before. It was a woman's voice this time, stern, commanding and not altogether pleasant. 'This is WPC Snyffe,' she said. 'Come quietly, sir, it'll be better all round.'

'Christ almighty!' he cried, his mind in a whirl as he jumped between different thoughts and different accents. 'Who invited you to ze party?'

'I think he's a German, sir!' said the voice at the other end, clearly speaking to someone else in the room.

'I'm not a German!' yelled Ticke. 'I am Russian. From Mosscow!'

'No need for bad language, sir,' said the woman, giving him her full attention again. 'You're only making things worse. Now if we can have your name...'

'It's Ratt!' he yelled maliciously. 'Mervyn Ratt! But you'll never take me alive, coppers! I've left your agent for dead, now I'm coming for ze rest of you. Especially Bennad Lunt!' And then he laughed madly. It seemed the right thing to do, even if his accent was all over the place.

There were a few more things he wanted to say before he was done, but, with escape presently uppermost in his mind, he heaved the gears into reverse, jammed both feet onto the pedals, and, screaming at the searing pain that tore through his buttocks, sped back down the road, clipping two Volvos, a Toyota Corolla and narrowly missing a cat with one eye.

THIRTY THREE

For Colin Crimp, whose world lacked hope at the best of times, life had plumbed new depths of despair. Encased in a hessian sack, hands cuffed behind his back and with Myrtle Fling sitting on his head, he writhed, rolled, kicked and screamed, but to no avail.

When the weight on his head was finally lifted, his spirits briefly soared, only to be shot down in an instant when he was hoisted up and slung across a broad, beefy shoulder. (Myrtle had always wanted to be a fireman and felt a swell of excitement as she strode into the back bedroom, which now doubled up as Norah Plank's idea of a prison cell. The wallpaper from 'Dungeons "r" Us' had been lovingly recreated in a grey, stone brick motif. Norah had never seen the inside of a real dungeon, and hoped she never would. However, she was happy to take her suppliers' word for it that this was the real deal as 'authenticity is our middle name'.)

Borne aloft by a dangerously wobbling Myrtle, Colin continued to kick and squeal, even when Norah jabbed him in the kidneys with a long stick and told him to 'shut the hell up, you're disturbing the neighbours!' Disturbing the neighbours was, just then, uppermost on his mind, and he wasn't in the mood to apologise for calling for help.

Any hopes Colin entertained of escape were promptly dashed as Myrtle dumped him unceremoniously on the gravelled bedroom floor. (Gravel, Norah had been assured, 'completes the mood and, though it costs a little more, you'll recover your outlay in the first week'.) The buffalo who had subdued him (he saw no reason to change his view) landed with a thump on his chest, knocking all the wind from his lungs. His head swam and, for one blissful moment, he assured himself – much like Lambert Ticke before him on the other side of town – that this was a terrible dream from which, any second now, he would wake.

That happy prospect was pushed from his mind a moment later, when the hood was yanked away and, catching sight of Myrtle's face for the first time, Colin Crimp saw a vision of hell itself, leaning in close. Rank body odour drifted over him, as if she hadn't washed for a week, or possibly her entire life.

Blinking in the subdued lighting, Colin opened his mouth to scream again – a big mistake he realised, too late. The monster on his chest was holding something large and red in her hands and, the moment he opened his mouth to tell her she'd be hearing from his lawyer (not that he had one), she pushed a large rubber ball into it.

Shifting his gaze to the left, he saw Norah Plank – that other creature from the bowels of Hell – as she shuffled into view. She was holding a tube of silver duct tape, one length of which she stretched noisily between her hands. When he moved his head in the opposite direction, she moved with him. When he swivelled back, she did the same.

'Can't you keep still?' she inquired in an agitated voice, as if he was being unnecessarily awkward. 'It's only sticky tape!'

Colin wanted to tell her he didn't care what sort of tape it was, he didn't want it anywhere near his sodding mouth. Unfortunately, just then, all that emerged was a volley of muffled grunts, which simply confirmed Norah Plank's belief that she was dealing with a form of life lower than the beasts. After all, she reasoned, what sort of half-human creature would gain even a jot of pleasure from being treated like this? The man, she concluded, deserved all that was coming to him.

'Hold his head still, girl!' she told Myrtle. 'I'll have his eye out if I'm not careful. The pervert might pay us twice as much for the privilege, but I don't want to end up on an assault charge.'

Pervert! thought Colin. There was only one pervert here – no, make that, two – and he was neither of them. In God's name what was Henry Plank thinking of, sending him to this house of hell? He swore into the rubber ball-gag and kicked sharply; not that any amount of kicking could unseat the malformed monster perched on his chest.

One of his feet, jerking upwards, caught Norah a glancing blow on her ribcage, just below a large, free-swinging breast. She swore obscenely. 'Right, that's it, you bastard!' she yelled. 'I've tried being nice, but if you want to play it rough, try this for size!'

Colin was still trying to fathom how his treatment thus far merited the word 'nice', and wondering what sort of abuse might be regarded as 'vicious' in this madwoman's world, when he felt a thwack across his face and realised, to his surprise, that she had punched him in the jaw.

So far as Norah was concerned, her action served two purposes. First off, the man immediately went limp, allowing her – finally – to wind the tape over his mouth and around the back of his head, securing the ball-gag in place. Better still, it relieved the tension that had been building inside her for the past few minutes. She had had second thoughts about her new career *before* Cyril the Creep had popped in for a paid thrashing. All this kerfuffle, and being kicked in her boobie, only reinforced her conviction that domination wasn't all it was cracked up to be.

'Come on!' she urged Myrtle, who remained shocked by Norah's vehemence. She didn't have a lot of time for men herself, but drew the line at smashing them in the face. Colin, for his part, felt much the same way, and was fighting back the urge to vomit. There was blood in his mouth, and something floating around that hadn't been floating around before. He realised, miserably, just a moment before he passed out, that she had broken a tooth.

'You've killed him!' shrieked Myrtle, aware that Cyril the Creep had gone horribly limp.

'Don't be stupid, girl! He's all right!' yelled Norah, though without much conviction. He *had* gone rather limp, she realised.

Vaguely recalling a programme on Sky, advocating something similar when faced with a dying man on your carpet, she pulled Cyril the Creep into a sitting position and thumped him on his back.

'You *are* trying to kill him!' screamed Myrtle. 'I ain't doing people in for fifteen pounds an hour. I'd rather go back on the check-out!'

'No one's doing anyone in!' yelled Norah, who was beginning to have second thoughts, if not about her new profession, then certainly about her choice of staff.

Myrtle was having second thoughts, too. 'Don't shout at me!' she protested. 'Just 'cos I don't want to kill handsome young men.'

This last remark brought Norah up short. 'Handsome young men?' she repeated, pausing with her fist in the air, about to strike Colin a second time but frozen into immobility by Myrtle's words.

She looked Colin fully in the face, or as fully as she was able to in the circumstances. His head was lolling at an awkward angle, forcing her to strain her neck to look him in the eyelids. 'He's an ugly so-and-so, what are you talking about?' said Norah.

'He's not that bad!' said Myrtle, rushing to Colin's defence for no reason that she could readily identify. To be fair, her experience of men, handsome or otherwise, was rather limited.

Just then, before they could carry their argument into more dangerous waters, Colin stirred. At least he began to cough and splutter, though his eyes remained firmly shut.

'See, he's alive!' said Norah triumphantly, and feeling she had won the argument.

'No thanks to you,' countered Myrtle, as Colin began to cough more heavily. 'You wanted to kill him!'

'I didn't want to kill him!' insisted Norah. 'I was only going to make him clean the toilet. After he'd confessed to topping Princess Di.'

Myrtle looked puzzled. 'What makes you think he did for Princess Di?'

Norah sighed. 'He didn't. It's just that when he phoned, he said, "I want you to tie me up and make me confess I did something bad." He didn't say what, he just said, "I'll leave the details to you. And after that, I'll clean your bathroom." '

'You're mad, you are!' said Myrtle. 'And I must have been mad chucking my job at the check-out to come and kill innocent young men for a living.'

'No one's trying to kill anyone!' yelled Norah, who was seriously regretting her decision to employ the massive half-wit sitting opposite her, squeezed into a tight rubber basque at least three sizes too small. It might be what some of these men craved for excitement, but if she stood up too fast it could easily explode, leaving her stark naked, which, Norah decided, was unlikely to be a pretty sight.

Colin, meanwhile, was turning blue, the reason being that he had swallowed not just his own blood, which, thanks to the gag, had nowhere to escape, but his recently detached tooth. Both were blocking his airways and he was slowly, and with absolute certainty, choking to death. Had he been awake to appreciate his parlous state of health, he might have concluded that it wasn't his day.

It was at that moment that Myrtle made a grab for him, closing her big, meaty arms around his midriff and dragging him towards her. Myrtle had never heard of the Heimlich manoeuvre, and, to be fair, her actions fell short of any recorded variation. But though not executed to perfection, her exertions achieved much the same end. Mercifully dislodged, the tooth came flying up into Colin's mouth. His eyes flew open and he roared miserably.

'We'll have to let him go!' said Myrtle. 'He's not well.'

'He hasn't paid us yet,' Norah reminded her. 'I should

have insisted on money up front. I'm too trusting, that's my trouble.'

Somehow, in his blind panic, Colin managed to shift the ball-gag a fraction. The blood in his mouth spewed through the gaps and onto the fabric of the cheap tape wound around his face. Very quickly, the silver-grey surface began to discolour. A moment later, his tooth flew up, hit the roof of his mouth and went flying back down into his throat. Colin sat bolt upright, heaving furiously. Norah, spotting the blood around his lips, and recognising what appeared to be her first client's final death throes, was at last convinced that things were not going well. Not having yet received payment might prove to be the least of her worries. A dead man on the premises was probably worse.

She reached behind Cyril the Creep's head and tried frantically to remove the sticky tape. Unfortunately, in her haste to get the job done in the first place, she had made a mess of things and the tape defied all her efforts to unpick it. To complicate matters, the tape had stuck to Colin's hair. The more she tugged, the more he yelped. And the more he yelped, the more awkwardly he moved, making her task all but impossible.

'Get me a knife, girl!' she yelled at the mortified Myrtle.

'You're not going to cut his throat, are you?' she yelled back. ''Cos I've told you, I ain't helping you commit murder. Not for fifteen pounds an hour!'

'I think you've made that clear!' cried Norah, exasperated. Things were getting out of hand. Even she could tell that this idiot of a man was in danger of choking to death. 'I just want to cut the bloody tape off.'

Myrtle struggled to her feet. She was not, as Norah knew, a woman built for speed. 'Wouldn't scissors be better?' she suggested.

'Yes they would,' agreed Norah. 'Only you know where the knife drawer is and the scissors aren't in it. They went out in the bin, along with my husband's suits.'

'Why did you throw them away?' asked Myrtle, perplexed.

'I didn't throw them away!' said Norah, frustrated. 'They went out by mistake. I was angry. I wasn't thinking straight.' She paused to collect herself. 'Could we have this conversation later? And preferably not over a dead man on the carpet.'

Close to delirious, the words 'dead man on the carpet' were loud enough to penetrate Colin's tortured mind. It sparked him into one last, urgent burst of movement, as he catapulted himself to his feet and sent Myrtle flying. As her full weight hit the floor, her legs flew apart, and the rubber basque tore in several places at once, rendering her instantly, and quite horribly, naked from the waist down.

Colin averted his eyes and, in so doing, crashed into a table burdened with several instruments of torture, the like of which he had never seen before and hoped never to see again – even in his worst nightmares.

He fell headfirst to the floor, and, with his hands still tied behind his back, and unable to protect himself, he struck the carpet with a sickening thud.

Norah jumped up and ran from the room, returning, a few moments later, clutching a huge carving knife. Colin lifted his head a fraction, saw her approaching him at speed, and finally gave up the ghost. His mind, never at its strongest, even on a good day, shut down completely, propelling him towards a sweet and peaceful oblivion.

THIRTY FOUR

Bernard Lunt was in the foulest of moods.

'What do you mean a madman's been asking for me?' he shouted, baring a row of yellow, tombstone teeth.

Superintendent Troy had no idea why a lunatic would be inquiring after Bernard Lunt, but he was not about to tell him so. Not to his face, at any rate.

'Who knows what one of our less intellectually able citizens might want with the police,' he replied, extending his arms expansively. 'Assistance perhaps.'

Lunt shook his head and gave a dismissive huff. He knew the assistance he was ready to give to a loonie, and it was more likely into a busy road than across it.

'He said his name was Mervyn Ratt,' explained Troy.

'Ratt?' repeated Lunt, and felt the hairs bristle at the back of his neck. 'That's the bloke Ticke was looking for.'

'I know,' said Troy,' who knew nothing of the sort or, if he had, had managed to forget it.

'The odd thing is...' Troy gave a nervous cough. 'The number Ratt phoned from is a mobile – registered to your man.'

Lunt's face, already an unhealthy shade of puce, darkened further. 'What do you mean, "My man"? He's not my fucking man. The bastard was foisted on me. He's your man, not mine.'

'He's yours if you're still looking for that Leeds posting,' Troy reminded him, though he took the precaution of pushing his chair back as Lunt advanced.

Lunt stopped in his tracks, straightened his back, and said,

'What's this Ratt bloke doing, phoning from Ticke's mobile?'

Troy hesitated before continuing in a voice as calm as if he were passing on the latest weather report. 'He said he'd – erm – well, he said he'd killed him.'

'Killed Ticke?' repeated Lunt, his interest sparked. 'What's he done that for?'

'We have no idea, he didn't say. He didn't say much, apparently. Very short and sweet, here's the transcript – from Emergency Services. Apparently he was very rude to one of their girls. Said he wanted to look at her – well – we needn't go into that.'

Lunt wasn't listening. He was reading the A4 sheet of paper that Troy had pushed across the desk.

'"You'll never take me alive. I've done for Ticke and I'm coming for the rest of you coppers!"' Lunt looked up. 'What the hell's that supposed to mean?'

Troy said nothing. He assumed Lunt's question was rhetorical; besides, he disapproved of Lunt's language, which rarely seemed to rise above the gutter. He'd recently checked his arrest rate. It was unusually high, given that Fetherton was a sleepy backwater, not known for its thriving criminal underworld, and wondered why he hadn't recommended his transfer to the city years ago. The man was bad news, and a source of grief, however you looked at it.

'The language has been tidied up. They've recorded it, of course, so we can listen later. But they think he might be German.'

'German?' repeated Lunt blankly.

'And from Moscow, apparently,' added Troy. 'It's all very international, isn't it?'

'It's bloody stupid, that's what it is,' said Lunt. 'A German from Moscow. Not very likely, is it? They hate each other's guts, the bloody Krauts and Reds.'

'There's another thing,' said Troy, keen to change the subject. 'We've had reports of an explosion.'

'Explosion?' repeated Lunt, struggling to keep up.

'Well, when I say explosion, it would appear that a house has been completely demolished.'

Lunt shrugged his shoulders. 'Probably someone's boiler. It usually is.'

'Possibly,' said Troy. 'However, if you'll look further down the page you'll see this fellow Ratt says he did it.'

'Blew up a house?' muttered Lunt, still trying to process this fresh turn of events. 'Why would he do that?'

'To kill Ticke, apparently.'

Lunt scanned the page as fast as excitement would allow. '"*I blew the bastard up and you won't find a bit of him anywhere.*"' He looked up. 'Well, he doesn't do things by halves, does he?'

'What puzzles me is that we've got the address now and it's not registered to anyone called Ratt – it belongs to a Colin Crimp. Ring any bells?'

'Never heard of him,' said Lunt, trying not to get too excited at the thought that Ticke might be out of his hair for good.

'I can't believe Ticke's dead,' he said at last.

'We don't have a body yet,' Troy reminded him.

'No, that's true,' said Lunt, and his spirits dropped a little.

*****

Norah Plank gazed down at Colin Crimp's senseless body, sprawled across her dungeon floor. Having checked his pulse and held a mirror to his mouth, she was pretty sure he was still alive. That was the main thing. He was safe enough now as long as he didn't come round, say something rude, and she lost her temper and hit him again.

Myrtle had fled to her room, announcing, in a stricken voice, that she wanted nothing to do with murder and might have to reconsider her position, even if the job did come with a comfortable bed and three home-cooked meals a day.

Left alone, Norah, fortified with another large whisky, pondered her next move as clearly as inebriation would allow. The first thing she had done was to fetch some rope and tie the man's legs together. She didn't want him waking up and trying to kick her breasts again, or any other part of her within reach of his ugly size nines. With some difficulty, she managed to remove the tape from around Colin's mouth, though at considerable cost to the hair at the back of his head – or, more accurately, to the hair that *used* to be at the back of his head. He looked as if he'd been scalped by a Comanche who was still learning on the job. Still, that apart he seemed OK, albeit, judging from the small object lying in a puddle of blood next to him, minus a tooth.

He hadn't paid her yet and, from what she'd seen of him, she didn't hold out great hopes that he would. Bending down, she rifled through his jacket. Finding his wallet, she opened it to discover just thirty pounds – nowhere near what they had agreed upon. Still, it was better than nothing and, extracting the crumpled notes, she tucked them into her blouse.

The more she thought about it, the more she realised it was madness to wait for the man to come round. She couldn't untie him, that wouldn't be safe. Better to get him out of here fast, before he stirred. He might turn violent on waking – even restrained – and she had no wish to knock him out a second time, however much he deserved it.

He was too heavy for her to move by herself; she would need to enlist Myrtle's help, whatever the girl's misgivings – at least as far as her car. She would have to drive him somewhere far away and dump him in the woods, or maybe a gutter if she could find one that wasn't in full view of someone's house.

The problem was, she wasn't sober, and Myrtle, she knew for a fact, couldn't drive. The more she thought about it, the more Norah realised that what she needed to resolve this latest problem was another drink. Cyril the Creep could wait. He wasn't going anywhere, not trussed up like a Sunday roast. She'd sit down and have a think about it over a good malt. It would give Myrtle time to calm down, too. Time, she told herself, time is what I need. She suddenly shivered, as if a ghost had walked over her grave. It had turned cold, and she shivered again. Turning her back on the distasteful sight of Cyril the Creep sprawled on her back bedroom floor, Norah hurried off to the sitting room. Extinguishing the foul-smelling candles (she'd be asking for her money back on those), she switched on the gas fire, poured herself a large whisky and leaned back in her favourite armchair to contemplate her next move.

About a minute after that, she fell fast asleep, the problem still unresolved.

*****

Lambert Ticke's day, he conceded miserably, was going from bad to worse. Having driven off at speed, in a van he didn't own and which had doubtless already been reported as stolen, he went over his new plan, searching for its flaws, which appeared to be many. Why he had decided to become Russian – or possibly German – was beyond even him. With all this talk of secret agents and killing people, it had seemed like the obvious thing to do, but he hoped he hadn't complicated matters. And all the while, he careered down roads he didn't recognise in a town he didn't know, until, at last, he was forced to accept that he was completely lost.

He had said a few more things into the mobile phone, and hoped it was enough to confuse the police. But more than that, he hoped it had bought him some time.

It was only when he turned onto a main road, realised it was one way and that he was heading in the wrong direction, that the enormity of his plight hit him fully.

Screeching to a halt, as several vehicles, obeying the legal strictures of the Highway Code, swerved to avoid him, Lambert Ticke reached another decision. The police could trace a man through his mobile phone. He wasn't sure how he knew that, but he was pretty sure they could and he didn't want them to trace him. Not yet.

Retrieving the phone, he jumped from the van (failing, in the process, to stifle an agonising scream of pain), looked around and spotted a drain. Perfect. He immediately squeezed the phone through the grating and heard a satisfying plop as it hit water (or possibly something worse – he wasn't sure what passed through the drains, it was outside his area of expertise).

Climbing back into the driver's cab, one knee on the seat and the other leg groping for the pedals, Ticke rammed the accelerator, screamed again, and continued on his way, ignoring all the idiots travelling in the opposite direction.

It was when he saw a lorry heading towards him that a nagging doubt entered his head. Slamming on the brakes once again, he squealed to a halt. The lorry, by contrast, failed to do so, and continued on its way without concern. Not for Lambert Ticke, at least. Even in his currently confused state, Ticke knew this called for evasive action, and as fast as possible.

Leaping from the cab, Ticke slipped, landed on his arse and screamed again. He had just enough time to clamber to his feet, and hurry down the ginnel between a small newsagents and an even smaller chemists, when his recently vacated van was hit head on. The impact sent it spinning across the pavement and straight through the front door of 'Pills 'r' Us', where it parked itself conveniently between 'Homeopathic cold cures' and 'Spectacles on a family budget'.

Without a care for the latest disaster he had left in his wake, Lambert Ticke reached the far end of the alley, turned right and kept running. He hardly knew where he was heading now, and cared even less. The world was not a good place. He had done his best to make it a better one, and this was his reward – a viciously serrated rear-end and the police closing in. He was running blindly, largely because the pain from his exposed and glass-riddled backside had reached his eyes and they were raw with tears.

He heard the sound of another vehicle, screeching to a halt, and a horn blaring angrily. Someone screamed, someone swore and then he was aware of a loud bang, followed by the sound of glass shattering. Behind his firmly closed eyes, he had the sensation, for the second time that day, of flying through the air and, worse than that, through another bloody window.

In the few moments before he drifted into blissful oblivion, he realised that it was he who had both screamed and sworn. As for the loud bang which, he belatedly grasped, had preceded the other events (with the exception possibly, of the furious horn), that appeared to be something hard and fast striking him in what was already, he felt, a horribly war-damaged part of his anatomy. The glass breaking around him had a familiar quality, too.

Life was a bitch, he concluded, and enough was enough. An instant later, as if finally abandoning their tasks as no longer worth the effort, his brain, and then his body – like Colin Crimp's before him – switched off for a well-earned rest.

THIRTY FIVE

Some ten minutes after Norah Plank had fallen asleep, Colin Crimp came round and realised, to his despair, that he had not been dreaming after all. Either that, or he had not properly woken up. Having given the matter some thought, he reluctantly conceded that he was definitely awake, and the world around him was real enough.

His hands were fastened behind his back and a length of rope had been knotted around his ankles. His head hurt, and felt curiously cold in places, as if it had been shaved. That was a ridiculous thought, of course, who on earth would want to shave him while he slept?

He was still considering his plight when a dark shadow fell across an already gloomy room. On hearing the patter of approaching footsteps, he feared the worst: Norah Plank was back to torture him. Looking up, he didn't know whether to be relieved or concerned to see that it wasn't Norah, but the foul-smelling giantess who had almost caved his head in. It crossed his mind to scream for help but she would probably hit him. That seemed to be the standard procedure in this house.

As his mind began to clear, he gave some small thanks to see that the woman was no longer clad in her hideous rubber basque. (Or, he recalled with a grim shudder, what little had remained of it after the thing had ruptured around her.) The dress and leggings she now wore might not have made her any the more appealing – bulging and stretching as they did in every conceivable direction – but at least she no longer looked likely to explode at any moment.

'Are you awake?' asked Myrtle pointlessly.

'Yes,' said Colin in a thin voice, and wondered if he'd come to regret it.

'You're not going to do anything silly?'

He struggled with his answer. It must be obvious, surely, even to this brain-dead ogre, that he was in no position to do anything at all just now.

'Do you want me to let you go?' she inquired, which was not what he was expecting to hear.

'Yes, please,' he replied, as calmly as possible, not wanting to get his hopes up. He half-expected her to say, 'I bet you do,' then kick him where it hurt.

'You've had enough, then?' she said, looking almost as confused as he felt. 'You don't want to clean the toilet or anything before you go?'

'Clean the toilet?' muttered Colin, alarmed. He wondered, perhaps, if he hadn't woken up, after all.

'You might feel better, when you get home,' said Myrtle, 'knowing you've done a good job. 'Specially as you've paid for it.'

She'd lost him completely now. He'd been punched in the face, tied up, sat on and was missing a tooth. Now the bitch wanted to know if he'd like to clean the bog before he left. And what did she mean about him paying for it?

It was only as he struggled to fashion a reply that another thought struck him. This was a bungalow. The toilet, bathroom, whatever, would be on the ground floor. With a window. A window he could escape through. All supposing it hadn't been nailed down, which, given all that had happened to him since he'd arrived, was more than likely.

He didn't trust her to let him go. The offer was probably a ruse, and she was testing him. Perhaps the proper answer *was* to agree to clean out her filthy toilet.

'All right,' he said, making up his mind and throwing caution to the wind. 'I'll clean the bathroom, but you'll have to untie me first.'

'As long as you promise to be good,' she replied cautiously.

'I promise,' he said, not bothering to cross his fingers behind his back.

She regarded him thoughtfully for several seconds, struggling to make up her mind. Finally, she said, 'I don't know why you do it. Was your mum unkind to you?'

Colin felt his grip on the real world weaken again. What the hell was she on about now?

'Yes, she was,' he lied, guessing that was the correct answer. It felt like playing chess, but with no idea where any of the pieces were on the board.

'You poor thing,' said Myrtle sympathetically. 'No wonder you became a pervert.'

Colin's mouth opened, then shut again just as quickly. No point in denying the charge, he knew, the woman was bonkers and that was an end to it.

It took her no time at all to release him. The cuffs clicked open when Myrtle pressed two small studs, and Norah had been so drunk when she had tied his legs that the knots fell away quickly.

Colin eased himself to his feet. He ached all over, and his jaw, noticeably swollen, had begun to throb. He could still taste the blood on his lips and longed for a glass of water to rinse out his mouth.

With great difficulty, he resisted the temptation to flee. The front door might be locked and, for all he knew, Norah Plank was standing outside with a rolling pin.

'Follow me,' said Myrtle, leading the way. Once outside the room, she took him along a short landing and stopped outside another door, which she promptly pushed open. Beyond it was a brightly coloured and, it seemed, perfectly ordinary bathroom, complete with bath, separate shower, sink, toilet and – to his surprise – a bidet. He had never imagined Henry to be a bidet man, it didn't seem his style at all.

Of more interest to him, just then, was the long, rectangular window over the sink and which, even from a cursory glance, looked ideal for his escape.

'Do you want me to watch you do the cleaning?' asked Myrtle, 'And hit you on the bottom if you're not doing it properly?'

'Not really,' said Colin, trying to keep the alarm out of his voice.

'Well, as long as you're sure,' said Myrtle. 'But I don't mind. If you think it would help, just give me a shout.' She gestured vaguely with her thumb. 'I'm only in the room next door, so if you want me to hit you, you only have to ask.'

Once again, Colin found his mouth opening and closing but to no purpose. Why the hell she imagined he might want her to hit him, in this world or the next, was a mystery.

'Right,' he said at last. 'That all sounds perfect. If I find myself slacking, I'll let you know.'

'There's a brush and a bucket in the corner,' said Myrtle, with another vague gesture. 'And a few flannels for doing the shower.'

'Brilliant!' said Colin. 'I can't wait.'

'Is it getting you excited?' asked Myrtle. 'You know,' and she waved shyly in the general area of his groin. 'Down there. Are you losing control?'

It took a moment or two for the implication to hit home. When it did, Colin felt a chill in his stomach. 'Dear God, no!' he squealed. 'I mean, yes.' He wasn't sure what the proper response was.

Myrtle shook her head sadly. 'It must be really hard being a pervert. And you look so normal, too.'

'Well, that's us perverts for you,' said Colin still hoping, somewhere at the back of his mind, that he really *would* wake up at any minute. 'Anyhow,' he added, rubbing his hands in a pretend show of enthusiasm for the job in hand, 'time to crack on.'

Myrtle regarded him affectionately. He wasn't so bad, she thought, for a pervert. It was a shame, really, if he'd been normal she might have asked if he'd like to come back to her room for a cuddle.

As the door shut behind her, it crossed Myrtle's mind that she should let Mrs Plank know what she'd done. They hadn't parted on the best of terms, what with her employer wanting to kill her client and she, Myrtle, not being so keen on the idea. Better put her in the picture, she decided, in case the other woman found him in the bathroom, thought he'd acted out of turn and tried to gut him with a carving knife.

Waddling to the far side of the house, she saw that the sitting room door was shut and knew what that meant. The old dear was taking a nap, and probably tipsy into the bargain. Myrtle didn't approve of alcohol, she'd seen what it had done to her mother. True, Mrs Plank didn't bring men home at all hours or run around the garden naked at midnight, but that didn't make it any the better.

Cautiously, she pushed the door open and saw Norah Plank sprawled fast asleep in the armchair. The old lady was snoring loudly, which was never a good sign. When Mrs Plank snored, as Myrtle knew, she often slept for hours. Oh, well, no point disturbing her. Myrtle sniffed. There was a funny smell in the air. She sniffed again and tried to work out what it was. Belatedly she sniffed under her arm and decided, incorrectly, that it was her. The moment the pervert had finished tidying up the bathroom, she vowed, she would take a shower and freshen herself up. Her decision made, she closed the door and waddled back to her bedroom.

*****

Back in the bathroom, Colin Crimp had made an appalling discovery. The moment Myrtle had left him on his own, he had turned on the cold water tap and given his mouth a good rinse. Feeling dreadfully unclean, he had washed his hands and face, too, in a failed attempt to lighten his mood. It was then, as he looked in the mirror to check how presentable he was before making a bid for freedom, that he saw that his earlier fears were not unfounded.

There were several chunks missing from his hair. Dear God! *They'd scalped him in his sleep!* This really was a madhouse and the sooner he got out of it the better. Trying the latch on the window, he felt a surge of relief when it moved easily. Opening it as wide as the fittings allowed, he knew that, though it would be a tight fit, there was enough room for him to squeeze through.

Taking a deep breath, he hauled himself up onto the ledge, swung first one leg over, then the other, and dropped onto the concrete path outside.

He was at the rear of the house, which suited him perfectly. Returning to the main road was too great a risk. If either Mrs Plank or her giant helper spotted him, they would probably give chase and drag him back. Should that happen he doubted that he'd ever see the light of day again.

At the far side of the garden was a large parkland area, the fence fitted with a door that gave easy access to the world beyond.

His heart pounding, and a light breeze cooling the bald spots on his head, Colin Crimp darted across the garden, slipped the latch on the door and, a moment later, was running as fast as he had ever run to the safety of a bank of trees in the distance.

THIRTY SIX

A lunatic by the name of Mervyn Ratt might well have been asking for Bernard Lunt a short time earlier but now, it seemed, he had gone to ground. Bernard wasn't much bothered, he had other things on his mind.

Just now, he was standing outside what had, until recently, been Number 78 Arcadia Avenue, Fetherton. Over the years, he'd seen more than one house reduced to rubble by explosion from a faulty gas appliance. But this was the first time he had ever seen a house eviscerated. Nothing was standing. It was just a pile of rubble. This was serious damage. He didn't like to admit it but, if that transcript he'd read was anything to go on, there was more to this than met the eye.

The house was owned, as Troy had told him, by someone called Colin Crimp. No Mervyn Ratt on the title deeds, or anywhere else for that matter because he'd checked. Perhaps it was an alias. He wondered if Ticke had considered that. He probably hadn't, or he'd have said something. Ratt might be Crimp, or Crimp, Ratt, who the hell knew? Why couldn't people just use the name they'd been given at birth, it would make his job simpler.

The fire brigade were there, of course, sifting through the wreckage, and a camera crew had already assembled. The buggers had got there before him, which was never a good start. It put them one up, which, in his experience, rarely augured well.

He had barely heaved himself from his car before the jackals had pounced.

'Inspector Lunt! Michael Jason, *Fetherton News.* Any leads

on what might be behind this disaster?'

'I'd hardly call it a disaster,' Lunt had replied, immediately regretting his choice of words. 'Well, obviously, it's a bit of a blow for the householder. A tragedy, in fact,' he had added, trying to claw back some ground.

'Tragedy?' repeated Michael Jason. 'So we *are* talking loss of life? Do we know how many?'

'We don't know anything as yet,' replied Lunt honestly, biting back the urge to add, 'I'm not a bloody fortune-teller.'

'Any chance it could have been a bomb?' asked Michael Jason.

'Bomb?' repeated Lunt, not wanting to give anything away until he knew more himself. "Course it's not a bomb. Why would anyone want to bomb a house in Fetherton?'

'So you're ruling out terrorism?'

'Of course I'm f—' began Lunt, before reining himself in again. He wasn't ruling it out at all, but he couldn't tell the press that, not until he was sure. They'd have a field day if he was wrong, and an even bigger one if he wasn't. 'We're keeping an open mind. The investigation is at an early stage. I can't say more than that.'

And, having said no more than that, he had ducked under a length of police tape. A few yards away, three firemen huddled close, examining something on the ground. Lunt recognised the senior man at once – Frank Gubble, always a pain in the proverbial. He looked up as Lunt approached, and took a step forward.

'We've found a body,' he announced, grim-faced. (Frank was always grim.)

Lunt crossed his fingers. 'Man?' he inquired hopefully.

Frank shook his head. 'Too badly burned to be sure, but we think it's a woman. Looks like she was wearing a skirt.'

'Bugger,' muttered Lunt, his hopes dashed. 'Couldn't be a man wearing a skirt, I suppose?' he asked. Ticke was a weird one, he wouldn't put anything past him.

'A man in a skirt?' said Frank, not caring to hide his

surprise. 'Why the hell should it be a man in a skirt?'

Lunt shrugged. 'Well, these days, you know, anything goes. Could be one of those transgentle blokes.'

'Trans–' began the fireman, then let it drop. He knew Lunt as well as Lunt knew him, and their opinions of each other matched. No point in trying to engage the idiot in sensible conversation. Not if he was looking for a man in a dress.

'Perhaps you'd like to have a look?' he suggested.

'I suppose I'd better,' said Lunt reluctantly.

Threading his way forward, he gazed at the mangled heap that had once been Amy Horris. There wasn't much left of her, but from what little remained she appeared to be more woman than man and, to his regret, nothing like Lambert Ticke.

'No other bodies?' he inquired.

'Not that we can tell,' said Frank glumly. 'Mind you, it's all bloody rubble. Could be anything under here. Never seen anything like it. Looks like a frigging bomb hit it.'

'Yes, well, we'll know more after forensics give it the once over,' said Lunt, trying to inject some authority into his voice.

'Good luck with that,' said Frank, ignoring the attempt. 'Funny thing is…' he began, then shrugged, as if he'd lost interest already.

'What?' said Lunt, who was in no mood for games.

'We found a bit of car. Just over there. In that pile of rubble.' He gestured vaguely, which only served to rile Lunt further. It all looked like rubble to him. The fireman strolled over to where he'd evidently been pointing and Lunt was forced to follow. Bending down, the fireman tugged a shard of metal from under the bricks and held it up for Lunt's inspection. It was buckled and grey, with the remains of a headlamp clinging to it gamely. 'Doesn't make a lot of sense,' said the fireman.

'What do you mean?' said Lunt, who wasn't sure what part of anything he'd seen so far *did* make sense.

'Well, unless this car was parked in the front room, there's no reason we should have found it here, even if the house blew up. It's in the wrong place.'

I know the feeling thought Lunt miserably.

'Maybe it was just a bit of car to begin with,' suggested Lunt. 'Maybe it was a souvenir, I don't know.'

'Bloody stupid souvenir,' said the fireman, chucking it back onto the bricks.

'That could be evidence,' said Lunt, and immediately regretted it.

'Make up your mind,' said the fireman, and didn't regret it at all.

Lunt reached down, retrieved the hunk of metal and rubbed the dust from one corner. Two letters and a number were just about visible: TL1. He hadn't taken much notice of Ticke's car, but he remembered its number plate well enough. What part of it was doing in what used to be some poor sod's house defeated him entirely.

It was at that moment that the phone rang in his pocket. He pulled it out and saw that it was Reginald Blight, the station desk sergeant. Frank Gubble's phone rang at almost the same time. Both men walked in opposite directions through the rubble to take their calls in private. Like two enemies duelling, they turned at the same time and faced each other across an ocean of nothingness.

'You have got to be kidding me!' they responded together, spitting out the words like bullets aimed at each other's hearts.

THIRTY SEVEN

Henry Plank had been sitting in his car for over two hours and something, he knew, wasn't right. His backside, for a start, which had gone to sleep some thirty minutes previously, followed, more recently, by one of his legs. His head hurt, too, but he put that down to the three whiskies he had knocked back from the empty hip flask now discarded on top of the dashboard.

It had been a long morning and he had no wish to make it a long afternoon. He had spent almost an hour closeted away with that idiot, Cupperby. His will redrawn, signed and witnessed – much, it seemed, to Cupperby's dismay – he had officially left everything he owned to Colin Crimp, including his share of the company. In truth, he had no intention of actually going through with any of it, the document was just for show. That was unless Norah refused to play ball, of course, in which case all bets were off. He was certain that if – as was likely – Colin failed to win her round, then the threat of leaving everything to a perfect stranger (especially if he, Henry, were to predecease her) would do the job instead. It was worth a shot, certainly.

Returning to the office, he had learned from Karen that he had missed Colin by just a few minutes and that the poor fellow had 'gone to the dentist'. Trusting that his house-mate had not in fact had a change of heart, Henry – taking his car on this occasion – had driven to Shangri-La and parked out of sight in a side road which gave a clear view of the bungalow. Arriving just a short time after Colin, Henry had seen the poor lad march up and down the road for several minutes before finally plucking up the courage to ring the bell.

Henry had imagined the job would be over and done with in no more than half an hour. Either Norah would see sense and agree to have him back, or she would chuck Colin out on his ear. Henry was keen to know the outcome either way and was ready to pick Colin up the moment he left. The fact that, having entered the house at 11.15, there was still no sign of him by half past one was a tad worrying.

Given Colin's reluctance to accept the task in the first place, Henry found it difficult to believe that he and Mrs Plank had shared a convivial cup of coffee that had spilled over into an early lunch.

There was only so much of this a man could take and he had taken it. Girding his loins – the prospect of bearding Mrs Plank in her den was no more appealing to him than it had been to Colin – Henry took a deep breath and stepped out of the car. Crossing the road, he marched up to the front door and pressed the bell several times. It was important to put the bitch off her stroke, he told himself, and nothing would do that better, he was certain, than making an infernal racket.

Inside the house, Myrtle Fling was dealing with problems of her own. Having left Norah Plank fast asleep in an armchair, she had returned to her room with every intention of doing nothing in particular. It was only when she looked out of her window and saw a familiar figure scurry across the lawn that she realised Cyril the Creep had made a run for it. Waddling into the bathroom, she spotted the open window and swore. She wondered how Mrs Plank would react to her client running off, especially when he hadn't started on the cleaning.

Myrtle was still trying to make up her mind what to do next when the doorbell rang rather loudly. It couldn't be another client, she knew, they only had the one booked in for today. Hurrying over to the front door, she peered through the spyhole and thought again. The man outside looked decidedly seedy – even in her limited experience. His hair hadn't been combed and there was egg on his tie. He must be another pervert, she thought, chancing his arm; someone who had seen the advert in *Thrasher's Weekly* and was calling on spec. Myrtle mulled the matter over. There was no point in calling for Mrs Plank, she was dead to the world. She would have to make an executive decision.

Having done so, she opened the front door and was about to tell the man he would need an appointment, when he brushed past her with a brisk, 'Morning, young lady, where's the old bag hiding, then?'

'You're drunk,' said Myrtle, catching the stale smell of whisky on his breath. There was too much drinking in this house for her liking. A glass or two was perfectly acceptable once or twice a year (though she didn't indulge herself), but some people appeared to have no limits.

'Yes, I am,' said the man, and hiccupped. 'Only way to get through to some people. Name's Henry Plank.' He hiccupped again. 'That's *my* name, of course. Not hers.'

'Mrs Plank?' said Myrtle, catching up but not very quickly.

'That's the ticket,' said Henry. 'Ugly old woman, no interest in sex, likes to beat men up for ready cash.' He sniffed loudly. 'Or so I've heard.'

'She's not at home to visitors,' said Myrtle, though if he really was who he said he was, she didn't imagine she was on very firm ground.

'Looking for a man, too. Youngish fella. Waltzed in a while back, silly sod, haven't seen him since.' Henry puffed out his cheeks as he got into his stride. 'Hasn't killed the poor bugger, has she?'

Without waiting for an answer, Henry advanced on the sitting room. It seemed as likely a place as any to find his wife. Myrtle waddled as fast as she could to keep up and, with an effort that surprised even her, managed to fling herself forward, blocking him at the entrance.

'I should go in first,' she said loyally. 'Make sure Mrs P is respectable.'

'Respectable?' echoed Henry, with another huff that sent

fresh waves of whisky-laced breath into Myrtle's face. 'Bit late for that, I'd have thought.'

'Even so,' said Myrtle. 'Best to be safe.'

'Suit yourself,' said Henry, with a weary shrug.

While Myrtle prised open the door as far as was needed for her to squeeze herself through without opening it fully – which, given her wide girth, was almost as much – Henry reached into his jacket pocket and removed his pipe. Now that he was as close as dammit to the moment of truth, his courage – even fuelled by several small whiskies – had begun to ebb away. The pipe would help to calm him down and focus his mind.

Inside the sitting room, it occurred, even to Myrtle, that something was not right. It was the smell for a start, and this time even she realised, rather quickly, that it had nothing to do with her. She sniffed again. Possibly it was those candles that had stunk out the room earlier on. Or perhaps Mrs Plank had broken wind, she couldn't be sure.

The old dear herself was lying flat out on the armchair, in the same position Myrtle had last seen her – her mouth wide open and arms dangling loosely by her sides. Myrtle took a deep breath, still trying to work out what the smell was, and felt immediately giddy. From somewhere nearby she caught a faint hissing sound, but couldn't place what it meant.

Henry, who had stepped into the room without waiting to be summoned, couldn't place what it all meant, either. Nor, with his atrocious sense of smell, was he even aware that anything was wrong. Like Myrtle, he swayed a little giddily but put it down to the whisky. He struck a match to light his pipe, but the damn thing broke, so he tried another. That broke, too. He wasn't having much luck, he considered. Had he known the true state of affairs just then, he would have realised he was, in fact, having a great deal of luck and all of it very good.

It was just as he removed a third match that the dreadful truth struck Myrtle. Mrs Plank had switched on the ruddy fire, but the thing hadn't lit.

'Oh, bloody hell!' she squealed, on realising, as she swayed even more giddily than before, that the room was full of gas. Alerted to Henry's presence, she turned towards him, with the general idea of passing on the bad news. As she did, she saw the small box in his hand and the triumphant look on his face as he drove a third match across the dark little strip and, for the tiniest fraction of a second, saw the beginning of a spark that would become a flame.

The words, 'You bloody idiot!' formed on her lips at almost the same time, but never left her mouth as, an instant after that, her entire world erupted and, for the second time that day, a house in Fetherton exploded.

THIRTY EIGHT

Bernard Lunt had seen it all now. He was beginning to wonder if Leeds might be a disappointment after Fetherton. The place was beginning to pick up in a big way. Of course, parts of it seemed to be disappearing in a big way, too. At this rate, there'd be nothing of it left by teatime.

Staring at the ruins of Shangri-La, he had a horrible sense of *deja vu*. A familiar figure groped his way towards him across the debris.

'We're having a busy day,' said Frank Gubble, idly kicking at a brick. 'Body count's going up, too.'

'Any idea what caused this one?' asked Lunt, keen to discuss causes before corpses.

'I can't be sure,' said the other man, 'but I'd say it looks like gas. The way the house has gone down, most of it intact, too.'

Lunt looked around and found it hard to think of what used to be a detached bungalow in a sleepy suburb of Fetherton being intact in any acceptable sense of the word.

'You mentioned a body,' he muttered carelessly. 'Man or woman?'

'Both,' said Frank laconically.

'Are you being funny?' said Lunt, recalling their conversation at the other house.

'I mean there's more than one body,' said the fireman. 'Two women, one man. Interesting collection, too. One blown to death, one burned to death and one flattened like a bloody pancake.'

'Wall hit him?' said Lunt, assuming the obvious.

'More like a woman,' said Frank. 'About twenty stone of her

at a guess, moving at speed, too. Never stood a chance, poor sod.'

Having seen it all, Lunt felt now he'd probably heard it all, too.

'What do mean – crushed to death?'

'Take a look,' said the fireman and gestured for Lunt to follow as he strolled towards the centre of the ruins.

Wearily, Lunt wandered through the rubble, drawing up short at the sight that greeted him when he reached his destination.

He immediately saw what the other man meant. The deceased female – what was left of her seemed to leave her sex in no doubt if the giant breasts were anything to go by – was lying flat on her back and on top of what looked like an overcooked side of beef.

'Are you sure it's a man?' said Lunt, who couldn't be sure and didn't want to take a closer look.

'Could be an ugly woman,' said Frank. 'Not my cup of tea at any rate. But that's a jacket he's wearing, and trousers, too. Not a dress, so I'm guessing it's a man.'

'Doesn't have to be a man,' said Lunt, 'not these days.'

'Maybe in Leeds,' said Frank, not wishing to be deflected. 'But not here in Fetherton.' He sniffed. 'Not unless he's a tourist.'

'I'll send forensics in,' said Lunt. 'See what they make of it.'

'They're having a busy day,' said Frank.

'We all are,' said Lunt, and felt the weight of the world rest a little more heavily on his shoulders.

*****

On the other side of town, Colin Crimp felt much the same way.

It had taken him three hours to make the journey home. Having left Shangri-La in a hurry – and not by the same route he had used to arrive there – it had taken him some time to navigate his way back to a main road. Only then did he discover that he had no money in his wallet. He'd been robbed! The women must have gone through his pockets while he was out for the count. Hearing a distant rumble of thunder, he looked up and was surprised to see a cloudless blue sky. That was odd. Had he looked behind him, he would have noticed a plume of smoke rising above Shangri-La, suggesting that all was not well at the house from which he had just escaped. However, Colin had other things on his mind just then. He considered the possibility of phoning for a taxi but, following his recent ordeal, there was something about the open air that felt preferable. Having Googled directions on his phone, he found that he was eight miles from home and the route, on foot, was not a complicated one. He had no wish to return to the office and the exercise, he concluded, would do him good.

Whether that was true or not was now beside the point. He *was* home and, at that moment, gazing into a hole in the ground that had, until recently, been 78 Arcadia Avenue, Fetherton. The emptiness was surrounded by bright yellow tape, the fluttering lengths of plastic broken up by an occasional official sign yelling, 'POLICE! KEEP OUT!' Somewhere beyond it, three constables appeared to be wandering aimlessly.

He closed his eyes for a few seconds, hoping, when he opened them again, to find that the world had returned to normal. Perhaps he was having a panic attack, anxiety brought on by the morning's events. It wasn't every day that one woman sat on his head while another punched him in the face before insisting he clean her toilet prior to another sound beating. The balance of his mind might be temporarily disturbed leading him to believe, for some unaccountable reason, that his house no longer existed. Possibly the image was symbolic, and something Hugo Lake could explain to him in return for another fat cheque from the NHS.

Opening his eyes to discover his immediate world had not taken a turn for the better, Colin felt a turn of his own come on. When one of the policemen who, from his fresh-faced looks and build, was scarcely more than twelve years old, walked over and asked him to 'move along, sir, there's nothing to see here', he did something even he could not have anticipated.

The words, 'I can see there's nothing! That's the whole bloody point, you bastard!' left his mouth at roughly the same moment his fist flew into the policeman's face and sent him flying.

A moment later, Colin himself went flying as the young man's companions – two somewhat larger and considerably more aggressive police constables – launched themselves at him with such force that, for the second time that day, his gums parted company with a tooth. He fought back, kicking, punching and biting as if his life depended on it. Something hit him on the back of the head and, a moment after that, and also for the second time that day, Colin mercifully blacked out.

THIRTY NINE

Lambert Ticke was lying on a hospital bed, feeling sorry for himself. He ached all over and his left leg, encased in plaster, hovered above a starched white sheet, restrained by several thin wires. He didn't like the look of the set-up, it didn't inspire confidence. His bottom burned, and his back throbbed as if a dozen pairs of feet had walked across it. No wonder he felt miserable. And that was before a familiar figure had squeezed through a gap in the screens set up to give him privacy.

'You're lucky to be alive,' said Bernard Lunt, in a tone that suggested it wasn't the best news he'd heard all day.

'Who are you?' asked Ticke, wishing the question had been truthful, not an opening gambit. It would be nice to think that he had never met the oaf at the foot of his bed, life would be simpler. But his mind was made up. He mustn't be connected with the disaster at 78 Arcadia Avenue, and – until he knew the official police line – he had no wish to be questioned on the matter. True, his spur-of-the-moment decision to threaten Lunt and most of the Fetherton constabulary, while suggesting that he himself had been done away with, might not, in hindsight, have been the best idea he had ever had, but he had panicked and was forced to shoulder the consequences. Stuck in a hospital bed, with no idea when he might be discharged, he must play for time.

'What do you mean "Who am I?"' said Lunt, who, though not anticipating the friendliest of welcomes from a man he had recently kicked in the goolies, hadn't expected no greeting at all.

'Have we met?' said Ticke anxiously. 'Are you my friend?'

He wasn't sure why that had slipped out, but it seemed to discomfort Lunt and that emboldened him further.

'You look like a nice man,' he continued, opting to lay it on with a trowel. 'I can see why we'd be friends. Have you come to take me home?'

That last line popped out too quickly and Ticke instantly regretted it. He had no wish for Lunt to take him back to what currently passed for his home. To be out of this frying pan would do him nicely – but not if that meant being thrown back into the Lunts' hellish pit of fire.

'No, we're not bloody friends!' said Lunt quickly. 'I'm a policeman,' he added, his eyes narrowing suspiciously. 'Have you lost your memory? Don't you know who you are?'

'No,' said Ticke and saw Lunt's brow crease sharply.

'What do you mean "No,"' said Lunt. '"No," you haven't lost your memory? Or "No," you don't know who you are?'

'I don't know who I are – am,' responded Ticke, who had begun to tire of the game already. He looked around him. 'Where am I?' he asked as if he didn't have a clue.

'You're in Fetherton General,' said Lunt, feeling on safer ground. 'You had an accident. Got hit by a car – went straight through a bloody window. Ended up in some poor bugger's sitting room.'

'Did you get their number?' asked Ticke. 'I might want to press charges.'

'You might want to what?' began Lunt, then stopped himself. 'You ran out in front of the poor sod. Wrecked his bonnet with your arse. You're lucky *he's* not pressing charges!'

Ticke looked indignant, but was saved the bother of replying as a young man in a white coat, heavy-eyed and with the look of someone who wasn't entirely sure where he was, pulled back the screen to join them.

'Everything OK?' asked his latest visitor in a voice that suggested he wasn't much bothered either way.

'He says he's lost his memory,' muttered Lunt. 'Doesn't know who I am.'

'Who are you?' asked the other man, giving Lunt an uncomfortable sense of *déjà vu*.

'Don't you start,' said Lunt, who was in no mood to be questioned. 'I'm a bloody policeman, that's who I am. Who are you?'

The other man gestured indignantly at his white coat. 'Well, I'm not the bloody milkman,' he answered, happy to give as good as he got. He waved a clipboard in Lambert Ticke's direction. 'Is he under arrest? Is it safe to go near him?'

'He's with me,' said Lunt, though it gave him no pleasure to admit it. 'He just can't remember.'

'It's not uncommon,' said the other, 'in cases like this. He'll be suffering from trauma. His brain has shut down, tried to distance itself from the memories.'

Lunt knew the feeling. He wouldn't mind his brain shutting down just now and distancing him from Lambert Ticke.

'How long before he gets it back?' he asked, without enthusiasm. 'His memory, I mean. Hours? Days?'

The doctor shrugged. 'Hard to say,' he muttered, playing for time because, quite frankly, he had no idea. 'Could be years.'

'Years?' squealed Lunt. That wasn't what he wanted to hear. It might affect his posting to Leeds, that wouldn't do at all.

'Could be sooner,' said the doctor, offering hope, though without any justification. 'There's no hard and fast rule in these cases.' He studied his notes. 'Won't be leaving here for a couple of days, though. Not till we're sure his wounds don't turn septic. Backside's cut to ribbons and he's fractured a bone in his leg. Lucky it wasn't worse, mind, given the nature of his accident.' He frowned. 'We found chemicals in the cuts. Very odd, that. Ran them through the hospital lab, just to be sure.'

'Drugs?' said Lunt, who didn't have Ticke down as a user, but was happy to hold it against him if he could.

'Nitrogen, phosphorous, potassium,' said the other man, reeling off a list from his clipboard. Lunt opened his mouth to ask how unusual that was, but the doctor hadn't finished.

'Boron, chlorine, copper, iron, nickel, zinc and manganese.'

Lunt opened his mouth again, hesitated then, when the doctor looked up, apparently out of words, said, 'Could he have got that lot from landing on a junkie's carpet?' It was a stupid question, and he knew it. He'd spoken to the woman whose house Ticke had, via her sitting room window, entered without permission. She was 83 years old and, until Ticke had joined her on the settee halfway through that afternoon's 'Countdown', had lived an apparently blameless life with three cats and a budgie.

'I doubt it,' said the doctor. 'I garden a bit. If I didn't know better, I'd say it looks like fertiliser.'

'Fertiliser?' said Lunt and glanced at Ticke, hopeful that he might be able to shed some light. Ticke, for his part, simply shrugged and looked away.

'Just my opinion, of course, I could be wrong. Then again...'

'Yes?' Lunt was keen for any help he could get. He didn't much care where it came from.

'There were two thicknesses of glass in the wounds. I'm no policeman, but–'

Lunt *was* a policeman, but just then he was struggling to keep up. 'Yes?' he muttered again.

'I'd say he's been through two different windows today.'

'*Two* bloody windows?' said Lunt, astonished, then shook his head. He looked at Ticke, but the latter refused to meet his gaze.

'Anyhow, we'll keep an eye on your man, he's in good hands.' He clicked his biro. 'What's his name? For our records.'

'Ticke,' said Lunt, without enthusiasm. 'Lambert Ticke. With an "E",' he sniffed. 'For your records.'

The doctor made a quick note. 'Right,' he said, 'I think that's everything. I'll leave you two alone.'

'Aren't you going to give him any pills?' asked Lunt. 'Or something with electrics? See if it jogs his memory?'

At the mention of 'electrics', Ticke sat up quickly and immediately regretted it. His backside stung like hell.

'A good night's sleep often works wonders,' said the doctor and then, as if that was an end to the matter, vanished through a gap in the screen, leaving the two men alone.

Lunt gave a resigned shrug. 'And you still can't remember anything?' he asked, regarding Ticke suspiciously.

'I'm afraid not,' said Ticke. 'But I'm sure it will all come back. It's just a matter of time.'

'I bet it is,' said Lunt sourly. He rolled his tongue and mulled things over. Something wasn't right here, he felt it in his gut.

'We had a call you were dead,' he continued at last. 'Man called Ratt. Phoned the station, said he'd done for you.'

'Well it looks like I had a lucky escape,' said Ticke, wincing as his backside stung again.

'I wouldn't call it lucky,' muttered Lunt. 'Arse like a sieve and one leg in the air.'

At the mention of his leg, Ticke felt a toe begin to itch. That was all he needed.

'So you don't remember being attacked? Or running away?' Lunt paused. 'Or stealing a car?'

'Stealing a car?' repeated Ticke, and squirmed uncomfortably as the itch spread along his foot.

'We had reports of a man stealing a car, then a van. The van was found near the hospital. Where you were found,' he added accusingly. 'The description matched you, too.'

Ticke shrugged and tried to put the itch from his mind. It wasn't easy, it seemed to be creeping up his leg.

'I don't remember,' he said. 'Then again...'

'Yes?' Lunt tried to keep the hope out of his voice, he didn't want to sound desperate.

Ticke was thinking on his feet now, or, more accurately, on his bottom. He couldn't see the harm in letting a few crumbs drop onto Lunt's table.

'I seem to remember a man. Oldish fella, may have been Ratt, I can't be sure. It's all a bit vague.'

'Where?' asked Lunt, cautiously.

'I don't know,' said Ticke, dashing his hopes before they'd drawn breath. 'He said something about a bomb. I'm sure of it.' He shook his head. 'I can't recall anything else. Hopefully it will come back to me tomorrow. After a good night's sleep.'

'Yes, let's hope so,' said Lunt doubtfully. He was wondering whether to call it a day when his phone rang loudly in his pocket.

'That shouldn't be on in here,' said Ticke reprovingly. 'It's a hospital.'

'Lunt,' said Lunt, as he pulled out his phone and scowled at the other man.

He was grateful for the interruption, it gave him something to do. Saved him from thumping Ticke, at any rate.

'You what?' he spat into the mouthpiece and his scowl deepened. 'He's done what? No, I've finished here, I'll be right back.'

Ticke was glad of the interruption, too. The itch in his foot was driving him mad. He needed a stick. Something long and thin at any rate, he wasn't sure how much more of this he could take. He hoped Lunt would clear off soon so he could call for a nurse. It was a relief to him when the policeman jumped up and said, 'Right, I'm off!'" before hesitating at the screens, looking for the way out. Where the hell was a door when you wanted one?

Turning briefly, he glared at Ticke, unable to shift the nagging feeling that there was something going on here. Ticke was an odd sort, he wouldn't put anything past him.

'I'll be back tomorrow!' he barked. 'Don't go anywhere!'

And then, like the doctor before him, he forced his way through a gap in the screen, and left Lambert Ticke free to call for a nurse. Preferably one with a very long pencil in her pocket.

FORTY

'The bastard nearly had my nose off!' said PC Gilbert, aggrieved. A recent recruit with a degree in business studies, he hadn't expected to be bitten on the job. His language was usually more restrained but, having almost lost a nostril, he was entertaining second thoughts about his career choice.

'Put a plaster on it,' said an unsympathetic Lunt, who had never been bitten in the line of duty and had no time for anyone who had – in this instance, a pasty-faced mother's boy who would come off second best in a fist-fight with a blind dwarf.

It had been a long day, and Lunt was in no mood to take prisoners, not after his recent catch-up with Lambert Ticke. Fortunately, someone else had taken one for him – that prisoner being Colin Crimp, a man with a taste for nibbling noses and who had possibly blown up at least one house in Fetherton.

Crimp was currently lodged in a holding cell where, having woken up, he was making a racket to raise the dead. Lunt was none too sure he wanted to question him in person, especially if, as seemed likely, he was a certified lunatic. The men who had brought him in had gone through his pockets and found enough to identify him. A card in his wallet indicated that he was under the care of a shrink by the name of Hugo Lake. He was probably barmy, too, reflected Lunt. Nut-doctors usually were, convinced that everyone had been locked in the shed as a child and abused by their parents as a matter of course.

That made things easier. If Crimp *was* a loony, they could get him banged up sharpish. Two people had already phoned in to claim they'd seen someone matching his description in the vicinity of the late Shangri-La – reconnoitring the house a few hours before it went up in smoke, then legging it over a field as if the devil himself was on his back just before it blew up. That put him in the frame and no mistake.

Crimp's own house had gone for a burton, too; a house in which Lunt knew Lambert Ticke had shown an interest. When you threw in the theft of two vehicles – one of which had wound up in a bloody chemists, and the other not far from Crimp's place – plus eye witness accounts suggesting that Ticke had been seen, half-naked, in the vicinity of at least one crime scene – and it was hard not to draw the obvious conclusion: the two men were in cahoots. Every instinct in his policeman's fists told him so. What the hell they were up to, of course, was another matter. But houses didn't blow up without a reason. Not in Fetherton. Nor anywhere else, probably – but anywhere else wasn't his concern.

'He didn't say anything more?' asked Lunt as the younger policeman dabbed at his nose with a hanky. 'Before he passed out? Or after he woke up and started biting you again?'

'He swore a lot,' said PC Gilbert. 'And told me my mother was a–' His voice drifted away, like feathers in a breeze. He had no wish to repeat what Crimp had said about his mother. He was pretty sure it was actionable and a judge would find for him in court. As for the suggestion that animals had been involved… His shoulders shook as if a spider had crawled over his back.

'So he didn't say anything about blowing up his house? Or anyone else's?' asked Lunt, whose patience was wearing thin.

'No, sir,' said PC Gilbert, whose patience was also wearing thin, though largely because his shift had ended an hour ago and he feared his nose was turning green.

Bernard brought his hands together and crunched his knuckles. 'Well,' he said, wondering what the chances were of being able to administer a good kicking before the night was over, 'let's go and speak to our suspect, shall we?'

'I'd rather not,' said PC Gilbert, who hadn't quite grasped the nature of his role at the station.

'Do you have a family you'd like to see again?' asked Lunt quietly, 'possibly one last time before you die in a ditch with my boot up your arse?'

'But he's a homicidal maniac,' protested PC Gilbert, in the hope that would cut some ice with his miserable superior.

'And he's not the only bleedin' one round here,' said Lunt, and crunched his hands again.

PC Gilbert opened his mouth to say something about his shift having long since been over and his mother feeling nervous if he was out after dark. One look at Lunt's forbidding face and even he had the sense to accept defeat.

'Yes, sir,' he said, and made a mental note to Google what jobs were available for a keen young man with a degree in business studies, but possibly lacking a sense of smell should he not get to see a doctor in time.

*****

As it transpired, Lunt's luck was out that evening. At least where the possibility of administering a good kicking was concerned. Indeed, if anyone was likely to be on the receiving end of violence, it seemed likely to be him, given the nature of the prisoner in holding cell J. The man was making such a racket – even after two hours' incarceration – that no one was willing to go near him for fear of losing something vital, even when Lunt told them he'd make their life hell if they didn't 'restrain the loony so I can ask him a few questions'. Eventually, he was forced to admit defeat and, when Crimp, exhausted by his efforts, finally nodded off, Bernard decided to have him transferred to Fetherton General, though it had taken four constables and a dog to get him into the car.

The moment he was through the hospital door, Colin – briefly subdued – had revived dramatically, provoked by an NSPCC poster that suggested all children were angels sent from heaven to walk amongst us, and began to lash out again. The poster was illustrated by a photograph of a lad who looked suspiciously like Wayne Winkley. It had taken three porters and a large syringe to bring Colin under control. (Even then, he had had to be jabbed six times during the night to ensure he didn't haul himself – and the bed to which he was strapped – out through the hospital car park, and into the world beyond.)

'I've never seen anything like it,' said Dr Fosdyke – the hospital's head of practice – shortly after Colin had been rendered senseless for the first time. In truth, in the sheltered environment of Fetherton General, the ineffective Fosdyke had rarely seen anything more complex than a swollen prostate or the occasional haemorrhoid. Lacking secure facilities for the mentally deranged, he was keen to phone Leeds and dump the problem on them, but Lunt wouldn't hear of it. Two Fetherton properties had vanished in a puff of smoke and Crimp, he knew, was somehow connected to both. This was big, he was sure, and every instinct in his gut confirmed it. He didn't want Leeds in the loop, not yet. Getting to the bottom of this case would be a feather in his cap before Troy put through his transfer. That would be one hell of a way to announce his arrival in the city, and he didn't want to lose it.

Fortunately, Dr Fosdyke was the sort of man on whom it was easy to pull rank, even if, being in different professions, Lunt didn't, strictly speaking, outrank him.

'I need Crimp to stay here,' he insisted. 'I've spoken to Leeds and they think it's best.' He had done nothing of the sort, but the truth, he knew, would only complicate matters.

'It seems rather irregular,' said Dr Fosdyke, fretting. 'We don't have the staff, no-one trained for the job. One of our nurses has an A-level in psychology. I suppose I could ask her to take a look.'

'No need,' Lunt had assured him. 'He's under the care of a Hugo Lake. Psychiatrist. Leading man in his field. I've given him a bell.' (He hadn't, just then, but saw no reason to tell Fosdyke that.) 'He'll look in on the bast- – the patient –

tomorrow. He'll take full responsibility. Nothing for you to worry about.'

'Well, if you think it's for the best,' said Dr Fosdyke, with all the glumness of a man who didn't believe it at all.

'I do,' said Lunt. 'Leave it to me. Us. Just keep Crimp drugged up. I'll put a man on the door. Don't want him coming round again and trying to bite his way out.'

'No, certainly not,' said Dr Fosdyke, happy to be relieved of the burden. It crossed his mind to have something put in writing, to be on the safe side. One look at Lunt and he dismissed the idea. Instead, he did what he'd always done, in a career spanning three decades and more than 1500 operations, some of them successful. He crossed his fingers and hoped for the best.

FORTY ONE

'So let me get this right,' said Bernard Lunt. 'Your patient is a nutter.'

It was the following morning and, after a restless night, Lunt was not in the best of moods.

'I wouldn't put it quite like that,' said Hugo Lake, shifting awkwardly. He had felt confident enough when he had arrived at the station, excited even for reasons he ought to have been ashamed of, but wasn't. Any sense of delight had been swiftly kicked into touch by the brusque, plain-speaking policeman with whom he was currently struggling to converse.

'How *would* you put it?' asked Bernard Lunt. 'I mean, he either is or he isn't – so which one is it?'

'He is, in my opinion,' said Hugo Lake – fighting to regain the higher ground – 'suffering from PTSD.'

Bernard's face tightened. 'What? *Women's problems*?' he snorted derisively. 'So he *is* a nutter!'

'Post-traumatic Stress Disorder,' said Hugo Lake, with as much conviction as he could muster, given his feeble grasp of the condition. Colin *had* suffered several shocks in his life, from verbal abuse as a teacher in the past (which had certainly taken its toll) to going out yesterday morning and – from what he had now learned – returning home to find his house had been vaporised. It was enough to cause anyone stress, post- or otherwise.

'That as well?' muttered Bernard, with a huff, 'No wonder he's off his head.'

Hugo Lake abandoned the battle. 'The important thing,' he said, choosing not to add that it was important for him, rather than Colin Crimp, 'is that I'm familiar with his case and that's what he needs right now. Someone who is there for him.'

Fortunately for Hugo Lake, it was what Bernard Lunt needed, too. He had told Dr Fosdyke at Fetherton General that Crimp was under the care of a 'top man', though from what he had seen so far of the pillock on the other side of his desk, Lake was far from that. Still, that wasn't important. What was important was keeping Crimp within easy kicking distance of either or both of his boots, and if that meant inflating the ego of an idiot nut-doctor, then so be it.

'Could he have blown up a house?' he prompted. 'Two, even? In his condition? With his PMT?'

Hugo Lake opened his mouth to correct the policeman, then thought better of it. That wouldn't do, he needed to keep on Lunt's good side, all supposing he had one. What he really needed, though, was time alone with Colin Crimp. Time to ask questions, scribble notes, formulate a theory that would make his name in the medical world. There were those, he knew, who didn't regard him as a proper doctor just because he'd done all his training on the internet and been given all his qualifications by a man who lived in California and who had once been a priest. This would change their minds. From what little he already knew – and it was admittedly little enough – there might be a book in this. A book that would make his name.

'Is he violent?' asked Lunt, hoping the answer was yes, because violence, for him, was always a good starting-point.

'He could be,' said Hugo Lake, with no evidence to support the view, but keen to hedge his bets. 'It depends on the provocation,' he added, for no particular reason other than that it made him sound as if he knew what he was talking about.

'It's possible he's killed,' said Lunt, recalling the mangled corpses at Shangri-La, and what looked like a woman at Crimp's house. 'Anything in his background make that likely?'

'He does have anger issues,' said Lake, struggling to contain his excitement at this latest news, 'though I can't say more at this point.' He wasn't convinced that a man writing letters to get things off his chest was what the grim-faced Inspector had in mind. 'Patient privilege, I'm sorry,' he added quickly.

Lunt curled his lip and looked distinctly miffed.

'We'll need you in with us,' he said. 'Once he wakes up. Keep him calm, so he doesn't do anything silly.'

'I'll need some time with him alone,' said Hugo Lake, 'to evaluate the situation.'

'You can evaluate whatever you like,' said Lunt. 'Just as long as we get a confession out of him. For all our sakes.'

Lake liked the sound of that. A confession would be good for book sales.

'Be at Fetherton General this afternoon,' said Lunt wearily. 'Two o'clock. We'll take it from there.' He'd had enough of Hugo Lake for the moment, and there were other fish to fry.

A car had been found across the road from Shangri-La, registered to the late Henry Plank, and documents recovered from inside had opened up a new line of inquiry. Two officers had called on Henry Plank (Publishers) Ltd first thing and confirmed that there were only three employees, one of whom was currently in Fetherton General, heavily sedated and clearly off his head. The others were a man and a woman, one of whom, according to Sergeant Danvers, 'didn't seem that bright'. That was a bit rich coming from Sergeant Danvers who'd struggle to match Prince Harry in a 'Guess your own name' competition. The upshot was that they were coming in at mid-day to be interviewed, in the hope of throwing more light on Colin Crimp's activities.

FORTY TWO

'I think we may have got off on the wrong foot,' said Linda Lunt, leaning in close. Lambert Ticke shuddered. Though he tried to back away, trapped in a hospital bed and with one leg hoisted high, his scope for retreat was limited.

'You were tiddly and tried to interfere with me,' she lied, daring him – as a man with no memory of recent events – to contradict her. It was galling in the extreme but he had made his bed and – for the moment at least – must lie on it. He just hoped to God the dreadful woman wouldn't try to climb in on top of him.

'I understand why,' she purred, attempting demure innocence, but – with her large, and fleshy, cheekbones – achieving more the pained expression of a constipated hamster. 'You're a man with needs.' She licked her lips in a vain attempt at sensuality. 'And I'm a woman.' She leaned in closer still, and he felt her scented breath wash over him. She'd been eating garlic and it almost turned his stomach. 'With needs of my own,' she added.

Lambert Ticke felt a surge of revulsion, and not just from the smell of garlic. He had no wish to be reminded of this dreadful woman's needs which, he recalled, had led to her first drugging, then very nearly raping him, after which her lunatic husband had beaten him over the head and kicked him in the testicles.

Linda Lunt was not good for his health. She had almost given him a heart attack on appearing at his bedside, bearing grapes and – having unbuttoned her coat – baring most of her bosom, too. Her free-wheeling breasts had greatly distressed him the first time she had tried to foist them on him, and time had not dimmed the awful memory.

'I'm sorry, I don't think we've met,' he attempted, regretting that he had ever considered amnesia as a cunning ploy to play for time.

'Don't you worry yourself over that,' said Linda, who had worked out her plan of campaign and was in no mood to be derailed. When Bernard had returned the previous evening and told her that Ticke had been hospitalised and couldn't remember his own name, it seemed that fate had played into her hands.

The moment her husband had left for work, Linda Lunt had come to a decision, one that would have made Mrs Palona, author of *Seize the Moment!*, immensely proud. Fate had thrown its Bouquet of Happiness at Linda Lunt and she had caught it with both hands – or planned to, now, at any rate.

'We came to an arrangement,' she said, having rehearsed her lines all morning until she'd got them vaguely right.

'Did we?' said Ticke, who didn't like the sound of this. He would have to tread carefully, he knew, hampered, as he was, by the need to feign forgetfulness.

'You asked me to run away with you,' said Linda, upping the stakes dramatically. Lambert Ticke almost choked. 'You said you wanted to take me back to London and make an honest woman of me.'

Stunned into silence, Ticke regarded her vacantly, much like a rabbit caught in the headlights of a truck driven by a heavily armed hunter. One who specialised in slaughtering rabbits. If honesty was her aim, he thought miserably, they would both have their work cut out to make her happy.

'I don't remember,' he muttered, taking refuge in the truth. If there was something he knew he'd never said, and so couldn't possibly recall it under any circumstances, it was a promise to throw in his lot with a woman so vile she would give a sex-crazed harpy a run for her money.

'Well you did,' she insisted, reaching out to stroke his face.

Ticke felt chilly fingers tighten around his heart as well as his cheek. Though he was fairly certain that, biologically, it was impossible for human blood to turn to ice while the rest of the body still thrived, he was equally certain that his was doing its best to prove biology wrong.

'You mustn't worry about a thing,' said Linda softly. 'You must leave all the worrying to me.'

Just then he really wished he could. For a woman who wanted to lighten the load on his shoulders, she was doing a first-rate job of heaping on a few extra pounds.

'I may never get my memory back,' said Ticke desperately. 'It wouldn't be fair on you. Not if I can't remember who you are.'

'Love will find a way, Lambert,' she whispered and bared two rows of snowy-white teeth. They put him in mind of tombstones beneath which she was planning to bury the rest of his life.

'I'm feeling sleepy,' he said, and closed his eyes in the hope she would get the message and leave. When he opened them half a minute later, she was still there, gazing at him much like Dracula might have gazed at an unblemished neck.

'I could look at you forever,' she whispered and realised, to her surprise, that she meant it.

'I'm still very tired,' he muttered anxiously. 'I'd rather you left now, I really need to sleep.'

'Only if you say that you love me,' demanded Linda, keen to press home her advantage.

'I don't see how I can,' said Ticke truthfully. If he survived through to the end of time, he couldn't foresee any future existence in which he would come remotely close to loving this wretched woman.

'Then I shall remain at your bedside until you do,' said Linda Lunt, recalling more pertinent advice from *Seize the Moment!*: 'When faced with a closed door, don't waste any time looking for the key. Just kick it down!' If Lambert Ticke wouldn't give her the key, decided Linda, she would kick down his manly door, however long it took.

Ticke gazed back at her, a battle raging within. He thought about calling for a nurse, a doctor – a hospital porter even, he didn't much care – but there was something about Linda Lunt that terrified him and, he suspected, would terrify them, too. She was a woman who wouldn't take no for an answer. Possibly, she was clinically insane, it wouldn't surprise him. Years of living in the same house as her Neanderthal husband would unhinge the strongest of minds, and he doubted hers was up to much to begin with.

He had never told anyone he loved them, not even his mother – and he had no wish to open his account with a sex-obsessed siren who had drugged, poisoned and done her best to ravish him on her sitting room settee. Reason had always been his ally in times of stress, and reason was his strongest weapon now. If he loved anything in his life he loved reason – and reason had come to his rescue. He knew the way ahead, though it pained him dreadfully.

'I love you,' he said, visualising – as only he could – the image of the Greek goddess, Metis, mother of wisdom and deep thought – standing before him, eager for a worship he was more than willing to bestow. What he put from his mind altogether was the red-lipsticked, bosom-wobbling Linda Lunt, the very antithesis of logic and sound thought.

'That's easy for you to say,' said Linda, unaware that it was anything but easy for Lambert Ticke. 'It's just words.'

Lambert Ticke felt the earth yawn open beneath him. How the hell did she think humans generally communicated if not through words?

'I want to hear you say, "Linda, darling, I – Lambert Ticke – love you with all my heart and want to be by your side until the sands of time run dry."'

It had taken her several hours to come up with that particular wording and it pleased her enormously.

'Just once, my sweet,' she gushed, losing herself in her fantasy, and all but turning his stomach. "Linda, darling, I –

Lambert Ticke,'" she repeated, "'love you with all my heart and want to be by your side until the sands of time run dry.'"

'And you promise you'll leave?' he asked, ready to prostitute himself if that was what was needed to get the wretched woman out of here.

'I will,' she said. 'I promise.'

Lambert Ticke took a deep breath, and hurled himself into the abyss.

"Linda, darling,' he began, forcing the words from his mouth with as much difficulty as if he had been Sisyphus, rolling his boulder up the proverbial hill with a broken back. 'I – Lambert Ticke – love you with all my heart...' He ground to a halt, took another deep breath and hurried on to the bitter, miserable end. '... and want to be by your side until the sands of time run dry.'

'Oh, Lambert, darling!' she shrieked happily. 'We're going to be perfect together. I don't care how many people you've murdered – you're the only man for me now.'

How many people I've murdered? thought Ticke. *Dear God! What was it with this woman and wholesale slaughter?*

Which was when a desperate notion came to him. What if he told her that he *had* killed people? Lots of them, in fact. Murdered them in their beds, and, after that, slaughtered their children, too – while they were watching something educational on the telly. It was all very well the lunatic bitch entertaining fantasies about his prowess on the killing field, but what if he filled in a few blanks – might it put her off?

To hell with it, decided Lambert Ticke – there was only one way to find out.

'You really don't mind?' he asked, leaning forward. Though distance was preferable where Linda Lunt was concerned – and as much of it as humanly possible – a certain closeness would, he knew, enhance the conspiratorial ambience he needed to convey. 'Even though...'

He allowed the sentence to trail away, largely because he hadn't made up his mind how to continue. From the changed expression on her face, however, it had the desired result of luring the awful woman in.

'Even though what?' inquired Linda, her voice suggesting an eagerness laced with caution.

Ticke shook his head sadly, as if the memory still pained him. He raised his arms a fraction and spread his palms. 'I've killed a hundred men, women…' He hesitated briefly, then went for broke. ' … and children, too.' He took a deep breath. 'Strangled them all to death … *with these very hands!*'

He wriggled his fingers in the hope of conveying to her that he hadn't finished yet – that there were more innocent souls out there waiting for his homicidal wrath to fall upon them. Starting with her if she didn't have the sense to leave him alone. To his despair, the horror that briefly registered in her eyes gave way to a look of genuine interest, as if, having given her the general gist, he might now supply a few corroborative details, the more unsavoury the better. He had read about women like Linda Lunt. They wrote to serial killers in America, preferably ones who had been sentenced to death or a hundred years' imprisonment and had never shown remorse for their crimes. They married them if they could and tried to have their babies. That's what the world needed more of, they seemed to imagine, lots of infant killers in waiting, ready to carry on the family tradition.

'I've murdered animals, too,' said Ticke, desperately. It was his last throw of the dice. There were many people, he knew, who didn't give a fig about human misery, but would gut a nun in her sleep if they thought she'd frightened a cat.

Linda shrugged. 'I'm sure they deserved it,' she said quietly, which was not the answer he had been hoping for.

'I killed a woman yesterday,' said Ticke, scooping up his final die and rolling it once again. His mind flitted back to the bathroom at 78 Arcadia Avenue. 'Drowned her in the toilet,' he continued, a manic gleam coming naturally into his eyes as he remembered the terrible scene, 'then set fire to her hair just to make sure.'

Linda Lunt stood up, a determined look on her face. 'You did what you had to do,' she said calmly, ending what little hope remained. 'And now you need your rest. I'll leave you in peace.'

Ticke's head dropped onto his pillow. *Did what I had to do?* he thought miserably. Dear God, was there nothing he could say that would deter this monstrous harridan? But at least she was finally buggering off. Perhaps, once she was away from here, she would reflect on what he had told her and think again. All supposing there was anything in that thick, vacant head of hers capable of thought.

It wasn't much to hope for, he told himself as, blowing him a kiss and winking crudely, she wafted across the room and mercifully vanished from sight.

It was only then, too late, that something else occurred to him. He had recalled and recounted a ridiculously detailed amount of information for a man with no memory of recent events. Still, with luck, it would have passed the idiot woman completely by.

*****

Sitting in her car, Linda Lunt took several minutes to calm down, and, even then, she scarcely managed it. Her heart was beating so fast it was a wonder it didn't burst through her chest. She had obeyed Mrs Palona's instructions to the letter – or at least the sage advice she had handed out in Chapter 3 of *Seize the Moment!*:

'Leave no stone unturned in pursuit of your goal. In matters of the heart, it may, on occasion, be necessary to "get the goods" on your soul's desire, especially if he is not as keen on the union as yourself. Carry a voice recorder with you at all times. (The standard app on your mobile phone is particularly useful and will generally go unnoticed. I heartily recommend it!) Have no scruples in gathering admissions of wrongdoing – or other slips of the tongue – that can

be used to your advantage. Victory is not just to the brave – but to the cunning, also. Be cunning in your pursuit of all things – and make me proud!'

Though it couldn't be denied that, on occasion, Mrs Palona's advice sailed close to the wind, Linda was happy to acknowledge its wisdom. Pressing 'playback', she listened with a mixture of dread and delight as Lambert Ticke confessed first to his undying love for her, and then to murder on a grand scale. She had no doubt that whatever butchery he had been party to had been necessary to preserve the nation's safety and ensure that people like her could sleep soundly at night. Even so, he would hardly want his actions broadcast to the world at large. Especially as, for reasons she couldn't yet fathom – and here she felt huge joy to know something that Bernard didn't – her darling Lambert was just pretending to have lost his memory. If not, how could he have remembered everything he had told her? She wasn't yet sure how or when this information would prove useful – and part of her hoped fervently that it never would – but it was there if she needed it and, as Mrs Palona had wisely urged, to be used to her advantage if push came to shove.

Switching off the device, Linda sighed contentedly. It wouldn't be long now, she told herself, before she was shot of her husband for good, and off to a new and exciting life in London. And beyond that, wherever in the world Lambert Ticke was posted to despatch the nation's enemies.

Linda Lunt could hardly recall the last time she had entertained such bright hopes for the future, but she entertained them now and it was a lovely feeling. Bugger Bernard, she thought happily, and bugger sleepy Fetherton where nothing interesting had ever happened until Lambert Ticke had driven into town.

FORTY THREE

'Colin's not a violent man,' said Karen. 'I don't know why you'd think he was.'

'We have evidence to suggest he may have blown up two houses,' said Bernard Lunt, who felt that was reason enough. He wanted a quick result, not a case for the defence.

He had already interviewed her work colleague, Bob (a man who, if anything, appeared to have fewer functioning brain cells than even Sergeant Danvers had given him credit for). What he had learned from the lad made this second interview potentially more productive.

'I believe you're engaged to the suspect?' he said, and noticed the way she flinched.

'Who told you that?' Karen asked, as if he had accused her of having a mole on her left buttock in the shape of a cock.

'Your work colleague, Mr...' and here Lunt paused, as if fearful of a wind-up, despite his running it through records and finding it ridiculously genuine. 'Mr Robert Bobb.'

'Oh, Bob,' said Karen, with a resigned air.

'Yes Bobb,' said Lunt, more formally. He cracked his knuckles and watched as Karen retreated a little into her chair. 'He said your fiancé threatened to kill him.'

'Nonsense,' said Karen. 'I've told you already, Colin's not a violent man.'

'You seem very sure of that,' said Lunt.

Karen frowned. 'Why wouldn't I be?'

'So you didn't say he'd kill him? He's making it up. Now why would he do that?'

Karen hesitated, struggling to fashion an adequate

response. When one eluded her, she was forced to tell the truth.

'*I* made it up,' she admitted.

'*You* made it up?' repeated Lunt. 'He didn't. *You* did?'

'Yes, *I* did,' she said again and hoped that was an end to it. It wasn't.

'Why?' asked Lunt, who couldn't think of a good reason himself.

'I didn't want Bob telling him we were getting married.'

'What?' said Lunt, already lost. 'Didn't he know?'

'It's complicated,' she said.

'It bloody sounds it,' said Lunt, who had never favoured complication.

'I didn't want him telling Colin,' said Karen, still struggling. 'That we'd, well – you know– '

'Had it away in a filing cabinet?' said Lunt, not caring to mince his words.

'It wasn't a filing cabinet,' protested Karen. 'Who on earth could do it in a filing cabinet?' She shook her head, as if pondering the possibility, then said, just to make it clear, 'It was a stationery cupboard.'

'Which makes it all right, does it?' said Lunt, though he didn't give a damn either way.

'I didn't mean that,' said Karen, increasingly flustered.

'What *did* you mean?' asked Lunt, who wasn't really sure what he himself meant just then.

'I meant – I told Bob that Colin would kill him just to keep him quiet.'

'He'd certainly be quiet if he was dead,' said Lunt. 'That's usually par for the course when you're dead.'

'I meant it would keep Bob quiet – so he wouldn't tell Colin. If I said Colin would kill him.'

Lunt sighed. This interview was giving him a headache. 'Wasn't it a bit over the top,' he inquired, 'telling the poor lad that your fiancé would try to blow him up?' He knew she'd said nothing of the sort, but decided to chance his arm.

'Who said anything about being blown up?' said Karen, who couldn't recall mentioning explosives.

'That wasn't how he was going to kill him, then?' he said, trying to back her into a corner.

'Certainly not!' she replied angrily.

'So how *was* he planning to do it?'

'He wasn't planning to do it at all,' said Karen. 'I keep telling you. Colin's not like that. He's a sweet little man.'

'They said that about Crippen,' sniffed Lunt, who had never heard anyone say that about Crippen, but saw no reason to admit it. He could see the young woman was rattled and when people were rattled they generally said whatever he wanted them to say. Eventually.

'Colin's not like Crippen,' said Karen defensively. 'That's not a nice thing to say.'

'Murder isn't nice,' said Lunt. 'Not for the victim – though the killer often finds it amusing.'

'My Colin wouldn't hurt a fly,' insisted Karen, refusing to buckle.

'Maybe not a fly,' said Lunt, 'but what about a woman in a dress? Or what was left of one?'

'A woman in a dress?' repeated Karen who was beginning to feel she'd somehow wandered into a different conversation.

'Three women, to be precise,' said Lunt. 'And your employer, Henry Plank.'

'That's ridiculous,' said Karen, completely lost now.

'So you deny that your fiancé set out to commit mass murder?'

'Of course, I deny it,' said Karen. 'And you can't make me say otherwise. A fiancée can't be forced to testify against her intended in a court of law.'

'That's not true,' said Lunt. 'If you know anything that can help the police in their inquiries, it's your duty to reveal it, whatever your carnal cravings for another human being.'

Karen opened her mouth to respond, but nothing emerged. She shut it again and prepared for his next move. She didn't have long to wait.

Lunt consulted his notes. 'Mr Bobb says that after you and he did something you shouldn't have done in the stationery cupboard, you said your fiancé would kill him if he ever found out. Because he had a terrible temper.'

'I told you,' said Karen, 'It was just to keep him quiet. Colin doesn't have a temper. How many times do I have to say it?'

'He bit one of my officers,' said Lunt sourly. 'On the nose,' as if that confirmed the gravity of the assault. 'It took four of my men – and a dog – to bring him under control. If that's not a bloke with a temper, I wouldn't want to meet him on a bad day.'

'He'll have been provoked,' said Karen, and immediately regretted it.

'So he *does* have a temper?' snapped Lunt, seizing on the admission.

'I didn't mean it like that.'

'So how did you mean it?'

'I don't know,' said Karen. 'You're getting me confused.'

'How long have you been engaged?' asked Lunt, changing the subject quickly. He often found the tactic derailed a suspect – or witness in this case – and made them more talkative.

'A few days,' she answered.

'A few days?' repeated Lunt, not caring to hide his surprise. 'You've only been engaged for a few days?'

Karen shrugged. 'Does it matter?'

'That depends,' said Lunt, and chose not to finish the sentence. That was yet another tactic, pretending he had something more to say, when, actually, he *had* finished.

Just then, he was thinking about the documents they had recovered from Henry Plank's car, papers making it clear that, in the event of his death, Colin would inherit the dead man's estate, including his share of Henry Plank (Publishers) Ltd. In the event of his wife's death, Lunt had since learned – following a short call to Henry's lawyer, who had drawn up the paperwork – there was every possibility Crimp would inherit the entire kit and caboodle. That would leave him very comfortably off. Throw in the likely insurance money for the evisceration of both his house and all his worldly goods – not to mention that of Shangri-La – and he had every reason to wish the Planks dead. As for the woman across the desk, she seemed harmless enough, but, given the fortune heading Crimp's way, she stood to gain, too.

Karen Fletcher was undeniably attractive – what some men (including, he had to admit, himself) would describe as 'physically alluring'. From what the improbably named Bob Bobb had told him, she had an insatiable sexual appetite and wasn't beyond seducing half-wits over a sheet of Xerox. (He wasn't entirely sure that wasn't an offence, but it didn't top his list of crimes to investigate just now.) To date, he'd only seen Crimp at his worst, gibbering ape-like with an unnatural taste for noses. Even so, he struggled to see why a woman like Karen would be interested in him. He was nothing much to look at and, as he'd since discovered, was officially a nutter. Mind you, money was a powerful motivator, and maybe there was more to this than met the eye.

Lunt looked at his watch, it was nearly half past one. He was due at the hospital by two to meet up with that other lunatic, Hugo Lake. This interview was getting him nowhere, it was time to wind it up. Let her stew, he decided. If she was innocent, there was no point wasting further time. If she wasn't, well, that could wait, too.

'That'll be all,' he said, 'for the moment. I'll let you know if I need to speak to you again.' He stood up quickly and couldn't help but notice that she stood up just as fast.

FORTY FOUR

'Can he be questioned?' asked Bernard Lunt, addressing Hugo Lake in much the same tone he might have employed had the latter been top of his suspect list.

'That's hard to say,' said the other man. He'd only spoken to Colin for ten minutes, and it hadn't been that productive. The latter, heavily sedated, had spent much of the time swearing, in-between mumbling something unpleasant he hoped to do to several policemen if they ever let him out of here. Other than that, he was making no sense whatsoever.

'It's a murder inquiry,' said Lunt sharply, keen to bring the case to a swift conclusion. It wouldn't do for Crimp to be transferred to a proper psychiatric ward before he got the chance to beat a confession out of him.

'When you say "murder",' Lake inquired tentatively, aware that at least one death had occurred but still hazy on the detail, 'are we talking something particularly serious, or...' He would have let the sentence trail away, but Bernard rendered his hesitancy academic by leaping in swiftly and removing all doubt.

'In my experience,' Lunt growled, 'murder is always fucking serious.'

'I didn't mean,' began Hugo Lake apologetically, but was saved the bother of completing his sentence for a second time.

'He's in the frame for multiple homicide,' said the policeman. 'Four killings. That do you for serious?' He wasn't in the mood for debate.

'Goodness me,' said Hugo Lake, struggling to keep the excitement out of his voice. Four killings would make Crimp a mass murderer and guarantee any book he wrote on the subject bestseller status not only here in the UK but in America, too, where carnage and madness were certain to shift copies. This was more than he had hoped for.

'So can he be questioned?' asked Lunt again. 'In the presence of his psychiatrist, naturally,' he added. 'We'll need you to guide us.'

Lunt, of course, had no intention of being guided by anyone, least of all a man who was probably just as barmy as his patients. That said, for all his love of administering a good kicking – whether deserved or not – he was fly enough to know when a tickle under the chin worked equally well. And Hugo Lake was clearly a man who would respond to a bit of pampering.

'When you put it like that, said Hugo Lake, nibbling happily on the worm Lunt had tossed him, 'I can't see any problems, once–'

'He's compost mentis?' asked Lunt quickly.

'I wouldn't say that,' replied Lake, whose grasp of Latin was only marginally better than the policeman's, 'but as long I'm present to – shall we say "interpret", as it were – then I'm sure everything will be fine.'

In truth, he wasn't much bothered either way. What he was hoping for now were a few juicy facts that he could file away for future use. He wondered whether knives had been involved, possibly an axe to chop up the bodies before destroying all the evidence in a fire that had razed two buildings to the ground. That would make for a good read and probably have the *Daily Mail* badgering him for serial rights.

'Excellent,' said Lunt, rubbing his hands happily.

'There's only one problem,' said Hugo Lake. 'He's still heavily sedated. I doubt he'll make much sense for a few hours. Maybe not for the rest of the day.'

Lunt cracked a knuckle. That wasn't what he wanted to hear, but perhaps there was a silver lining. As long as this was kept under wraps – away from Leeds, at any rate – it gave him time to build a case. And maybe not just against Crimp. Ticke was in this up to his neck. Which gave him another idea, and one that cheered him greatly.

'There's another patient here,' he said, dropping his voice conspiratorially. It had the desired effect, as Lake leaned in a little closer. 'Someone we feel may be connected with the case.' He lowered his voice to a whisper. 'But that's between the two of us, understand?'

'Of course,' said Hugo Lake, who didn't understand at all.

'Ticke's the name. Lambert Ticke. I'd like you to keep an eye on him. He's a bit of a nutjob, right up your street.'

Hugo Lake wasn't sure what to make of that but wasn't about to say so.

'Conspiracy theorist from London. Lost his memory, needs help getting it back.' He glanced about as if fearful of being overheard. Lake took the bait and leaned in closer still. 'We think he might have been planning to kill the PM, something went wrong, we don't know what.'

'You want me to find out?' asked Lake, scarcely able to believe his luck. A mass murderer *and* a man who hoped to kill the PM. That could be two separate books – or one really big one to cover all his options.

'Exactly,' said Lunt. 'But play it carefully. He mustn't know what you're up to.'

'Leave it to me,' said Lake happily.

'I intend to,' said Lunt, even more happily. He looked at his watch. There was nothing to be gained by his remaining here any longer. He had no wish to speak to Ticke again – not for the moment – and he'd get nothing out of Colin Crimp, except possibly a lacerated nostril for his trouble. Might as well shove off, get stuck into the paperwork. Build a case that couldn't be broken – before he came back and gave the guilty pair the kicking they deserved.

FORTY FIVE

Conrad Blag was not a happy man.

'There's something going on,' he said, chewing the nail on his thumb and idly heaping sugar into a mug. It was his third coffee of the morning and had done nothing to improve his mood. 'I don't like it.'

Hapgood regarded the other man with his usual mix of weariness and confusion. In his experience, Blag was rarely happier than when something appeared to be 'going on'. What generally ruined his peace of mind was the all-too-frequent discovery that nothing, in fact, *was* going on. London was not the most exciting posting in the world, aside from the distractions – for Hapgood at least – of the lovely Miss Lulu de Flame. The Brits played things close to their collective chests and struggled to get worked up over threats to the free world. They took the view that everything would turn out fine as long as no one lost their temper during lunch, and always laughed at the vicar's jokes. Something like that.

'Two houses have been blown up and Grogan's disappeared,' muttered Blag grimly.

'You think they're connected?' inquired Hapgood, who had a feeling it was going to be a long day.

'What do you think?' said Blag, defying his assistant to suggest otherwise.

'It could just be coincidence,' suggested Hapgood, testing the waters.

'Coincidence, my ass!' exploded Blag. 'This Tit fella's only been up there five minutes and half the town's in ruins. If you ask me...' His voice trailed away.

'Yes?' prompted Hapgood, who was pretty sure he already knew the answer to his question.

'Tit was building a bomb. Testing it out in a couple of safe houses.'

'Hardly safe,' remarked Hapgood. 'He's ended up in hospital by all accounts.'

'Which proves my point,' said Blag. 'Something went wrong. And why did it go wrong, eh? Why?'

Hapgood shrugged. He wasn't sure if it was a rhetorical question, but ventured an answer anyway.

'He made a mistake, got something wrong. Or perhaps he was just in the wrong place at the wrong time. Perhaps there was no bomb? Perhaps it was just an accident?'

Blag huffed and muttered something else about his ass which Hapgood didn't catch.

'Someone stopped him,' he hurried on, 'before he could do any harm. Someone who knew what he was up to.'

'We can't be sure he was up to anything,' said Hapgood, though he wondered why he was making the effort.

Blag's withering gaze had its intended result and Hapgood finally abandoned his objections.

'If you ask me,' said Blag, 'we won't be hearing from Grogan again...'

He pressed a hand to his chest, over where he imagined his heart to be, though missing it by several inches. 'He's taken a bullet for the free world,' he said in a quiet voice. 'No other explanation.' He sighed and added reverently, 'The bastard has done for him.'

Familiar with Grogan's chequered past and aware of his tendency to work outside any box into which he had been placed, Hapgood could think of several explanations to account for the other man's absence, but he wisely kept them to himself.

'So what now?' he said, trying another tack. 'Do we pass this on to MI5? Let them get on with it?'

'Jesus, no,' replied Blag. 'It's too big for the Brits. They'd just pussyfoot around, offer to understand the swine, then send him on his way.'

'But if it's their PM he's after, is it any of our business?'

Blag gave Hapgood another withering gaze. 'Their PM today, our President tomorrow,' he said sharply. 'Tit's got to be stopped.'

'But he's safe enough in hospital, surely?' said Hapgood. 'He can't do any harm from there.'

'Don't you believe it,' said Blag. 'Man like that will have a back-up plan. Butchers always do.'

'Butchers?' repeated Hapgood, wondering how they'd wandered into tradesmen's territory.

Blag gave an exasperated huff. 'Grogan's last report – before he went MIA. Tit kept boasting about how many people he'd murdered. According to Grogan, those perverts he was staying with were so turned on they ended up screwing each other's brains out.' His face clouded over. 'He's got the police in his pocket. They'll spring him if they have to. The bastard could vanish before we know it.'

'So what do we do?' inquired Hapgood, repeating his earlier question but, as far as he could manage it, in a less questioning tone of voice.

'We may need to bring in The Team,' said Blag ominously.

Hapgood felt a shiver creep down his spine. No one brought in 'The Team' unless several balloons were going up at the same time. They extricated hostages, had blown up more buildings than the busiest demolition company in Baghdad, and wiped out entire armies behind enemy lines. All without anyone ever knowing they even existed in the first place.

As the first panicked wave ebbed away, Hapgood relaxed a little. Only the President could authorise a mission by 'The Team' and that was surely unlikely. The fact that Fetherton boasted two fewer houses this morning than it had the previous day might be a source of concern for local planners but it was hardly a matter of interest to the United States government.

Even so, Blag had that look on his face that rarely augured well. True, it often meant they wasted days, weeks and sometimes months pursuing pointless leads. That was fine. Theirs was one of many small bases operating around the country, most of which had been set up years ago and generally forgotten about. As long as they kept their noses clean and reported back from time to time with titbits of interest (often gleaned from left-wing journals like the *Guardian*, which frequently published articles by radicals keen to overthrow the elected government – as long as it was Tory – and who, to show their even-mindedness, were none too keen on whichever poor sod had most recently drawn the straw to lead the Labour Party), they were left in peace.

The last thing they needed, thought Hapgood, was to make a fuss about a couple of minor incidents in a quiet northern market town. Especially when their main suspect was a civil servant against whom there existed no more damning evidence than his peculiar-sounding name, an eclectic browser history, and an interest in garden fertiliser. Once the suits in Washington were briefed, it might open all sorts of doors best kept closed and bolted.

True, Grogan had filed several reports to the effect that Ticke was up to no good, since when two houses had been razed to the ground and Grogan himself had gone AWOL. (Or, as Blag insisted on labelling him, 'Missing In Action'.) Ticke seemed to have an unusually powerful sex drive – astonishingly varied, too, if Grogan's reports were even halfway accurate. But that just meant he was normal in Hapgood's book – and even a man to be envied. It certainly didn't make him a dangerous Russian subversive.

Besides which, Grogan wasn't the most reliable of informants. He had once reported back that a convent of nuns was planning to detonate a dirty bomb in the centre of New York. It transpired that their Mother Superior – in an earthy Brooklyn accent – had suggested designating the centre of the city as a good place to bring the word of God to its 'dirty bums'.

A soup kitchen, set up to feed a thousand vagrants, in between praising the Almighty, had been subsequently tear-gassed into oblivion, with three nuns blinded for life and several more consigned to a hospital for the criminally insane. (Which, quite frankly, was where Hapgood would have consigned Grogan if it had been in his power to do so.)

It was the New York 'incident' that had led to Grogan being posted overseas, where it was felt he would do less harm to the American people – unless, of course, they were unfortunate enough to be taking their annual vacation in the wrong place at the wrong time.

Hardly surprising, thought Hapgood glumly, that he was less than convinced by Grogan's reports. Then again, two houses had, it seemed, exploded, and with – as yet – no obvious explanation. And Grogan *had* gone missing. Even so, he felt uneasy, and mention of 'The Team' did nothing to calm his mind. He wondered, idly, if he could seek political asylum if it all went hideously wrong. The Brits were famously keen to take in strangers, especially if they posed a risk to life and limb and had no visible means of support – both of which might describe him perfectly if Conrad Blag had his way.

Clinging to the thought, like a man on a plank in a shark-infested sea – who had cut his leg and couldn't swim – Hapgood conjured up another soothing image of Miss Lulu de Flame and wondered what her rates might be for a refugee on benefits.

*****

Thirty miles to the north of Fetherton, Chuck Grogan surveyed his work with satisfaction. Though it was a source of some distress to him that Lambert Ticke had evaded American justice, even if his Russkie safe house had not, he was not a man to dwell for long on setbacks. The moment he had lost sight of Ticke and realised that pursuit was pointless, he had swung into action.

Having fired his missile, vaporising both it and the house

into which it had been launched (along with Ticke's car, for good measure), Chuck Grogan knew that he needed a new plan. Though he had no great respect for British surveillance, he was aware that his van might have been picked up on camera. With that in mind, he promptly headed north, parking in a quiet stretch of woodland outside Richmond. Waiting for nightfall, and, having examined the area with thermal imaging to ensure he would not be disturbed, Chuck Grogan set up four large spotlights, and began work. Over the next seven hours, from 11pm until 6 the following morning, he painstakingly resprayed the blue transit van in a fresh coat of white paint until, as the sun rose on a grey Yorkshire day, he had very nearly succeeded in transforming 'Gertie'. All that remained was to replace her number plates with one of several spares he kept for emergencies and he was once again ready for the fray.

Chuck Grogan had not slept for almost 36 hours, and even he knew that he needed to be as sharp as a surgeon's knife to bring the next stage of his mission to a successful conclusion. Having ensured 'Gertie' was out of sight and not likely to be stumbled on any time soon, he injected himself with an experimental dose of BIDEN45, curled up on his camp-bed and, five seconds later, was completely out for the count.

FORTY SIX

Forty-eight hours on from the first explosion, and Bernard Lunt was making progress – progress that surprised even him. As reports came in – from forensics, fire services, and finally pathology – a disturbing picture had begun to emerge.

Three bodies were now confirmed dead at the former Shangri-La: those of the owners, Henry and Norah Plank, and a woman by the name of Myrtle Fling, a former checkout girl, who seemed to be in the Planks' employ. According to neighbours, the couple – Henry and Norah – had recently separated, following what one of them, a fierce old biddy in a wig that didn't fit and a face that would curdle cheese, described as 'a sexual scandal'. Having discovered a copy of a pornographic magazine – *Thrasher's Weekly* – in Henry Plank's car (found parked nearby), matters had taken a more salacious turn. Norah Plank, it seemed, was running a domination den, where men could be beaten senseless in return for ready cash. Various items of clothing – basques, peep-hole bras and underwear with slits where slits shouldn't be, together with what looked suspiciously like instruments of torture – had been found in the charred ruins, confirming the establishment's seedy purpose.

Things had taken a darker turn still when the contents of the late Henry Plank's briefcase had also thrown up a copy of a legally binding will appointing Colin Crimp as his sole heir. The bizarre injuries Colin Crimp had sustained – a missing tooth and absent hair that none of Bernard's men were willing to claim the credit for – seemed to confirm that the pervert had enjoyed a sound thrashing that day. It only remained to be determined whether he had gone on to murder both Planks in order to inherit their estate or in a moment of madness brought on by excessive sexual pleasure. Either way, he was as guilty as sin.

As for the suspect's old place – the one that had been almost vaporised – the picture was stranger still. Bill Thomson, who ran forensics, said he'd never seen anything like it – except on a course he'd taken years ago and never had to make use of. In his opinion the house had been blown up by a heat-seeking missile, probably made in China but fired by an American warplane.

Lunt hadn't bothered to check how many warplanes were flying over Fetherton on the day in question, though he had got on the phone to Bill to ask how much he'd had to drink before compiling his report, while suggesting he adopt a healthier lifestyle if he didn't want his liver to go the way of Colin Crimp's house. Bill had seemed put out and insisted he hadn't had so much as a small sherry since Christmas. He said he stood by his report, and had no idea what could have caused that sort of damage other than an explosive device of military origin.

'Could it have been a home-made bomb?' asked Lunt, keen to head Bill off at the pass.

The other man had relented at that stage and said he doubted that very much but if Lunt's only concern was to convict a man, regardless of the facts, then, yes, it could have been a home-made bomb.

Lunt wrote 'Forensics indicate a home-made bomb' on the official file, happy to live with that until a better explanation came along.

FORTY SEVEN

'It's hard to believe Mr Crimp's a murderer,' said Bob, 'but the policeman seemed so sure it must be true.'

He and Karen were sitting on a park bench, close to the office. Henry Plank (Publishers) Ltd was currently shut and, given the demise of both its owners, it seemed unlikely it would open again.

It had been Karen's idea to get together, though she had told Bob he wasn't to read anything into it, they were just meeting up as friends. The meeting was more for Bob's benefit than hers. She wasn't convinced that their interviews had gone well – in fact, she knew they hadn't – and was keen to ensure they got their stories straight should the sour-faced policeman want to talk to them again, which he surely would. She had no idea how Colin had got himself into such a mess, but she didn't for a moment believe he was an arsonist, let alone a murderer.

Looking over at Bob, who seemed more interested in a passing squirrel than he was in her, Karen realised, not for the first time, that innocence was a powerful aphrodisiac. She had a key to the office and, though she knew it wasn't the right thing to do, she couldn't help but reminisce over the stationery cupboard and how nice it had been to be inside it with Bob. And with Bob inside her, too, if she was going to be completely honest.

When all was said and done, it wasn't as if she was actually engaged, and, if Colin *was* found guilty, she might not see him again for another 20 years, by which time she would be past child-bearing age, whatever chemicals they could pump into your womb these days. Not that she'd previously given any thought to babies, and wasn't sure she really wanted to even now.

'I think we should check out the office,' she said, making up her mind. 'Make sure no one's broken in.'

Bob frowned. 'Why would anyone want to break in?' he inquired.

'They might want to steal our pens,' said Karen. 'Pens can fetch a lot on the black market.'

'Can they?' said Bob, who had never given it much thought before.

'Yes, they can,' said Karen who, having made up her mind to be ravished in the very near future, didn't want to waste any time getting down to it.

'Well, if you're sure,' said Bob, standing up at the same time that she did.

'Oh, I'm very sure,' said Karen, doing her best to justify what she had in mind on the grounds that she was very possibly engaged to a serial killer who was going down for a very long time, and not on her. It wouldn't hurt to hedge her bets.

FORTY EIGHT

Hugo Lake was having the time of his life. True, that wasn't how others viewed the arrangement but he wasn't overly concerned. He had been given *carte blanche* to run the new psychiatric wing of Fetherton General Hospital. That the new wing consisted of two adjacent rooms, one of which had until recently served as a storage facility for the hospital's janitor and was now home to Colin Crimp, was neither here nor there. Dr Fosdyke, the hospital's administrator, was content to hand over responsibility for his two unwanted guests to his internet-qualified colleague, as long as, in return, he was absolved from all blame should the experiment end badly, which he was pretty sure it would.

In the room next door to Colin Crimp, Lambert Ticke remained blissfully unaware of his neighbour's identity, which was probably for the best. It was bad enough that he had been given into the care of a man who appeared to know as much about traumatic memory loss as he did. Fortunate, then, he told himself, that he wasn't actually suffering from memory loss. A part of him wished that he was, it would have helped him pass the time more comfortably. Had he known that the man he had travelled north to unmask was just the other side of a thin plaster wall, it would have ensured a restless night on top of a tiring day spent fending off questions about his childhood, parents' sexual appetites and whether an aunt had ever interfered with him.

That last suggestion brought back unpleasant memories of his recent assault at the hands of Linda Lunt. Her husband, too, when all was said and done. One benefit of his current incarceration – a private room with, he had learned, a police guard outside – was that he had not been troubled by further visits from that monstrous harridan with her unnatural carnal longings. That he had been forced to accept her version of the recent past – and a threat of a grisly future together – had weighed heavily on his mind ever since they had spoken. At some point he would have to announce to the world – and to Bernard Lunt in particular – that his memory had returned, it was the only way to save himself. But the moment he did, he would have to account for his whereabouts on the day a certain house had gone up in smoke. (Just then, he had no idea that a second one had joined its ranks, which was probably just as well.) Feigning amnesia bought him time, but it didn't get him out of the hole he had dug.

It crossed his mind that he should call Roger Caspin. His boss had pulled several strings to get him up here in the first place, and could, perhaps, pull a few more to get him out again. Reluctantly, he dismissed the idea, still hoping to extricate himself with the least amount of bother, whilst holding the idea in reserve, should all else fail. For the present, he must keep a clear head and bide his time. Having blown up a house and almost certainly killed a woman of dubious repute – as well as being forced to profess true love for another – he consoled himself with the knowledge that things couldn't get any worse.

*****

In the room next door, Colin Crimp was of a different mind altogether, inasmuch as he had any mind left. It was bad enough that he had been rudely interfered with by an elderly tart and her clinically obese assistant. In his absence, his house had been eviscerated, after which he had been arrested, assaulted, and taken to a police station where he had been assaulted again. As if a malign Fate had only been teasing him up to that point, he had been promptly carted off to hospital where several large men had jabbed him in both buttocks and at regular intervals throughout the night. Compounding his misery was a vague memory of having seen Wayne Winkley, the pubescent schoolboy who had come between him and Maggie Henderson – literally as it turned out. Finally, he had emerged from a drug-induced coma to see Hugo Lake peering over him. The latter appeared to be under the impression that he, Colin Crimp, harboured homicidal tendencies which, after an hour in the quack doctor's company, he was ready to confess that he did. Had Lake not left at that point, apparently with 'other patients to see', Colin was pretty sure he would have been facing a more serious charge than that of simply examining the remains of his house. (Though why that was now an offence under English criminal law was something he'd be writing to his MP about the moment he was out of here.)

There was, he had learned, a constable outside his door. Lake had let that nugget slip, in between asking how many knives he owned and was there anyone else he'd like to kill. Lake apart, no one immediately sprang to mind, or at least no one he was ready to name with a policeman close by and buttocks that had had more than their fill of hypodermic needles.

How had things come to this pass, he wondered? Only a short time ago, his fortunes were soaring. He was engaged to the love of his life – though admittedly she didn't see it that way – and Henry Plank was close to leaving his house for good. On the plus side, he no longer had a house, so Henry would certainly have to find other accommodation, hopefully back with his gargoyle of a wife. With luck, she'd give him a damn good thrashing, too. It was the least he deserved.

Lake had inquired more than once if he regarded Henry as a father-figure. That was a dreadful enough prospect, but when the quack went on to ask if Henry had ever come between Colin and his mother and had he viewed him as a rival for the latter's breasts, Colin had very nearly thrown up.

In an attempt to change the subject, Colin had asked where Henry was, at which point Lake had become evasive and said he mustn't worry about that now, nor must be blame himself. That puzzled him as he saw nothing to blame himself for. Quite the contrary. To help his employer he had endured all manner of physical abuse and lost his house into the bargain. If there was any apologising to do, he felt, not unreasonably, he should be on the receiving end, not the other.

That was another thing. His house hadn't disappeared without help, and he was pretty sure it wasn't his fault. That appeared to leave Henry as the likely culprit. Colin had insurance but what if Henry had started a bonfire in his bedroom to toast a teacake? OK, perhaps not even Henry was that careless, but he might have left the iron on, or discarded a lit cigarette in bed. Insurance companies weren't known for settling up at the best of times. If Henry had done something he shouldn't have done, the consequences could be incalculable. The fact that he hadn't dropped in for a visit spoke volumes. And Lake's evasiveness suggested he knew rather more than he was letting on.

Karen hadn't dropped in, either, which was a tad more upsetting, especially as they were engaged. He hoped she hadn't been so upset on hearing what had happened to him that she had turned to Bob for comfort. Losing one's house in an unexplained conflagration was one thing, but being arrested and confined to hospital under the care of a medical charlatan might not cast him in the best possible light as a future husband.

Colin's spirits slumped and, a moment later, so did he. Reflecting Lambert Ticke's unfounded hopes on the other side of the wall, he assured himself that at least things couldn't get any worse.

FORTY NINE

Linda Lunt's preparations were coming along nicely. She had no wish to remain in Fetherton for the rest of her days. She deserved more out of life and Lambert Ticke was the man to give it to her – whether he liked it or not.

Fate had thrown a debonair assassin into her hands and she had no intention of throwing him back. As Mrs Palona advised on page 243 of *Seize the Moment!*, 'When it comes to your own happiness – take no prisoners!' Though not entirely sure what that meant, Linda was convinced it applied here. From what she knew of Lambert Ticke, he took no prisoners himself, so would surely approve.

His memory loss – whether feigned or otherwise – was fortuitous. She could press on with plans for their lives together and fill him in on the details later. Stage One of her scheme involved cramming as many of her clothes as she could into two large suitcases. Returning both cases to the cupboard where they were permanently stored (Bernard not having taken her on holiday – a weekend in Morecambe aside – for the past seven years), she felt a girlish thrill of excitement. Bernard walked past the cupboard every day (generally on his way to the toilet in the middle of the night). She giggled mischievously at the thought that the next time he did so he would have no idea that he was walking past her future – and passed his past, also. He had no interest in her wardrobe, and even less in her panties drawer, so there was no chance of him spotting all the gaps and drawing the obvious conclusion. (Though Bernard's obvious conclusion would probably have been that she didn't own as many clothes as he thought she did.)

Going online, she opened up their bank accounts and checked the details. Bernard hated computers and limited his involvement with their finances to visiting the cashpoint once a week to draw out drinking money. She knew that because, having worked out his password – 'Fuckoff!' (the exclamation mark raised it from 'weak' to 'not very strong') – she kept a regular eye on his expenditure, and siphoned off a sum each month into a private account she had set up on her laptop (a purchase she had made with the first month's transfer). Bernard would have had a fit had he known that, at any given time, he had barely enough to meet all their direct debits and two weeks' worth of his alcohol needs. Once, when he had withdrawn a little more than she had expected, the account had briefly gone into overdraft and incurred a fine. She had taken more care after that and upped his beer and curry money from its previous one-week level to a fortnight's potential outlay, just to be on the safe side.

Having given the matter some thought, and not wishing to be mean about it, Linda calculated how much was required to meet one month's bills plus £25 for her husband's personal needs, and promptly transferred the rest into her own name. Though she was sure that a man like Lambert Ticke would be comfortably off, she recalled Mrs Palona's pertinent injunction on page 312 of *Seize the Moment*! ('the modern woman is an independent woman') and didn't want to bring a begging bowl to her second marriage.

Now it was simply a case of waiting for Lambert Ticke to be discharged from hospital. Hopefully before his memory returned – all supposing he had lost it in the first place, which, from what he had told her, she seriously doubted. She had his confession on tape – useful insurance should he have an attack of nerves – but hopefully she would never have to use it. She had confidence in her womanly charms to win the day, though blackmail was always a useful back-up if push came to shove and Lambert needed convincing.

She hoped it wouldn't be too long now. She was no longer a young woman and her biological clock was ticking down. She wondered if Lambert had any preferences for children's names. It would be an interesting topic for conversation on their way back to London and the new life she had planned for the two of them.

Again, whether he liked it or not.

FIFTY

Unknown to Linda Lunt, Lambert Ticke's eventual discharge from hospital was as much on her husband's mind as it was on hers. Indeed, Bernard had thought about little else since arriving at the station that morning and assessing the state of play. It was the phone call from a man called Sidney Wainwright, of Wainwright's Independent Printers and Business Services in Leeds, that had ticked his final box and convinced him that the time for action had come.

It still concerned him that the case might be taken out of his hands before he could bring it to a satisfactory conclusion. That Crimp and Ticke were up to their necks in this together, he didn't doubt at all. He was increasingly convinced, also, that there was nothing wrong with Ticke's memory and that the idiot was playing for time. Well, he reflected happily, if time was what he wanted he'd soon have enough of it on his hands. Twenty years at least unless the judge was in a bad mood, when thirty might be on the cards. A pretty boy like Ticke wouldn't last long in prison. Whatever sex-starved inmates he made friends with in the shower would think all their Christmases had come early the first time he dropped the soap. Crimp was an ugly sod and, being a loony into the bargain, might find himself banged up in a completely different establishment, though probably also for the rest of his natural.

Be that as it may, if he didn't get a confession out of the two of them, it could still prove academic. If they insisted on lawyers and kept quiet in the meantime, Leeds would certainly get to hear of it and that would be that. Checking over the paperwork one last time, and still giddy with excitement following his recent call from Sidney Wainwright, Bernard made up his mind.

It was time to bring in the two men and interrogate them with all due kindness and consideration in according with PACE and any relevant Geneva Code.

And, if that didn't work, he would hold them by their balls until they screamed – and cheerfully confessed to everything on oath.

*****

An hour later, he was standing in a tiny, foul-smelling room at Fetherton General – not at all keen to know to what purpose it had previously been put before being pressed into service as Hugo Lake's office – and laying down the law to the irritated quack. The latter had been hoping for longer to grill his patients and get the first few chapters of his book down on tape.

'I need to interview the two of them,' insisted Lunt. 'Back at the station. Now. It can't wait. There's been a significant development.'

'In my professional opinion,' began Lake, hoping to stall for time.

'I don't give a stuff about your opinion,' said Lunt honestly. He opened a briefcase and extracted a sheet of paper. He had had it typed up before he left the station. From a glance, the sixteen-year-old trainee secretary to whom he had entrusted the job had not numbered an English GCSE among her accomplishments. Or at least he hoped she hadn't if her spelling was anything to go by. Given the current levels of schooling in the country, he rather feared she had passed with an A and was top in her year.

'My name's not Luke,' objected Lake, as he ran his eye over the page. 'And what's this about "tea and crumpets"?'

Lunt snatched back the document, pulled out a biro and made the necessary alteration.

'Oh, Ticke and Crimp,' muttered Lake as he read the page a second time.

'It says you give your permission for the two guilty men – suspects,' said Lunt, hastily correcting himself. 'The two suspects to be interviewed – in your presence – at the police station.'

'Well I suppose if I'm going to be with them,' said Lake, though again without enthusiasm.

'All above board,' insisted Lunt, with two fingers crossed behind his back. He had no problem with Lake being present if the two men played ball. But if they didn't, he'd get rid of the idiot nut-doctor and get to work on them properly.

'Well, I suppose it's all right,' said Lake doubtfully.

'If you could just sign there, there and there,' said Lunt, indicating the relevant boxes. 'That'll do nicely.'

Hugo Lake studied the document with all the attention of a man with his mind on other things and reluctantly signed wherever Lunt pointed.

'I can take notes?' he inquired, with his hand poised over the third and final signature.

'You can write a bloody book on the subject as far as I'm concerned,' said Lunt, prompting Lake to sign so quickly he almost snapped the pen in half.

FIFTY ONE

Chuck Grogan sat back in his chair and cursed a malevolent fate. Three days had passed since he had left Fetherton. He had planned to return much sooner but the drugs he had taken to snatch some much-needed sleep had proved more potent than he had anticipated. Waking up in a pool of his own urine had been the first clue to the fact that he had been unconscious for more than one night. Logging into 'Gertie's' on-board computer confirmed the fact.

As he monitored classified reports from around the world most, if not all of which, he had no right to listen into, his heart sank.

During his time asleep, there had, it seemed, been significant 'movement on the ground'. Back in London, Conrad Blag (or 'Comrade' Blag as Grogan preferred to call him, having once heard that he favoured a quick shooting over slow lethal injection for killers on Death Row) had been in touch with Washington. Though everything was in code and his manuals (illegally obtained some years ago) were mostly out of date, Grogan was pretty sure that 'The Team' had been put on immediate standby. If that was the case, it was for one of two reasons. Either they were about to step in and steal his thunder, or events had moved on in his absence from Fetherton. If the latter was the case – and he was inclined to believe it must be – it meant the situation was now grave and it was every hand to the pump. Or, in his case, every finger on the button.

Setting out at once, he arrived back in Fetherton at a little after five in the afternoon. En route, he had steeled himself for the battle ahead. What he had not steeled himself for was the fact that he was hungry, having not eaten for the past three days, and out of burgers. If there was a war coming, and Grogan didn't doubt it for a moment, a hungry man's aim was not to be trusted. And so he pushed back his chair and swore loudly.

Glancing at his watch, he pondered his dilemma. He was parked in a narrow road off the high street, and as close to Fetherton Police Station as he could safely manage. Any closer, and he might have raised even the suspicion of the British bobby who, he knew, was not noted for his perspicacity, a word he had read one day, liked the sound of, looked up in a dictionary and subsequently committed to memory.

His guts were rumbling, and rumbled even more at the thought of a plump hamburger, complete with relish and mustard, and accompanied by a side order of French fries, with apple pie and a cold root beer to follow.

Grogan was aware that the British version of each and every one of these was a poor substitute for the real thing, but needs must. He was on field duty and would have to rough it for now. There must be somewhere close by that could do a halfway decent job of feeding him, even in this God-forsaken town. Slipping his pistol into his inside jacket holder, he secured 'Gertie' and headed down the road in hope if not expectation.

*****

Meanwhile, back in London, Conrad Blag paced the floor with more energy than usual. Hapgood felt distinctly uncomfortable. Despite his objections, The Team was going in. Satellite observation had thrown up activity in the general area of the police station. From monitoring radio reports, it seemed that the two suspects in the recent terrorist bombings, Lambert Ticke and Colin Crimp, were being taken from Fetherton General to the police station for questioning. That was some small mercy. For Blag, having suggested that this was a job for America's most lethal (and occasionally accident-prone) squad of trained killers, the prospect of them shooting up a British police station with serious loss of life was not as horrific as the idea of several helpless hospital patients being slaughtered in their beds.

Hapgood was more pessimistic. In his view, this was bound to end badly, however you tossed the coin. Grogan was still unaccounted for, which hadn't gone down well in Washington. In the latter's opinion – voiced forcefully by a General with several medals from his time in Iran, Iraq and Afghanistan – 'If those bastards have killed one of our own, they'll get everything that's coming to them.' Given Grogan's track record, Hapgood wasn't convinced the renegade agent had come to any harm. But even if he had, he was equally unconvinced that it was a bad thing and/or deserving of retribution.

Still, it was out of his hands now. The Team was going in, all hell was about to break loose and, as far as he could tell from his internet research, his only viable route to asylum-seeker status was to relocate to Calais, and trust in the RNLI to rescue him halfway across the Channel in a rubber bathtub.

*****

Chuck Grogan was replete. Three quarter-pounders and a mega-size portion of chips and onion rings from 'Danny's Eaterie' had filled the sizable hole in his stomach. Why this Goddamn country couldn't run to a decent root beer was beyond him, but two cokes had washed the sour taste of a British burger from his mouth and he was ready to take on the world in a way he had not been 45 minutes previously.

He turned the corner into the road where he had parked 'Gertie' in time to see the unthinkable happening. His van had been loaded onto the back of a large pick-up truck and was, at that moment, being slowly towed away. He dropped his half-eaten bucket of chips and ran as fast as he could, which, given his bulk and recent feeding frenzy, wasn't very fast at all.

As he reached the spot where 'Gertie' had recently been parked, he almost collided with a thin man in a checkered hat, busily jotting something onto a clipboard.

'That was yours, was it?" said the man in a voice that suggested he didn't much care either way.

'You better believe it,' said Grogan, his anger rising.

Before the fellow had a chance to say another word, Grogan grabbed him by the throat and rammed him up against a wall.

'Where the sweet Jesus are they taking her?' he screamed into a pair of bulging eyeballs.

It took Grogan a few seconds to realise that blocking a man's windpipe with near-lethal force was not the best way to extract an answer. At least not one he could understand. Reluctantly, he eased the pressure, a little at a time, until the man was able, albeit with difficulty, to speak. Grogan heard something about 'the pound' and was about to give the fellow a good kicking for wanting to discuss the economy, when the latter gave up the fight and passed out.

Dropping his victim onto the pavement, Grogan rifled through his pockets and found a plastic card that identified him as one Norris Plunge, an operative of the Fetherton Car Pound, 66 Westlake Crescent, wherever the hell that was.

Still thinking things through, Grogan felt inside his own jacket for his Smith and Weston .36 repeater. It was probably a mistake to remove it just as three elderly ladies rounded the corner on their way to early evening bingo. At the sight of one man sprawled on the pavement, apparently lifeless, and another standing over him holding the biggest (and admittedly only) gun any of them had ever seen in their lives, they screamed, dropped their bags, and ran away as fast as four arthritic legs and a pacemaker between them would allow.

Grogan watched their departure with mixed feelings. Even at this distance, he felt sure he could bring down two of the women with a single shot, then make it to the corner in time to aim at, and eliminate, the third. But even his trigger-happy nature recoiled at the thought of gunning down three unarmed British pensioners. Besides, the sound of gunfire would only alert others and complicate things further.

Allowing them to flee unmolested, he turned his attention to a more pressing need: how to recover his vehicle with the minimum of fuss and as rapidly as possible. 'Gertie' was his little piece of American soil in this God-forsaken land. Not to mention home to an armoury of lethal heat-seeking missiles he would have serious need of very shortly.

Reaching into another pocket, he extracted a small tracking device. A tiny green dot flashed across its screen, travelling in a vaguely northerly direction. Fetherton was a small town and, with luck, 'the pound' was not far away. It crossed his mind to commandeer a passing car. Then again, shooting its driver, even in a just cause, might attract unwanted attention. Best to advance on foot, he decided, and hope he didn't have far to walk. If he was wrong, all bets might be off.

As it turned out, his destination proved to be no more than half a mile away, and, though he was labouring a little by the time he reached the locked, heavy gates on which a sign announced that the pound was 'closed until 6am tomorrow morning', he saw, just thirty feet away from him, on the far side of a tall metal barrier, his beloved 'Gertie'.

FIFTY TWO

Fetherton Police Station had been built on the ruins of Fetherton Castle, a Cavalier stronghold, razed to the ground by syphilitic Roundheads in 1647. All that remained of the original structure was the castle's dungeon: two large, claustrophobic chambers – windowless and below ground level. One now served as a storage facility – housing records of unsolved crimes, burglaries that had never been looked into, and copies of pornographic magazines that one day, it was hoped, might fetch a fortune on the black market. The second had been converted into a games room, where the police team liked to practise for its darts matches. (Generally for half an hour maximum, after which time alcohol consumption and poor lighting rendered training sessions potentially hazardous; at least one officer had been obliged to take early retirement after losing an eye, and a second denied his chance of fatherhood following two strikes to the groin.)

Bernard himself had long held the view that either dungeon would make the perfect interrogation room: a place where confessions could be secured in the absence of lawyers and other archaic procedures designed to protect the accused, whether they were guilty or not.

Given that it was a Tuesday afternoon and that, on Tuesday afternoons, Chief Superintendent Troy teed off with his pals at Fetherton Golf Club, Lunt had snatched at the chance to make his dream come true. The scale of the offences committed, and his eagerness to have both parties banged up before midnight, demanded nothing less. With that in mind, he had had three constables board over the games room's snooker table to serve as a desk, on one side of which he was now seated, with Hugo Lake to his immediate right and Ticke and Crimp directly opposite. The seats were made from heavy oak, not easy to shift, and each man had one arm cuffed to a chair to ensure his immobility. Given that one of Ticke's legs was encased in plaster, he was unlikely to make a run for it, but Bernard saw no reason to take any chances. The room itself was gloomily lit, imbuing it with a grim atmosphere which, he hoped, would hasten their confessions.

He had decided on the unusual step of interviewing both guilty parties at the same time. (He saw no reason to give them the benefit of any doubt.) Separately, they might deny the allegations, and force him to ask the same questions twice. That would be a criminal waste of time and police resources. Besides, he was hopeful that, keen to avoid conviction, it wouldn't be long before they turned on each other in the hope of securing a deal.

'Right,' he began, leaning forward and addressing them in a loud voice. 'I know the pair of you are in this up to your necks, and the sooner you admit everything the sooner we'll all be out of here and tucked up comfy in our beds.'

'I don't know what you're talking about,' said Colin Crimp, squinting across the table. He glanced about him. 'Why is it so dark in here?'

'I'll ask the questions, not you,' said Bernard huffily.

Colin looked around and his eyes narrowed further. 'You need to change those bulbs. They're not the right wattage. It's like being in a dungeon.'

'It *is* a fucking dungeon!' said Bernard, and immediately regretted his outburst. He didn't want to lose the upper hand. He needed to remain cool, calm and collected. At least until he could get the nut-doctor out of the room and continue these interviews in private. Just him and the two condemned men.

'He's right, though,' said Lambert Ticke, who was also having trouble in the gloom. 'I had bulbs like this once. The new ones. They weren't very good in the early days. They make better ones now. They'd brighten up the room no end and make it more comfortable.'

'It's not supposed to be fucking comfortable!' yelled Bernard, who was already rethinking his need to remain cool, calm and collected.

'Shouldn't you have switched on the tape recorder?' asked Hugo Lake, feeling a little left out.

'That's for confessions,' said Bernard sharply. 'Once we've warmed up. No point in using it yet. Waste of electricity.'

Hugo Lake appeared doubtful but decided to err on the side of caution. He wasn't much bothered as to the innocence or otherwise of the men on the far side of the table. To be honest, it suited him for them to be found guilty. Any other verdict might render pointless the book he was planning to write on the subject of deranged and homicidal serial killers.

'OK,' said Bernard, in what he hoped was his most menacing voice, 'which one of you bastards wants to confess first?'

'I haven't done anything,' objected Colin. He might have demanded to see a solicitor, had he not viewed lawyers as a stain on the nation's conscience. It put him in something of a moral dilemma: much like a Nazi, he imagined, being told not to shoot a roomful of judges. Having considered the matter carefully, he opted to rely on his innocence and bugger the miserable looking policeman who glowered at him from the far side of the curiously large table at which they were sitting.

'That's for me to decide,' said Lunt unfairly. 'You wouldn't be here if you hadn't done anything.'

He turned to Ticke, who looked as if he was about to say something. Or perhaps it was just a trick of the light. Not that there was much light in this God-forsaken pit, but then that was why he'd chosen it.

As for Ticke, he was torn between protesting his own innocence, implicating Crimp without damaging his own cause, and keeping completely shtum because he was supposed to have lost his memory so should have no idea what was going on.

'I don't know who I am,' he said, and couldn't help wishing, just then, that he was telling the truth.

'You're a lying toe-rag!' snapped Lunt, not so much dispensing with any remaining niceties as strangling them at birth, then ramming them through a meat-grinder.

This time Lake opened his mouth as if to say something, then promptly thought better of it.

Lunt looked from one man to the other, tipped half a dozen documents from a folder, and stabbed his finger at the pages in no particular order.

'One house going up like a tart's fanny at a vicar's leaving do is one thing, he snarled. 'But two is just taking the piss!'

He ignored the confused look on both men's faces and turned his attention to Ticke.

'You ponce up from London with some cock-eyed story about the Prime Minister being murdered, break into my house in the middle of the night, give me a good kicking, then throw up over my favourite armchair.'

Ticke kept his mouth shut, though it pained him to do so. The catalogue of events just described was an unsavoury broth of truths and untruths, thrown together in an order that made no sense, but, in the circumstances, he could hardly refute them.

Lunt, meanwhile, was happy to plough on.

'We've got camera footage – local CCTV – showing you in the vicinity of 78 Arcadia Avenue, a short time after it went to meet its Maker.' He pushed forward a snapshot. 'There you are, that's you!' he said accusingly. 'In your sodding underpants!'

'I must have been attacked!' said Lambert Ticke, recoiling at the blurred photo which, though he would have liked to deny it, was most definitely of him. 'That's how I lost my memory. Something terrible must have happened to me.'

'Not as terrible as what's going to happen to you!' snapped Lunt. He lowered his voice to a whisper. 'Pretty boy like you in the prison showers,' he said menacingly, 'doesn't bear thinking about.'

He swivelled to face the other man. Pick them off one at a time, that was the way to do it. Let one bleed out on the floor while he kneed his mate in the groin.

'We've got you, too,' he announced triumphantly, pushing forward a second snapshot. 'About half a mile away from the other house. And an eye witness who says he saw you legging it over the fields – about ten minutes before the place went up in smoke.'

Lunt leaned back, and his vicious grin widened. 'Bit of a coincidence, that. Your house goes up first and milady here's seen running away in his knickers. Meanwhile, you're halfway across town blowing up your boss's gaff.'

Colin's face paled. He was struggling to grasp the full impact of everything he had just heard. This was the first he had heard of Henry Plank's house going up in smoke, but he knew what had happened to his. And if what this cretin of a policeman was saying was true, the man responsible was sitting right next to him.

He turned to address Lambert Ticke. 'Did you blow up my house?' he asked indignantly.

'Of course not,' said Ticke, backing away as much as the seating, his leg and the one cuffed arm would allow. In the circumstances, he considered, it was never going to be far enough.

'How do you know?' piped up Lunt, unhelpfully. 'If you've lost your memory? You might have blown it up and just forgotten.'

Ticke's face tightened as he struggled for the right words. 'I didn't blow up anyone's house!' he insisted, hoping that if he repeated it enough times, it would take on a semblance of truth.

'Then what were you doing running away in your undies?' asked Lunt gleefully.

Ticke threw his tormentor a baleful look. Lunt seemed to

be taking an unnatural delight over his state of undress. 'I'm innocent,' was all he could think to say, in the hope that it would mollify the man seated next to him.

It didn't.

'You bastard!' screamed Colin and lunged with his free arm in a bid to strangle Ticke one-handed. Ticke immediately brought up his own free hand to defend himself. The duo being equally unsuited to combat, their ensuing tussle, to Lunt's mind at least, looked more like a pair of Morris dancers in full flow, than two enemies fighting to the death.

'Cut it out!' he yelled, and his raised voice had the desired effect. Both men, already exhausted, disentangled themselves, though the air remained heavy with menace.

Lunt sighed. This might prove to be a longer night than he had anticipated.

FIFTY THREE

On the other side of town, Chuck Grogan studied a pair of locked gates, and pondered his options. It occurred to him that he could shoot his way through. The padlock and bolts would be no match for his .36 repeater. Then again, several rounds of high-velocity ammunition being loosed off in a quiet part of Fetherton might draw the crowds. Reluctantly, he decided to think again.

To one side of 'Gertie' sat a low, wooden hut and, through its square, brightly lit window, he could see a fat, balding man hunched over a desk.

Taking hold of the gates, Grogan gave them a powerful shake, and the man immediately stirred. Grogan pointed towards 'Gertie', then gave a thumbs-up sign which, he hoped, would draw the watchman from his hut and quickly reunite him with his armoury. Instead, the man pointed to his watch, dismissed Grogan with a finger and tugged down a slatted blind, shutting him out completely.

Grogan told the man what he thought of his mother's sexual preferences, then cast around for his next move. A spiked echelon spanned the top of the gates, making it impossible to climb over – not that Grogan was a man built for climbing stairs let alone anything more challenging.

Stepping back, he examined the car pound for weaknesses and found none. He needed another way in, and quickly.

And then he saw it: a manhole cover, off to one side, an entry point, he assumed, to the sewerage system. Returning his attention to the far side of the gates, he saw a similar cover to the right of the hut in which his enemy was currently entrenched. His spirits immediately rose.

Lifting the cover, Grogan peered into the gloom below. He caught a whiff of foul air and wondered if he should, perhaps, take his chances with the gate. He had done some peculiar things for his country, but climbing into a British sewer had not, until now, been one of them. Making up his mind – and not without difficulty – he lowered himself into the darkness. Given his considerable bulk, it wasn't easy and he was forced to press on his stomach several times as he wriggled his way down. Once through, rungs fixed into the wall offered a makeshift ladder and the drop was not as deep as he had feared. Very soon, by the less than piercing light of a fading pocket torch, he was trotting along a dung-filled trench towards the pound. He reached his destination quickly and began to climb. This time, the cover proved more awkward and, though he put his shoulder into it and heaved with all his strength, it wouldn't shift.

Inside the hut, Frank Sturgeon was in need of a cigarette. Though he would have preferred to have lit up at the desk, while warming his toes on his three-bar heater, he knew he didn't dare. His replacement, Avril Trench, came on at 5.30 next morning and was a staunch anti-smoker. One whiff of stale air and she would have his guts for garters. Literally, as she was a large woman, whose hobby was power-lifting, and with a temper as short as a policeman's cock.

Tucking the newspaper under his arm – he liked to have something to do while wrecking his lungs and the quick crossword was proving anything but tonight – he opened the door and stepped outside. Walking to one side of the hut, he glanced over to the gates. Relieved to see that the irate man who had recently hailed him was no longer there, he lit up, and sucked happily. The world could often be a dark and miserable place, he mused, but there was nothing in it so bad that a couple of fags couldn't make better.

*****

Down in the stool-ridden bowels of Fetherton, Chuck Grogan had come to regret his decision to launch a subterranean attack.

His first attempt at shifting the manhole cover had ended badly. Putting his shoulder into the task, he had overbalanced and lost his footing. The torch beneath his chin had fallen into the turd-infested waters, and he had promptly followed.

Emerging from the thick brown slime, he had lost his footing a second time and ended up head-first in a stew of festering crap. Having made the mistake of trying to wipe his mouth clean with a sleeve that was, if anything, filthier than his face, he threw up twice and almost passed out. It was only the thought of where that would leave him that lent him the strength to cling on to consciousness.

Taking a deep breath – which, in the circumstances, didn't help at all – he began to climb again. The stink was unbearable and his trousers were soaked in something obscene from the knees down. He just wanted to get out of this rat-infested hole (literally – he had seen three of the buggers scampering for cover as he and his torch advanced) just as fast as humanly possible. They could park a tank on top of the Goddamn manhole cover, he told himself with feeling, and he'd shift it this time.

*****

Out in the fresh-air world, Frank Sturgeon sucked happily on his cigarette and mused on the nature of his rather dull existence. He had been working in the pound for six months now, and it had been six months too long for him. This wasn't what he had been put on earth for. There must be more to his life than watching over other people's cars, before taking both their money and abuse in return for handing them back.

It was while Frank was standing there, contemplating his

pointless time on earth, that two things happened in quick succession. The first was that he noticed, to his surprise, that someone had shifted a manhole cover out in the street. He knew what that manhole cover was for, and he knew you didn't shift it – not unless you were legally qualified and had a large van with 'Fetherton Sewerage' printed on the side.

The next thing that Frank noticed was that the ground was moving beneath him. Frank was a large man – fifteen stone seven pounds at his last doctors' appointment – and not used to the ground shifting under his feet. At first, the movement was ever so slight, but then it became more urgent, as if someone – or some *thing* – was trying to push its way to freedom. Frank was not a quick-witted man, but even he was able to put two and two together and occasionally do the maths. There had been a wild-eyed stranger banging on the gates. Though he appeared to have vanished, a manhole cover that wasn't open before was open now. And the one beneath his feet was shaking. Dear God, in heaven! It didn't take a genius to work out what was going on. *The lunatic was down in the sewers!*

The movement beneath his feet was becoming increasingly insistent, leaving him in no doubt that someone was trying to push the cover up. He turned things over in his mind as quickly as he could. He needed to contain this madman – and anyone ready to go through a stinking sewer just to get his car back a few hours early was clearly a madman. But how? He needed reinforcements. Reaching into his pocket, he extracted his cell phone and stabbed in the three easiest numbers he could think of – 999. This was an emergency. He was under attack. It was time to call in the heavy brigade.

*****

Inside the sewer, Chuck Grogan was beginning to experience something he had never experienced before: panic. He clung to the ladder by one hand, which made shifting the cover even more difficult. A big man, even he had trouble pushing up on a cast-iron weight with just the one arm, and in complete darkness. If he hadn't known it was a crazy notion even by his standards of craziness, he would have sworn someone was standing on top of the manhole cover and trying hard to keep him trapped inside this dark, stinking dungeon. He decided to rest for a few minutes, before gathering his strength and hoping to force his way to freedom one last time.

*****

When a minute had passed and there had been no movement from beneath his feet, Frank wondered if it was safe to step away. A woman had come through on the 999 line to inquire if he was drunk. He had said he wasn't and would be grateful if they could despatch an armed police unit to Fetherton Car Pound as soon as possible.

'You're standing on a manhole cover and someone is trying to get out?' she repeated, convinced she must have misheard at some point.

'That's right!' he snapped, his nerves on edge as he waited for the cover to shift again.

'You think it could be a man who wants his car back, but, if not, it could be some form of extra-terrestrial life?'

Frank ignored the sarcasm in her voice. Though it was probably the man he'd seen before, he had watched enough 'B' movie horror films in his youth to know that sometimes things crept out of the earth in the hope of taking over the world. She would be the fool, not him, if something not-quite-human emerged from the sewers and tried to eat her brain while she was still using it.

'Are you possibly on some form of medication?' inquired the woman, attempting to tick all her boxes.

'I'm not on any sodding pills!' screamed Frank, though he feared he might well soon be. It had belatedly occurred to him that the keys to the gates were on his desk. He wondered what the chances were of him being able to run back into the hut, grab the keys, then run out again and open the gates before the nutter down in the sewers made another bid for freedom.

'Let's go over this one last time,' said the woman, at which point Frank's nerve cracked. He shoved his phone back into his pocket and ran towards the hut.

Less than half a minute later, he was at the gates, fumbling awkwardly at the padlock, stabbing the key everywhere but into the lock itself. Behind him, and to his absolute horror, he heard the wheezy grate of the manhole cover as, having gathered his strength one last time, Chuck Grogan heaved it up and to one side. As the key slid into place, and he was able to fling open the gate, Frank hurried through, turning only briefly to glance past his shoulder and scream without shame at the hideous brown creature whose head (he assumed it was a head) had emerged from beneath the ground and into the early evening gloom. A moment after that, Frank was hurtling down the street at a speed he had not achieved since he was nine years old and had come last in his school's egg and spoon race.

*****

Hauling himself with some difficulty into the fast-fading light, Chuck Grogan sucked at the air and threw up for a third time. Staggering towards 'Gertie', he delved into his jacket pocket and fumbled in the stinking mess for the keys he prayed to God were still there. Finding them – eventually – he pressed the fob button and gave a squeal of joy when 'Gertie's' lights flashed on and off and he heard the door click open.

Climbing into the driver's seat, he pulled back the dividing panel and heaved himself past the gap and into the control room beyond. Trudging filthy slime behind him, he made for his built-in sink and prayed there was enough water in the tank to wash off the layers of crap that clung to him like a drunken aunt on New Year's Eve.

Turning on the tap, he clutched at the water, hugging it to his face, clearing the muck from his nose, mouth and eyes. He was an agent of his country, used to deprivation in the field (though in truth that deprivation rarely amounted to more than a couple of hours without coffee). But what he had recently suffered went beyond anything he had ever endured. To feel clean again was something that was now at the core of his being. Indeed, there was a part of him that wondered if he would ever feel clean again.

Throwing off his rancid clothes, he filled the sink to overflowing and squeezed a bottle of washing-up liquid into the warm water. It wasn't enough – it could never be enough – but it was the best he could manage. Plunging his arms and face into the frothy mess, he rejoiced to feel the thick, brown gunk sluicing from his flesh. If the basin had been large enough (and he so small that dwarves would have looked down on him), he would have jumped in and immersed himself completely. As it was, he was forced to compromise and, although he did his best to immerse his entire frame, it was in stages: an elbow here, a wrist there, a kneecap followed by a thigh and finally the toes of both feet.

It was only at that point, sopping wet and stark naked, that Chuck Grogan realised he didn't carry a change of clothing – other than a spare pair of underpants which he had used once already, for a week at least, and woken up in that very morning, soaked through. Drying himself down with a towel, he wrapped it around his lower half, in a pointless concession to modesty, and climbed back into the driving seat.

At which moment, a fresh problem presented itself.

Though not convinced that Frank Sturgeon was anything other than a drug-addled alcoholic, with nothing better to do than waste police time, Gladys Rack, the emergency response operative to whom Frank had pitched his ridiculous tale of mutant car owners crawling from the earth to wreak havoc on mankind, had decided to err on the side of caution and inform Fetherton Police Station that a madman was on the loose. She wasn't sure who the madman was – Frank, or his imaginary friend – but she was off duty after this call, and had a hot date tonight, so sod the lot of them.

By the time Chuck Grogan had climbed into the driving seat again, clad only in a damp towel, a local patrol car had arrived at the pound, carrying with it two unarmed officers who had spent most of the day driving around town aimlessly and were keen to see some action.

What they saw, as they parked outside the car pound, was a big white transit van exiting at speed – driven, it seemed, by a fat naked man, with what looked suspiciously like a sausage in his hair.

If their first mistake had been to get up that morning, their second was to draw their truncheons and wave them eagerly as he approached. Aware that he was under attack – albeit from nothing more threatening than a couple of sticks, Chuck Grogan reached for his own weapon, still lying on the passenger seat where he had thrown it on entering the cab, and fired off three rounds in their general direction.

Fortunately, for the two men, the American's inability to both shoot and drive straight at the same time meant that the bullets shattered their windscreen and petrol tank, but damaged nothing else.

As 'Gertie' hurtled around the corner and out of sight, the two men first thanked their lucky stars, then sent out an APB to all surrounding units that an armed, dangerous – and apparently naked – man was at large in Fetherton, and heading in the general direction of the police station.

FIFTY FOUR

Battalion Commander Steve 'Scotty' Assmann could hardly believe his ears. The helicopter carrying his 11-strong Team of elite fighting men had landed two minutes earlier on deserted farmland, four miles outside Fetherton. Three unmarked cars were waiting to ferry them to the local police station where their mission was to extract a suspected red Jihadist by the name of Lamp-pole Tit. As well as plotting the assassination of both the British Prime Minister and the American President, he had apparently butchered one of their own, CIA agent Chuck Grogan. The maniac was a one-man killing machine and had to be captured at all costs.

Their arrival had been timed to take advantage of night cover, in the hope that they could enter, snatch Tit and exit the station with a minimum loss of life. Since taking off from RAF Leeming, where they had arrived from the Middle East an hour earlier, they had monitored all radio coverage in and out of Fetherton Police Station, as well as satellite reports of movements in and around a three-mile exclusion zone.

From what they knew, Tit had recently been taken to the station from a local hospital. He had been accompanied by another man, Colin Crimp, who, if their intelligence was correct, was part of the same terrorist cell as Tit and went by the code name, 'Mervyn Ratt'. Though Tit was to be taken alive, their orders for Crimp were 'extract or kill'. Given the difficulty of capturing just one man without serious loss of life, Battalion Commander Assmann leaned towards just shooting Crimp the first chance they got and had informed his men accordingly.

Again, from what they had been told, it seemed likely that the police station itself was a Jihadist 'safe house', with every officer on site to be regarded as a potential threat.

Now, it seemed, there was a further complication. A third man, identity unknown, and in a vehicle not showing up on any of their records, was heading into town at speed. The reports they had hacked into suggested he was armed, dangerous and had already tried to take out two police officers.

Though the information to hand was sketchy and inconclusive, its import was clear enough. The man was almost certainly part of the same revolutionary cell as Crimp and Tit, and it seemed just as likely that he was heading to the station to extract them first.

'We'll see about that!' muttered Battalion Commander Assmann, as he bundled his men into the three cars, put his foot down hard and sent his lead vehicle screaming towards the centre of Fetherton with all the speed the good God above was happy to allow him.

FIFTY FIVE

Bernard Lunt was not best pleased. He had given orders that he was not to be disturbed until he emerged, victorious, from the interview room, with the heads of his suspects on a stick. The fact that an armed and, apparently, naked man had emerged from a sewer and was driving around Fetherton shooting at policemen didn't concern him unduly. It was probably some drunken crackhead from Leeds. The Pope himself could be flashing his tackle at the local girls' school and it wouldn't distract him this evening. He told Reginald Blight as much, and in language he knew his desk sergeant would understand, before returning to the dungeon to continue his questioning.

'Right,' he said, dropping into his chair, 'this bollocks has gone on long enough.' He glanced from one man to the other, as if they were something he had recently scraped off his shoe and didn't like the look of.

Addressing Ticke first, he leaned forward and ground his knuckles noisily. Over the course of the past hour he had thrown evidence at the men higgledy-piggledy, hoping to catch them off-guard. However, they had stood firm and denied everything. Now it was time to put his facts into order and end this nonsense. If they continued to mess him around, he'd get rid of Hugo Lake for twenty minutes and let his fists finish the job his mouth had begun.

'You came up here, with some cock-arsed story about a bloke called Mervyn Ratt wanting to kill the Prime Minister.' From the corner of his eye he saw Colin Crimp flinch, the way he'd seen him flinch more than once when the name Mervyn Ratt had been mentioned. 'Next thing we know, a house goes up in smoke and you're seen running away naked.'

Lunt paused, daring Ticke to deny the accusation – as he had on previous occasions – but he just slumped, like a boxer on the ropes who had taken one punch too many to his goolies.

'Five minutes later, some poor sod says his car's been pinched – by a naked weirdo who looks just like you. Minute after that, said pervert nicks another car, crashes it into a chemists then pitches up at the local hospital claiming to have lost his memory. Ring any bells?'

When it didn't, Lunt paused again, but only to catch his breath. 'Meanwhile,' he continued, turning his attention to Colin Crimp, 'the plot thickens. One Colin Crimp, aka Mervyn Ratt, is seen exiting a bungalow by the name of Shangri-La – a few minutes before it, too, goes belly up. On closer inspection, said building turns out to be a whore house, where men pay to be thrashed senseless by a fat old bag called Norah Plank, and an even fatter one called Myrtle Fling.' He lowered his voice for a moment. 'God rest their souls', he muttered, then picked things up a notch. 'Lo and behold, said older whore is the wife – now late – of the just as late Henry Plank, proprietor of Henry Plank (Publishers) Ltd, where one Colin Crimp – a certifiable nutter as one Doctor Hugo Lake is happy to confirm – is employed.'

Lake opened his mouth to voice an objection, but a glare from the other man immediately silenced him.

'Documents retrieved from the late Henry Plank's car,' continued Lunt, 'found parked outside his house, show that he had – only a few hours earlier – made one Colin Crimp the sole beneficiary of his estate, should he be unlucky enough to die first. Which he has – making Colin Crimp a potentially comfortably off young man.'

Lunt paused again. He was in danger of losing his thread, but, returning briefly to Lambert Ticke, he gathered himself for a final push.

'CCTV footage from Fetherton Agricultural Centre shows a man in a beard that's obviously not his own purchasing several bags of fertiliser 24 hours before the first Fetherton house goes sky-high. Fertiliser is a common component in home-made bombs which, we have reason to believe, were to be constructed and used in said previously referred-to attempt on the Prime Minister's life, said PM being the local MP and who was due to visit the area next week.'

Again, he saw Colin Crimp scowl and, as before, struggle to keep his hands on the table, rather than where he clearly preferred them to be – around Lambert Ticke's neck.

'It gets better,' said Lunt, who was feeling almost as overwhelmed by the information at his disposal as he hoped the men opposite him were.

'When you were admitted to Fetherton General,' he said, addressing Ticke directly, 'you were covered in chemicals consistent with having been in close contact with fertiliser. Exploding fertiliser!' he added for good measure, and was disappointed when Ticke didn't immediately break down and confess.

For Colin Crimp, however, those last two words were the final straw. His free hand came up and, for the second time that day, he tried his best to strangle the man sitting next to him, though, as before, by leaning backwards just a fraction his enemy remained tantalisingly out of reach.

Ignoring the fracas across the table, Lunt marched on. He could smell victory and had no intention of stopping now.

'And that's without all the other sodding evidence that screws you two bastards into the ground!' he snarled. When the two men appeared to ignore him, he yelled the name 'Frederick Tipson' and Colin Crimp span round, his mouth open like a goldfish at feeding time.

'I thought that would ring a bell,' said Lunt gleefully. 'That's where you got the idea, isn't it? To blow up Henry Plank's house.'

Colin shook his head. 'I don't know what you mean.'

'I think you do,' said Lunt. *'Crime of Passion!* by Frederick Tipson. I had a call from Sidney Wainwright, of Wainwright's

Independent Printers and Business Services. He just happens to play in the local darts league, saw what had happened up here, read Tipson's book – which you'd sent on to him – and put two and two together.'

'I didn't read the book,' said Colin, not sure where this was going, but not liking the sound of it.

'A likely story,' said Lunt, and huffed for good measure. 'But not as likely as this one. Seems it's all about this bloke that gets put in someone's will, then blows up his house to inherit.'

The colour drained from Colin's face. He couldn't believe what he had just heard. Frederick Tipson of all people. This couldn't be happening. It was like something out of a bad novel. In fact it *was* something out of a bad novel!

'You see, it was him all along, not me,' said Ticke, snatching at what looked like a straw, though he wasn't sure how long it might prove to be.

Lunt had one more bullet in his gun – the CD they'd found in what was left of Colin Crimp's house, confirming Ticke's allegation of an assassination plot by a man called Mervyn Ratt, Crimp's alias. He wasn't sure how that tied the two men together, and there were a few other gaps in his case, but he knew he was almost there. He had them by the short and curlies, and, by God, he was going to twist their knackers off if they didn't confess to everything in the next minute.

It was just then, as he stood on the verge – he was certain – of total victory that they all heard a large bang overhead, followed by several epic thuds. A moment later, the ceiling fell in and, a moment after that, none of them remembered very much at all.

FIFTY SIX

While Bernard Lunt was pursuing justice in his own, inimitable fashion, the wider world had not been waiting on the outcome.

Chuck Grogan, for one, had wasted no time – engine screaming, tyres burning – as he and 'Gertie' hurtled towards their date with destiny.

Approaching from the opposite direction, Battalion Commander Steve 'Scotty' Assman and his men were no less sluggish. Having reached their jumping off point, a quiet cul-de-sac to the rear of Fetherton Police Station, The Team robed themselves in Arab thawbs and checkered ghutras. Though attacking under the cover of darkness, it was vital that whatever memory anyone retained of the assault, it would not be that of twelve American soldiers blasting their way through a British police station – but a dozen heavily armed Saudi assassins in search of their place in heaven.

Meanwhile, sitting almost naked in 'Gertie's' control room, Chuck Grogan's mind was in turmoil. Having shot his way through half the town, he knew that time was short. Hacking into every spying satellite currently circling the UK, he raided their contents for all he could find on that corner of Fetherton that was shortly to become his final battleground. And what he saw was worse than he could have imagined.

Infra-red spying devices – most of them Russian or Chinese (but on this occasion he passed no judgment) – revealed blurred red images of policemen roaming the inky cloud of the station. That was all pretty normal. What was not were the twelve fuzzy blobs creeping around the rear of the building, their brighter hue suggesting the presence of serious firepower. Zooming in, he saw the unmistakeable swirl of gowns and headgear and knew, at once, from where this new foe hailed.

If there was one thing worse than a commie or an Arab, it was an Arab commie – and here were a dozen of the camel-shaggers worming their way into a British police station, and for only one purpose he could fathom. To spring a man with more lives than a Goddamn cat – a man he'd felt certain he had killed but who had somehow got away. Well not again. Not this time, no siree!

With a speed at which even he had not imagined himself capable, Chuck Grogan fired up every weapon in 'Gertie's' armoury – and prepared to unleash the full, unforgiving fury of American justice.

*****

When the first of Grogan's missiles tore through the double front doors of Fetherton Police Station, bypassing Desk Sergeant Reginald Blight as he bent down to pick up a biscuit, then continued on its way, miraculously causing no loss of life, before exiting through a wall at the back and bringing down half a ton of bricks on the two unlucky Team members tasked with securing their retreat, Battalion Commander Steve 'Scotty' Assman wondered what the hell had happened. His confusion lasted just as long as the time it took for a second missile to be unleashed, causing marginally less damage than the first, only because there was no wall to impede its progress as it hurtled first through, then out of the station and into a 1960s' branch of the NatWest Bank that no one had much cared for in the first place.

As his battle-hardened instincts kicked in, Steve 'Scotty' Assmann knew at once that the 'third man' had arrived and launched his own rescue mission. Given the direction of the missiles that had seared the hair from his eyebrows and taken out two of his best men, the enemy was located directly opposite the police station.

The element of surprise now lost, he spat a single word of command into his radio. 'Attack!' he yelled, giving every member of The Team licence to do whatever they judged necessary to move in, extract the target and get the hell out of here as fast as they could.

It didn't help that no one, just then, had any idea where anyone else was – Lamp-pole Tit, in particular. It was chaos, as the crack US unit rushed around aimlessly, shooting anything that moved (and very often didn't). But if they imagined things couldn't get worse, they were about to learn otherwise.

By chance, when the APB had gone out from Fetherton Car Pound, warning that an armed and naked man had escaped from the sewers and was shooting his way into town, a five-strong unit from the nearby Army base had been returning by helicopter following three nights' manoeuvres on Grimsley Moor, twenty miles away. Sensing action, after 72 hours worrying sheep and sleeping in his own pee, Captain Rupert French (an unfortunate name for a proud British officer) had promptly ordered the pilot to change course and, as luck would have it, they spotted Grogan as he rounded a particularly sharp bend and very nearly blinded a jogger with a rapid round of gunfire.

This was more like it, thought Captain French, as he unholstered his pistol and took careful aim, missing all four of 'Gertie's' tyres but wounding the jogger in the foot as he leaned against a letterbox and thanked his lucky stars for still being able to see.

A moment later, Grogan was out of sight, but the chase was on. When the van came back into view and – to the pilot's relief (flying across moors was one thing, but through badly-lit streets was just asking for trouble) – screeched to a halt outside the police station, Captain French readied his men for action.

They were still taking aim, though wondering at what or at whom, when Grogan fired off the first of his missiles. As the rear of the station vanished in a fireball, Captain French knew his time had come.

'Take the swine out!' he yelled, a moment before the second missile flew from 'Gertie's' undercarriage and spiralled through the station on its way to the NatWest.

As gunfire peppered the white van, Grogan turned his attention from the station to whatever the hell was happening overhead. 'Gertie's' bullet-proof casing offered some protection, but even she could only take so much and, when several rounds found their way through the roof and made short work of the sink, Grogan knew that he was under attack from a lethal source. The Arabs, he reasoned mistakenly, must have air support. There was nothing for it. He was out of missiles anyway, and a sitting duck now.

Jumping up, he grabbed his rapid-fire M16, ten belts of ammunition and a grenade launcher. Flinging everything across his shoulder, he climbed back into the driver's cab. A moment later, he had revved up the engine, pulled sharply into the road and turned to face the police station. As bullets continued to rain down on 'Gertie', tearing her to shreds around him, Chuck Grogan steeled himself for what was to come.

'Remember the Alamo!' he cried pointlessly, jammed his foot down hard on the gas and shot, like the missiles he had previously unleashed, towards the steeply tiered entrance to what was left of the police station. As 'Gertie' jerked up the steps, and groaned with every advancing inch of progress, Chuck Grogan leaned out of the window, spotted the helicopter as it swayed drunkenly overhead, and fired off two grenades. One missed completely, but the second caught a rotor blade and immediately exploded.

'Abandon ship!' yelled Captain French, unable to recall a more airborne-appropriate order to evacuate. Not that it would have helped. They were too far up to risk jumping, and there was nowhere to jump to, even if they could. As flames licked down into the fuselage, the men continued to shoot wildly, finally taking out three of 'Gertie's' tyres as she reached level ground. Rapidly losing height, the helicopter swung out over the police station, just in time to catch the attention of two US soldiers dressed as Arabs, as they peered through a hole in the ceiling – the result of Grogan's stray grenade, which had finally found a target.

Convinced they were under attack from above, the Americans opened fire, catching one of the still-functioning rotor blades and sending the helicopter into a frenzied tailspin. The British soldiers, in turn, though unable to see who they were shooting at, fired off several rounds of their own, one lucky bullet catching a Team member who had paused for breath by a water cooler in reception and who would never take another one again.

As the helicopter's pilot finally abandoned all hope and watched his 37 years of life pass quickly in front of his eyes, Captain French loosed off a final shot and yelled triumphantly as an American's head exploded twenty feet below him. A moment after that, the helicopter turned belly up and plunged heavily through the roof, eviscerating what little remained of reception. The last thing Captain French saw, a moment before the helicopter itself relinquished its shaky hold on life, was a fat, naked man sitting at the wheel of a van as it careered into reception and straight through a wall into whatever realms of hell lay beyond.

FIFTY SEVEN

Chuck Grogan was having the time of his life.

This is what he had dreamed of, from his very first day in the US Secret Service, to make the world a better place. And there was only one way to do that: you had to shoot as many of the bastards who didn't want to make the world a better place as was humanly possible, given restrictive rules of engagement and limited ammunition.

But even he knew the odds were against him. He was one patriotic American against an army of Arab communist liberal Trotsky-ites, not only here inside the police station, but outside in the skies above. And they were led by a man who couldn't be killed, even by a heat-seeking missile. It was time to call in help, even if it did mean sharing the glory.

Though the bulk of his equipment lay wrecked and out of reach in the ruined rear of the van, its dashboard remained intact. Sliding back a small panel, he exposed a state-of-the-art communication device into which he had programmed one set of contact details. As the world erupted around him, Chuck Grogan leaned forward and pressed a button marked 'Home'.

*****

'You have got to be fucking kidding me!' yelled Conrad Blag, on hearing the voice of a man he had presumed dead and whose demise, he quickly hoped, could still be arranged in the next few seconds.

'You're breaking up!' said Chuck Grogan, though breaking down was a more accurate description of how the man in

London felt just then.

Since late afternoon, both Blag, and the long-suffering Hapgood, had been on tenterhooks. A call had come through on their most heavily encrypted line: The Team was going in and would extract Lamp-pole Tit that evening.

Possibly the corruption of their target's name was a coding error, Blag wasn't much bothered. The Team was on the case and his faith in them – unlike that of his less-than-confident deputy – was absolute.

That heartfelt belief had lasted only as long as it took The Team to fly from Leeming Bar. As they touched down outside Fetherton and word came in of a large, naked terrorist shooting at the local police, Blag felt a moment of panic, while Hapgood all but passed out.

Ever since then, via satellite, they had been monitoring events as they unfolded. They had seen the missiles that had shredded the police station, heard the screams of US soldiers as they went about their lawful business in the dark, and gaped in disbelief at the helicopter that had appeared from nowhere, adding its own share of devastation to the mounting carnage.

And now, out of the blue, and clearly responsible for everything that had gone so horribly wrong in the last few minutes, was the very man they had sent in to 'keep an eye on things', and ensure that nothing untoward happened.

'I told you he was unstable,' said Hapgood quietly, wondering if there was still any chance of extricating himself from this mess.

'The hell you did!' yelled Conrad Blag, who hadn't forgotten it was Hapgood's suggestion in the first place.

'I need back-up!' yelled Chuck Grogan, his voice almost silenced by the background roar of gunfire and exploding helicopters.

'Back-up?' screamed Conrad Blag, his face almost puce with rage. 'Those people you're shooting at *are* your fucking back-up!'

'You want me to keep shooting till I get back-up?' yelled

Grogan, struggling to make sense of what little he could hear.

'No!' screamed Blag. 'I want you to *stop* shooting! You're killing American soldiers, you mindless piece of crap!'

Another volley of gunfire, and another scream suggested things were not improving at the other end even if, by keeping Chuck Grogan talking, Conrad Blag was at least doing his bit to keep the body count down.

Christ! thought Blag grimly, this was an international incident to end all international incidents. The British government would put up with a shed-load of collateral damage to keep its favourite ally onside, but even they, he reasoned, would have difficulty explaining to their electorate, and, more importantly, the tabloid press, the demolition of a police station, and the wholesale slaughter of everyone inside it, by American soldiers. His country was still paying the price for screwing up Iraq – they didn't need it put about that they were bombing the crap out of Yorkshire just for the hell of it.

'You have to give yourself up!' yelled Conrad Blag, changing tack.

'Do what?' yelled Grogan, aware, just then, that 'Gertie' had caught fire and there was an acrid smell of petrol in the air. He was pretty sure his tank had taken a direct hit from an Arab shell.

'Give yourself up!' repeated Blag hopefully. 'Tie a hanky to your gun and wave it in the air, so they know you've surrendered.'

'They'll shoot him if he does that!' objected Hapgood, from the corner of the room into which he had retreated. The further away he was from this disaster, the better.

'I know what I'm doing!' snarled Blag, who was rather counting on the fact that a man waving a gun in the middle of a fire-fight wouldn't be seen as a friend come to visit. They'd give Grogan a medal and send his remains back to his mother. The idiot had done enough damage for several lifetimes. This would get him off the hook lightly.

At that moment, however, any future conversation became

redundant. Taking a deep sniff of the air around him, Chuck Grogan knew that 'Gertie's' last moments had come. With a quick prayer for her eternal soul, he leapt naked from the van and had just enough time to get clear before 'Gertie' erupted in a ball of fire, blowing a hole in the nearest wall, on the other side of which Battalion Commander Steve 'Scotty' Assmann had been taking a moment to compose himself.

*****

Naked, and without a shred of fear, Chuck Grogan stormed through the burning ruins, blasting carelessly at anything that caught his eye. Friend or foe no longer mattered in the world through which he tumbled. Unleashing grenades, bullets and prayers to protect his beloved homeland from the enemies of democracy, he revelled in the carnage around him. Somewhere in this hellish nightmare, lurking like the coward he was, was a man who couldn't be killed – Lambert Ticke, the evil mastermind who had set all of this in train. Well, Chuck Grogan vowed, he would find him now and kill him if it was the last thing he did.

It was just then, as a pungent smell of burning flesh and smouldering concrete seeped into his lungs and made him giddy with excitement, that a figure hobbled towards him out of the smoke.

Chuck raised his gun to fire, then paused. The man was unarmed, his hair matted and spiked, his features bruised and bloody. One leg appeared larger than the other, stiff and straight as if wrapped in a tube. As he emerged from the gloom, Chuck Grogan found himself staring into the maddened and barely recognisable face of Lambert Ticke.

The fat American took a moment to savour victory, then aimed his gun at the heart of a man whom he knew to be the most debauched, evil swine of a terrorist in the world. Even Putin didn't get a look-in when this maniac was around.

'Hello,' said Ticke in a thin, feeble voice. 'Do you know who

I am?'

The words, 'You're a dead man, that's who you are,' were on Chuck Grogan's lips, when a second figure drifted into view through the smog. With its equally bloodied features and curious network of bald spots on a square, monkey-like head, he didn't immediately recognise the latest arrival. Then something clicked at the back of his mind. *It was Ratt's rent boy!* Though he had only seen him the once, Chuck Grogan prided himself on never forgetting a face. And this face, he had to concede, was harder to forget than most.

Why the hell he was here, Chuck couldn't rightly say. But that he was involved with Ticke seemed obvious enough and made him as worthy of a bullet as his Russian masters. He was deliberating which of the two to shoot first, when the rent boy released an ear-piercing scream and hurled himself at Lambert Ticke.

'You bastard!' Chuck heard him cry, a moment before the pair of them hit the ground, the rent boy's hands around the other's neck.

The fat American was in a quandary. Linked together, as the two men were, he could take them out with a single shot. But that would rob him of his moment of glory – staring into Ticke's eyes as his enemy went down under a hail of fire. Then again, from the way the rent boy was holding onto Ticke's throat – the veins in his head now bulging in a serious way – Ticke might go to meet his Maker long before he, Grogan, was able to put a bullet through his heart.

Reaching a decision, Grogan shouldered his weapon and came forward, lunging at the pair like a teacher hoping to separate two lads fighting in the playground. It was at that point that yet another figure hove into view, if anything more fearsome-looking than its predecessors. There was nothing Bernard Lunt enjoyed more than a good scrap, and, still dazed from the blast that had wrecked the old dungeon, he reacted instinctively on spotting three men wriggling on the floor. At least he thought they were three men. Dazed, and in the blackened fog that swirled around him, he was no longer sure of anything. One of the men, he saw to his horror, was stark bollock naked – which put a different, and more hideous, complexion on matters. Nudity was all very well in the bathroom – as long as a bath was involved – but not in a police station. A primitive need took hold and he readied himself to administer a good kicking – once he could work out where it was legal for him to begin.

As for Colin Crimp, he had long since reached the point of no return. After weeks of misery living with Henry Plank – a treacherous sex maniac – he had been tortured by the man's equally depraved wife, sat on by the fattest woman he had ever met, and partially scalped in his sleep. Next, his home had been reduced to rubble and he had been incarcerated in a hospital, where he had been questioned by an unqualified charlatan about his mother's breasts. On top of all that, he had been accused of being the architect of his own misfortune, a murderer and a con-artist to boot. Finally, to rub it all in, he had been chained to a desk in the bowels of the earth alongside a man who, for reasons which, even now, he couldn't fathom, had wrecked his house, his life and, quite possibly, his sanity. Oh, and then a party, or parties, unknown had bombed the police station to buggery and the roof had fallen in on his head.

Someone was going to pay for everything he had been through and that person, he concluded happily, was the man around whose throat his hands were currently locked.

Bernard Lunt saw things differently as, just then, did Chuck Grogan. What Bernard saw, as his vision briefly cleared, was a large and obscenely naked man attempting to wrestle with his two prime suspects. Or perhaps, given what he knew about Crimp's proclivities, he was attempting something far worse, and – worse again – in the sanctity of what remained of Fetherton Police Station. In normal circumstances, Bernard would have had no hesitation in hurling himself into the fray, but he had never fought a naked man before and had no wish to start now. Instead, he settled for a vicious swing with his favourite boot, catching Grogan in the belly and briefly winding him.

Vaguely aware that he was under attack, and had suffered a blow perilously close to his groin – which even he was prepared to admit was his potential weak spot – Chuck Grogan closed his mind to the pain and heaved again, forcing his enemies apart. Ticke squealed as the hands that had previously threatened to choke him to death now threatened, instead, to tear the Adam's apple from his throat. Colin Crimp, for his part, squealed even more pitifully as what looked like a grilled frankfurter flew past his face. Bernard, meanwhile, gave a squeal of joy as he lashed out once more and caught the American on his left buttock, marking him for life – or at least what now remained of it.

As Chuck Grogan somehow clambered to his feet and staggered backwards, Bernard landed a final blow, this time catching the fat American squarely between the legs. Chuck released a keening howl and his eyes watered so badly that he swivelled full circle as he dragged his weapon off his shoulder and pointed it at no one in particular. A moment after that, he howled again, threw back his head and fired randomly at the ceiling.

The roof above him – having done sterling work to maintain its dignity in the face of all the bombs, missiles, helicopters and assorted weaponry that had been thrown at it in the past half an hour – finally abandoned the good fight and plunged down in one gigantic chunk, rendering Chuck Grogan as flat in death as the pancakes he had once sampled in Alabama and pronounced, rather fittingly, 'good enough to die for'.

FIFTY EIGHT

'What do you mean it was a gas explosion?' queried Bernard Lunt.

He was lying in a hospital bed, both legs in plaster and his arm in a sling.

A few hours earlier, along with Lambert Ticke and Colin Crimp, he had woken for a second time, covered in concrete, dazed, damaged and not a little confused, to discover that Fetherton Police Station had, for all practical purposes, been razed to the ground.

'Quick thinking of yours to get the suspects to safety,' said Chief Superintendent Troy, changing the subject. 'Saved their lives – yours, too,' he added, though without enthusiasm.

Lunt looked as if he was about to deny the fact, then thought better of it.

'I shouldn't be surprised if they give you a medal,' added Troy. He hoped it wouldn't come to that, but the powers-that-be had leaned on the chief constable, and he, in turn, had leaned on Troy. Given Lunt's tendency to punch first and ask questions later, Troy himself had deemed it unwise to lean on the Inspector but flattery, he hoped, would do the job for him. Rather distressingly, it had been intimated that Lunt might well get a medal, as might all the surviving members of Fetherton Police Force – both those still *compos mentis* and those who, sadly, had lost their minds and would never read *The Sun* again.

In the hours that had followed the disaster, matters had moved quickly. In the wake of frenzied communications that criss-crossed the Atlantic, US senators, cabinet ministers, army officers, intelligence teams and even, at one point, a plumber in the Oval Office who had been mistaken for the Secretary of State and asked for his views on nuking Iran as a means of distracting the press, came together to get their stories straight. A DSMA Notice in the UK (rushed through overnight) kept a lid on most of what had happened, while authorities both sides of the Atlantic swiftly came up with something they could all agree on.

Al-Qaeda, it seemed, had decided to attack a small British police station which, coincidentally, just happened to lie within the Prime Minister's constituency. The police had fought back bravely, led by a plucky Inspector, Bernard Lunt, who was widely praised for his quick thinking in guessing that the rooms below ground – previously part of a disused dungeon network – would offer safe refuge for the station's two prisoners and their mental health provider. It was just a pity that when the ceiling had fallen in, Hugo Lake had taken its full force and not escaped himself.

Fortunately for all concerned – the terrorists aside – a stray bullet had ruptured a gas pipe and the station had been all but obliterated in the resulting explosion. That Fetherton Police Station was all-electric, and had been for the past five years, was overlooked in the excitement.

Eye-witness accounts from a handful of residents who had claimed to have seen a UFO hovering over the station at the time of the explosion were quickly dismissed, while the Army was happy for it not to be put about that one of its helicopters had added a match to the flames. As for the Americans, they were quick to offer sympathy, and cash to rebuild the station in support of a brave ally. On top of that, a lucrative trade deal that had previously stalled due to concerns over radioactive cheese was promptly signed, much to the distress of dairy lovers everywhere.

The complete loss of one of their most feared fighting units, largely at the hands of a rogue and naked CIA agent, was not something the American Army wanted widely talked about and they, too, were ready to sit this one out.

Those police officers who had survived the disaster were either pensioned off, or relocated to quieter parts of the country where they could teach road safety to school children or take photographs of motorists travelling at 31 mph in a 30 mph zone.

As for Al-Qaeda, they were delighted to learn they had breached British security with such success that they had laid waste to half of central Fetherton and most of its police station. On the debit side, they were none too pleased to be told that everyone involved had been killed. In the end they decided to cut their losses, accepting praise for the attack while announcing the arrival of new 'martyrs' in heaven.

Having marshalled his men in stout defence, unarmed throughout while leading others to safety, Inspector Bernard Lunt was hailed a conquering hero. After giving the matter a good hour's thought, and consulting Chapter 28 of *Seize the Moment!* ('the modern woman is an adaptable woman'), Linda Lunt promptly ended her 'engagement' to Lambert Ticke, unpacked her bags and prepared to bask in her husband's glory. When it was announced, to great fanfare, that he was to be awarded the George Medal for bravery, she went online to see if that made her a Lady. Though disappointed to discover that it didn't – and that *Seize the Moment!* offered no advice on the subject – she reasoned, contentedly, that being married to a man with the George Medal was almost as good as having one herself. It would certainly open doors in the future, and Linda Lunt was happy to walk through as many of them as she could.

Although, had he known otherwise, Bernard Lunt would have been happy for his wife to run off with an idiot civil servant, his eventual posting to Leeds – and his enhanced reputation as a war hero – helped compensate for any disappointment. His only regret was moving from the frantic world of Fetherton to what now seemed like a quieter part of the country.

As for Lambert Ticke, any joy he might have taken at escaping from Linda Lunt and Fetherton was tempered by the fact that, having emerged from a smoke-filled bunker only to be confronted by an obese and naked man, then all-but strangled to death by someone whose face seemed vaguely familiar but whose name still escaped him, he had lost his memory for real. Subsequently pensioned off, and with only his book for company, he later moved to the seaside, where he did his best to speak to as few people as possible.

Roger Caspin's delight, on learning that Lambert Ticke would never return to the office, lasted only as long as it took for a dismissal notice to land on his desk, accusing him of a criminal failure of care in sending Ticke north and threatening to sue the shirt off his back should he come within fifty miles of Whitehall ever again.

Chief Superintendent Troy, meanwhile, prayed for guidance following what the chief constable insisted on calling his 'Fetherton Fuck-Up', and took early retirement within the year.

Rather remarkably, Conrad Blag and Felix Hapgood weathered the storm, though vowed from that day on to keep their heads down and report back on as little as possible. It seemed the best approach. Deciding to chance his arm, Hapgood asked Miss Lulu de Flame if he could make an honest woman of her. She told him he couldn't, and, on reflection, he was more relieved than he had imagined he would be.

In the short term, Colin Crimp – the unsuspecting catalyst for everything that had happened to everyone else – suffered more than most. But, in the long term, things weren't so bad.

Waking, like Lunt, for a second time, and finding himself herded from a smoking police station, with memories of a large, naked man trying to climb on top of him, he feared the worst. To his surprise, the next day, while, again like Lunt and Ticke, he recovered in hospital, he was told no charges would be brought. Indeed, his arrest had, apparently, been a dreadful misunderstanding, for which a considerable sum in damages was swiftly paid into his bank account in return for his signing an agreement never to speak of the matter again.

He had no wish to speak of the matter again and signed everywhere he was asked to and in at least two places that he wasn't. To learn that the money had come from the American Treasury and not the British taxpayer would have pleased him no end, had it not fallen under the heading 'Classified Information – Not To Be Released Until The Year 4022 (to be on the safe side)'.

Readmission to the mental wing of the hospital in which he had spent time in the past gave him a much-needed break from the real world and, when he eventually resurfaced six months later, it was to discover that all the necessary paperwork had been completed and he was now the proud owner of Henry and Norah Plank's combined estate, including Henry Plank (Publishers) Ltd.

Finding himself uncomfortably well off, he sold the company, gave one half of the proceeds to Bob, and the other to Karen. She had long since called off their engagement and promptly left Fetherton to travel the world without him. He wasn't much bothered. Though it surprised him at first, he quickly realised that he had had a lucky escape. A woman who gave herself to a man in a stationery cupboard – especially when that man wasn't him – was not a woman of whom his late mother would have approved, whatever the size of her breasts.

Colin Crimp had learned much from his time at Henry Plank (Publishers) Ltd, and these last few months in particular. And what he had learned was that the world was full of mad, bad and stupid people and that, in his opinion – and greatly to his surprise – he was none of them.

So, all in all, everything ended happily.

A MESSAGE FROM THE AUTHOR

Hello. If you've read this far, I do hope you've enjoyed my book and would like to read more of my work. A list of my previous titles appears at the start. They're a varied bunch, from crime to gentle comedy, but my plan, for the immediate future, is to write more in the Tom Sharpe-ish vein of *The Alienated Assassin*.

It's often difficult for a relatively unknown author to become more widely known. If you were able to leave me a review or rating on Amazon (or Goodreads) it would be a huge help – and I'd be very grateful.

If you would like to be added to my email list and notified about future books, please email me at: james@jamesward.co.uk.

The list will not be shared and will only be used to notify you about future books.

Take care, and thank you for your interest.

James

www.jamesward.co.uk

Printed in Great Britain
by Amazon